DAWN TILL DUSK

GENESIS CRYSTAL SAGA BOOK 1

T. Hackett

Irene

TYFFANY HACKETT
BECKY MOYNIHAN

20 20
FEATHER INK
PUBLISHING

ISBN-13: 978-1-7347972-0-6
ISBN-10: 1-7347972-0-7

Printed in the United States of America

Feather Ink Publishing
http://www.beckymoynihan.com
http://www.tyffanyhackett.com

• Cover Design by Becky Moynihan
www.beckymoynihan.com

• Interior Design by Tyffany Hackett
www.tyffanyhackett.com

• Feather/Music Images via
www.freepik.com

• Interior Illustration by Hanna Sandvig
www.hannasandvig.com

To the tomato haters of the world:
tread carefully.
No, really. Watch your step.
You never know . . .

Content Warning

This is a New Adult series recommended for 17+. While the language and gore are relatively minimal, we do invoke and address harder topics and issues. We try to handle them with sensitivity, but we want our readers to be aware that they are there, in case of potential triggers. <3

Dawn Till Dusk contain themes of: child harm/death, reference to sexual assault, parental abuse, self-harm, and suicidal ideation.

PRONUNCIATIONS

CHARACTER NAMES:

- TARIK — *T-air-ik*
- REAGAN — *Ray-gan*
- NEVAEH — *Nev-eye-uh*
- MORDECAI — *Mor-di-kye*
- ALEC — *Al-ik*
- BENJI — *Ben-gee*
- HAVEN — *Hay-vin*
- LEILANI — *Lay-lon-ee*
- JOCELYN — *Joss-ill-in*
- SEBASTIAN — *Seb-as-tee-in*
- ELIAS — *Ill-eye-is*
- MICAH — *My-kuh*
- MALACHI — *Mal-uh-k-eye*
- CASPAR — *Cass-per*
- AKENO — *Ah-ki-no*
- Flynn — *Fl-in*
- CALLIE — *Cal-ee*

LOCATION/GENERAL:

- NATHRA — *Nath-ruh*
- DARANIL — *Dar-uh-nil*

“Hatred paralyzes life; love releases it.
Hatred confuses life; love harmonizes it.
Hatred darkens life; love illuminates it.”

— *Martin Luther King, Jr.* —

CHAPTER 1

Tarik

Staying out past curfew and surrounding myself with enemies were two habits I needed to break.

One of these days I'd wisen up, but not tonight.

I yawned, wide enough to crack my jaw. The dim ambient lighting of the place made my eyelids droop, and the heavy stench of cigarette smoke dulled my usually sharp senses. What I wouldn't give for a coffee right now.

Coffee wasn't served in the warehouse district, though. Only hard liquor and about every form of drug imaginable. To my right, a rainbow array of bottles lined a black shelf behind the bar. I looked away from the tempting assortment as a slim shape sashayed toward my table. The girl, long-legged and way too young to be working this joint, sidled up beside me and trailed her fingers along my exposed forearm. I stiffened, but she didn't take the hint.

"I've heard about you," she purred, walking her pointed, red-lacquered nails up my bicep. Her other hand flicked aside strands of the red hair shadowing my face. I kept my expression neutral, reining in the sneer that threatened to twist my lips.

She wanted something from me—all shifters did. But I wasn't here for *that*. Never that. "Tarik. Or should I say *ScarFae*?"

I hated that name. Why not just call me Scarface?

The shifters who frequented The Pit loved their cheesy nicknames, though—the cheesier the better. But you'd think they could have come up with a more creative name for this seedy establishment.

Practically everyone here went by a pet moniker. Pets. That's what my race called them. Shapeshifters had one master and waited with pricked ears for his call, like obedient lap dogs.

Sickening.

"Go home," I muttered, watching the girl from my peripheral. She was pretty—for a shifter. I could acknowledge that. But young. Too young. "This place will pick apart your flesh and spit out your bones when it's finished with you."

Short fur suddenly darkened her soft pale cheeks. The pupils of her light brown eyes slitted. Long nails became talons, jabbing into my skin. I yanked my arm from her clutches and knocked my stool over as I stepped back. She laughed, the sound throaty and self-assured. "I'm not the one who should go home, *Fae*."

She walked away before I could, her miniskirt-clad hips swaying so hard, I wondered how gravity hadn't taken her out by now. Most of her kind knew to avoid me on nights like these—she must have missed the memo. I came to The Pit for one purpose: to fight in the cages.

I needed the release, the pure natural hum of adrenaline coursing through my veins. Better than any artificial drug. Sometimes I won, but more often than not, I lost. Didn't matter. I would always be a loser in their eyes anyway. Lesser. They only put up with me because I was a curiosity—an anomaly. No other Fae dared step inside this shifter-infested den.

"ScarFae, man, you're up next," someone yelled over the thumping music. A hand clapped my shoulder and I almost lost my cool. The worst part about coming down here was the touching—and the nakedness. Shifters had no shame.

I strode through the scantily-clad crowd toward my assigned cage. A literal cage, with chain links and a steel lock keeping the fighters contained. I checked to see if my opponent was inside. He was. Stocky, tatted up, already vibrating with adrenaline from being surrounded by his kind. Typical shifter.

After I slipped through the gate, a bouncer clicked the lock shut, sealing us inside. Besides being knocked unconscious, there was only one way to lose a cage fight: using your abilities. But that was a joke. Shifters carried their abilities with them wherever they went. They were naturally strong, even in human form. Their reflexes surpassed humans and Fae alike.

That's why Shapeshifters were top dog in this dirty city, and why I didn't bother giving myself a pep talk. I wouldn't win, but I would sink my fist into this shifter's gut tonight—maybe break his nose if I was lucky. My blood sang at the thought.

A voice boomed through the underground, shaking me from my growing bloodlust. "My fellow beasties and the rest of you foul creatures, next up is Wolf Man and his challenger, ScarFae!" He drew out my moniker, making the word sound tough. But my concentration was solely on my competitor. Wolf Man? I snorted. And I thought *my* nickname was lame.

The barrel-chested dude must be a wolf shifter then. I held in a wince, already knowing how this night would end—with me limping home, a couple dozen bruises decorating my body. I was quick for a Fae—definitely faster than a human—but my tall, lean frame was no match for this guy's muscular build. He was going to make puppy chow out of me.

When his yellow eyes met mine, I gave him the slow lip curl, the one that always freaked out my competition. Like they thought I was preparing to cast a spell on them. I stifled an eye roll. Shifters and their superstitions. Somehow they'd gotten the idea that Fae were also witches. Ruffling their feathers—or fur—was far too easy. He flashed his teeth at me when nothing happened. What, did he expect a light show?

Maybe he was hoping I'd reveal my wings. At the thought, an ache pulsed between my shoulder blades. I hadn't released them in so long. The temptation was great—especially when I knew his reaction would be epic. But it wasn't happening. He could grind me to minced meat and I still wouldn't unleash my wings. The last time a Fae had broken the city's wing ban rule, they'd been executed. A quick slice to the throat by the devil dragon himself.

I didn't want to go out that way.

"You're going down," Wolf Man sneered.

How cute. We were thinking the same thing.

"I know." I shrugged and he blinked, surprised. Point one for me. As the match began, there was no fanfare, no chick in a bikini to announce the rounds. Not even an official ref. At least I wasn't forced to strip half naked, thank Gaia. That didn't stop Wolf Man from doing so—he wore tight black shorts and nothing else.

The sight burned my retinas.

A rail thin man—ferret shifter was my guess—quickly recited the rules. Simple: knock out your opponent and win.

"You two ready?" the man asked in a reedy voice. I nodded. "Then in five . . ."

At that, a heady dose of adrenaline surged through my body.

"Four . . ." I settled onto the balls of my feet. "Three . . ." My eyes found Wolf Man's. I winked. His nose wrinkled. "Two . . ."

Whatever you do, don't stop. You're the master of your pain.

"One. *Fight!*"

My vision bled red.

Thoughts switched off.

Instinct kicked in.

Kill the shifter.

I rushed forward, barreling my right shoulder into Wolf Man's eight pack. He shuffled back a few steps, then flung me off him. I rolled but popped up, ready for more. Always more. I never wanted this feeling to end, this blinding blaze of hatred.

He came at me. Swung a brick-sized fist. Missed. I slipped past his guard, driving my own fist into his unprotected side. A second later, I paid the price for getting so close to a dominant wolf shifter. He drove his elbow into my sternum.

The impact almost caved in my bones and crushed my heart. I staggered but focused on my defense, ignoring the fire surging through my chest. The fight had just begun. I wouldn't black out now. My body yearned to make contact with his, brutally, savagely. No mercy. Never mercy. None of them deserved mercy.

Not after the way they had pinned her down and—

Wolf Man struck at my face, but I blocked—kept my arms up, chin tucked close to my shoulder, waiting. My feet danced, taunting him. No one could dance quite like Fae-kind. I swiveled around the guy, sneaking in jabs from behind, from the sides. He threw his head back and bellowed as I made contact with the same spot on his ribs for the third time. A dusky bruise formed on his deeply tanned skin.

"You're slow," I deadpanned, avoiding another killer swing. Given the opportunity, one of those hits would knock me out cold. And maybe I would never get up again. But wasn't that what I wanted?

"Hold still and fight me, you prancing pony," he snarled and fell for my fake jab, leaving his ribs unprotected once more. What was with this guy? Dumb as toe jam. I rammed a fist into that dark purple spot, the impact splitting the skin at my knuckles. Sharp pain sped up my arm, sending my pulse into overdrive.

Finally.

After months of losing, I'd finally hit my stride. I could win this match now that my veins were engorged with the sweet thrill of revenge. No one could stop me, not when I felt like *this.* Invincible. Powerful. Stronger than a Shapeshifter.

"Too bad you're not allowed to show me the *real* you," I taunted. Baited him. "Your human form is weak and pathetic." He lunged and managed to snag a handful of shirt. The linen fabric tore, exposing a section of my torso and back. My scars. Pure rage fueled my next move as I whirled and leapt, my bare heel pounding his jaw.

He roared. Several shifters outside the cage roared back. *Good. Communicate. Connect to your animal. Change.*

Change! Black fur sprouted on his arms.

"No abilities," Ferret Man warned. But his words had no impact on the slowly-morphing beast man. Shifter's strength lay in their animal forms, but therein lay their weakness. Sometimes they fell prey to their animalistic instincts, human rationalism but an annoying buzz in their furry ears.

I was counting on that tonight.

"Come out and play, little pup." I crooked a finger at the now half man, half wolf. The fact that he hadn't fully shifted was kind of impressive. At least he was smart enough to resist the urge. He was hideously ugly in this half form, though, large canines pushing past thinning human lips. His comrades shouted at him, demanding he change back, but he was too far gone.

With a wicked grin, I launched myself at him.

His claws lashed out and raked across my chest. That didn't stop me. Ferret Man demanded we separate. The match was over. Wolf Man didn't hear him and I pretended not to either. The win wasn't the prize, *this* was: fighting a fully-formed shifter.

"Show me what you got," I snarled, all bravado stripped away. I had what I wanted, what I *needed*, and I wasn't going to waste this ripe opportunity. The human part of the man disappeared completely—only a large black wolf remained. The creature growled, baring massive teeth. I growled, too. "Fight me!"

And then hands were suddenly on my biceps, holding me back. No. *No!* I struggled, shaggy hair slapping my cheeks as I twisted out of their grasp. But my moment was gone. Stolen from me yet again. Wolf Man was already more human than animal as his comrades coaxed the beast into his tattooed skin cage.

My gut spasmed as the hair receded. Disgusting.

"Wolf Man forfeits, you win. Get outta here before we string you up, Fae." A wad of cash was shoved against my chest, scratching my new wounds. I barely felt the pain. I only wanted my fight, but the night was ending all too soon and I wasn't satiated. When I didn't leave, the hand on my chest pressed harder. "Don't make me call the Night Enforcer again. Didn't she threaten to tear your throat out last time?"

"I'm not afraid of her." I spat on the ground near the bouncer's shoe and, surprisingly, he didn't deck me.

"You should be," he continued, forcing me out of the cage. "Haven't you seen her lion?"

I hadn't. All I'd seen was a tiny girl with a strong voice that couldn't disguise her short stature. With a dismissive wave, I balled the money in my fist and pushed past the hovering crowd, making for the exit.

This whole evening had been a colossal disappointment.

I charged through the back door, not caring that the metal banged off the stairwell's cement wall. My bare feet took the stairs two at a time, and a moment later, I burst free of the accursed underground. The damp night air sent a chill racing over my sweaty skin. Maybe I'd jog back to my apartment, release some of the excess fire in my veins before taking a cold shower.

The dank alleyway appeared deserted, spattered with rusted garbage cans and bits of trash no one ever picked up. On either side of me, the dull brick buildings covered in garish graffiti cast long shadows that hid rats and who knew what else. As my sharp Fae ears picked up a slight shuffling noise a few yards behind me, I slowed, making a show of studying a detailed Shapeshifter painting.

The drawing was incredible, really, capturing the almost iridescent quality of pure white wings. Attached to the wings was the hulking body of a—

"Fae trash, what are you doing loitering in shifter territory?" The comment was meant to offend, maybe even confuse, but I knew they had followed me from the underground. Knew that they hated the fact I had walked away with the win. With their betting money.

I turned my back on that terrifying creature painted on the wall, and acted surprised. "Shifter territory? Is that what this rank craphole is?" I scratched my nose with my middle finger. "I should have known better. Even the dingiest part of the Fae slums doesn't smell this bad."

I knew how they would react: like hot-headed idiots. All shifters were the same. My blood thrummed once again, excitement a live wire beneath my skin. The odds weren't great—three on one—but I'd dealt with worse. At least the incessant rage I carried would be depleted tonight. I didn't know if I'd make my early-morning shift on time, though, not with the world of hurt I'd soon be in.

The largest of the three stepped forward, illuminated by a weak circle of orange light. He was bigger than Wolf Man. "What did you say, filth?"

"I said," I enunciated slowly, "that your territory smells like a sewer exploding with animal dung. Oh wait, that's what you are. *Animals*. Does your kind not use bathrooms? I didn't realize you were *that* primitive."

All three of their switches flipped like clockwork. Too easy.

They prowled forward, fur of varying hues rippling along their tattooed forearms. They wouldn't fully shift, though, I knew that much. In beast form, they couldn't savor the pain that would soon be inflicted on me. I carefully rolled up the money and, with a smirk, slid the wad into my front pants pocket.

"Come and get me, hairy beasts." I widened my stance, keeping all three men in sight. One more blink and they were on me. Too many limbs. Too quick. I loosed the fiery rage on them anyway. My knuckles cracked against a nose. In return, a fist rammed into my left eye, swelling the lid shut in seconds.

After that, I began to enjoy the pain. Sweet, savory pain. A rib snapped and the world went black. The itch to fix what was broken hummed beneath my skin. I smothered the feeling. With my one good eye, I blinked the darkness away. Not yet. I didn't deserve peace yet. My foot lashed out and dislocated a kneecap—the crunch of shifting cartilage rang in my ears.

Gaia, that felt good.

Two of the men trounced me, wrestling my arms behind my back. A kick to the back of my knee drove me to the crumbling asphalt. "Strip him naked," one of them said. "We'll tie him up and make an example out of him. No one cheats in the cage fights."

A stab of panic pierced my chest. I could endure any form of physical torture but that. *Anything* but that. I whipped my head back and connected with a groin, almost wincing when the man let out a weak whimper. With a yank, I freed my arms and rolled away. But not fast enough. A steel-toed boot struck my cheekbone.

The pain was exquisite but way too distracting. I tasted copper on my tongue. I couldn't see anymore. Groaning, I rolled again and a foot stomped on my spine. "Take his pants off while I've got him pinned like the cockroach he is."

That's when I lost control of the anger. Rage burned so hot, so intensely, it consumed me completely.

I blacked out.

CHAPTER 2
Reagan

I took a long drag from my cigarette. Held my breath. Exhaled.

White smoke rose in front of me, a soft cloud that curled and twisted into the night air. A chill shivered up my spine, the alley's brick wall cold against my back. My nose wrinkled, the burnt scent mingling with the pungent odor of trash from a pair of dumpsters wedged against the far wall of the dead-end street.

My attention was focused on the slender girl in front of me. I hummed softly, a tune I didn't quite remember the name of, spinning a lock of blue hair around my finger as I watched her work. I didn't make a habit of standing in grungy alleys—Nevaeh liked to slap graffiti all over the rundown walls in the slums of Nathra City. Especially when I was on patrol.

Nevaeh's work was masterful, though. I loved watching her paint. My best friend didn't only illustrate walls; she was a talented sketch artist and she had done all of my tattoo work. Unfortunately, she didn't want to make a career of her talent. I had offered to give her the startup funds, to open a shop or to take art classes if she wanted.

"I don't want to paint for money," she had said. "This world is too dark already. I want to add some beauty to it."

I couldn't blame her. Still. Her skill was undeniable.

With a heavy sigh I tapped my cigarette, shaking free the ashes gathering on the end. Nevaeh's brush paused over the rough stone as she shoved strands of long, lavender hair from her eyes. Her illustration was little more than an outline at the moment, a large snake slowly taking form. He was less intricate than most of her other designs, likely an homage to some shifter conquest of hers. I envied her ability to stay detached. Maybe it was because she had a rule against kissing them—a form of shifter intimacy that was for more than casual hookups.

Nevaeh only did what made her happy, end of story. I had never quite managed that level of aloof iciness. When I found someone interesting, I latched on hard and fast. Every time.

Which was why I was standing in a dark alley in the middle of the night, watching my only friend paint yet another mural on the wall. I had long ago given up hope that people wouldn't disappoint me. Nevaeh was the exception.

My gaze snagged on her outfit, an almost identical copy of my own—tiny black jean shorts, fishnets too torn to be new, and a vintage t-shirt cut down to a crop top. The only real difference was the black and white canvas shoes on her feet.

As if she could feel my scrutiny, Nevaeh turned where she squatted and leaned back onto her heels.

"You don't have to stay, you know." She grinned, blowing a giant bubble with her gum before nodding pointedly at the pile of cigarette butts at my feet. "You're going to burn through a week's pay at that rate."

I rolled my eyes. "Mordecai pays me excessively. Might as well treat myself."

"Yeah, to lung cancer."

"Beats living under his thumb the rest of my life." I glanced around the alley. "I suppose I should do *something* tonight."

"You are doing something. You're watching me work and keeping this alley safe."

"And failing." I waved my cigarette at her art. "You're defacing the wall."

"I call it improving." Nevaeh huffed, loosening a band from her wrist and looping her hair into a bun. Even in the dim light from the street lamps her silver and brown eyes sparkled with glee.

Truthfully, I should have stopped her. I had been told by Mordecai to find the artist responsible for "vandalizing" his city and report them. But who was I to step in? My Enforcer position had very few perks. Not reporting my best friend was certainly one of them.

I dropped the last bit of my cigarette to the ground, stomping out the orange ember with the toe of my slick black combat boot. Stars glittered in the sky above us; brighter here, toward the Fae district. We couldn't see them at all in the main shifter areas.

Pressure tickled along my spine—my wings threatening to break free, daring me to shift, telling me to go find trouble instead of waiting for trouble to find me. *Not yet.* I didn't really feel like patrolling tonight. Mordecai trusted me at least enough that as long as the night stayed quiet, I could do absolutely nothing if I wanted.

Unless Alec told him.

I ran the thought over in my mind. Mordecai's son would definitely report me if he caught me relaxing in the alley. But he should be sleeping.

Should be.

Nathra City had a Night Enforcer and a Day Enforcer. I covered nights, Alec days. Shifters were cruel, and the most bloodthirsty ones loved to find unassuming Fae to pick on. As Enforcers, we were to make sure things didn't get out of hand—that the Fae weren't being slaughtered pointlessly and the shifters weren't being generally unruly. The laws were no sympathy of Mordecai's—in fact, most of his rules were instilled to keep the Fae under as much control as possible.

Still, the Fae worked too many critical jobs in the city to allow the shifters to do as they pleased. Not that they had much choice. Mordecai had set traps all around the city, an invisible fence. The perimeter was a minefield with an enormous detonation radius. Escape was nearly impossible, and the few times any of the Fae had tried, Alec had dragged their bodies back into the city to use as an example.

No one escaped the dragons.

From the position of a shifter and an Enforcer, I knew we had too much power. Too much freedom. An unpopular opinion, and one I couldn't vocalize, but it was the truth.

Once, the Fae and shifters had lived side by side. Or, at least, that's what I understood from the small bits of history I had gathered on my own.

Two decades ago, Mordecai had changed that.

He had power but wanted more. A veritable army of shifters answered to him and they saw the Fae as no more than animals. If Mordecai and Alec treated the Fae like lower class citizens, why wouldn't the rest of the Nathra shifter population follow their lead?

Mordecai was already powerful—too powerful—and his mind was a dark and twisted place I wanted nothing to do with. I knew firsthand what he was willing to do to innocent Fae for his own sick version of pleasure. And control. The same way he would do anything to keep *me* in line. A shiver raced up my spine.

Shouts lit up the night. Nevaeh paused her work, moving to stand beside me. She cocked her head, the street lights casting an amber glow across her light brown skin.

"What do you hear?" I asked.

Her ears rounded, sliding upward on her head. My friend halted the transformation right before her face began to lengthen, but whiskers still poked from her cheekbones.

She paused, ears twitching. "That Fae is at The Pit again tonight."

"Well that's not unusual."

"He won."

My brow pinched. I tugged at the silver ring in my lip. "Who did he fight, the ferret? He never wins."

"Wolf Man. He shifted. The fight was a forfeit, not an earned win."

"So what's the problem?"

"A few shifters didn't take too kindly to his victory."

"Of course they didn't." I sighed and pushed off the wall, breaking into a jog. My heartbeat rose with each step.

Nevaeh was talking about a very specific Fae, one who couldn't seem to stay out of trouble. I had found him more than once in the shifter districts, snarling and picking fights.

Mostly, he kept to The Pit. His fights were legal and relatively unmonitored. This wasn't the first time I'd had to chase him out of our territory, though. Probably wouldn't be the last. I usually circled this alley several times a night. The Pit caused me far more grief than anywhere else in the city.

As often as I could, I spared the Fae from real punishment. He and the rest of his kind didn't deserve the abuse they suffered. I was an Enforcer, I could do that much. I could stop the shifters.

Still, I had a part to play. If I didn't perform well, the cost wouldn't be worth the effort. Mordecai made sure of that. At the very least I would lose my position, which meant my ability to help. At most . . . I tried not to think about that end of the spectrum.

I rounded the corner, cracking my neck and stretching my fingers in front of me, Nevaeh close on my heels.

The scene that met my eyes stopped me cold.

Three shifters had that antagonistic Fae pinned to the ground and were kicking the life from him. I wasn't even sure he was still conscious. He didn't so much as flinch when the alpha of the group slammed a steel-toed boot into his side.

I cleared my throat loudly, rolling back my shoulders. "What the hell is going on here?"

Nevaeh straightened her posture to match my own, mimicking my pace as we strode from the shadows. She paused and I passed her, narrowing my eyes on the three shifters. They had stopped their assault the moment I had spoken, but one gripped the Fae's throat, holding him up for another round of blows.

The alpha cracked a wicked grin in my direction. "We're teaching this Fae his place."

"He's learning a lot while he's unconscious, huh?" Nevaeh spat. I raised a hand, shooting her a glance. Her jaw snapped shut, fire still glinting in her eyes.

"Do you know who I am?" I kept my voice low, calm. My heart pounded in my ears, though, and I tried to determine the state of the Fae. Blood splattered the ground around him. His face was swollen almost beyond recognition. Thankfully that shock of red hair was one-of-a-kind in this city. But he was so still . . .

"Of course we do. And? You really want us to leave this Fae be?"

"There are laws against Fae brutality," I said carefully, beginning a slow circle around the group.

"He's a troublemaker."

"I don't care."

"He took shifter money. He's a nuisance. We're doing you a favor."

"I'm paid to deal with him, am I not?" I snapped. "Leave. Now. Before I report all three of you to the Great Dragon for misplaced Fae aggression."

The alpha shifter shoved the Fae to the ground. His head bounced off the asphalt. I restrained a wince as he said, "Fine. He's your problem."

One of his companions raised a boot to deliver another blow. A small tug pulled at my throat, the smallest of shifts, and I growled. Low, threatening, lethal . . .

Inhuman.

All three shifters eyed me, considering, before they stepped away from the Fae. Muttered curses reached my ears as the men disappeared into The Pit. I hurried to the wounded Fae, sliding a hand to his wrist. His pulse tapped at my fingertips, weak but steady. I released a long breath.

"I have to take him back to the penthouse," I whispered to Nevaeh. "I'm going to shift. Put him on my back."

"But Reagan—"

"If I don't get him out of here, those shifters will kill him. If they don't, and I leave him, another shifter will. You know that."

"If you're caught you'll be tried for treason. You're already pushing your luck helping so many this month. If he catches you, Mordecai will kill you *both*."

"Let him try," I growled.

"You say that now," Nevaeh pleaded, "but you know what's happened when he's caught you before. I can't watch you get hurt like that again."

"He won't hurt me again. He won't catch me." My nostrils flared, but she was right. I wasn't as brave as I sounded. I didn't want her to talk me out of this, though. Helping the Fae . . . this was all I had.

I didn't give her a chance to respond, dropping my lighter and cigarette case to the ground before I kicked off my boots. Stepping farther into the lane, I closed my eyes. Took a long breath.

A burst of electricity zipped through my veins.

Searing pain blazed to life in parallel lines along either side of my spine. I didn't know why the wings always came first; they were the only partial shift I had never managed, but even if I had the weight of them was agony for my human form to hold up. A soft grunt slipped from my lips. Nevaeh shot a concerned glance in my direction. I gritted my teeth, ignoring the cracks as my bones extended and my frame widened. A low growl rumbled from my throat as my teeth extended, sharp against my tongue.

My whole transformation took maybe a minute. Bones, fur, wings . . . I let myself adjust to the new form, panting heavily. Shreds of fabric littered the ground around me. My clothing.

Oops. Forgot about those.

I stretched my spine, each of my paws, curled my toes. Lifting my wings, I shook myself and growled at Nevaeh.

She rolled her eyes and grinned. "The mighty winged lion might scare anyone else, but you're only a cute wittle kitty cat to me," she cooed.

I scowled, as much as a lion could. Nevaeh lifted the Fae without issue. She might be tiny, and a rat shifter, but the strength of our kind wasn't based on our animal forms. We were all incredibly strong, especially compared to humans and Fae. When he was between my wing joints, she paused to stare at his immobile form.

"He'll fall," Nevaeh warned, crossing her arms over her chest. I looked pointedly at the belt she had looped twice around her torso. Her silver and brown eyes narrowed. "Not a chance in hell. This is brand new."

Rounding my eyes, I stepped closer, nudging her arm with my nose. When I rubbed the top of my head against her side, she groaned and tugged the belt free. "You're buying me a new one."

I jerked my head in imitation of a nod, the weight of my mane adjusting with the motion. The second I heard the belt snap into place, I huffed a soft breath and bolted down the blacktop lane. When the buildings parted enough that I could open my wings, I spread them wide, letting them carry me into the sky.

The Fae moved slightly and I held my breath. Waited. He stayed in place and I relaxed. I could fly faster if I didn't have to worry about him falling off; and I needed to move. His blood was already seeping into my white fur.

I carried Fae back to my apartment more often than I should admit. Only when they were near death, only when I thought there was no way I could save them hastily. Occasionally, the Fae were grateful. Many were afraid, and a few seemed so numbed by their heinous lifestyles that they were utterly indifferent to their own survival.

This one though . . . This Fae was going to be angry, I knew already. He was a different breed. He was aggressive, an attacker. A provoker. I had never met a Fae like him. I could see the rage in his eyes every time we met, the bloodlust. More than once I had wondered if he was tempted to attack me, to try resisting with more than the saucy mouth he couldn't seem to control.

He adjusted again and I glanced over my shoulder. I wondered what kind of inner pain could fuel the kind of violence he held. Mordecai and Alec had so little regard for the Fae, and had hurt or killed so many without thought, that nothing would surprise me.

Stillness suited him though. The lines of his face softened, the anger smoothed into peace. He looked innocent. Gentle. Almost handsome, even.

Almost.

Air huffed through my nose at the thought. I flapped my wings gently, careful not to shake him too hard. Nathra City twinkled below, a constellation of lights that spanned the entire shifter district. Thankfully, I didn't live too far from The Pit. Mordecai decided that, if I wasn't going to live at the manor with him and Alec, he wanted his Enforcers on both ends of the city—so my penthouse was on the southern end, closer to the Fae homes.

Mordecai claimed he was being generous allowing the Fae to have dwellings at all. Generous would be allowing them to leave, not treating them like cattle. I didn't believe the drivel he fed the other shifters, the ones all too eager to eat up the nasty stories he spewed about the Fae.

I had studied their dwellings in my circles over the city; the crumbling buildings, the high risers covered in meager gardens. Fae abhorred technology, alongside the processed foods and materials that many shifters hoarded. Myself included. I loved my cell phone, when I had the time to enjoy owning one. I couldn't imagine a life without music at my fingertips.

The Fae took their distaste to a whole new level though, covering every spare inch of their territory in plants of all kinds. Maybe they did it for survival. I had to admit, the ruinous buildings they inhabited held a certain beauty capped in new, green life. I couldn't shake my guilt though, going back to a shiny penthouse when I knew there were Fae without the basics.

I did what I could. Snuck food and medicine down, left full bags on random doorsteps. I helped Fae who were caught in the hands of more vindictive shifters, even though the aggression made no sense to me. We had everything. Why kick a dead horse, after all. The Fae couldn't get any lower; Mordecai made sure of that. He reminded us regularly that the other shifter cities around us would never tolerate Fae presence.

I wouldn't know. He had strictly forbidden me from leaving Nathra City. I was the Night Enforcer and apparently too vital to the city to leave, even for a day. Seemed like another lie to me. He needed shepherds to tend his flock, to make sure his beasts didn't devour his prisoners. Sneaking out wasn't an option, either. Those traps of his weren't ones you could fly over.

A growl escaped my throat and I shook myself, bits of white mane fluttering across my vision. This wasn't the time. The Fae needed bandages and I needed to focus. I couldn't tell how much blood he had lost and, if the purple of his face was any indication, the shifters hadn't spared a blow.

The balcony outside my penthouse rose in front of me. I flapped once more, tucking my wings into my sides upon landing, and nudged the sliding glass door open with a claw. Across the hall from my own bedroom was an empty guest room. I sidled in, climbing onto the bed as gently as I could before I rolled to my side and bit through the belt. The weight of the Fae pinned my wing. I struggled to move him off, grunting softly.

This Fae is a pain in my—

He groaned. I stilled. I didn't know what he would do if he woke and saw a winged lion sprawled on a strange bed beside him, but "*nothing good*" echoed through my mind. He didn't wake, though, only shuffled a little. Enough that my wing slid free. Blood smeared the quilt and I grimaced. I had already replaced the damned bedding three times this month from stains I couldn't steam out.

With a final glance, I crossed the hall and shifted back. Swapping to human form was a much faster and easier transformation. I could rapid-shift, but the act was incredibly draining; I used double the energy to speed the process. In a day, I could only manage a small handful of them.

I ducked into my bathroom, digging through my large stash of bandages and cleansers. After my arms were loaded, I moved for the guest room, halting only long enough to tug on a pair of thick gray leggings and an oversized cotton sweater. The Fae were always more appalled by my lack of clothing than the fact that I was a shifter.

So strange, their level of discomfort around skin.

The Fae was sprawled on his back when I returned. I scanned his body, taking stock of his wounds. His muscular torso was exposed, his lightly tanned skin scattered with the same freckles that dusted his face. Bruises blended with the tiny specks, a patchwork of purple across his flesh. The button on his pants was undone, and I didn't recall seeing a shirt near him. Those shifters must have taken that.

What the hell were they going to do to him?

I grumbled in agitation. They always went for the tall ones too, as if their superior height made them more of a threat to shifter dominance. I snorted. More like a threat to their delicate shifter *egos*. Even if he had won tonight's match, he didn't win them often. One lucky night didn't warrant a beating this excessive.

The long claw marks that raked his chest seemed to be the worst of his injuries, so I set to work. I cleaned them gently before I sewed stitches along the deepest wounds, resting cloth strips in yarrow and honey over his skin when I was finished. A more natural healing method than I would use on myself, but I tried to make the Fae in my care as comfortable as possible.

The mix was effective enough; the swelling would be reduced, as well as the risk of infection. I would have to change the bandages though, to keep them cool.

My attention fell to his cheekbone next. I wiped away the excess blood, finally able to assess the damage. Fractured, at the very least. Another cold poultice went to the spot before I moved on. The rest of his face didn't seem as damaged—a swollen left eye and a knot where his head had struck the blacktop—so I laid strips of cloth across them as well, wishing I could do more.

An older set of scars ran down his right cheek, clipping off on his jaw. I traced a finger across the smooth, raised marks. Their spacing was too perfect, like a shifter had dragged claws down his face. The scars were mimicked in smaller forms across his arms and torso, over and over, raised marks that marred his otherwise smooth skin. My heart clenched.

Were they from the cage fights? Another shifter encounter? His hatred for shifters was glaringly obvious, and theirs for him. Not that I could particularly blame him, especially right now.

The shifters who attacked him tonight deserved far worse than being left to wander the streets. I clenched my jaw as my nostrils flared. Every single mark on his skin was unnecessary. I was familiar with his attitude and, even still, he had never said anything to warrant this severe a response. A corner of my mind dared me to get up, go back to The Pit, and kick the living piss out of all three of them. Reporting them to Mordecai in the morning would have to suffice.

The Fae coughed, drawing my attention to the swollen spot on the right side of his torso. Almost certainly a broken rib. Not much I could do for that. He would have to stop fighting long enough for that one to heal.

His bloodied knuckles were last, a mess that I cleaned and bandaged quickly. Split knuckles were child's play in my healing repertoire. Mordecai had taught me how to attend them early on. We healed no faster than humans, after all, and shifters were notorious brawlers.

"And dicks," I grumbled to myself. I cast another long look at the red-headed Fae sprawled before me, seeking any missed wounds. He seemed a bit more relaxed. Cleaner, at the very least. I shook my head and sighed, closing the door to the guest room as I strode out. He was going to be hell incarnate when he woke up.

I jumped into a quick shower while I waited for the inevitable. Pocketing my phone from the kitchen counter, I grabbed a soda and wandered to the living room. As I flopped onto the couch, I clicked the television to a cheesy soap opera and settled in. Flipping the can tab, I snorted. Let him wake up and try to give me trouble. I would show him the meaning of *hell incarnate*.

CHAPTER 3

Tarik

Snap. Whoosh. Snap. Whoosh.

The sound boomed in my head—a head ready to burst. When the repetitive noise wouldn't let up, I cracked my eyes open. Well, one of them anyway. The other wouldn't work. Had someone glued my lids shut? No, that wasn't right. My body tilted, moving against something warm and . . . furry?

Blinking sluggishly, I peered down at what looked like fur of purest white. A sensation similar to caressing fingers feathered up and down my right arm. My vision grew hazy then, but I swore I saw wings. *White* wings. Almost iridescent like in the painting. Was I dreaming?

Gaia, am I dead?

An angel was winging me up to heaven.

At least I wasn't going to the *other* place.

With that thought, my single-working eye drifted shut and my mind blanked. I hadn't felt peace like this in a long time.

When I woke again, the first thing I noticed was a slight breeze on my bare skin.

The second thing was white scraps resting on my chest. My *naked* chest. Was this my angel garb? I thought they wore floor-length robes. I lifted the cloth to find tiny black stitches holding my skin together. Then I saw the scars littering my torso. Was I to be cursed with these reminders even in death? Maybe they would be my penance for failing.

I deserved to remember. I deserved the pain.

Talking about pain, it was everywhere. I hissed between my teeth at the sensations flaring awake.

Something tickled my face and I reached a hand up, dragging a sweet-and-spicy-smelling cloth from my left eye. Right away, I recognized the natural healing aromas, ingredients the Fae used far too often. My eyelids were still swollen, but at least I could crack them open now. Which meant . . .

My brain slowly clicked together the pieces of last night: the disappointing fight, the alley encounter, the thrill of unleashing myself on those mangy fleabags, the angel dream.

I paused on that memory. When had I ever dreamt of angels? And those *wings*. So white, so real. I could still imagine how they felt against my skin.

My brain caught on a new revelation: morning light streamed through the transparent blue curtains covering a tall window. A *clean* window. Not mine. My eyes raced over the rest of the room. Pristine white walls with blue and silver accent pieces. Definitely not mine.

And not a hospital. At least not one I'd ever been to before, and I'd been to a few. I forced my battered body into a roll and landed with a dull thud on soft white carpet. At the sight, a rock settled in my gut. Fae couldn't afford white carpet. They wouldn't want it anyway since most of us walked around barefoot. The cleaning bill would be disastrous.

That meant I wasn't in Fae territory.

Cursing, I stumbled to my feet, a groan sliding up my throat as my rib cage pulsed with pain. *That's right. I have a broken rib.* Healing the bone would take a lot of energy, and my abilities didn't work well when unconscious. As fast as my aching body would allow, I strode to the window and yanked back the curtains. Several swears flew from my mouth. How did I get up here?

I was a good ten stories off the ground, and in the ritzy, high rise section of the shifter district, no less. Exiting through the window wasn't an option. Maybe I could bulldoze my way out of this place, catch my kidnapper unaware.

Solid plan.

On silent feet, I crept to the door and tried the handle. Unlocked. What was going on? Now wasn't the time to question my luck. I jerked the door open and was met with a hallway. My head whipped right, then left. I went left. Although I walked with purpose, my steps were whisper soft on the snowy carpet.

I hated myself for the thought, but the plush floor on my calloused soles sure beat hard cement. The hallway dumped me into a large open-plan living area. I slunk past a sleek dark kitchen counter-top, snatching an orange from a bowl along the way. The apartment's main door—my portal to freedom—was only a few steps ahead to the right, but I made my first mistake.

I glanced left.

And that's when I saw her.

Asleep on a white leather couch was the Night Enforcer. Dressed so casually, so *normally*, I almost didn't recognize her. But the blue and black hair spilling over the couch's edge gave her away.

Oh Gaia, not *her!* What in all blazes was happening? Was this her apartment? My second mistake was not seeing the small table with a blue and white vase perched on top. My thigh bumped the table and the vase swayed. I lunged with the hand that held the pilfered orange. And missed.

Crash!

I skid to a halt, gaping in shock. The carpet had given way to tile, and now the mosaic was covered in broken ceramic bits.

"Really? You'd think someone who loves to fight would have a little more grace."

The annoyed voice came from *her*, and I made my third mistake, the worst of them all: I faced her and opened my stupid mouth. "At least I know how to decorate. What a dumb spot for a table with a fragile vase."

The little spitfire flashed hands on hips before retorting, "It's Feng Shui."

I stared, slack-jawed. Fae worried about a room's energy, not shifters. I shoved the random thought aside, muttering, "I don't have time for this," and nimbly navigated the mess I'd made.

When I was two steps away from the door, she said, "You're welcome," before adding a mumbled "Ungrateful prick" under her breath.

I paused. Heat slowly crawled up my neck. *Walk away. Walk away and don't look back.* I turned, scattering pieces of ceramic as I marched up to that glaring upturned face.

"For *what?*" I snarled, holding nothing back. "For driving my kind to the edges of your precious city? For beating them up when they step out of line?"

Her two-toned gold and sapphire eyes darkened. "I don't—"

"Of course you do," I spat. "You're an Enforcer. And I'm supposed to *thank* you?" I pressed nearer to her, trying for intimidation. It was high time she got a piece of Fae malcontent up close and personal. But she didn't budge. She had balls, I'd give her that. "You're what's wrong with this city."

Before I swiveled on my heel, I saw her mouth pop open. Saw her hands curl into fists. If she were male, I would have stuck around. Seen what kind of damage we could wreak on this expensive waste of space. I wrapped my hand around the door handle right as she barked, "Stop!"

And, Gaia help me, I did. What was wrong with me? Now was not the time to pick a fight. Not with *her*. I looked over my shoulder at the five-foot-nothing slip of a girl. And when I saw the scowl she was giving me, like she could twist my balls off with one hand, my body flushed cold. Then heated. *Make up your mind.* "Yes, almighty Enforcer?"

She prowled toward me with feline preciseness, hips swaying. What was with female shifters and their hips? "You'll never get to Fae territory without being seen."

I snorted. "I'll survive."

She finally stopped a foot away, brow furrowing as she reached toward my face, gliding her fingers over my swollen cheek. "They'll find you again and this time you'll *die*."

I jerked away from her touch, the blood in my veins simmering. "They can try. Haven't succeeded yet. And what concern is my safety to you? Don't they follow your example?"

Her hand, still raised in the air, formed a fist. I waited, expecting her to bash me in the face, but she was frozen. No, not quite. Her chest rose and fell sharply, like she wanted nothing more than to hit me, but was trying not to. I wondered why she didn't. "I'll take you where you need to go."

"Don't bother. You've done enough." At that, her lips thinned, the action wrinkling her pert little nose. The look was almost—Nope. Not going there. Not ever. "Because of *you*, I've probably lost my job. So, if you don't mind, I'm leaving."

I finally wrenched the door open and stuck my head into the hallway. All clear. But before I could make my grand exit, having said my piece, she muttered, "You're *alive* because of me."

One last time—I swore this would be the last—I looked at her. "No." I shook my head, putting as much loathing as I could behind my next words. "I'm *dead* because of you."

I hated that she'd saved me last night.

Why couldn't she have left me to my fate? Then this *nightmare* I couldn't wake from would be over. And maybe, just maybe—Gaia willing—I'd see *her* again. She had been the exact opposite of the spunky little Enforcer. Tall and willowy, not short with killer curves. Long blonde hair that glittered in the sun, and a bright smile that never failed to punch me in the gut.

My heart throbbed. I had to stop and focus on my breathing. I leaned against an alley wall strewn with shifter propaganda—some old news about the Great Dragon Mordecai, their lord and savior, freeing them from oppressive Fae control two decades ago. Apparently, the first Fae who had settled in this city forty years ago were explorers. With their pointed ears and raven-like wings sharp as any blade, they'd been revered. Many thought them to be guardian angels.

But they were different than the Fae of modern day. They held a strength greater than the strongest Shapeshifter. And that wasn't all. With a single touch, they could perform miracles. At least, that's what humans and shifters *used* to think. After a while, there were whispers of dark magic. Witchcraft. Those Fae who had risen to power were seen as evil mind manipulators, so they'd been executed. War ensued.

But then something happened. The Fae began losing their strength, their abilities. Shifters saw this as a sign that their gods had cast them out. So Fae became the outcasts. When Mordecai rose to power, he said we were a blight. That we didn't belong in this realm. You would think he'd let us leave, then, but no. Not that any of us even knew where to find our ancestral land if we had the freedom to choose.

In Nathra City, we were simply guests. Permanent, unwanted guests meant to serve our hosts. The Shift, they called the segregation of our two races.

A bunch of crock, the whole ordeal. Mordecai was a warmonger, plain and simple.

I dug a finger underneath the edge of a poster and ripped the lies off the wall. If only my actions made a lick of difference. Still, I enjoyed crumbling the paper and chucking the ball down the street.

That Enforcer—Reagan, I'd heard her called—would ream my hide for tearing off the poster. Not that it would hurt. How much damage could a girl that size do? Her lion form must not be very substantial either considering she'd never shifted in my presence when I'd been making trouble. I grunted and mentally punched myself. Why was I still thinking of her? Despite what she'd said, she hadn't done me any favors. And now? Now I was late to my job for the third time this month.

No way would I be given grace again, but I had to try—after I grabbed a shirt, of course. And healed the worst of my injuries.

An hour later, I was jogging toward Smithfield Press where I'd managed to hold down a job for six solid months. A record for me. I had depleted my small well of healing magic, focusing a steady stream on my broken rib—now mended but still aching—and my left eye. Call me vain but a black swollen eye socket was gross to look at.

The stitched scratches on my chest had been free of infection—the Enforcer's rudimentary administrations might have had something to do with that. All in all, I didn't look too bad considering how close to death I'd been twelve hours ago.

Behind me, the pattering of little feet distracted my train of thought. I knew who they belonged to without turning around. "Get lost, kid." I jumped over a broken crate discarded on the sidewalk.

He continued to pursue me like a lost puppy. "You're late for work. Where were you last night? I could hear Callie meowing all morning, dude. You forgot to feed her again."

"I'm serious, Benji, get out of here. I'm not in the mood for your questions. Catch." I tossed him the orange I'd snatched earlier, knowing he needed the sustenance more than I did. Curly blond hair fell over his eyes as he whooped and hollered, like I'd gifted him a toy from his Christmas list.

Normally, Fae were strict vegetarians. We didn't consume animal meat like a ravenous pack of wolves—that was the shifter's thing. Our options were limited, especially since we weren't allowed to shop in their stores. Fruit was a rare commodity in our territory, which made our lifestyle that much more of a challenge.

For the next several blocks, I ignored Benji and his firecracker mouth. He finally grew bored and skipped off, leaving me to my thoughts. With his mom always taking ill, he was practically an orphan. I had snuck into their shoddy apartment across from mine on more than one occasion and tried to heal her. But her sickness was beyond my abilities. If she didn't get well soon, Benji would be out on the streets to fend for himself. Or worse, taken to the Fae orphanage.

A shudder rippled through me. When I'd come of age five years ago, I freed myself of those walls, but I still had nightmares. Although the kid was a pest at times, I didn't want that life for him. And I couldn't take him in. I could barely take care of my cat, let alone an energetic eight-year-old boy.

By the time I made it to Smithfield Press, harsh breaths sawed in and out of my lungs. Maybe my rib needed another blast of healing. *No time.* I slipped through the back door and clocked in. Quickly throwing on an apron, I got to work and prayed to Gaia that the boss was on lunch break. Maybe he'd chalk up the late timestamp to faulty machinery. Most of the machines in this miserable factory were on their last legs anyway.

But ten minutes later, as I was lifting a fifty pound stack of paper, I felt his presence behind me. More like smelled him. I didn't think he owned a bar of soap.

"Tarik, you're late again."

With a grunt, I heaved my load onto the assembly belt. "Sorry, boss. A couple of shifters got the drop on me last night. I won't let it happen again."

I faced him and my chest tightened. He had that look, the one that said I had screwed up for the last time. "If you didn't pick fights in their territory after dark, you wouldn't be having these problems. Oh, you didn't think I knew about that? I had to ask around, but I finally got the scoop." He muttered incoherently for several seconds as I braced for the inevitable blow. "The thing is, Tarik, you're a troublemaker and I don't need that in my workplace. If the wrong kind of shifters found out I let you stay on after three strikes, public discipline would be the least of our worries."

He blew out a breath, raking salt-and-pepper hair behind his pointed Fae ears. "I can't jeopardize my position in Nathra for you. Do you have any idea how hard it is for a Fae to climb up the corporate ladder? No, of course you don't," he said, shaking his head in disappointment. "Get out of here, Tarik. You're done."

My stomach rolled. Not again. "But, sir—"

"No. No more chances. You're fired. I want to see you gone in five minutes or I'll have Sully kick you out." With that, he turned, shaking his head some more.

Bad luck. That's all I was. All I'd ever be.

I ripped my apron off. Wadding it into a ball, I chucked the cloth as hard as I could. My bones vibrated with the need to punch the life out of something, but there was only paper. Lots and lots of paper spewing nothing but crap about Fae and praise for the animals who ran this city. Good enough. I grabbed the fifty pound stack and, with a growl, flung the whole thing in the air. Paper burst everywhere, rattling, fluttering to the cement in a disorderly heap.

A small kernel of satisfaction bloomed in my gut. I had wanted to do that for six long months. A Fae employee ground to a halt in front of me, bug-eyed and slack-jawed. I straightened, then snarled, "What are you looking at?"

"You—you're going to get us all killed," he stammered, staring at the mess I'd made.

The words almost knocked me over. Grisly images, ones that wouldn't stop haunting me, rapid-fired through my brain. I struggled to keep my angry mask firmly in place. "Get out of here before I kill you myself," I barked.

He skittered away. Loud breaths heaved from my chest. I needed to leave before I destroyed something else and Sully came after me. That guy was scary big for a Fae, but I didn't want to fight my own kind.

I forced myself toward the exit, stomping on paper as I went. One stuck to the bottom of my bare foot and I bent to rip the sheet off. I prepared to crumple the ad when a word caught my eye: "Wanted."

Reading further, my eyes widened. I didn't have time to stew over the ad's contents, though, not when someone yelled for the boss and jabbed a finger at the mess. Fisting the paper, I stalked out of the printing press.

I didn't bother saying farewell to anyone. They wouldn't miss me anyway because they were right. I caused destruction wherever I went. My departure was probably the highlight of their day.

CHAPTER 4
Reagan

Spoiled, stubborn, rotten . . .

A string of names, each worse than the last, slurred through my mind. I screamed into the silence of my apartment. My hands trembled at my sides and I clenched them into fists, ignoring the light prick of angry tears growing behind my eyes. I was nothing like the shifters in this city. The accusation stung.

His opinion doesn't matter. At least he's alive to have one.

Across the room my cell phone vibrated on the coffee table. Probably Nevaeh dying for an update. She could wait a few more minutes.

Shattered bits of ceramic stared up at me, mocking me from the entryway floor. I glared bitterly at the mess, then at the door. I should go after him. If any shifters saw him in his current state, they wouldn't think twice about taking advantage and killing him. Alec wouldn't stop them. The prick was an easy target.

I tugged on my lip ring, considering my options. If anyone saw that Fae barreling from the building, they would likely report him to Mordecai. I didn't need my adoptive father tracing his presence back to me. But, on the upside, most shifters in my building should be at work or asleep right now. The odds were in my favor. Decent, even. That Fae, though . . .

Damnit, conscience.

He was in rough shape. Rarely did a fight get that far without my intervention, and usually this Fae held his own long enough that a stern warning would see both sides on their way. Three on one though? Even he didn't stand much of a chance. Part of me admired his tenacity, that he didn't just accept his lot in life as his final place.

Maybe the Fae didn't want or ask for my help, but they *needed* it. And that man in particular . . . hell, he might be angry about my help, but if I didn't save him he was going to end up in an alley, lost and forgotten.

The thought was a lead weight in my stomach.

With a sigh, I grabbed the broom from the corner and swept the mess into a dustpan. He could have a head start. I wasn't keen to relive the last time a vase had broken across my floor—I had forgotten about the mess when I returned hours later, and was rewarded with bare feet full of tiny clear splinters. Moving the vase would mean redoing the entire apartment, but that Fae was right . . . this was a terrible spot for a vase.

The shards clinked together as I poured them in the trash can, but they were drowned out by a loud thump on the balcony. I flicked a glance at the sliding doors. The dark silhouette of a man strode forward, his body shaking as sharp scales retracted into his skin. He slid the door aside, mouth cracking into a wide grin.

"Hey, Reagan." I didn't like the way my name rolled on his

tongue. He wagged an eyebrow.

I frowned. "Alec. What are you doing here?"

"I came to see you, of course," Alec purred. He leaned across the kitchen counter-top, noisily biting into a stolen apple. "You look like crap, by the way."

"You're cheerful this morning. Do you have a purpose for this visit or are you going to"—I grimaced as my gaze flicked to his bare waist before landing back on his growing smile—"hang out?"

"Little bit of both."

"Little bit is right," I muttered, rolling my eyes.

Of course Alec dodged giving me a straight answer. He seemed to think no one was impervious to his alleged charms—including me. I could admit he was handsome, in that generic movie star type of way. Sun-tanned skin, toned abs covered in the best tattoo work money could buy, and bright blue eyes. The sides of his head were shaved, the dark brown hair on top long and currently ruffled, strands of which curled down onto his forehead. His beauty was superficial, though. Alec was exactly like his father, equally cruel and malicious.

"I have places to be, so . . ." I stared pointedly at the door.

"I did say I had a purpose for being here," Alec started. "I heard some rumors and I was curious. Judging by the state of your hair, I'm assuming they're true."

"What's wrong with my hair?" I reached up, patting the matted clump on top of my head. *Great.* Frowning, I ran my fingers through the blue and black strands, tying them back into a hairband.

"Did you really bring a Fae back to your penthouse last night?"

I stared at him, schooling my expression into careful amusement even as my mind raced. "Why would I bring a Fae up here? I had to chase that redhead from The Pit again. When I got home I was too hopped up to go right to sleep."

Alec stepped around the counter. "What happened to your vase?"

"I knocked into the table, right before you showed up. Thus the broom. The shards are in the trash. Anything else, Sherlock?"

His eyes fell to the trash can and my lips pressed into a thin line of annoyance. When he looked up again, he seemed sated. Not enough though, when the next words from his lips were, "Where are you going then, if you didn't sleep?"

"I need a new set of earbuds," I said evenly. "You know damned well I don't sleep without them, and I'm exhausted."

Alec stepped closer, a predatory glint in his eyes. I knew his routine and still fell into step, not moving fast enough to stop him from trapping me against the counter-top. Gritting my teeth, I stared up at him and crossed my arms over my chest. He licked his lips.

"You know, if sleep is a problem . . . I can help you with that."

"Ew. You're like my brother."

"Adopted brother, doesn't count." He grinned. "And we were never close siblings anyway."

"You're disgusting." I gagged, placing my hands against his bare chest and shoving him backward. He resisted for a moment, then stepped away with a shrug.

"I have to run my patrol. Maybe tomorrow morning?" Alec winked and chucked his mostly eaten apple at me. I caught the wet core at the last second, right before he strode to the balcony. His wings extended, arms and legs shortening. Within moments, he changed into a shimmering, dark blue dragon that flapped once and disappeared.

I almost went to bed. I almost decided that the asinine, mouthy Fae didn't deserve my help. Or my precious sleeping time.

But some part of me felt responsible for that Fae. I had rescued him, after all. I knew what condition he was in. I really should have insisted he stay; let him throw his tantrum, maybe learn his name so I didn't have to keep calling him "that Fae."

"Prick" could do as a filler.

I snorted. He wouldn't have stayed without a real fuss and Alec would have murdered him in a second flat. A male anywhere near me? Alec was as possessive as his father, and they both seemed to think I had some sort of property value to them. Once, I had even overheard them talking about how many children I would bear Alec. I shivered. No thanks.

Shoving those unpleasant thoughts aside, I tugged on my boots and punched the elevator button for the bottom floor. If Alec hadn't been so suspicious I could have asked him where this Fae worked. The streets weren't overly busy this early in the day, but searching on foot could still take a while. Using my bike would draw too much attention, though.

All I had to do was see him safely to his own district. No engagement needed. Then I was free.

I was going to regret cutting my sleep on patrol tonight.

The thought echoed in my mind again when ten minutes passed with no luck. Twenty. An empty soda can clattered away from the toe of my shoe and I sighed, searching the doors and streets around me. I was on the verge of returning home when the door of Smithfield Press banged open. A shock of red hair caught my eye. I ducked around the side of the building, seeking a hiding spot. The roads in this part of the city were narrow, mostly used by foot traffic, so my options were limited. If I crossed the street, he would see me; playing the invisible guardian would be far preferable to dealing with that nasty temper again.

Rough concrete bit into my palm as I leaned out, peering around the corner. He wasn't moving quickly. His head was downturned, like he was staring at something in his hands.

I took advantage of his distraction to creep closer, crouching behind a line of trash bins. He looked up, as if he could hear the thunder of my pulse. My heart skittered, but he turned, oblivious to his tail. I waited for another chance to move. His right hand was balled into a fist at his side, his shoulders trembling—angry. Again. Always, with this one, always so angry.

In my peripheral, a coyote shifter prowled the borderline, almost parallel to where the Fae was walking. He didn't notice me, his attention locked on his distracted target. I bit back the growl that rose in my throat. Alec should be watching this area, but as I scanned the skies all I saw were puffs of white drifting across clear blue.

No shifters should be this close to the Fae district unsupervised. There were rules and, as usual, Alec was disregarding them. I could clear the shifter out easy enough—most of them weren't willing to tango with an Enforcer—but if I moved, the Fae would be alerted immediately. He would know I was basically stalking him.

In my distraction, I missed the coyote shifter moving forward. The animal was mangy, its tail flicking back and forth. I shivered. That patchy, clumped fur . . . what if he carried diseases? Uncertainty jumped around in my stomach. I could stop him right here. Reveal myself.

And that Fae wasn't in any condition to fight today. The coyote would tear him to shreds. Releasing a string of swears under my breath I stepped out from my shelter, cracking my knuckles. Dark eyes met mine as the coyote's ears caught the sound.

"Why are you on Fae territory?"

His eyes darted from mine, seeking an escape, but I prowled closer. He tensed, then shifted into human form. "I'm sorry, Enforcer. I'm a bit lost."

"Lost? In the only part of the city shifters aren't allowed unescorted?" I loosed the growl I had been holding, watching as fear shivered up his spine. Good. He should be afraid. I moved closer and said quietly, "If I catch you anywhere near this district again you'll wish the dragons had found you first."

He nodded and fled, but I didn't miss the glance he shot over my shoulder. Another shifter with a vendetta against this Fae. I sighed. Alec was going to catch hell from me for not watching the border. When the coyote shifter was almost out of sight, my shoulders relaxed.

Then tensed again when a voice behind me snarled, "What are you, my personal stalker now?"

I spun on my heel. A muscle ticked along the line of his jaw, his expression blazing with anger. His fist tightened around a piece of paper. I scanned the purple marks that darkened his skin—and paused. The bruises on his face and arms were significantly better. More so than they should have been, even with my aid. "How did you heal so quickly?"

The Fae crossed his arms, hiding the paper from view. "I asked you a question first." He raised his eyebrows mockingly.

"I followed you, yes. I wanted to make sure no shifters tried to bother you. And good thing I did too." I motioned behind me, at the spot where the coyote shifter had been.

He clenched and unclenched his jaw, green eyes narrowing. "Let's make something crystal clear: I'm not breaking any laws, so butt out. You're crossing a line, Enforcer."

"You're absolutely right. I *am* crossing a line. The Fae-shifter borderline." I hopped back and forth over a crack in the sidewalk to emphasize my point, grinning as I added, "And I'm paid quite well to be here. But don't worry. You've cashed in your last favor."

I turned on my heel to leave. Sleep and a soft pile of blankets were calling my name.

"You cost me my *job*. So keep your nosy self out of my business."

I stiffened, rolling my shoulders back as I turned to face him once more. "You cost yourself your job, you mean. Picking fights like you do . . ." I shrugged. "Mordecai has rules about Fae jobs. I *know* one tardy isn't enough to get you fired. Nice try, but you can't put this one on me."

My hands slid to my hips, heat simmering through my blood. He didn't have to want or accept my help, but to put his job loss on me? I wasn't about to take the blame for that. He started to open his mouth, but before he could speak I snapped,

"Remember who you're addressing. Watch your mouth."

His expression changed then. He looked almost . . . comfortable. Like he was settling in for a fight. Sure enough, he opened his mouth and off he went.

"Oh. My bad. Remind me again what exactly you do?" I gritted my teeth, trying to ignore him. I couldn't remember the last time I wanted to hit anyone as much as I wanted to deck him right now. He smirked. "For an Enforcer, you're quite the pushover. Why don't you hit me already for being—"

I didn't know what came over me. Exhaustion, maybe, but that was no excuse.

One moment my Enforcer training was carefully reined behind shaking fists and gritted teeth. The next? Venom exploded in my veins and I—

I slapped him.

Hard.

Shock lit up his eyes, likely to match my own, and the muscles in his arms tensed. I shook my head, blinking away the red.

"What is your problem?" I growled, even as my mind reeled. I hit him. *I hit him.* What the hell was wrong with *me*? I reined in my riotous emotions long enough to add, "Why are you so angry all the time?"

Slowly, he raised a hand to his cheek, eyes wide as if he couldn't believe what I had done. *That makes two of us.* I had never actually hit him before. Threatened to, once or twice, but I had never intended to follow through.

He suddenly laughed. Not a belly laugh, but a demonic one, cold and cruel. "See? Everyone has the instinct to be angry. To inflict violence on others. I rest my case."

He brushed past me and, for a moment, I stood frozen. He

was right. I knew he was right. I was furious that he had provoked me so easily, livid that after all the time I had spent restraining myself and fighting for the Fae, this one bad egg was trying to spoil the lot. He poked and I exploded; acting exactly the way shifters were supposed to. But I didn't want to be like them. I had seen the things Mordecai had done in the name of "the greater good."

Honey-colored eyes sparkling with all the brightness of childhood curiosity filled my mind. I clamped down on the image. No. I couldn't let those memories back in, because if I did . . .

"Fine. You're right. We all make mistakes." That was the closest I could bring myself to offering an apology. I shrugged and added, "But not everything has to be a fight."

The Fae stopped in his tracks. Maybe I was finally getting through to him. "You're right," he said, and a flicker of hope warmed my chest. Then, "But if your kind doesn't control their urges to beat up my kind, then why should I? Leave me alone, stalker." And with that, he turned to stride away.

But the paper fell free and I bent, plucking the folded sheet from the ground. "What's this?"

The Fae whirled, fire in his eyes. I was pushing my luck. Hard. He closed in quickly and I shoved the paper into my bra, giving him an *I dare you* smirk. He froze, eyes locked onto my chest. With a blink, he tore his gaze away, lips twisting as if the sight repulsed him. Heat blazed in my cheeks, but I held my ground. I didn't know what was inside this paper, but he wanted it and I wanted information. I wasn't about to pass that off.

I narrowed my eyes. "Or don't talk and I'll take the paper back to my penthouse. Either way . . ."

He frowned as he considered his options. Fight or flight? I was shocked when he said, "You know what? Keep the paper. I'm out of here."

Ugh. What a diva. I pulled the paper free, quickly scanning the contents. *Mordecai. Job opening. Fae only.* I blinked. *What?*

"Here," I said as he pushed past me. "I was only teasing you. Trying to clear the air a little. You can have this back." Questions flooded my mind. Any inquiries I had for this Fae could wait until I solved this new mystery. Folding the sheet in half, I extended my hand toward his retreating form. I paused, then asked, "What's your name?"

He didn't turn around. "My name? I'm surprised you don't know already, being a stalker and all. And I don't need the ad anymore. My puny Fae brain has already memorized the words. If you really need a name though," he said, head swiveling enough to meet my eyes, "call me ScarFae."

"I hate those stupid Pit monikers," I muttered, raising my voice to add, "And you're as pathetic as your dumb nickname."

I spun in a huff, dropping the slip of paper over my shoulder as I went. Fae prick. If he responded, I didn't hear him. I had more pressing matters to attend to. Questions I needed answered.

I paced the foyer of Mordecai's mansion, flicking cigarette ashes on the flecked marble floor. My hands were jittery from dealing with the Fae and I knew if Mordecai noticed, he would have my hide.

"No Fae should be able to spook my daughter."

Adopted daughter. Theoretically the same thing. And I wasn't spooked, I was infuriated. I couldn't remember the last time I had been so angry from a handful of sentences. That Fae had me teetering a dangerous line between helper and Enforcer, and I didn't like the feeling.

"Your father will see you now." An older gentleman—one I had dubbed Squirrel Butler so long ago the name was ingrained—played doorman to the mansion. Mordecai said his shifter form was harmless, but I wasn't entirely sure what the doorman actually was. With his mousy face, puff of red-brown hair, and bottomless pocket of sunflower seeds, I had to get creative. He was wiry, thin, and twitchy. Squirrel made sense.

I began the climb to the second story, up an elaborate staircase made from the same marble as the floor below. Mordecai spared no expense on this place. Alec had an entire wing to himself now. I had been offered the same, but I had passed under the pretense that I needed more quiet to sleep during the day. Mordecai agreed, and paid the expense for my penthouse, but only so long as I remained on as an Enforcer. The last bit was formality; I didn't actually have a choice in the matter.

His office was down a long hallway, carpeted in black velvet and scattered with silver light fixtures; the same thematic colors he used downstairs and in all the public rooms of the mansion. Mordecai had decked his own suites in green and silver, Alec choosing red and gold. Both had massive balconies attached to their private chambers, larger even than mine. Dragon shifters took up more space, they claimed. I scoffed. Alec's "mighty" dragon was puny next to my lion.

Mordecai's huge office door was dark, solid kingwood,

engraved with a dragon curled around a shard of crystal. His signet. I twisted the silver handle and shoved, groaning at the weight.

My eyes fell first to the walls and the beautiful bookcases that circled the room. Mordecai's desk sat in the center on a garish, woven rug. He was tapping away at his laptop when I entered, but he paused to look up expectantly. I dipped to one knee.

"In loyalty and service to the Great Dragon." I lowered my head.

Mordecai snapped his fingers and I stood. "Sit. I'll only be a moment."

I did, lounging in the chair in front of his desk. Resting might have been a mistake. The moment my feet left the ground, my eyelids began to droop, my mind slowing. I straightened, planting my boots firmly on the floor.

"Father, can I ask you about a flier I saw at Smithfield Press this afternoon?"

Mordecai's eyes flicked up. He and Alec shared that icy blue color, though his were a tad lighter than his son's. They even had similar hairstyles, though Mordecai's was noticeably shorter, black, and peppered with gray. A long scar stretched from the left corner of his mouth to his jaw. I didn't know where the mark had come from—one of the stories he swore he would never tell. From what I knew of wounds, I could only guess that someone had sliced his mouth wide open.

"What did you see at the press, my darling?"

I balked at the strange pet name, so easy to mistake for real affection. Mordecai had never been shy about his terms of endearment; always the doting father until he needed to punish me. I didn't fall for the act anymore, not often anyway. Alec and I had grown up the same, with every comfort and privilege, but having seen the sheer brutality they dealt innocent Fae for small things like stealing food, I couldn't bring myself to share their ideals.

I swallowed. "I saw that you're opening a new position to Fae employees? I was curious as to what, and why? You've always shown so much favor to the shifters—if you have this many new jobs, shouldn't they be approached too?"

He probably wants to repress the Fae a bit more, I thought bitterly.

Mordecai leaned back, his wooden chair groaning at the weight change as he steepled his fingertips. The three silver bands in each of his ears clicked together. He slowly nodded. "I think we should try to repair a bit of the damage that's been done. Allow the Fae to take better-paying positions if they're up to the task. Mend fences, if you will."

"But why? And why now?"

"I have mines in need of workers. The Fae have workers in need of jobs. I thought you of all people would appreciate a move toward bettering Fae livelihoods." His tone was a challenge, daring me to defend the Fae. Asking for a reason to reprimand me, or worse.

"Yes, well, we both know you keep the Fae in the city to do the jobs shifters don't want."

His eyes flashed. I was pushing my luck. But I would handle a lashing if I could squeeze more information from him. "I'm in need of laborers. Why do you care where I acquire them?" My hands shook and I tugged a cigarette free, lighting the end and taking a long drag. Mordecai scowled. "You're not to smoke in my office. You know this."

"I do," I agreed, eyeing him. The best way to get Mordecai off me was to send him after his son. My brow lifted as I said, "I've had extra Enforcer duties all day. On Alec's watch. I think I'm entitled to a little leniency."

"What do you mean on Alec's watch?" Mordecai's scowl deepened, but his shoulders relaxed. "That boy is as useless as wet bread."

"There was a shifter in Fae territory. A coyote. Don't worry, I handled him."

"I'll have a word with Alec," he growled. "Go home, rest. I need you in top shape tonight. I hear there's a Fae making trouble at The Pit."

"I've handled him," I said casually, standing. "That's all this new job is? Mining positions?"

Mordecai shrugged, his expression a touch too innocent to be believed. "That's all, sweetheart."

I strode out onto the balcony, smashing my cigarette onto the banister before I shifted. Part of me suspected he knew what I did for the Fae, but I had to believe he would have punished me if he did. He never seemed to miss the opportunity, and I wasn't always the one to pay the price. Then again, his hatred for the Fae was the reason Alec and I had been trained as Enforcers.

To do whatever is necessary to teach them their place.

I growled at the thought. Whatever these mining jobs were, they were almost certainly not going to benefit the Fae. If Mordecai was even being honest about the positions in the first place. I had my doubts. I guess I'd have to be a little more *nosy.*

When my fur finally settled into place, I took flight, my aim the soft bed that called my name.

CHAPTER 5

Tarik

The last twenty-four hours had royally sucked. Getting beat up sucked. Losing my job sucked. Getting carried away by the Night Enforcer who happened to be a foot shorter than me—and probably a hundred pounds lighter—

Sucked.

Carried . . . Yeah, I still didn't know how I'd gotten into her apartment. The bouncer's warning about her lion form resurfaced. I snorted and tossed the notion aside. She was too small. There was no way.

As I took a swig of whiskey, I stewed over the mystery, but my brain was buzzing too hard to help me solve the case. I knew fighting at The Pit so soon after my win would only land me in a ditch, so I was playing nice. For now. No one bothered me as I sat in a corner booth of the warehouse's underground, slowly getting drunk and pretending to watch the fights.

I saw nothing.

My head was too full of what-ifs and booze. Earlier in the evening, a few shifters had approached me—tried to bait me into entering the cages. But no, as much as I wanted to numb the pain, I couldn't risk another beating. Alcohol would have to do. So, after staring at my unblinking face for a few minutes, they called me a piece of Fae trash and left me to my vices. Deep down, somewhere in the far recesses of my being, I was relieved. I doubted the Night Enforcer had any desire to rescue me a second time—not after the way I had treated her.

I really was a prick sometimes. The thought made me want to laugh. I gnawed on my lip instead. If everyone just left me alone, my word choices wouldn't be an issue. It had taken years of social suicide on my part, but not many noticed me anymore. Except Benji, and now this Enforcer. What was her deal?

My mood was especially sour tonight—didn't help that I'd been stuck in a downpour on my way over. This city was the worst: wet, dirty, and smelling of shifter musk. If I had more money, I'd leave this craphole behind for good and find a small corner of the world that accepted Fae as equals.

But that was the problem. I didn't know if such a corner existed, and finding a shifter knowledgeable enough and willing to escort me past the minefields so I didn't get blown to bits was probably impossible—especially with my bad rep. More likely, they'd laugh, shoot me in the face, then pocket my money.

Humans had been smart enough to clear out of this city around the time of The Shift—I hadn't seen one since before my days spent locked in that sad excuse for an orphanage. The humans had been treated fairly and were allowed jobs with decent wages, but they'd still left en masse after witnessing so many executions.

They were lucky. Mordecai had allowed them to leave, and other cities would accept them. But here I was, stuck, fresh out of a job, and money wasn't coming anytime soon. That was why I chose not to fight tonight, despite my body's cravings.

Money. A necessary evil.

I had stashed away the roll I'd won last night, but the cash wasn't enough to solve my problems—unless drowning my problems in whiskey counted. I laid a hand over my right pants pocket where the wanted flyer now rested. Open interviews started at noon tomorrow and I was determined to be first in line. My blood heated when I realized who I would no doubt face. Who I would directly work for. For the first time that I knew of, the devil dragon himself was offering a position to Fae. The pay would undoubtedly be better than any I'd had previously.

But the thought of Mordecai peering over my shoulder while I worked, correcting my every stupid Fae move, made my blood boil. I slammed my empty mug down on the sticky, claw-marked table, and the cheap glass shattered. Someone nearby cursed and threw an insult my way. Another urge to laugh swept over me.

"Hey, you," I said to a passing Pit girl, the words a bit slurred. "Another whiskey on the rocks."

She wrinkled her nose, but went to do my bidding. I hoped. The buzz in my head was getting good now—heavy, like a nest of swarming honey bees. My problems were but pesky little bubbles, and if I squinted hard enough, I could pop them. Make them disappear.

Another glass of amber liquid thunked on the table and I wasted no time knocking the drink back. After two more, the world started to swirl. Maybe I shouldn't have had that last one. Getting home was going to be interesting. With a lurch and slight stumble, I was on my feet. Somehow I had to keep my cool as I weaved through the undulating crowd.

Were they dancing?

I had never seen anyone dance in this joint before. They had no idea what they were missing out on. An urge to sway to the thumping bass consumed me. I bobbed my head and shuffled my feet. Only for a minute. Shaggy hair fell over my face like a curtain, hiding me from the others. If they couldn't see me, they couldn't bother me. I was alone with the music, the vibrating beat, alcohol warming my insides and calming my normally rage-filled mind.

The moment was rudely interrupted as my back hit a wall. I swung around, almost tilting too far, but I grabbed onto a pole. Or rather, an arm covered in swirly green art.

"Pretty." I focused on the wall that had ruined my dance moves, but was greeted by a two-headed monster instead. I blinked and the heads squished into one. Then split into two again. He *looked* human. Sort of. "Ugly."

Two mouths pulled back to reveal hideously yellow teeth. "What did you call me, Fae scum?"

I stumbled back a step, waving a hand in front of my face. "Dude." I coughed. "Didn't your mom ever tell you to brush your teeth?"

The teeth elongated and I stared, fascinated. How did he do that? Then he started talking again and more laughter bubbled up my chest, escaping through my nose. "You shouldn't have come to a shifter joint if you can't hold your liquor, boy. Now the floor is about to get real messy."

I watched, curious, as he took off his shirt, revealing a large tattoo of a mermaid. But the drawing had—I squinted—three heads. I pointed at the fuzzy image. "Is that your girl? She's uglier than you."

The two-headed monster roared, sounding like a constipated walrus. His rotten egg breath washed over me a second time and my gut roiled. I held up a hand, the other gripping at my stomach. "Whoa, I think you're right. Keep doing that and the floor is going to get messy. Maybe your shoes, too."

Out of nowhere, something struck my face. My head whipped to the side and so did the rest of my body. Another pole broke my fall though. No, not a pole. Some of the fog receded, enough for me to see a furious shifter holding me upright. A second later, I was thrust backward, right into another wall.

The whiskey in my stomach sloshed back and forth. I groaned. "Time out, guys. Give me a second. I don't think my stomach likes being tossed around by an ugly pack of shifters." I belched, my body's way of agreeing.

But I should have known better. Shifters didn't play fair.

One second I was swaying on my feet, the next rolling on the floor as a boot struck my back. My spine throbbed, the ache sharpening my awareness. Shifters. Shifters everywhere. At least a dozen glaring down at me. Another kick, right between the shoulder blades, wrenched the buzz away.

I scrambled to my feet, blinking rapidly as the dozen faces became fifty. *Snap out of it before they snap you in half!* Barely dodging another kick, I let fly a fist—my knuckles smashed into a nose. *Crunch!*

Everyone paused, gaping as a shifter cradled his broken nose, blood streaming between his fingers. I clenched my teeth, knowing that whatever happened next would be bad. Maybe I'd finally managed to provoke them into not letting me walk away again. The end had come for me at long last.

At the finality of the thought, my stomach twisted, and not because of the alcohol. Maybe, now that the end stared me in the face, I wasn't quite ready. The realization came too late. In the next moment, hell was unleashed as several hands grabbed me, dragging me to the putrid floor.

Fists and feet and elbows and knees rained down on me. No way was I surviving this. My entire body was on fire, receiving blow after blow.

"Stop!"

The shout was strong, authoritative, and decidedly female. But the beating didn't let up, only intensified. Everything changed when a roar shook the building, vibrating through the cement beneath my cheek and into my bones. Silence. Frozen silence. Shuffling feet, and then . . .

Then . . .

I frowned. From my place on the floor, I saw the crowd part, giving me the perfect view of . . . the alley wall painting? White wings. And attached to the white wings was an enormous white lion. My eyes failed me then as the terrifying creature shrank inward. Shaping, reshaping, bones snapping, fur receding, until a few short moments later, a girl stood in place of the lion.

A very naked girl.

She straightened, revealing pale skin covered in colorful tattoos. This wasn't the first time I'd seen a naked female at The Pit, but when my eyes traveled up to blue and black hair, I wanted to die. Someone needed to put me out of my misery and fast because the Night Enforcer's nude image was now forever imprinted on my brain.

I grimaced as her keen gaze swung my way, no doubt taking in my fresh new bruises and weakened state. Her thoughts practically shouted: *The idiot Fae needs my help again. But will I save him this time? He's a complete prick after all.*

My lips curled mockingly. Then I rolled to a stand—one of the hardest things I'd ever done. Somehow I didn't cry out, despite the shooting pains lancing up and down my body. I swaggered to her—well, more of a swerve than a swagger. I noticed the shifters openly curse and grumble at having their fun interrupted, but they made no move to stop me. Were they afraid of the big bad kitty cat? I wasn't. Far from it. The only thing I felt was annoyance.

Leaning in close to her, I murmured, "I don't need your help, stalker."

I strode for the exit and held my breath so I wouldn't hunch over my aching ribs like the injured sap that I was. On my way out, I swiped a half empty beer bottle off a table, the owner too shell-shocked from the almighty lion's appearance to protest.

At last, after huffing up a flight of stairs, I emerged from the place that had nearly cost me my pathetic life. Again. *I think I have a death wish.* As the night's incessant downpour further washed the alcoholic haze from my mind, I groaned, thunking my head against the warehouse's outer brick wall.

"This isn't a safe spot to rest. Or wallow. Whichever one you're doing."

That *voice!* Would she ever leave me alone?

"Noted," I mumbled, peeking at her through my damp hair. I shouldn't have. My stupid male eyes went straight to her chest for the second time today. And this time all I saw was skin and more skin, and a red-and-black heart tattoo right between her—

"Do you want my help, or do you want to stand there gawking all night?"

My eyes snapped to hers and I scowled. "Neither."

"Not an option. I'm taking you home." She planted her hands on her hips and I quickly looked away.

I took a slow sip of beer, grimacing at the thought of shifter lips having touched that same rim, then settled more comfortably against the bricks. "You take your babysitting duties quite seriously. But no. I'm not ready to go home yet, and I sure wouldn't let *you* know where that is."

Leaning against the wall beside me, she crossed her arms and slid one leg over the other. "You're literally the most impossible Fae I've ever tried to help. Why is that?"

Oh, she thought this was unburden my heart time? That wasn't happening.

"Look," I said, drilling holes into her eyes in an attempt to keep my gaze from wandering. "This city is crawling with Fae who would trip over themselves for some help. So help *them*, not me. I'm not your problem. You do, on the other hand, seem to have a stalking problem. It's not attractive, I'll say that much."

Being as she was female, I expected the slight to offend her. But my attempts at getting rid of her once and for all failed yet again. She simply stood there, looking annoyed. Definitely not stomping away in a huff like I'd hoped. Like I *needed.* Time to up my game. She was giving me no choice.

I rose from my slouch and faced her fully, putting as much hatred and loathing as I could behind my words as I said, "You don't seem to understand subtleties, so I'm going to say this as clearly as I can: I. Hate. Shifters. Every single one of you. The sight of you. The smell of you. Standing next to you repulses me. So the last thing, the very last thing I want is to be your charity case. In fact, if you ever see me beaten half to death in an alley, *don't* rescue me. Never again. Got that?"

She stared at me, lips pressed into a thin line. Her breathing was even as she unfalteringly met my eyes. And then she sighed. "Yeah, I hear you. I mean, if you're so eager to die, taking one of Mordecai's shady jobs is a sure way to do it. But you're right—you're a waste of my time." She spun on her heel and stepped away.

Instead of victory, shock zipped through me. I had anticipated dozens of reactions—anger, hurt, disgust—but not sadness. The look she had given me . . . Not pity, exactly. More like acceptance. Like I was a lost cause. Like I really was a waste of time.

Gaia. Watching her walk away was worse than a punch in the gut. *Let her go. Good riddance. Go after her.* My brain fired off conflicting commands and I shoved a hand through my hair, yanking on the ends. What was wrong with me? She was a *shifter!*

"There's this boy," I began, then blew out an exasperated breath. Why was I still talking? She paused, one pale foot off the ground. Didn't turn around, but she was listening. My mouth started blabbing again. "His name is Benji. Eight years old and never shuts up."

Her other foot lowered. "I may have seen him once or twice. There aren't many Fae children anymore."

For some reason—maybe because she was acknowledging me after what I had said—I continued. "You're right, there aren't. Too many lose their parents and get shoved into the Fae orphanage, myself included. That hellhole is barely livable—dirty, the children malnourished with hardly any supervision. Most don't survive. And that's where Benji's heading if his mom doesn't get better. That's . . . that's why I'm applying for the job on that flyer. She needs the money, and he needs his mom. So, yeah."

I was all kinds of uncomfortable after dumping those facts into her . . . lap. My eyes dipped down her spine, low, lower, until they rested on a fiery red and orange bird tattooed across her hips. A Phoenix. The tail feathers swooped over her right—

I needed to get out of here.

"Look, I get it. The tattooed skin, the Enforcer title . . . what I can become. You look at me and all you see is what people like me have done to yours. To you. But you don't actually know anything about *me*." She paused, shuffling her feet, then cast a nervous glance around. "Mordecai is my father by law, not blood. I don't agree with the majority of things he does and says, but you try disagreeing with the *Great Dragon*. I do what I can, though. And what I can do right now is warn you that whatever this job is, Mordecai is up to something. I don't know what, but I don't trust the information he gave me. Do with that what you will."

Goosebumps rose on my arms and the back of my neck. She spoke treason. I could easily report her and—I huffed, shaking my head. I was such an idiot. "You're a spy, aren't you." I didn't phrase the words as a question. No shifter would willingly trust a Fae. "What game are you playing at?"

"I don't play games. Like I said, I do what I can. I see an injustice, I try to help. I'm in a position where I have that option, and we all know Alec isn't going to save any Fae." She moved closer to a motorcycle leaning against the far wall of the alley, street lights catching the vibrant blue paint. Glancing around as though checking for prying eyes, she leaned over the bike and dug into the saddle bags. Clothing. She had spare clothing. Thank Gaia. "Look, if you don't want my help, fine. There are other Fae who do. But you seem to find the most trouble."

She slipped a shirt and shorts on and faced me once again. My shoulders loosened, then tightened as light caught the arch of her throat. Twin marks ran lengthwise across her neck. Scars. Shaking my head, I replied, "You'd better believe I find trouble, because I see the injustice too and won't sit back while shifters abuse our kind."

"And you think The Pit—"

"Yes," I interrupted her. "Because the cage fights help *me!*" Her eyes widened as she digested that blurted piece of information. I sighed, tipping back the beer bottle for one last swallow. I was such an idiot. "Here's the thing, Enforcer: when your back's to a wall, you're willing to risk more. I didn't choose this life, but nothing will keep me from that job interview tomorrow. A position like that is the only chance I have at bettering the crap life I've been forced into."

I pushed off the wall and turned from her, beginning the trek back to Fae territory. I'd probably regret this conversation in the morning. We had both been too honest, too *real.*

"Reagan."

I peered over my shoulder at her. "What?"

"My name's Reagan, not Enforcer."

Right then and there, I knew I was going to do something incredibly stupid. Probably the dumbest thing I'd ever done in all twenty-three years of my life. My traitorous tongue formed one word: "Tarik."

I gave the stalker shifter my name.

CHAPTER 6

Reagan

Mordecai and Alec were in a particularly foul mood today. I trailed behind them, scuffing my boots across the asphalt, flicking the cap of my lighter with my thumb. A nervous habit. They hadn't explained why they had requested my presence. Two Enforcers and the Great Dragon seemed like overkill for Fae matters, and I doubted highly that they cared about my fifteenth birthday tomorrow.

I glanced up, squinting under the bright sun. Whatever was going on, this was Alec's patrol. He should be able to handle this without me.

"Keep up, Reagan, I don't have all day." Mordecai's clipped tone broke through my thoughts. I wasn't sure why he was seeing to this personally, either. He never left the mansion unless something went terribly wrong.

A chill ran the length of my spine, warning bells toning in my mind.

My lighter clicked open again. The urge to light a cigarette twitched through my fingers, tension tightening my shoulders. Each step we took toward the Fae district shot ice through my veins. This wasn't standard procedure. I racked my brain, scanning the last week's events for anything that might clue me in. Nothing. Nothing abnormal, anyway.

Except—

"So what's this all about?" I asked, struggling to conceal the tremor in my voice.

"You'll see soon enough." Mordecai turned his head to grin at me.

The matching expression on Alec's face sent my stomach plummeting. He had been a friend, once. My best friend. We had spent more hours than I could count working on his vintage motorcycles; hell, Alec taught me how to ride my own bike. But the last few years he was too much like his father. Power and ambition were his hobbies, and our friendship had fallen to the wayside. Doubly so when he started to think he was entitled to more. To me.

And now he was here, for whatever this was. I had a really bad feeling.

Only one thing had gone wrong this week. My back and hips still ached from the raw lashes I carried as punishment. I had already paid the price though. The mistakes were mine. Surely he wouldn't . . .

My heart stuttered, then clenched. Mordecai stopped before a torn-down apartment building and led us up two short sets of stairs. Crumbling concrete rained from under our feet, bouncing down to the floor below. My breaths came in short bursts, the air fire in my lungs. The rhythm of my heart was a drumbeat in my ears.

He wouldn't.

He couldn't.

At the end of the hallway, he stopped before a door. A crooked "3" hung from beneath a caved peephole. Mordecai waited until I caught up, then slammed his boot into the door handle.

The weak wood splintered and collapsed under the force. A small Fae family sat around a table—a tall, slender woman with dark walnut-toned hair, her partner with blue eyes that glittered in the afternoon light, and two small children.

The eldest was almost six.

I only knew that because I had been punished for passing food to that six-year-old. She was malnourished, thin, frail. But her spirit—I had been drawn to her the moment she smiled, unafraid, when I had been patrolling one afternoon. I wanted to help her, to nourish the bright light that sparkled in her amber eyes.

The same eyes that now widened in confusion, framed by red-brown curls. I froze in the door frame, watched the questions on her face morph to betrayal.

My heart shattered, the jagged shards tearing at my chest from the inside.

Alec extended his claws. I moved to shift but Mordecai anticipated my interference. He slammed me against the wall, a sharp blade pressed to my throat.

"We don't help the Fae, Reagan." He cast a glance over his shoulder. "And I don't abide those who willingly take from my coffers. Alec, if you would."

I struggled, the blade biting into my skin. Blood trickled onto my chest as I blurted, "Please, don't. I forced her to take the supplies. She didn't want to."

First mistake. A confession.

Alec extended his claws and attacked. The father lunged to protect his children and took the full brunt of Alec's dragon claws as they shredded his chest apart. Bile rose up my throat, stomach heaving when the small boy fell beside him. Sobs filled the room as the mother gripped the girl tightly against her side.

"Please," I begged. "Please don't do this."

Second mistake. Pleading.

Mordecai ignored my tears and lifted the blade long enough to motion for his son to continue. I tried to free myself, pressure trembling against my spine as my wings threatened to punch free. Cold steel found a new mark on my neck, a new line of blood springing up right below the first.

"Let this be a lesson to you. I don't tolerate mistakes, Reagan."

At the end of the sentence the girl's mother fell, her throat slit. I swallowed. Met those honey-toned eyes.

A sob shuddered through me when she crumpled into the spreading pool of blood. Mordecai released me then and I shoved past him, gathering the small girl to my chest. Tears fell unrestrained down my cheeks. My body shook so hard I almost lost my grip on the poor child.

This young, innocent Fae . . . her death was my fault. Her family's deaths . . . My fault. Her blood was on my—

"One minute," Mordecai said, his cold voice cutting through my sorrows. "If you're not outside in one minute, I'll slaughter every other Fae in this building and burn it to the ground. You're emotional, Reagan. Weak. Maybe this will teach you to be strong."

His footsteps retreated, tailed by Alec's. I spared a glance at the girl's eyes but they were dull, lifeless, and my chest ached as tears welled up again. Gently, I brushed them closed and lowered her back to the ground. I would find a way to make sure they were buried properly, even if I had to sneak back myself. I glanced down at my clothing, to the crimson splattered and smeared across my own skin. Blood.

Her blood, mingling with mine.

A gasp tore from my lungs—a dream. I knew it was a dream. I had lived this moment a thousand times. And still, as the memory played out, I was powerless to change anything.

Powerless to silence my own mind.

My fingers slipped to my throat, traced the thin scars that Mordecai's knife left as a permanent reminder. I wiped at the tears that always followed that dream, reducing them to dark spots on my sleeve.

Four years had passed since that day, and every time the dream came the emotions were as strong as the first time. The pain in my chest was still raw agony, my heart clenched tight beneath my ribs. My nightmares had been worse, once. When I moved from the mansion they had lessened, gradually. Now they visited only once or twice a month, if I was lucky.

Still too much. That day should have never happened. I had been sloppy, and their lost lives were still my biggest regret. The girl and the bright, sparkling life in her beautiful eyes . . . gone.

And it had been my fault.

I blew out a breath, scrubbing my palms over my face. My eyes fell to my cell phone. Nine-thirty. In my waking frenzy, I had torn my earbuds out. I freed them from my blankets, shoving them back into place.

Without them—without music—I never would have managed to sleep again. I buried my face into my pillow and tugged the blankets over my head.

"Reagan." The sound was foggy. Who would interrupt my sleep? No one had access to my— "You look a little cold. Want to use me as a blanket?"

Oh, hell no.

"Alec, get out of my room."

"Are you sure? I could—"

"Whatever you're thinking, stop. Get out."

I heard the small huff, the retreating footsteps. Blinking, I glanced at the clock beside my bed. Eleven? Like, eleven *in the morning?* This better be good. Alec had pulled an earbud from my ear and I plucked the other free, dropping them onto my comforter beside my phone.

Shoving off the covers, I rolled out of bed and pulled a long t-shirt over gray leggings. I stormed down the hall, eyes narrowed. Alec leaned against the kitchen counter, helping himself to the cupboard.

"Why did you wake me up? What do you want?"

He cast a long look my way, eyes traveling head-to-toe and back. "Not too bad. Would be better—"

I growled, the low lion tone rumbling from my throat. Alec cut himself off as I snarled, "What do you want?"

"I don't. Mordecai wants you at the mansion." He shuffled

a box aside and snapped the cabinet shut. "The shifters have been rowdy since the mining job hit the papers this morning. He needs me to make sure the Fae get safely in and out. While I lead them along the border, he needs you to secure the manor, since the interviews will be held in the mines."

"In the mines? Why?"

Alec shrugged. "Something about wanting to be sure the Fae know what their working conditions will be?"

I really didn't like the sound of this. "When does he need me?"

"Eleven forty-five." He glanced at the oven clock and grinned. "So, twenty minutes?"

"Fine. Go. I have to shower."

"I could—"

"Go."

I showered quickly and dropped into lion form. Mordecai would have clothing waiting for me. I stepped out onto the balcony, sun beaming warmth across my skin as I shifted and leapt into the air. Spreading my wings, I glided toward the mansion at the northern edge of the city.

Unsurprisingly, a shock of red hair waited inside the foyer as I prowled in. I tucked my wings in tight, but Mordecai had designed the room for himself, so my caution was unnecessary. As I maneuvered over to Squirrel Butler, my gaze turned to the manor doors. Tarik leaned against the wall, first in line. He was determined, I could give him that.

The shift back into human form took longer than usual. Exhaustion. Unfortunately, Enforcers didn't get days off. Mordecai didn't believe in them. Apparently he didn't believe in rest today, either. I glanced at Tarik again and smirked as I gathered the clothing held out to me.

"Hi, *Tarik*," I cooed. "Enjoying the view?"

His eyes widened comically when he caught sight of me. As if pulled by some magnetic force, his gaze wrenched downward, landing on my chest. He had done that three times now. And like the last two, he quickly looked away, blinking rapidly. A new detail caught my attention this time, though; a blush that crept up the back of his neck.

He reached a hand up and scratched at the growing red stain, as if trying to scrub the blush away. My smirk grew.

"Bravo, you remembered my name. I didn't know you had other talents besides stalking," he said sarcastically.

Interesting. Deflecting because he was uncomfortable. My thoughts skipped to his temper. What was *that* a coping method for?

I mentally shook myself, turning my attention to the clasp of my shorts before fastening the buttons on my top. This wasn't the time for a psychological profile. Squirrel Butler passed me a tablet and I slid my finger across the screen. Flipping the device over, I showed him where his name blinked at the top of the list.

"Hail? Tarik Hail?" My lip twitched as I considered. "Seems fitting that you're named after chunks of ice that like to bludgeon people."

His eyes rolled to the ceiling as he muttered, "Never heard *that* one before."

My fingers danced across the screen, checking his credentials. Name, age, etcetera etcetera. I looked up again, a reluctant sigh falling from my lips.

"Are you sure about this?" At his nod, I shrugged. "All right, follow me."

I led him to the rear entrance of the manor but, instead of opening the door leading outside, I took a sharp left and followed the wall to a door farther along. Through that, a staircase spiraled downward, the only surface entrance to the mines below. Or, at least, the only one I knew of.

Round, silver-edged lights lined the rough stone walls. I hadn't considered having to climb these stairs a couple dozen times today. My head lowered in defeat, the groan I released far louder than intended. A small snort of laughter caught my ear from behind.

"Keep laughing. I'll make you climb these stairs with me—and I'm going to be escorting applicants *all* day."

Chatter echoed up the stairs from below. I hadn't anticipated Mordecai being alone, but I couldn't imagine who he would enlist to help him with the interviews either. The staircase widened out into a cavern of stone that narrowed into a hallway on the far side. According to the tablet, the Fae would work in a room farther along—a room filled with green crystals. Genesis Crystal.

I hated coming down here. The mines always made my stomach uneasy and my hands shake. I couldn't decide if the feeling was a weird side effect of the crystals, or my conscience screaming about the wrongness of the mines in general.

Mordecai hoarded the Genesis Crystal. I didn't know what the green rocks did, or why he wanted them, but I was certain they had value I couldn't see. Especially with the amount of money he put into the lab designed to research them. I did know that the bombs surrounding Nathra City had chips of the crystal in them, and that I wasn't allowed to touch the stuff.

Maybe they were easily detonated?

I shot a glance to where Tarik walked behind me. Even in the dim glow of the lights he looked pale. Did he feel the same way I did? Or was he nervous about the interview?

I led him farther into the cavernous room, to a grooved cutout in the wall where Mordecai had set up a makeshift office. My eyes slid to Tarik again as we approached, my stomach recoiling at what I was about to do. This certainly wouldn't win me any brownie points.

Do I really care what he thinks?

Still, I swallowed hard when Mordecai stared at me expectantly—and I knelt. "In loyalty and service to the Great Dragon."

My throat tightened. I couldn't bring myself to look at the Fae beside me, even after Mordecai snapped his fingers so I could rise. The flutters in my chest sped up to a painful pace. I could almost feel Tarik's distrust thrumming off him. Mordecai's eyes danced over him before he motioned to the woman at his side.

"My new assistant, Jocelyn. She'll be overseeing our new employees."

I studied the woman, not recognizing the name. Ruby-painted lips, bronze skin, long ebony hair. She was dressed for business in a tight A-line skirt and button-up blouse. Jocelyn's lips widened into a welcoming smile.

"Reagan, so nice to meet you. I've heard so much." She glanced at Tarik. "And this must be our first applicant?"

"Yes, ma'am." I handed her my tablet, which she scanned and passed back.

Mordecai glanced down at his own device. "Tarik Hail, am

I correct?"

Tarik's complexion had paled even further, but his eyes were sharp and wholly trained on Mordecai. He looked . . . Oh no. I closed my eyes and braced for impact.

"Yes, your *grace*, that's me."

I glanced between the two. Mordecai lifted his chin, studying Tarik down the line of his nose. "Mordecai will do. What's your interest in this position, Tarik?"

"Well, sir, I couldn't pass up this once-in-a-lifetime opportunity. What an honor for us lowly Fae to be offered jobs from the esteemed dragon himself." Tarik plastered a fake smile on his face—I fought to stifle a laugh at the absurdity.

Mordecai shoved his chair back, eyes narrowing as he stepped around the table. My stomach dropped, humor gone. He swooped into a predatory stance, circling Tarik slowly, examining the Fae from head to toe. When he stopped he was right in front of him, a tad too close for my own comfort.

"And is there truth to the rumors that you can't seem to hold a job?" The small smile on Mordecai's lips sent a shiver down my spine, but he continued. "And that you regularly cause issues for my daughter and the other shifters who frequent The Pit?"

Tarik's eyes practically glittered. A muscle jumped in his jaw. "More like they can't handle all of this." He made a gesture spanning the length of his body, adding as an afterthought, "Your highness."

Mordecai licked his lips. He stared into Tarik's eyes for a moment, then blinked. I knew that look. That decisiveness.

"You're awfully arrogant to come asking for a job and then present yourself in such a manner." Mordecai stepped away, circling back to his perch behind the desk. His smirk was vile. "But I'll tell you what. Find one shifter. One. Who will vouch for you. And you can have this job."

I stared a little too hard at the uneven floor, swallowing the knot in my throat. No other shifter was going to speak in his favor. Not one. But if *I* did, what would Mordecai think? Had Alec told him about that Fae rumor, so now he was fact checking me?

The silence in the room was palpable. My eyes finally lifted to Tarik's face, to the tension lining his shoulders, to the fists trembling at his sides. *Damnit.* I tried to imagine myself in his shoes, with that little boy, Benji, needing him. His mouth slid open and I took a step forward. "Father, I'll speak for him."

Tarik's troublemaker mouth snapped shut. Mordecai's stare locked onto mine, his voice low when he asked, "Why?"

"The shifters at The Pit might complain about him, but they like that he's there. They can bet on the fights and Tarik gets to blow off steam. I'm the one who deals with the problems down there every night. I've seen what goes on myself." I licked my lips, bought myself the split second I needed to come up with an excuse. *In for a penny . . .* "And I was the reason he lost his last job. I pissed off a couple of the shifters when I told them to lay off him. They found him later. He wasn't able to work the next day. If I had done my job properly, he wouldn't have been late."

Mordecai stared at me—really stared—and I squirmed at the carefully bottled fury lurking in his eyes. There would be a discussion later. Probably a punishment. I had teetered over that line of getting too close to the Fae, and he had warned me. My fingers slid to the scars at my throat, before I realized and jerked them away. Still, I couldn't let Tarik lose this job now that I knew what—or who—the position was really for. Even if he couldn't keep his damned mouth shut, and Mordecai was playing games.

Punishment or no.

"So be it," Mordecai said quietly. Jocelyn bounced around the desk and extended a hand toward Tarik.

"Welcome aboard," she said. Her widespread, toothy grin reminded me of the clowns I had been afraid of as a child. Innocent enough, until they were standing over you in your sleep. A shiver raced up my spine. If Mordecai trusted her, I didn't.

"Be here first thing tomorrow morning. Eight. Do not be late, and leave your attitude at home." Mordecai's voice was still too soft, too low. I could vomit.

Without a word I motioned at Tarik to follow, clutching the tablet a little too close to my chest as I led him up the spiral staircase. He remained silent. For once. Back in the foyer, the next Fae applicant stood waiting inside the doorway.

"Wait." Spoken so softly, I almost missed the word. I turned to find Tarik studying me, a crease bisecting his brows. "Why did you do that for me? After all the things I've said to you?"

"I don't know." I stared at the floor. My stomach still felt wrong, and not because of the mines this time. Mordecai was *angry*. And all because of a Fae I had been dead set and determined to abandon last night. He had a death wish and I didn't have the heart to watch another light get snuffed out by this city. But his tiny revelation about the boy had given me pause. So here I was, opening my big mouth . . . "Come on, there's other applicants for me to take down."

Before brushing past me, he paused, then said, "I'm not forgetting who you are, but I'm not forgetting what you've done, either." He parted with, "See you around, stalker."

I watched him leave, the door closing heavily behind him. What had I done? I had helped him, despite his attitude and all his protests. The next Fae followed me when I gestured, verifying his name before I settled back into my thoughts. I had set out to help him and I had accomplished that.

But what will be the cost?

My blood ran cold. Tarik was trouble, and I gravitated to trouble. To the dying, the sick, the abused. To the one Fae in the city who seemed to want to fight back, who I wanted to keep alive because . . . because his fire was motivating. I didn't feel so alone, knowing that another soul in Nathra was battling against the shifter oppression, and I couldn't help but want him to keep fighting.

And, selfishly, deep in my gut I had this feeling that if I could convince this one Fae I was good, maybe I wouldn't have to feel so guilty all the time. That maybe Tarik, who seemed to hate the shifters more than any other Fae, could grant me some small peace and forgive the stupid title which plagued my steps and ruined my predetermined life. I had trained for this job since I could walk. There were no options in the matter; I was always meant to be an Enforcer. I didn't realize what that entailed, what Mordecai and Alec actually did, until I was far older. Until the damage was already done. Service and loyalty to my adoptive father were ingrained reflexes.

Speaking up for Tarik was worth the consequences, I chanted to myself. I stood behind my decision. Didn't I? My breath came in staggered bursts. I closed my eyes and inhaled slowly.

Worth it, I repeated.

So why didn't I believe myself?

The rest of the day passed in a blur. I kept to myself, quiet, and didn't interfere with any more interviews. Mordecai didn't let me forget his anger though. The fire in his eyes grew with each passing applicant. Late in the afternoon, when I had escorted the last Fae out, I turned to find him in the foyer with his arms crossed tightly over his chest.

His eyes narrowed on me. "What were you thinking, interfering with Fae dealings?" he spat. "Have I taught you nothing?"

"I was the reason he lost his job, Father. I felt guilty."

"You shouldn't. We do not *help* the Fae."

I paused. I hadn't expected him to confirm my suspicions about this job so easily. "Isn't that the whole purpose of your mining operation? To help the Fae?"

Oh. He didn't like being called out. Rage ignited his expression and I winced as he snarled, "My office, now."

Too far. I had pushed too far. Without response I turned to shuffle up the stairs, hurrying into the enclosed room. He didn't follow. My usual punishment was a couple dozen lashings. I could handle that. Even so, my chest tightened at the thought, blood pulsing in my ears. When the door finally opened I almost sobbed in relief.

Until I saw what was in his hand.

A long, thin metal rod.

One whose end was fashioned into a brand of his dragon insignia. I stared hard at the small bit of silver, then met his eyes.

Oh.

Oh.

"Father, wait—"

"I've been too lenient with you, Reagan. You're soft. You've always been soft. I've let you slip through the cracks for too long," he growled. "You are the Night Enforcer. You have a job and a duty, one that does not involve playing knight in shining armor to the Fae. Apparently you need a more permanent reminder of who you are and who you belong to."

I froze. He stuck the metal into the crackling flames of his fireplace. The instinct to shift clawed at my insides, but my body was too tired. Pressure grew along my spine and then faded. My wings never came. I was alone. No help to be had.

The silver glowed a hot orange.

"Kneel," Mordecai barked. Every inch of me trembled as I dropped to my knees, head bowed. He inched closer and shoved my head up, brushing my hair across the far shoulder. He tugged the collar of my shirt lower then gripped my hair, shoving my head away from him to expose my neck. I trembled in fear, in horror, as he met my eyes and said, "We do not help the Fae."

White hot pain lashed through the left side of my neck, splintering my vision. He held the brand there.

One second.

Two.

Three.

When he finished, I collapsed onto the rug. My breath came in long, frenzied gasps and I sobbed into the rough fabric that bit into my cheek. The mark thrummed angrily on my neck, pulsing along with the heartbeat that slammed into my ears.

"Get out," Mordecai bellowed.

I lifted myself, arms and legs trembling, and crawled to the door. I managed to turn the handle, to crawl into the hallway. The marble floor flew toward my face and the world went black.

CHAPTER 7

Tarik

Worst hangover ever.

I thought I'd slept off last night's stupidity, but the headache had increased after my interview with Mordecai, forcing me to take an afternoon nap—that hadn't helped. Maybe his mere presence had caused the migraine pulsing at my temples and the slight tremor in my bones. I snorted, hopping over a rain puddle which only made my head pound more. My healing magic all but begged me to soothe the ache, but I ignored the pull.

At the sight of Mordecai this morning, I'd lost my temper. Completely screwed up. The rage had taken control, unfurling from my mouth in the form of snark.

Somehow, I was still alive. For a hot second, I thought he'd morph into a fire-breathing dragon and burn me to ash. The look in his eyes . . .

And then Reagan had interfered. I shook my head, picking up the pace. My bare feet slapped against cracked concrete as I took a late evening jog along the Fae border. If not for her, I'd probably be in an unmarked grave right now. Up until last night, I thought I'd wanted that—to leave this cold, sadistic world behind. Go out with a bang. Show shifters what Fae were still capable of.

But now . . .

Now I realized what an idiot I was. Destroying my life in a blaze of glory would mean absolutely nothing to anyone, least of all the shifters. Except maybe one. Sweat trickled down my spine, reminding me of *her* spine, the way it dipped inward before tapering off, giving way to—

Crap. I couldn't stop picturing her naked. She really needed to quit parading around the city with nothing but a network of colorful tattoos splayed across her skin. My thoughts took a hike every time my eyes landed on those sinful curves.

I groaned, firmly shaking my head. Wrong. Looking at her that way was completely wrong. The screws holding together my dimwitted brain were coming loose, probably thanks to the recent cage fights and increased drinking. Maybe I should stay away from The Pit for awhile. That way I wouldn't run into *her*.

As I rounded a crumbling brick building with its smashed front window boarded up, there she was as if I'd conjured her. And then I literally ran into her. Our bodies collided and, on instinct, my arms wrapped around her back so she wouldn't tumble to the uneven pavement. A soft whimper left her lips and I immediately let go, jerking back a step.

I was breathing hard from my run, sweat stinging my eyes, so I couldn't get a proper read on her expression. After our last meeting, I wasn't sure what to expect. And for once . . . for once my mouth didn't fill with the acidic tang of disgust at the sight of a shifter. I quickly scanned her body, a sigh of relief puffing from me when I saw the black cropped shirt and shorts covering her frame.

"When I said 'See you around', I didn't think you'd run into me this soon, stalker." I flicked my eyes to hers, waiting for a reply, but none came. She just stared, like she'd seen a ghost or something. She almost looked . . . haunted.

Finally, she said, "Oh. Hi, Tarik," then slipped a cigarette between her lips, inhaling slowly. Her gaze grew distant as the cigarette glowed orange. A slight tremor shook her hand. She moved past me then, not really seeing. Simply walking.

I frowned, tracking her wraith-like movements. In all the times I'd stumbled across her on patrol, I'd never once seen her so distracted. Absent. A spark of concern flared in my chest.

"Are you . . . okay?" I swallowed, rubbing at my neck. I couldn't remember the last time I'd asked someone that question. And I knew how many times I'd asked a *shifter* that—none.

Attached to the building's corner was a thin rickety stairwell, and she climbed a few steps before gingerly taking a seat. I stood there, studying her. She looked fragile. Breakable. Something simmered in my gut then. Something I hadn't felt in a long time, not since—

My hands formed fists. *Walk away. She's not your problem. Don't get close. Only pain will come of this.* But, for once, I didn't listen to the voice in my head. I approached her warily, silently, unsure how she would react. "Reagan?"

Her lashes fluttered. She blinked, meeting my gaze as if seeing me for the very first time. "You said my name," she whispered. The cadence of her voice, so small and vulnerable-sounding, tugged at my humanity.

I couldn't stop myself from lowering onto the step below hers. With our height difference, my eyes were level with her neck. That's when I noticed a new mark faintly illuminated by a nearby street light—a red, angry brand seared into her blistered flesh. The shape reminded me of a . . . I squinted. As the image sharpened, heat surged through my veins.

"Who did that to you?" My voice was like a whip, harsh and biting.

She flinched and pulled her hair over her shoulder, hiding the brand from view. A barb of panic pierced me. The strong and mighty Night Enforcer *flinched?* I didn't know what to make of the movement. A minute later, she still hadn't responded, and I was left to form my own conclusions. I thought back to the day's events: her stepping in yet again to scare off a pack of shifters from killing me, her vouching for me in front of a seething—

Mordecai. That look he had swung her way.

Oh Gaia. That brand was my fault. She had suffered because of my stupid, hot-headed words. Because she'd vouched for a low-life Fae. I waited for vindication to wash over me—*needed* the surge of adrenaline—but the feeling never came. Instead, I felt rotten. She had helped me for some misguided reason, and all I brought her in return was pain.

You're bad luck, my mind jeered. This time I listened. But not before doing something I shouldn't. Slowly, carefully, I feathered a finger down her arm, the one inked with a koi fish the same hue as her eyes. Where my skin touched hers, I pushed my healing magic. Directed the thin threads toward her neck. Not a lot—I didn't want her to suspect. Only enough to cool some of the fire no doubt raging beneath that dragon brand.

"I'm sorry," I said, then stood and quietly walked away. The words should have tasted foul, but they didn't. They felt right.

"Tarik! Help me!"

Arms, hands, fingers ending in claws, held me back. Made me watch. The voices in my head, even after all these years, were crystal clear. But the sounds. The sounds were the worst. Tearing clothes, shredding flesh, breaking bones. And then the screams.

Desperate. Afraid. Helpless.

I couldn't get to her. I couldn't save her.

"Leilani!"

Her tortured gaze met mine, her mouth opening in a silent plea.

Agonizing guilt crashed over me and I cried out. Cried out as they—

The pounding echo jolted me awake. Dispelled the familiar nightmare. I inhaled sharply and blinked at my apartment's yellow, water-stained ceiling. After a few more deep breaths, my racing heart slowed. No matter how many times the dream gripped me, shaking the images loose never got easier. The knocking continued and I grunted, stumbling out of bed.

On my way to the door, I pulled on pants, not bothering with a shirt. I knew who was on the other side at this ungodly hour. Flicking the lock, I swung the door open and a shape hurtled inside, making a beeline for my bed.

"Morning, Benji," I drawled as he scooped Callie, my gray and white cat, into his arms.

"Hi, Tarik," he mumbled, clearly distracted. "Can Callie stay at my place today?"

"Sure, kid. But don't feed her so much catnip this time. She was yowling and jumping off my head all night." I ducked down, peering into the ancient mini fridge. Empty shelves stared back. I groaned, thunking the door closed. Shopping wasn't high on my priority list these days, but something besides tomatoes for breakfast would be a nice change.

"I'll be on the roof. Don't skip school today." At his grumble, I laced some authority into my words. "I'm serious, Benji."

He dragged Callie off the bed and scampered across the room, slamming the apartment door shut with a little too much force. I grimaced as the tenant above me shouted. With a click, I unlocked my window and slid the glass up, folding my body in half as I climbed onto my balcony. The small cement slab had been turned into a garden as all Fae itched to do with any available space given them.

Every surface was covered in green, the majority of the plants edible. I plucked a bright red tomato from the vine before swinging onto the rusty escape ladder that led to the building's flat roof. Once on top, I planted a foot on the roof's edge and bit into my breakfast, taking in the panoramic view. This early, the sky was still a dusky blue, only a slight yellowing at the horizon. The Fae district was old and rundown, unwanted by the shifters. Everything—from the buildings' dirty exteriors to a few rickety bikes in the pothole-riddled streets—spoke of poverty.

But, if anything, Fae were resourceful. Rain barrels dotted the flat rooftops as well as fruit-bearing trees in large pots. I could even see corn stalks swaying in the breeze on an adjacent high-rise apartment. My kind was downtrodden, but we managed. We always found a way to survive.

Even those of us who didn't want to.

And that's why I stayed away from them. I was the bad apple. The disease. Anyone who got close to me would sooner or later regret doing so. Those I'd once called friends had finally let me be. It helped that I spent most of my evenings at The Pit where no other Fae dared to go. I had tried, again and again, to discourage Benji from invading my personal space, but he was like a flea on a dog. Persistent. No matter how many times I plucked him off, he jumped back on.

But, besides him, I was alone. Well, I had Callie, but she wasn't really mine. Technically, she was—I stopped myself from thinking her name. Sucking in a breath, I pushed memories of wavy blonde hair and infectious laughter from my mind. They were always there. Always hovering. And that's why I came up to the roof every morning at dawn.

I settled cross-legged on the smooth, still-cool concrete, hands loosely resting on my knees. Closing my eyes, I sought the one thing that had eluded me for three solid years.

Inner peace.

"Go back to your territory, Fae scum!"

A rock sailed toward me and I didn't have time to duck. The pain was sharp and instant, a pulsing throb between my shoulder blades. I gritted my teeth but kept moving forward. Where was the Day Enforcer from yesterday? Lazy, good-for-nothing—

A dark blue dragon dropped from the sky and, with a boom, landed right in front of me. I stopped, searching the light blue eyes for signs of intelligent life. Was the Day Enforcer hungry? Maybe he hadn't eaten breakfast yet and was hankering after a piece of Fae meat.

His scales retracted—the tail and wings shrank, and the snout smooshed inward—until all that remained was a nude god. At least, that's what I assumed he thought of himself as he struck a pose. Didn't he feel even the slightest bit uncomfortable dangling in the wind like that?

"Are we done here?" he said, ignoring me entirely as he peered past my shoulder. The harassing shifters skittered off. That simple, huh? He finally looked at me. "You're welcome."

I stared at what I knew to be Mordecai's son, even if I'd never spoken to him before. He kept puffing out his chest, trying to look down his nose at me. I was taller than him. "Oh. Yeah," I drew out the word. "Thanks for the show. The sight of naked male shifter first thing in the morning gets me all hot and bothered."

"Doubtful," he said, sliding into a prowling circle reminiscent of his father's. "But I have heard some rumors. About a certain Night Enforcer getting you all hot and bothered."

At the insinuation, heat flushed up my neck. But admitting that I knew Reagan, even as an acquaintance, would set this guy off. Something unsettling glinted in his gaze. Creepy. "The Night Enforcer?" I pretended to think, scratching at the side of my head. "Never heard of him. I don't get out much past dinnertime. You know, being an early-riser and all."

"Yeah. You're full of crap." He scowled, rage now glittering in his eyes. "You see, I had a nice chat with my father yesterday. Because after running Fae up and down the border all day, I came home to find *my* Reagan slumped on the mansion floor. Unconscious. I carried her home, and then I found out about the interesting details of your interview, *ScarFae*."

I blinked. Crap. He had me there. But something he said snagged my attention. Not the fact that he knew about my Pit nickname or the botched interview, but that he had been there for Reagan. Had carried her away from the problems I had inflicted. That knowledge doused my simmering anger. And the preening peacock seemed to think Reagan was *his*. But what if . . .

"How do I know *you* didn't burn that mark into her neck? You're Mordecai's muscle. I mean, makes sense that he would ask you to do his dirty work."

The Day Enforcer's nostrils flared and he lowered his voice to a soft snarl. "I would *never* hurt Reagan. And I never said she was branded. How did you know that? Are you *stalking* her?"

Without warning, he swung. I wasn't expecting the brute to actually put his enforcer skills to use, so I couldn't avoid his fist in time. He slugged me right across the jaw. My teeth sank into my tongue, and with a groan, I spat blood on the ground. As he slipped into a fighting stance, I slowly settled onto the balls of my feet, knees slightly bent.

"Look, man, your job is to get me inside the mansion in one piece. Are you sure you want to do this right now? Besides, if you cared about Reagan so much, wouldn't you have saved her *before* she got hurt?"

"Reagan knows her place. She's known since she was a child. Sometimes she needs a reminder that Fae scum like you are trouble. She got what she deserved. We don't help the Fae."

The Enforcer paused, then added, "I wouldn't have saved her anyway, whether I like what our father did or not. He deals fair punishment and she knows that."

I straightened, completely mind-blown by the drivel leaving his dumb mouth. For a moment, I thought he might truly care for her, but *this* . . . this was sick. Fair punishment? A brand to the *neck* was fair punishment? Mordecai didn't even do that to the Fae, but he would brand his own daughter?

My stomach churned as I fought the urge to vomit all over this sorry excuse for a man. No, he needed worse than that. Far worse. I curled my hands into tight fists, ready to unleash every ounce of rage roaring through my blood. But, as I took that first step, right before I could end my life—because this Enforcer would no doubt have me killed after I struck him—a flash of light purple barreled toward me.

"Nooope, nope, not today," a female voice said loudly, halting my progress with a quick shove. Her next words were hushed, meant only for my ears. "Reagan saved your life at great personal risk. Don't you dare squander that on this piece of crap."

I made to go around her, too angry to think straight, but she persisted. Like a flea. Like a—Benji. I froze. What was I doing? This tiny, purple-haired woman was right. I couldn't throw my life away, not when Benji still needed me. I blew out a breath, glancing down at her heart-shaped face. Big brown eyes ringed in silver blinked up at me, almost pleading with me to walk away.

"You're right." I rolled my shoulders, tamping down the rage that still demanded I punch this guy's lights out. "He's a pile of crap. Thanks for setting the record straight."

"He is, and you're going to be late for work. Please. Please, go. Reagan is in enough trouble, and if you're late . . ." She huffed. "I'll deal with the puffed-up dragon boy. Go. I'm Nevaeh, by the way."

If there was one word I understood abundantly clear, it was trouble. And I didn't want to be the cause of more right now. Reagan had been through enough. "Tarik," I muttered without thought, peeking through my lashes at the irate Day Enforcer.

"I know," she said, shoving me some more. I looked at her, confused. How come this shifter knew so much about me? I had never seen her before. A bright pink tattoo on her left forearm caught my eye and I focused on the shape. When I realized what I was looking at, a bubble of laughter almost erupted from me. A chubby pig. With a rainbow unicorn horn on its forehead. I clamped my lips together and met her stare. As if reading my thoughts, she winked, and simply said, "I'm the best friend."

Despite her short stature and thin frame, she was quite strong. Nevaeh pushed me forward a step, and my legs did the rest. As she maneuvered me around the pompous dragon shifter, I couldn't resist glowering at him. He glared back with equal intensity. Great. I'd made a new friend.

Walking the rest of the way to the mansion without an escort proved hazardous to my health. Three more rocks struck me, and my shirt now sported a sticky green stain. What the substance was, I didn't care to know. When I arrived at the mansion—barely on time—a thin shifter with poofy, reddish-brown hair led me down the stairs to the mines.

I decided to nickname him Bushy.

Jocelyn—I couldn't even imagine what kind of shifter she

was . . . poodle, maybe—gave us the grand tour when the last Fae employee was accounted for. "And these are the required uniforms you will all be wearing. Go ahead, put them on. One size fits all."

I couldn't quite contain a small eyeroll. Uniforms? They were hazmat suits. Big and yellow and—

As I slid one on, I groaned. Hot. Stifling hot. If I didn't need the money so badly, I'd be charging up the stairs right about now. This job was going to be hell. I heard a few grunts and curses and glanced at my new coworkers. We all seemed to share a similar train of thought.

And that's when I noticed something a touch peculiar: Jocelyn was the only female in the room. Mordecai had only hired male Fae. The realization tasted bitter. Perhaps Reagan was on to something. Maybe there was more to this job than mining.

"All right, men." Jocelyn clapped like a spectator at a carnival. "This way, please."

As we shuffled after our mother hen, waddling like oversized chicks, she pointed out various nooks. "Here's where you'll find the mining tools. One pickaxe and shovel will be assigned to each worker. Treat your equipment kindly, because if you break anything, you'll be docked pay."

The bathrooms were next, then a long unlit room she dubbed 'In case of emergency.' What, like a cave-in? But she whisked us onward, the clack of her red heels echoing down the corridor.

"And here is where you'll be working," she said, stopping just shy of the entrance. Before continuing, she looked each of us in the eye, as if that would drive home her next words. "There is one rule that mustn't be broken if you wish to keep your job: never directly touch the Genesis Crystal. Understood?" At our nods, she stepped aside and allowed us to spill into a tall cavern, so large that walking to the other side would take a solid minute.

But the sheer size wasn't what had my mouth dropping in wonder. The cave was covered in green. Not pale green or even leaf green, but a rich emerald, deep and pure and—I swallowed with difficulty, my throat suddenly bone dry. The crystal was beautiful. Startled by a tugging sensation, I swiveled, half-expecting to find Jocelyn pulling at my suit. But no one was touching me.

Still, the tug persisted, calling, beckoning . . . draining. My eyelids drooped but I forced them open again. Maybe that punch to my jaw had caused a slight concussion. Before I could think more on the matter, Jocelyn clapped again, ushering us from the cavern and into a bright, impossibly clean-looking white room. I couldn't find a speck of dirt anywhere.

"This is our final destination for today, men. Claim an empty table and sit. Someone will be with you shortly." With that, she turned on her heel and left the big yellow blobs to gape at each other.

Sit? In these sweltering hot suits?

For the next several hours, I was poked and jabbed, stripped and humiliated by shifter doctors. I thought about fleeing the room many times. But, despite the ever-present rage simmering in my blood, I remained. I needed this job. Badly. Still, I questioned my sanity.

What had I gotten myself into?

CHAPTER 8

Reagan

". . . and then he had the nerve to tell me to butt out. Like, he wasn't doing his job in the first place. I had to. And he thought he could tell *me* what to do?"

Nevaeh had been chattering for almost an hour. Normally, listening to her gossip was soothing. She needed an ear and I was more than willing to offer one. This time was different. This time she was talking about Alec and Tarik, and the confrontation they'd had this morning. My mind kept circling back to her detailed description of Alec's fist hitting Tarik's jaw, and the image squeezed my chest. I coughed to clear my throat and Nevaeh paused, but I motioned her on.

What was he thinking, antagonizing Alec? What was Alec thinking, targeting one of the Fae who now worked for our father?

I tugged at the fraying hemline of my leggings, an older pair worn soft. Nevaeh had come over before I had woken, and I still hadn't showered. Part of me didn't really care if I did—the other part cringed at the wad of unwashed hair perched into a messy bun on top of my head. Showering felt like effort. I didn't have the energy for effort. My mind had been spinning since the interview, and even sleep hadn't given me rest. The Fae, Mordecai, Alec, Tarik . . . the storm in my mind was becoming a flood.

The brand was Mordecai's way of raising the stakes. What would he do if I kept sticking my nose where I was told it didn't belong? Or if Alec, or another shifter, reported me? I lifted my hand, instinctively reaching for the sore mark, but I balled my fist and withdrew. A dragon brand. My stomach curled. A permanent mark, a visible reminder that screamed who I was, who I belonged to.

I had been relieved when Nevaeh was the one to visit this morning, with no sign of Alec. But her words sent me plummeting further into myself and now . . . now I wanted to be alone. To wallow. To be as pathetic as I felt.

The only reason I'd had any joy in my Enforcer position over the years was my small ability to help. I *knew* there was a risk to my actions, knew that if I was caught . . . But the price was too high for the little I actually did. I should have learned that lesson four years ago. A brand was small, but if Mordecai caught me again . . .

If he caught me again, I wouldn't be the only one to suffer the consequences. Of that, I was certain.

My neck ached, as if reinforcing my thoughts. The mark was resisting the natural and medicinal cures I tried, and I had to wonder if Mordecai had put chemicals on the brand. Thankfully, the pain was more tolerable than it had been that first night. I had almost felt better after running—literally—into Tarik, but the feeling had been short-lived. Probably a placebo.

Imagined, like I imagined I could actually make a difference.

"Reagan. You okay?" I glanced up. Nevaeh studied me, her slender fingers sliding locks of her hair into a braid. "I think I lost you there for a minute."

"Sorry," I said. I reached for my cigarette case, resting on the couch arm beside me, and watched my fingers tremble as I went to light one.

"Are you all right?"

"Of course."

Nevaeh stared at me, eyes narrowing. "I know you better than that. You can't give up on them now. You've been doing this for years, and you rarely get caught. The Fae *need* you. And you started Tarik down a path. You can't abandon him now." She paused, her lips curving into a smirk. "Besides, he's kind of cute."

I groaned. The last thing I wanted to think about was the dusting of freckles on Tarik's nose, or the way his hair fell over those bright green eyes.

No.

Thinking about him beyond our tenuous acquaintanceship was dangerous territory. He had felt guilty yesterday when he pieced together what Mordecai had done. Guilt changed people's minds—but the feeling would fade. The rage would return. And while the thought of strategically avoiding him made me squirm, this relationship—if it could be called that—was too dangerous.

Even if I was making progress through the heavy facade he wore over his emotions.

I sighed. "If I keep helping him, you know what will happen. Mordecai isn't above murdering innocents."

"He's not exactly innocent, Reagan," Nevaeh protested. "He painted the target on himself in that interview. But you've saved his life twice. Can you really walk away and let him go into those mines suspecting that this job isn't what's advertised?"

She was right, of course. Tarik's troubles were only beginning. But he couldn't rely on me—that was dangerous too, would take him off his guard. He needed to be alert. I didn't trust Mordecai, but I couldn't watch him all the time. And after his slip-up, the Great Dragon was more of a threat than usual. Especially if he had both eyes pinned on Tarik.

My head was going to split in two.

"I don't know, Nevaeh. Maybe I can help from a distance. A great distance."

She shrugged, unconvinced, but I stood to retrieve a soda. The moment I did, a great thud shook the penthouse. I groaned.

"Hey, Reagan."

"Alec, I am not in the mood."

"Unsurprising. I saw your boyfriend today." Ah, so he wasn't in the mood either. Fine. He continued, "Taught him a little lesson: How to stay away from things that don't belong to him 101."

"I don't belong to *you*, either," I snapped. Anger bubbled in my chest. "Stay out of this, Alec, I'm warning you. What happened in that interview is between our father and me. You have a job too. Do you want me to tell him you disobeyed and attacked one of his new employees?"

Alec leaned against the couch. His gaze flicked to Nevaeh before he crossed his arms over his chest and spoke again. "You honestly think that you don't belong to anyone? Has Father taught you nothing about loyalty?"

"Loyalty is given. Ownership is taken."

"And in regards to our father, he holds the strings to both. You have a job to do, and I don't recall father's motto being 'join the Fae in baking cookies and singing kumbaya.'"

"Alec, get out," Nevaeh said, sitting up a bit straighter.

He disregarded her, instead moving closer to me. Nevaeh jumped to her feet as his chest inflated, but I waved her off. He was in my face when he said, "You'd rather have some random Fae scum than the son of the Great Dragon?"

"Is that what this is about? You puffed-up egomaniac, I'd rather be left alone by all of you. Now get out of my apartment."

He grabbed my arm. His mistake. I balled my fist and decked him square in the nose. Cartilage crunched under my knuckles and he released my arm to clutch his face, anger sparking in his eyes as he took a step back. I pointed at the balcony. This time, he listened, loosing a low snarl before striding to the door.

Nevaeh watched him retreat before she settled back onto the couch. Her eyes locked onto my trembling arms as she said, "Go shower. You'll feel better."

I nodded my gratitude. By the time the water ran cold, she was gone, a text blinking at me from my phone. She understood that I needed time alone. Maybe tonight's patrol would help. The wind under my wings, the stars glittering quietly above me. Peace—or the closest thing to peace I could find.

But first . . . the inevitable. I needed to see Tarik. To apologize and explain. I didn't want him to think he was a lost cause, but I couldn't be his hero.

I knew talking to him was potentially suicide. Mordecai

would probably be watching him a bit more carefully and, if not him, Alec. But the sun was already falling from the sky and I started my patrol early all the time. Doing so now wouldn't necessarily look suspicious. I shifted, jumping off the balcony and letting the wind catch my feathers. The gentle, familiar tug calmed my racing mind and rapid heartbeat.

Tarik wasn't along the borderline on the first flyover but, as I swooped back around closer to the manor, I saw the Fae employees leaving the mansion. No good. My patrol gave me an easy excuse to keep an eye on them, but Tarik would have to break off for me to stand a chance of getting a word in. I needed less eyes, especially at the moment.

The universe had a sense of humor. Or maybe I had won a small favor. Instinct wanted to call the odds a sign, but in the pit of my stomach I knew better. Anything that worked in my favor would come back to bite me. Fate or no, most of the Fae split from Tarik before they came too close to The Pit. By the time he was parallel to the building, he was alone.

I dropped out of the sky, rapid-shifting, worried my lion form would unnerve him. The blacktop bit into the bottoms of my feet and palms as I landed. For a long moment, we stood in silence. I scanned his face—the tired lines around his eyes, the way hair clung to his forehead. My gaze lingered on the purple bruise along his jaw. Inwardly, I flinched. Guilt poured over me in a wave, though I knew I wasn't technically responsible for the mark. Still. If I hadn't forced my way into his life, he wouldn't have an arrogant, possessive dragon shifter tailing him.

I took a step forward. And another. Then I asked quietly, "You're okay?"

He stared, wide-eyed and unblinking for what felt like an hour. I couldn't stand the silence. When I was almost certain he wasn't going to reply, I prepared to walk away. But then his mouth twisted into a sardonic grin.

"Oh, this?" He gestured at his bruised jaw. "I'm used to this. But . . ." His expression changed again, darkened. "I'm assuming your friend Nevaeh told you about what happened this morning?"

"Yeah." I dropped my eyes to the concrete, staring at a jagged crack that ran between us. I didn't miss the irony.

"Yeah, well, your brother is a piece of work, you know that?" He leaned forward, as if to step closer, then rocked back on his heels. "But what I want to know is if you believe the crock he spouts, about Mordecai dishing out fair punishment. Do you think *that*"—he jabbed a finger at my neck—"is fair?"

I huffed a small, half-hearted laugh. "If it's any consolation, I'm fairly sure I broke Alec's nose earlier. And *adopted* brother. He's not lucky enough to share blood." I paused, considering the rest of his words. Breathing seemed particularly hard when I said, "Honestly? If you'd asked me a few years ago, I would say the punishment was fair. But now . . . I'm not sure. I'm . . . confused."

His brow furrowed as his eyes shifted downward, then whipped up, as if noticing my naked state for the first time. "Here." He reached behind him and tugged off his shirt, exposing skin free of bruises yet still littered with faint white scars. How—? "Can you put this on for me?"

I snickered softly. "Um. Sure." He held the shirt out and I accepted, sliding the soft linen over my head. His scent washed over me like rain. No. Like the earth after rain. Mentally, I shook myself. "I'll never understand the Fae aversion to nudity."

A small smile tilted his lips, and part of me cracked at the sight.

"It's not an aversion—okay, maybe when we're talking about a two-hundred-pound sweaty male shifter, yes—but it's more a . . . distraction." He cleared his throat, hand creeping toward his neck. "Anyway, no one deserves to be punished like that. *No* one. Not even—" He cut himself off and glanced away, jaw clenching. Then sighed. "You're being abused, Reagan. Maybe *you* should be leaving your job, not me."

My breath skipped—the soft, airy hiccups that came before the wall of tears. Nope. That wasn't going to happen, even if I knew, deep down, that he was right. I questioned the words of protest that sprang into my mind, formed them carefully, then forced them back down. If this was truly the last time I was going to speak freely with him, there were things I wanted him to know. Needed him to, for my sanity. Or maybe I simply needed to hear myself say them.

"I moved out, you know. When I started to make my own salary. Mordecai insists on paying the rent. I understand why, now. Control. I didn't then." I struggled to still my trembling hands. "I thought that, as an Enforcer, I could help people. I thought maybe I could make a difference. Because I started to see things as I grew up and every time a Fae was harmed, my entire being wanted to recoil. I knew that no matter what sugar-coated reasons Mordecai and Alec gave, they were doing terrible things. But what he did to me? It's far from the worst thing he's ever done to punish me." I lowered my voice. "You might be right, but if I try to leave? Tarik . . . I don't have anywhere to go."

After a moment of heavy silence, he groaned, scrubbing both hands down his face. "Man, Reagan," he muttered, gaze pinging all over the place. His next words were strained, like they hurt to say. "The thing is, I'm the last person you should be getting help from. I'm—I'm no good. I'll only add to your troubles. I wish I could help, but . . ."

I stepped closer, until I could barely pass my arms between us. He was so tall. I lifted a hand, gently brushing the scars on his cheek.

"You're not the bad, evil person you make yourself out to be, Tarik. You've had horrible things done to you, probably beyond what I can imagine. I can tell the scars run deep." I withdrew, adding softly, "But I didn't come to you for help. In fact, the exact opposite. I may want to help you, but I'm only digging you in deeper. You kept getting yourself into trouble for no reason, and you looked so lost . . . like you needed a friend. But now there's an even bigger target on your back, and that's my fault. If I don't stop trying to help you, there will be no *you* left to help. So. Don't worry about me. I'll be okay. I have been all this time."

I offered a tight-lipped smile before I moved around him, taking slow steps down the alley. My heart and body ached. I didn't know if I was making the right decision.

Stop. Wait. Go back.

All Tarik really needed was a guiding light; the potential was all there, hidden beneath layers of thick defenses. In the back of my mind I *knew* he didn't want to be alone. That he needed someone, anyone, who could see him and pull him out of the darkness. To remind him that he mattered, even to one person. He had scars I couldn't see and I knew that with time, I could help mend them.

But I didn't have time. Mordecai made sure of that.

"You're not okay." The words gave me pause, but I didn't stop. Couldn't. "And you're not hurting me. You're saving me. You're saving me from myself, and . . . please don't leave."

I froze. Oh. *Oh no.* My voice cracked, tears springing free when I said, "I can't watch them kill you. I can't condemn you to that."

His voice was nearer the next time he spoke. "A few days ago, I was a dead man walking. I—I wanted them to kill me. Then you swooped in, literally. I wasn't happy about your interference, but now . . . maybe I want to stick around a little bit longer. And I wouldn't mind if you bugged me once in a while. On occasion. Not all the time, but . . ."

Damnit. I couldn't stay. I swallowed hard. "I thought you didn't want a personal stalker."

The warmth from his body touched my back as he said, "Maybe this stalker thing is growing on me."

"I don't know. I mean, I *am* a pushover Enforcer after all." Despite myself, I laughed quietly, the sound clipped by a small hiccup.

I felt a soft tug on my hair. Then, "You are, actually. But maybe I'm okay with that too."

My laugh was more genuine this time—still airy, but warmth sparked in my chest. Only for a moment. I stared at the dimming skyline, exhaling slowly. "I have to patrol. I can't make you any promises, Tarik. But, if I can, I'll find you in a couple days."

"Oh, I have faith in your stalker abilities."

"You haven't even had a taste." I grinned and turned around, still finding that my eyes wanted to look anywhere but at his. I tugged his shirt over my head. "Here, you need this. I have to shift. Sorry if it's . . . disconcerting?" My eyebrows pulled together. "And . . . thank you."

I stepped away from him and closed my eyes. Felt the pressure, the tingle, the savage crack of bone. I bit back the gasp that tried to escape when my ribs widened. *Why couldn't I be a cute, small shifter?* I tucked in my wings immediately, finally looking up to meet Tarik's eyes.

He squinted, peering into my face as if— "Can you hear me, Reagan? How many fingers am I holding up?" He lifted two digits in the air.

I huffed, a puff of air escaping my nose. Then I growled, two throaty rumbles that bounced off the walls of the alley around us.

With a slight grimace, he whispered, "That's gonna take some getting used to."

I stepped closer, slowly, tentatively. Lowering my head, I tried to make myself seem a tad smaller. I wasn't kidding anyone—even for a lion I was massive. I stopped in front of him, bumping his side with the top of my head.

"Whoa," he said, the word vibrating through my skull. His hands latched onto my ears and I shook my head, swatting at him. "Okay, okay." He backed up, palms facing outward. "Good . . . kitty?"

A small hum vibrated up my throat as I circled him, then nudged him backward. He moved without too much effort—wary, like he thought I might hurt him still—and when I had the space I needed, I spread my wings, stretching them to their full glory. I watched Tarik's jaw drop and growled with satisfaction before I sprang down the alley and shot into the sky.

Could I escape Nathra City? Leave Mordecai and Alec behind?

I spent a lot of the evening pondering the conversation I'd had with Tarik. In my gut I wondered if I should have told him so much. Spoken so poorly of Alec and Mordecai. Guilt clawed at me, gnawed at the parts that still felt the relentless tug of blind loyalty. Still, I couldn't deny there lay a certain relief in dropping those words into the world. Letting them fade away into the night air.

What he had said about abuse, though . . . the words stung. I knew he was right. Maybe. I mean, I knew the rules. *Right?* My chest tightened. I hated that I wasn't sure what could actually be termed abuse. Did the same terms apply when I knew the rules? If I committed an action, knowing the consequences, and was then punished . . . That couldn't be abuse, right?

As much of a challenge as Tarik was, I secretly enjoyed our spats, in a weird way. The challenge that being friends with him presented.

And underneath, there's a good man. I can feel it.

I closed my eyes, releasing a breath. Feeling so much, wanting to feel so little—I hated every second. His encouragement was the push I needed to keep me on the right path, though. But to do that I needed to find out exactly what I was saving him from.

Nevaeh and I spent an entire day gathering schedules from

around the mansion. The Fae worked fairly long hours, but Mordecai almost never oversaw them himself. Nevaeh's rat form was incredibly useful for this type of work—she was sneaky, and clever enough not to get caught—and the information she extracted was helpful.

When we had gathered all the intel we needed, we formed a plan. A day later, we set it into motion.

And even though I was reluctant to lose sleep, to leave the warmth of the sunshine above for the dark, unsettling mines, that's exactly where we were. Currently Nevaeh was perched on my shoulder, digging her claws into my shirt as payback for the cracker I was dangling above her. She was always hungry in rat form. Always. Torturing her with snacks endlessly entertained me.

She clamped her teeth around a strand of my hair, tugging sharply. My grin grew, but I relented, passing her the snack. Her eyes remained narrowed as she munched. Crumbs littered my shoulder—the rat shifter was intentionally making a mess. Karma, I supposed. Her fur caught a bit of light, pale lavender to match the color of her hair, a neat little trick I had always envied. She had been a rainbow of colors over the years, but the lavender suited her round, black eyes.

We crept down the staircase and into the shadowed edges of the mine's first cavern. There didn't seem to be anyone wandering around out here; lucky, given that we had chosen working hours to sneak down. We hoped the extra bodies would create distractions . . . but they came with added risk. I glanced at Nevaeh. She cocked her head at my silent question, her ears twitching as she listened ahead. Faint voices echoed from a chamber near us. The Fae must be in there. Nevaeh shook her head. Nothing abnormal.

I knew there was a medical room on the far side of the hallway and I made for that, pausing to peer around the corner when we reached what seemed to be a small lunchroom. A dozen or so Fae were scattered around the space with trays of food. Hopeful that no one would spot me, I darted past, slinking down the hallway.

The infirmary door wasn't locked or guarded, surprisingly. The room was simple enough. Clean. A sanitary station, filled with cabinets of medical supplies and lined with exam tables. Medicine was stored in a glass cabinet on the far wall. A drawer unit of clean, dry clothing sat next to a lonely shower head, marked with instructions for emergency use.

Odd. The Fae were mining crystals, right? Could the crystals harm them? Was that why they wore hazmat suits? My attention snagged on a counter tucked in the back corner, lined with microscopes, burners, and equipment I didn't recognize. The technology was state of the art. Mordecai's lab. I had never been allowed anywhere near his crystal experiments; I supposed that was why I hadn't considered that the lab would be down here. It wasn't marked on any of the maps, but clearly that had been done with intent. What better way to hide an expensive lab than under the guise of an infirmary that no one used?

Another glass cabinet caught my eye and I stepped closer. Test tubes sat in racks on the shelves; most were empty, some filled with liquids ranging from various shades of green to perfectly clear. What was Mordecai up to?

Regardless, I wasn't going to find answers here, not unless I learned how to break into the wall safe where I guessed the real trial results were hidden. Or maybe only the crystal he was testing with. Nothing else in the room stood out to me, except the computer perched on a corner desk. Maybe answers were there?

The screen flashed a "password required" warning.

Of course.

Nevaeh jumped from my shoulder and scoured the room, slipping into unlocked cabinets. I rummaged through the papers on the desk, mostly blood work results. Why had Mordecai run this much testing? Each employee had a small pile of paperwork to their name, an unnatural amount for a simple mining job.

Wait.

All the hired Fae were male, but at least half the applicants had been female. Did Mordecai make the selections intentionally, or did he think females were simply incapable of such jobs?

No one's blood work seemed abnormal, though. Regular readings on general health. They had run every test imaginable. All the applicants seemed to be Fae in their prime, with little to no nutrient deficiencies. That made sense—wouldn't want ill workers—but they were all in the same age range. Early to late twenties. Odd.

Nevaeh squeaked softly from the other side of the room before shifting into human form. The room was dark—even a passerby was unlikely to see her because I barely could. I crept to her side.

"Look at this."

She held out a floor plan that marked the medical room, the work rooms, the storage spaces. Mordecai's half office had been marked, and a room labeled "for emergencies only" that we had passed on our way in. My head spun in new waves of confusion. What kind of emergency were they anticipating that they needed an entire room set aside?

"What does that mean? For emergencies only?"

Nevaeh pursed her lips. "I don't know, but that's probably where we need to be looking."

I relayed the information I had found about the male applicants, and her forehead puckered. "This all feels off, right?" I asked quietly.

Nevaeh nodded. "I don't know what he's up to. But follow your instincts. You know him better than I do."

She dropped into her shifter form, climbing the counter and jumping to her perch on my shoulder. I slipped from the lab and peeked around the corner, listening. Safe. We headed for the room marked "for emergencies only."

The room was long, but I didn't dare turn on the main lights—the glow from the hall would have to do. I couldn't find anything that struck me as particularly special about the bathroom facilities toward the back, or the generic safety posters around the walls. The two dozen cots that were shoved into the small space caught my eye. What was Mordecai up to? I couldn't see an emergency situation where they would need so many beds. Nothing else raised any alarms in my mind, though—until I turned to leave.

The door to the room was thick, massive steel.

And hidden on the back was a line of deadbolts—that only activated from the outside.

I glanced at Nevaeh before I hurried out. Mining crystals didn't require security methods quite that stringent. Mordecai was definitely up to mischief—and I was starting to think I *really* didn't want to know what.

CHAPTER 9

Tarik

"You shouldn't be in here."

The voice at my ear startled me so badly that I almost swung a fist. Twisting around, I silently released a breath, relieved that I hadn't acted on my instincts. Jocelyn peered up at me, looking equally annoyed and fake friendly. She crossed her arms—which pushed up her disproportionately large chest—and arched a brow. Waiting.

Oh. This far into the work day, my mind was almost too foggy to form coherent sentences let alone excuses. I tried on a sheepish smile that probably made me look constipated. "Uh, I was looking for the bathroom but forgot where it was. Can you help me out here?"

Her lips pinched and I could tell she was trying really hard not to chew me out. Which made me wonder what her shifter form was again. My coworkers had a running tally: they thought she was a seal because of all the clapping. I could see that, her sleek black hair flowing into a slippery dark hide. But every time I imagined red lipstick on the creature, I busted out laughing.

I was imagining it right now.

"Something funny?" Her brown eyes narrowed.

I coughed and cleared my throat to hide my laughter. "No, ma'am, but I really need to pee."

Jocelyn grimaced, no longer pretending to be my best friend. Her expression practically shouted, *Dirty Fae*. She jabbed a finger down the corridor. "Second door on the right. Be back in five minutes or you'll be docked pay. Oh, and Tarik?" At my raised eyebrows, she finished with, "Don't let me catch you in the medical room again."

"Oh, you won't." She tapped a foot, so I added, "Ma'am." When she waltzed back into the Green Room—as the Fae were calling our new work zone—I muttered to myself, "You won't *catch* me next time."

On autopilot, I made for the bathroom, subtly peeking into each open door I passed. This was the second day in a row I had seen Reagan down here snooping around. At least, that's what I thought she was doing. I hadn't crossed paths with her since the evening she shifted into lion form right in front of me—which, I admit, was rather impressive.

That evening, though . . .

My steps slowed. I had thought about that meeting over and over until I'd memorized each and every word we had shared. Words I regretted. The guilt, the shame of knowing my actions had caused her harm . . . I'd had a weak moment. I had said things, opened myself up in a way I'd not done in years, and now I wished I could take the whole conversation back. The offer of truce, the false hope, the show of friendship.

Because seeing her wearing my shirt with the hem past her

mid thigh, feeling her soft hair between my fingers, had turned the dull ache I'd felt in my chest for the last three years into a sharp throb. And watching her wings splay wide, so white and pure and clean, had ripped the scars right open.

As she'd taken to the sky, I'd crashed to my knees, unable to draw air into my lungs for several agonizing seconds. The memories from that night three years ago still haunted me, never allowing me peace. And that evening with Reagan, I'd started down a path of making the same mistakes I'd sworn to myself I'd never repeat.

Getting too close to her was dangerous. Getting too close to *anyone* was dangerous. Something dark inside of me sought to destroy—and not just those who got too close. This black, oily presence wanted to snuff out every spark of joy I managed to light.

Bad luck.

Everything I touched turned to ash eventually. It was only a matter of time before the darkness inside me consumed the female lion shifter—who I had once thought an angel. A small smile tugged at my mouth. Took me long enough to figure out she'd flown me to her apartment the night I'd lost consciousness in that alley. She had risked so much and was already paying the price.

Branded. Like cattle. By her own father.

I stared unblinking at the glistening white bathroom wall. A hot wave of fury ignited my blood and I punched the tile, reveling in the bark of pain.

A branded angel. *If she's a white angel, then I'm the black demon in the shadows waiting to drag her down to hell.* My stained soul was already corrupting hers.

As I made my way back to the Green Room, there was still no sign of blue and black hair. But, even hours later—as my back screamed and head pounded, leaving my entire body sapped of strength—I kept an eye out. The sooner I saw her again, the sooner I could put an end to this torture.

"Tarik! Tarik, help!"

I wrenched my eyes open, for a horrified moment thinking my nightmare had come to life. After a few blinks, the soft morning sky and flat rooftop of my apartment building swam into view. A breath shuddered out of me. Benji's mop of unruly blond hair popped over the roof's edge. I frowned. He never came up here this early, knew this space was off-limits while I meditated.

"It's my mom! She fell again, and—and this time, I think she really hurt herself. Tarik, come on!"

In a flash, I was up and scrambling down the ladder after him. We ducked into my apartment before charging into his, the sound of soft whimpers coming from their small bathroom. I stopped cold when I saw her right ankle twisted at an unnatural angle. Gaia, no. This wasn't happening. Not now.

I blocked the view from Benji, ordering him to feed Callie. He complained but did as instructed when I said I'd forgotten to feed her yesterday. With him out of the room, I knelt next to his mom, running my gaze over her trembling body. A tangle of blue veins could be seen through translucent skin, her arms and legs rail thin.

In a word, she could be described as breakable. Her mysterious condition had grown worse this last year, to the point where she hardly ever went outdoors. For a Fae, that was almost worse than death. I carefully touched her arm, always worried that no matter how light the pressure, I'd leave behind bruises.

Her blonde lashes fluttered. "Tarik," she whispered. "I'm sorry."

I bit my lip, hard, frustrated and hating how she saw herself—as a burden. "Don't apologize, Haven. This isn't your fault." I bent so my face was near hers. "Can you put your arm around my neck? I'll get you into bed."

She tried. Gaia, she tried. But she was too weak. I gingerly draped her arm over my shoulders and prepared to lift her. The act took no effort—she was skin and bones—but she cried out in pain and I gritted my teeth. I didn't know how much longer her body could fight this illness, but I did what I could to ease her suffering.

It was the *least* I could do. I didn't really believe the gods had abandoned our kind, but I wholeheartedly believed that I was cursed. This healing ability of mine was proof of that. Why have it at all if I couldn't save anyone? The fact that I'd never met another Fae who could heal with a single touch made me wonder if my ability was indeed dark magic. Maybe instead of helping others, my touch made them worse.

But despite feeling a sickening twist in my stomach every time I tried to heal someone—worried that I was sinking poison into their veins—I couldn't stand the suffering. Couldn't stand hearing Haven's pain-filled moans and Benji's soft sniffles. If my curse had befallen them because of their close proximity to me, then the least I could do was remove some of the suffering.

Once Haven was tucked in bed, I got to work pushing my

healing magic into her broken ankle. Carefully. We never talked about the times I did this. I knew she could feel it—the sensation was like a gently moving current and the bone knitting back together wasn't pleasant—but we had an unspoken agreement that my unique ability shouldn't be discussed. If rumors of magic reached the shifters, I'd be accused of witchcraft and no doubt executed on the spot.

Not only did I refuse to go out that way, but the decade's old superstition that had started a war could reignite widespread panic and cause even more Fae persecution.

Halfway through fixing the break, sweat peppered my forehead and even more slid down my spine. A wave of exhaustion hit me and I hunched forward, my head too heavy to hold up. I closed my eyes and sighed. A bony hand on mine broke my concentration. "You've done enough, Tarik. Thank you. I can never thank you enough."

I leaned back, inspecting the break. The ankle was straight but the bone was barely fused together. "I'll come by after work and see how you're doing. Until then, stay in bed and ask Benji to get things for you. That kid has the energy of ten puppies."

She laughed, the thin sound ending in a cough. I smiled as best I could before taking my leave, knowing her thanks was misguided. If not for me—if not for my inability to reject Benji—she would no doubt be whole and healthy, laughing and chasing after her son under a clear blue sky.

Bad luck.

Diseased.

Everything I touched would eventually die.

The day only got worse.

Mordecai had extended our hours, saying we were already falling behind schedule. Some of us used pickaxes all day, chipping out the crystal from the cave's wall. Others carted, sorted, and cleaned the crystal, while a select few were tasked with sawing down the crystal to predetermined sizes. It was the latter that I felt most sorry for. Jocelyn hovered over them something fierce, critiquing each and every cut.

Less than a week on the job and exhaustion consumed us. Maybe because of the lack of sunlight or the stale filtered air. Whatever the reason, every time my coworkers and I went into the mines, we staggered out at the end of the day, barely able to make the trip home.

I had even considered black lung disease, but we weren't mining coal. Maybe crystal disease? Something was off and I was determined to find out what. I couldn't make the money I needed—that *Benji* needed—if I couldn't get out of bed in the morning.

I paused in my task, wiping sweat off my brow as Jocelyn clattered by. "Can I ask you a question?"

She whipped her head my direction, eyes rounding like I'd insulted her hair or something. "I'll answer if I can."

Well, then. Better than nothing. I leaned more fully on my pickaxe handle. "Are there side effects to working in these mines?"

She blinked owlishly. Maybe she was an owl shifter? "Not that I know of. I'd have to ask Mordecai. The doctors said you were all in perfect health. Why, are you not feeling well?"

I gave her a flat look, not bothering with subtlety. "Okay, I know we're all new to this job—including you—but I think we should have been informed if this task makes us sick."

Jocelyn stared like a deer in headlights—deer shifter? Laughter suddenly bubbled past her red lips. "Or maybe you're not accustomed to working for your pay? Yes, this is hard work, but your body will acclimate. Chin up, Tarik. The job will get easier, you'll see."

Her heels clipped smartly as she traipsed off. I rolled my eyes. What a quack. Duck shifter, perhaps? Now *that* one made sense. Right then, my stomach cramped with spasms and I groaned. Maybe the water down here was bad. Mordecai wouldn't poison us . . . would he?

Crap. Something wasn't right. I nudged the Fae next to me, pointing at my pickaxe. "Gotta pee, Holden. Watch this for me?" At his nod, I crossed the cavern, the trip taking longer than usual. My knees shook but I straightened my spine, resolved to complete this trek in one go, even if the effort killed me.

Maybe I was getting a normal sickness, like the flu or something. I shied away from that reasoning. My healing ability always cured me of ailments before they could take root. After relieving myself, I poked my head through each door I passed, still hoping to find Reagan slinking around.

The bright medical room beckoned like forbidden treasure, asking to be explored. Curiosity tugged and pulled at me, the need to discover what ailed me and the other Fae overcoming Jocelyn's earlier warning—even at the cost of my job. If the mines were slowly killing us, then this room seemed like the best place to find answers. After a thorough scan of my surroundings, I gave in.

The sterile room was empty, lined with examination tables

and shiny silver equipment. Against the far wall was a floor-to-ceiling glass cabinet. Locked. Filled with Fae blood and urine samples. Everything sat in labeled order: test tubes, syringes, bottles of—

What if the doctors injected us with something?

I had lost count of how many times they'd poked needles into me earlier this week. Maybe I and some of the others were having an adverse reaction to the mystery drugs. Or maybe they were instructed to pump us with poison. I made for the cabinet, searching for a key or tool I could use to pick the lock. I would even settle for smashing the glass at this point.

The room was too clean. Too perfect. I didn't trust it. I needed answers and I would bet they could be found behind that cabinet's thick sheet of glass.

"Well, Tarik Hail, I guess I shouldn't be surprised to find you in here."

That voice.

Ice froze the blood in my veins. I whirled to find Mordecai standing in the doorway. A dark head peeked over his shoulder. Jocelyn. My heart pumped double time. I should have known she'd run off to her boss after my probing questions. They'd caught me red-handed. I couldn't talk my way out of this one.

Even as a tremor worked its way through me, I strolled over to an exam table and sat, white paper crinkling as I settled in. Might as well be comfortable if I was about to get fired.

Mordecai said something to Jocelyn, who scampered off to do his bidding, then stepped inside the room and closed the door, locking us inside with a soft *snick*. Despite my efforts to play cool, my pulse thundered. I was alone in a room with the Great Dragon, the man who made our Fae existence hell.

My hands curled into fists where they rested on my thighs.

"I knew you were going to be more trouble than you're worth," he said, tucking tattooed hands out of sight as his arms crossed over a barrel chest. His human size was intimidating—I couldn't imagine how big his dragon form was. But in all my years trapped in this city, I'd never once seen him shift. Had never seen a massive dragon darkening the sky. Alec didn't count. His dragon was puny.

I shrugged. "Then why did you hire me?"

His upper lip curled, pulling at the jagged scar running across the left side of his face. Scary. I was glad I'd relieved myself a few minutes ago. "Because I need you. Only Fae can work this job. Strong Fae, like you. Unless . . . Jocelyn informs me that you're sick? Maybe I don't need you after all."

My spine stiffened. He wanted me to beg. I could see the command in those mocking blue eyes. His lips tipped up. Checkmate. Everything in me rebelled at the thought of pandering to this slave-driver, but an image of Haven, broken on the ground, held my tongue. I swallowed the retort that wanted nothing more than to punch this man's face. "No, sir," I said. "Ate a bad burrito for lunch is all. It upset my stomach."

His nostrils flared as he took a step closer. Only an exam table separated us now. "Regardless, you were caught for the second time entering a room strictly off limits. This can't go unpunished." He paused, studying me. My skin felt too tight, like I'd spent the whole day baking under a sweltering sun. "I doubt you'd respond well to my preferred methods, so I tell you what. Step out of line one more time, *one* more time, and Reagan pays the price."

My head spun as those words sucked all the oxygen out

of the room. If I wasn't sitting down, I might have fallen from abject shock at his threat. This guy was pure evil incarnate. The words on my tongue were boiling hot. I couldn't control them. I couldn't stop them. "What, you don't think one brand is enough? Does she need a twin on the other side of her neck?"

I'd done it now. Maybe I was imagining the fine wisps of smoke puffing from his ears. Lightning quick, he grabbed the exam table and flipped the whole thing in the air. Metal clanged against white tile as he stalked toward me, stopping only when his nose was almost pressed to mine. "The first thing I'll do is cut Reagan's tongue out. Maybe that'll shut you up."

The vile threat stomped my rage to a sputtering ember, then tossed buckets of ice water over any lingering heat. I lowered my eyes in a show of submission, even as my knuckles bled white. "You don't have to do that. I won't give you any more trouble."

He quickly straightened, adjusting his suit jacket in short, jerky movements. I peeked at his face, and wished I hadn't. *Victory*, his expression gloated. "See that you don't. I know your routine, Tarik. The places you haunt, the people you see. One more foul word out of that mouth, and I'll show you what misery is."

I didn't respond. Couldn't.

"Now get back to work. I'll see that half an hour's pay is docked from your wages."

Head still lowered, I slid off the table and left the room without a sound.

Gaia.

The miserable day wasn't done yet.

Now there was rain and the smell of overflowing sewage as I dodged muddy potholes and bags of garbage tossed into the streets. But I could see home. Only a few minutes more of this mess and I could sleep my troubles away.

What I wouldn't give for a stiff drink right now. The Pit was the last place I should be seen at, though. Mordecai was watching me. One false move and—

"Well, you look like crap."

Without turning, I knew she was behind me. I had memorized her low, gravelly voice. My heart skipped a beat and I inwardly cursed at the stupid thing. "Slogging through the rain for three miles will do that to a person. Even Jocelyn."

"It helps that she spends an obscene amount of time primping in the mansion bathrooms. Go into any one of them and there she is."

I snorted. "Yeah. There she is." I peered over at Reagan's soaked form and tried not to notice how good she looked. "Are we gonna discuss Jocelyn some more or did you have another reason for being here?"

"How was work?" Her tone was cautious. Nosy.

"Really?" I sighed and faced her, dragging hair out of my weary eyes. "Work sucks. There, happy?"

"You okay?" She frowned, fidgeting with the handles of her bike.

"Yeah, I'm peachy. Your father is sunshine and my job is rainbows," I snapped.

"Tarik, did he do something to you? Say something?" Reagan inched closer.

I laughed humorlessly, taking a step back. "You could say that. Threatened me, my job, and everything else he could think of. He even threatened—" Instead of finishing, I growled and kicked an empty trash can, sending the lid skittering across the street. I couldn't do this with her right now. Not when everything was falling down on my head, crushing me beneath its weight.

"He threatened your job?" Her eyes followed the silver disc, lips pressing together before she shrugged. "Well, honestly, you'd be better off if he fired you."

At those words, anger simmered beneath my skin. I almost walked away, too full of aggression and exhaustion to think clearly, but maybe this was best. Maybe if I expelled all the words, she would leave me be, once and for all, and Mordecai would remove the target from her back. I strode up to her, close enough to see the gold in her eyes.

"What makes you think you know what's best for me? You don't know what I have to deal with, the *responsibilities* I have. And we all know the blasted shifters running this joke of a city won't let dirty Fae near the *decent* jobs." She stared, and I watched as my words slowly sank in. I had to look away, otherwise I might do something stupid, like apologize. I backed up, putting much needed space between us. "Go patrol, Reagan. There's nothing to see here."

"Really? I have no idea about the responsibilities you shoulder?" she said, stepping closer again. She couldn't take a hint. "You know, I have a job too. And I'm not talking about my official one. So if you want to endure whatever terrible things Mordecai has planned for you, be my guest."

Leaning so far in that she had to tilt her head back, I growled,

"I won't be the one enduring the terrible things Mordecai has planned. *You* will. Especially if you don't give up this pipe dream of saving the Fae. Don't you understand? You need to lay low or he's going to hurt you again, and I can't—" I balled my hands at my sides so I wouldn't reach out and shake some sense into her. "You need to leave. Now."

"I can handle myself. You think I haven't already been punished a number of times? I accept that as part of the deal." Her eyes widened, then dropped to the ground. When she spoke again, the words were a soft mumble. "I knew his rules and got caught breaking them. I deserved his punishments."

That was too far. I could feel myself tipping over the edge, losing sight of what I was supposed to be saying and doing. I clamped both hands on her shoulders and yelled, "You don't deserve to be abused!"

She didn't even flinch. "You have no idea how much I've been able to do for the Fae over the years. Healing, food, intervening when the shifters just won't quit. I know the risks and I'm glad to take them. A brand is a small price for the things he does to your people. Who cares if he marked me? I knew I was breaking his rules, Tarik. But helping people? Helping you? *That's worth the risk.*" She swallowed. "I don't know what your problem is today. But I've had enough."

I yanked my hands off her and turned away, frustrated beyond belief. "And here I thought *I* was the one with a death wish. But you know what? I'm glad you've had enough, because I can't save you. So walk away and never look back. You're better off."

"Ha! You think *I'm* the damsel in distress in this situation? That's hilarious. I didn't ask for your help. I can handle myself.

I'm not the one who keeps trying to get myself killed for an adrenaline rush."

She's driving me insane! I threw a glare over my shoulder. "Yeah, that really is funny because I didn't ask for your help either! But go ahead, get yourself killed. I won't be there when you fall."

Reagan rolled her eyes. "Mordecai needs me. He would never kill me. And hell, I didn't earn the title of unwanted stalker for nothing."

"You think too highly of yourself," I bit out. "Mordecai threatened to cut out your tongue a few short hours ago."

"Okay?" She barked a laugh. "You know he threatens things like that all the time, right? Especially toward Alec. I could give you a list of the ways he's threatened his own son. He wouldn't kill me because I'm years of his hard work bundled into one neat little package. Wound or maim, sure. A tongue? That would interfere with my Enforcer duties. I'd be a damaged investment. He wouldn't dare."

I gaped at her incredulously. "Okay, I'm done," I said, backing away toward my apartment and a piece of sanity. "You're completely brainwashed and I don't think *I* can be the voice of reason in your head. Good luck being Mordecai's pet dog. Or lion. Whatever."

As I turned my back on her, I muttered, "And maybe someday you'll inherit this crap city and turn into a little Mordecai clone."

She gasped, then shouted, "What the hell did you say? You arrogant Fae prick!"

I heard a crash as her bike hit the ground, then she was on me, arms wrapped around my neck and legs straddling my waist. I froze when she let out an unearthly growl and sank her teeth into my shoulder. At first, I was too shocked to feel anything. Then pain shot through me with a vengeance. I roared and tried to shake her off, but she clung on like a leech, digging her teeth in deeper.

"You better not be using your fangs, shifter!" I bellowed. She wanted to play rough? Fine. My adrenaline rose to the occasion. While she was preoccupied with chewing on my shoulder, I wrenched one of her arms forward, sinking my own teeth into skin and muscle. I broke through and a coppery tang flooded my mouth.

Her teeth unlatched as she shrieked in fury. She jerked her arm away and I let her go, whipping around when she hopped off my back. Worst mistake ever. Her fist rained an uppercut into my chin. I tipped over, back smacking the ground with a great splash. Air whooshed out of me, not only from the fall but from the fist Reagan rammed into my gut a second later.

I probably looked like a gasping fish as I struggled to inhale oxygen, helpless to stop her from pounding me to raw meat. But that's what I'd wanted for three solid years—for a shifter to put me out of my misery and end this rat-race of an existence. And who better than her? She didn't deserve Mordecai's cruel punishments, but she deserved to end my pathetic life after everything I'd already put her through.

So I closed my eyes and relaxed my muscles, giving up the fight. Rain pelted my face as I waited. The rain stopped. I blinked, confused, only to find Reagan hovering above me, a wrinkle between her brows. What, was she concerned for me? This wasn't working. She wasn't leaving!

There was only one thing left to do then. She would never

forgive me for this, and my chest ached at the thought of what it would do to her.

What it would do to *me*.

But, Gaia, I knew it would work.

I snaked a hand around her neck and yanked, bringing her head down, down, down, then kissed her on the mouth. Hard. The action surprised her, as I'd assumed. Her body stiffened where it brushed against mine. But my plan started to backfire. The kiss lasted too long. I couldn't tear myself away. I desperately dug my fingers into her hair and pulled her back, breaking the connection.

When I met her wide gaze, I wanted to shoot myself. She almost looked . . . frightened. My mind screamed at me to apologize, to beg her forgiveness. Crap, I couldn't do this. But I *had* to. I dragged in air, my voice hoarse as I said, "That was goodbye." With a grunt, I shoved to my feet, effectively rolling her off me. She simply sat in a discarded heap, staring at the ground, looking lost.

I'm a monster.

"Tarik!" The excited child's voice was unmistakable and I stifled a groan. I moved away from Reagan, not wanting to add to her confusion.

"Benji, you shouldn't leave your mom alone. Is she okay?" I strode toward him, trying to block his view of the bedraggled Night Enforcer.

He leaned to the side, curious as a cat, and I grasped his shoulder. Finally, he blinked up at me. "She—she's crying a lot. I think her leg is really hurting her. She won't eat and she keeps saying strange things." His bottom lip quivered, the stress finally getting to him. He didn't cry often.

"Don't worry, kid, I'm coming in to check on her. Let's go." I wrapped an arm around his shoulders and firmly led him away from the havoc I had wreaked.

Another life I'd destroyed.

CHAPTER 10

Reagan

Tarik took five steps before I dove for my bike. I didn't know if he noticed, if he heard my bike as she roared to life under me, but my heart skipped with relief when she lurched forward. Main Street flew past, my tires skidding dangerously as I swerved to avoid potholes. Adrenaline shot through my system, almost enough to shake the other feeling, the one that sat like a weight in my chest. I needed distance, and now.

That kiss. That *stupid* kiss.

My first—did he know? Did he care? Shifters could be an affectionate race, even if the brutes in Nathra City made it hard to believe. We had a natural inclination to touch others, to stick together. As a race so open with every facet of our bodies, something had to remain sacred. A kiss? Uncharted territory for the girl locked away by a dragon. A valued moment of emotional intimacy that I had been robbed of, like he had taken a small piece of me. And not because he *wanted* to kiss me, or wanted me at all. No, he had wanted to steal a moment to crush between his hands, and he had chosen that one. A moment I couldn't replace. Because he wanted to *hurt* me.

My elbow almost bit blacktop when I took a turn too sharply. I kept going, trying to inhale against the fire in my lungs. The bite on my arm throbbed, my knees smarting from kneeling on hard concrete. Nothing hurt as badly as the ache in my chest, though. The tightness. My breaths came in painful, arduous gasps. I drove blindly, foot pressed heavily on the gas. I needed to stop, pull over, get off the bike. My thoughts were skittering across my mind like spilled marbles—driving in this state wasn't safe. I would wreck.

Swerving, I cut through an alley. A stray cat darted out of the way as I shot past, not slowing until I found the abandoned ruins of an old high rise. My favorite spot, when the days were hard or I had failed. When Alec went too far, and I couldn't do anything but watch as he brutalized innocent Fae. I ditched my bike on the street corner, jumping over the jagged edge of a rock wall. This building had collapsed years ago, before I had even left the mansion, one of the first to go in this district. The second floor had fallen shortly after, creating a small overhang above the rear corner.

My dark, quiet little corner. The one place in the entire city I knew no one but Nevaeh could find me.

The one place I could cry.

Hot, heavy tears fell noiselessly onto my legs, catching on the fishnets wrapped around them. My body shook, chest heaving under the effort to pull in air. I didn't know how else to react or process the flood of emotions.

He had to know what he'd done—he had acted with purpose.

One kiss.

Taken. Used for revenge.

What kind of cruel, cold-hearted person did that? Simply took what they wanted of a person, with no regard for their victim?

Heat simmered through my veins. If he never even *looked* at me again, I would be all too happy. And if he did, he had better keep his damned hands and cursed lips to himself. Because after that stunt, I didn't care if he lived or died.

Did I?

Love is pain, Reagan.

A scream of frustration tore from my throat. That *voice.* Mordecai's voice. I didn't want to hear him in my thoughts—now or ever again. He dictated every facet of my life. Every choice, every decision. Helping the Fae was my only solace, the only way I could cope with what I was.

Night Enforcer.

A title that literally brought fear wherever I went. But then, how could it not when my failures didn't only punish me?

I stifled a sob. I thought Tarik would be different. He was a Fae unlike any I had met before, one whom I thought might understand how I felt as the black sheep of my race. I had thought he might even be able to look past my title. That maybe Tarik—

I choked on the name.

Mordecai was right.

No. He wasn't.

I didn't love this Fae. My feelings weren't anywhere close. I might have liked him a little, though. Might have been drawn to his fire.

But at the end of the day, was he really so different from the shifters he proclaimed to hate? He, like them, disregarded the feelings of the people they hurt in an effort to lift themselves.

He was no better than the scum at The Pit.

My head throbbed. Fingers shaking, I struggled to pull my cigarette case free. My thumb brushed the embossed lion on the front, fumbling for the clasp on top. I took several deep, steady breaths, enough to even out my trembling, and snapped my lighter open. The bright flame flicked to life, casting a faint orange glow on the concrete rubble. I managed to spark the end of my cigarette, taking a long draw.

Better. Not really. A bandaid slapped over a gaping wound.

I kept replaying the fight, retracing each word, trying to find the exact moment things went south. Did I believe what I had said to Tarik? That Mordecai wouldn't kill me? I had never seriously considered him taking his anger that far. Lashings, sure. My fingers brushed the dragon mark on my neck, still achy. A reminder that Mordecai's punishments were escalating again. Every time I was caught, or learned more about my adoptive father, I gained a clearer picture of exactly what kind of monster he was. Did I deserve the brand? No. Maybe . . .

Hell.

I don't know.

My eyes fell to the still-bleeding wound on my arm. I deserved that. No question. Tarik had a way of poking at my temper, lighting the worst parts into a blazing rage. But I was an Enforcer. Losing control like I had was unacceptable. His words were cruel, but he had used words and I had resorted to violence. My behavior was unacceptable. Plus, my shifter abilities gave me an unfair advantage. Guilt rippled through my chest. I was supposed to be better than this. If I couldn't be, how could I hold him responsible for his own actions?

Because he had hurt me in return, then kept going. Because he had repaid every blow I had given him and I couldn't do the same. I didn't want to. My heart clenched. I hadn't deserved that, no matter what his reasons were. He stole something precious.

I'm done thinking about this.

Inhaling slowly, I forced my mind to wander, thoughts skipping back and forth until they landed on the boy. Benji. I didn't know much about him, and I had never met his mother, but clearly her health was worsening. Tarik wouldn't get paid for a few days yet—Mordecai had them on a biweekly cycle. Maybe I could help. I didn't know which apartment was hers, but I could leave the medicine with Tarik.

That would mean seeing him.

I winced.

No, thanks.

I took another drag from my cigarette and crushed the hot cherry into the broken concrete beside me. I could help Benji and his mother, Tarik be damned.

Climbing to my feet, I vaulted the half wall and threw my leg over the seat of my bike. She purred, raring to go, but I hesitated. My mind skimmed over the places that might have what Benji's mother would need. I had medicine in my penthouse, but no vitamins—and she would need those if she was struggling to heal. Buying them wasn't an option. Mordecai was likely tracking my purchases right now.

Damnit. There had to be more options.

My fingers drummed the handles of my bike as I looked around the quiet street. I tugged at my lip ring, lost in thought, gaze falling to the mansion that taunted me in the distance.

I can take the medicine from Mordecai.

He would never notice, and the irony would be sweet. His money, directly funding my efforts to save the Fae . . .

I huffed an airy laugh before I laid on the gas.

The mansion's doors loomed in front of me but I couldn't seem to move. Mordecai kept his first aid supplies in a bathroom near his office. If I went there, he'd see or hear me. I tapped my foot on the stone path, glancing at the small flower gardens that edged the lawn. Their presence was a travesty, the bright petals far too vibrant for a place holding so much darkness.

Darkness.

The mines. The medical room. I could steal the medicine from there. No one was down there right now, or should be. My patrol didn't start for an hour yet. I eyed the door handles that taunted me to pull them open.

Reaching out, I wrapped my fingers around the polished silver and waited for the soft click. No turning back now. I stepped through, nodding curtly at Squirrel Butler before I dipped down the rear hall. I took a roundabout path, stopping in random rooms, checking for people. No one seemed to be here, or at least not on the lower levels as I crept into the downstairs hallway. I paused outside the mine door to extend one of my claws. Picking the lock was the work of ten seconds.

Another minute and the bottom of my boots met the stone floor of the mines. The scent of sweat now mingled with the earthy smell I had grown used to. Everything felt *off* down here, and I wasn't talking about the unusual pull on my stomach. Even the stone walls seemed to understand that something terrible was going to happen. I swallowed hard and crept along. No voices echoed from the mining chambers, no click of heels resonated from Jocelyn's pacing. Everything was painfully, unnaturally silent.

I could see relatively well in the dark. Well enough that I wasn't concerned about light as I slunk into the dim lab room. The password warning flickered brightly from the computer in the corner.

"I'll deal with you next," I muttered.

Having a plan made me feel better. My chest tightened when I paused, so I simply kept moving. Tried to focus on my task. The fight with Tarik taunted my thoughts, images and words replaying in waves. I shoved them away roughly. Tarik's split second of hesitation before his final words to me pushed to the forefront, words he apparently thought I deserved.

That was goodbye.

My throat closed, a knot wedged in the middle. I tried to swallow and choked instead.

Focus. I needed to focus. The medicine cabinet was on the far wall. I moved forward and studied the case, rapping a finger against the glass. The tiny sound echoed, louder than I had expected. I stilled, listened. Silence. The glass was thick, and the lock didn't have a hole to pick. I drummed my fingertips across my forehead, whispering, "There has to be *something.*"

My eyes slid to the small metal hinges that ran down the side of the cabinet door. I pulled in a sharp breath. This could be risky. I scanned the shelves. Everything Benji's mother would need was here—vitamins, pain medicines, supplements.

Dark, auburn curls and amber eyes flooded my thoughts.

Skipping feet, a joyful laugh. My jaw clenched.

I had to do this.

But I wouldn't make the same mistakes as before. I wouldn't get caught.

Benji wouldn't become *her*.

With only a second of hesitation, I watched as my index finger shortened, a long claw extending from the end. I raked the point down the metal of the first hinge. The steel resisted, so I turned to the screws holding them in place. My nail was pointed enough that, with my shifter strength, I could twist the large screw loose. This was going to take a while.

I took my time though, one screw after another, carefully holding the door with my free hand. When the final hinge slipped loose I almost sighed in relief—until the full weight of the door shoved against my arm and I slipped.

The glass shattered.

Air froze in my lungs. My pulse flew to a thundering rhythm, drowning my thoughts. Echoes of the crash still reverberated through the room and caverns surrounding. I waited, positive that Squirrel Butler must have heard the crash. Seconds passed. Minutes, maybe. Then I heard them. Heeled shoes clacking across stone. I grimaced, searching the room.

The shower—bunched white curtains trailed the tile floor. I moved as quickly as I dared, pulling the sheet around me. The stifling scent of new plastic overwhelmed my senses. My heart raced as the heels stopped outside the room. Lights flicked on. I slowed my breathing, tried to still my arms and legs as they shook with adrenaline.

"What the hell—" Jocelyn's heels clicked closer before they faded into a soft shuffle—like she was on her toes. Silence fell, then a frustrated sigh. I didn't dare move.

More small shuffles reached my ears, and the clatter of glass shards, then the heels retreated from the room. This was too easy. All I had to do was grab what I needed and get out.

But the footsteps returned before I could move, and she wasn't alone this time.

". . . was coming to get you, sir."

"What happened?" Fresh waves of fear washed over me at the second voice. If Mordecai heard me, if he saw me . . . I begged my heart to be a little quieter.

"This cabinet door fell. I don't know how."

Glass crunched. More swearing. "Who installed this unit?"

"Um, I'm not sure, but I could check with the installation staff." Jocelyn's voice trembled.

"Fire anyone who had a hand in these cabinets. Execute one, make the others watch. Sloppy handiwork will not be tolerated in *my* city."

No . . .

A shifter would *die* for this? I swallowed the bile that raced up my throat. Damnit. This was the exact opposite of what I was trying to do.

"Yes, sir. I'll have one of the maintenance staff come down here in the morning and clean up the glass."

Mordecai's footsteps retreated a bit, then paused. The rapid tap of computer keys filled the silence. "See that you do. And order a replacement door."

"Yes, sir."

He left and a weight fell off my shoulders. The terror that had risen in my chest faded. Jocelyn was at the computer now, her fingers skimming over the keys. She was silent otherwise;

apparently Mordecai made her more nervous than she cared to say. Or maybe she hated that he had appointed her to pick a shifter for execution. An innocent employee.

And, since an Enforcer was required to be at executions, I would be the one to oversee it. Mordecai liked to remind me what he was capable of—and that I couldn't stop him. I shuddered to think what my punishment would be if I even tried.

Only a few minutes passed before she left, the lights snapping off. I waited until the sound of her heels faded away, and then a few more beats. Silence. Utter and complete silence. I inhaled, then slowly released the breath. Close. That was too close. Carefully, I pulled the curtain away, wiping small beads of sweat from my forehead. I snitched a small first aid bag from a side cabinet and shoved bottles inside, picking from the back so they hopefully wouldn't be missed. When the bag was full I crept for the door, my eyes sliding momentarily to the computer.

Jocelyn hadn't logged Mordecai out. My heart skipped. Lingering any longer would be asking for trouble. I had already almost been caught. I moved to leave.

And turned at the last moment, making a beeline for the desktop.

My fingers flew over the keys, pulling files, searching for anything that would tell me what they were doing down here. At first, there wasn't much related to the mines; shipping logs, trade deals for paper products, a map that showed an underground passage from the shifter district out past the city limits. That had to be how Mordecai imported goods; I had always been told that information wasn't my business. I would have to look into it when I had more time.

I clicked a yellow envelope buried deep in the documents folder.

All the employee files popped up. Blood work, personal data. Original applications. Deeper in were the official announcements as well as detailed sheets filled with rules and expectations.

In a file of their own, tucked into a corner I almost missed, were a bunch of files detailing experiments Mordecai had done on himself. I didn't have time to read them in depth but the notes I gathered from skimming were repulsive enough. They weren't what I was looking for. I closed them out and continued on.

At the bottom, right as I was starting to think that what I needed wasn't here, I clicked a lone folder.

Genesis Crystal—Trial One.

I skimmed the page, eyes widening the more I read. The details were horrifying. Outlines of lab procedures, tests meant to measure the effects of the Genesis Crystal in unwitting subjects after days of exposure to build their tolerance.

Mordecai was planning to trap the Fae he had hired. Cage them and experiment on them. My stomach twisted. Mordecai was a monster. An absolute monster. The brand on my neck twinged as if confirming the thought. Spreadsheets by the dozens filled the file, ready for the results of a multitude of blood tests, sample doses, and placebo scenarios. I swallowed. I had to tell Tarik.

He wanted this job.

I groaned in frustration. He didn't want *this*. No one would. But would he listen if I told him?

None of that mattered if I didn't get out of here. The longer I lingered the later I was going to be for my patrol. I was already late. If I didn't take to the sky soon, Alec would report me. He enjoyed making sure I was doing my job. Enjoyed *stalking* me, more like. Stalker. My chest panged. I shoved that word and its association aside, clicking my way through a set of red x's and signing Mordecai out.

You're welcome, Jocelyn.

I climbed the spiral staircase, careful to lock the mine door behind me before I bolted out the rear door of the mansion. Shedding and abandoning my clothes in the bushes, I stretched into lion form. Clouds trailed lazily over the bright moon, already high in the dark sky. I was late, so late. *Damnit.*

My wings stretched wide as I took flight, the first aid bag clenched tightly between my teeth. I flew straight for Tarik's apartment, glancing at his neighbor's windows as I landed and slid into a shift. No sign of Benji. I groaned, my eyes carefully tracing each building.

Fine.

I twisted the handle on Tarik's door, surprised when I heard the soft click and met no resistance. Yeah, that's safe. My heart stuttered when I saw him splayed across his bed, like he had collapsed from exhaustion. I knew he had been tired. An apology bubbled up in my throat.

Then his lips moved, parted. The sight reignited the fury in my veins, reminded me of that particularly painful hurt. In a moment of haste, I dumped the bottles on his sleeping form, not at all surprised when he didn't move. I threw the bag too and stormed out, taking to the sky.

Stupid, arrogant Fae prick.

Regret. I ached with regret.

I punched the shower tiles. Afternoon sun blazed through the bathroom window, meaning Tarik was already at work. Maybe today wasn't the day Mordecai planned to trap them. Maybe I still had time to tell him. Sure, seeing him would rip my soul apart. Again. But I couldn't keep letting him go into that mine without a proper warning, one based on *evidence* instead of vague concerns. My gut ached at the thought of facing him, but avoiding him would hurt more than my bruised heart—two dozen Fae would be condemned to a fate worse than death. I couldn't let Mordecai's twisted plans come to fruition.

Tarik had been right, though. If Mordecai was so willing to torture the Fae, I couldn't imagine what he would be willing to do to me. I had no doubts now that he would follow through on his threat to Tarik; if he thought harming me would keep that temperamental Fae in line, boy was he wrong. Still, his obsession with the Fae had gone too far if he was willing to run experiments on them.

Arrogant prick he may be, but Tarik was right. I didn't deserve the brand on my neck. Mordecai was abusive. Controlling.

I choked back a sob, but the tears fell anyway. Nevaeh would know what to do. I almost wanted to call her, but I knew what she would say. Talk to Tarik. Apologize. Or at least try.

But when I thought about that kiss, the angry press of his lips to mine, and the forceful way he had shoved me back. My tears renewed. I sat on the floor of my shower and let them fall.

Minutes passed before I swiped at my face, the effort wasted under the steady downpour. Time to get up. I needed to collect myself, take action. I could find him and tell him what Mordecai planned, and then, if I didn't want to, I never had to see him again. Right now, I could live with that. But I couldn't exactly walk up to him in the mines.

When the water ran cold, I dried off and climbed into bed. The warmth and comfort of my blankets sang a siren's song that was impossible to resist. I didn't want to go anywhere or see anyone, anyway. I set an alarm for half an hour after he should get out. Didn't want to be too much of a stalker.

I punched my pillow, burying my face in the impression my fist left.

A couple hours later the painfully cheerful chirp of my alarm woke me. My body was sluggish but my mind was ready to go. I had a plan. I dressed quickly and took the elevator instead of shifting. No time to deal with Fae modesty. I needed to spit the words out and be gone.

My mind was a carousel of emotions—angry, then sad, then hurt. Never at the same time. I glanced left and right, eyes skirting the route to the mansion. Abandoned, no Fae to be seen. *Come on. I want to get this over with.*

Under my hands, the handles of my bike vibrated; as though she could feel the tension squeezing my shoulders and wanted to get moving. I pushed her forward, racing toward Tarik's apartment, but the dark windows told me all I needed to know. No lights, no Tarik. My stomach lurched. Maybe I was too late. Maybe Mordecai had kept them today.

Damnit.

I can't be too late.

My fist met his rotted, wooden door frame. A distant shout echoed down the street and I realized that I had one final hope. The Pit. I kicked my bike into motion, flying across the worn blacktop.

The air around The Pit felt wrong tonight, the shifters eyeing me in a way I wasn't particularly comfortable with. Out for a fight, and the Night Enforcer was the perfect target. I set my kickstand and ignored them.

Not tonight boys, I'm not in the mood.

Tarik wasn't inside though. Frenzied anxiety roared through my veins.

Where is he?

I didn't want to be wrong, didn't want to be too late.

Please, please don't let me be too late.

As I climbed the stairs from The Pit, one of the angry-looking shifters sidled up beside me. The scent of whiskey was strong and upset the delicate balance of my stomach. I almost expelled the meager contents all over him.

"Aw, Enforcer, can't find your boyfriend?"

I puffed myself up. "Do you really want to instigate a fight you're not ready for? I don't have a boyfriend."

"Oh, no? We know all about you, dirty Fae-lover." His eyes locked on my face as he waited for me to confess my treasonous behavior.

I chuckled softly. "You might want to check your sources."

I turned to leave when he grabbed my arm. Rage spiked through my veins and I swung for his face, but he caught my fist. His eyes raked the length of my body and I shivered at the predatory glint that sparked to life. The scent of alcohol washed over me. Liquid courage.

"I have these friends . . . they're pretty reliable sources," he sneered, shoving me backward.

My back met warm bodies. I spun around. Shifters—the ones who had been prepared to kill Tarik several nights ago—lurked in the shadows. And they had brought friends. Too many. These odds weren't in my favor.

I'm not going down without a fight.

In my distraction, I missed the fist that flew at me. My body shook under the impact. Instinctively, I slid into a defensive position. I raised my hands to block another blow and a fist slammed into the back of my head. *Damnit.* I was completely boxed in. I dipped low and swept at the legs of the leader. He caught my foot, flipping me onto my back.

My heart pounded in my ears as I glared up at him. "You don't really want to piss off an Enforcer, do you?" Blood trickled over my lips.

His responding grin chilled my core. "No, but we'll gladly kill one."

CHAPTER 11

Tarik

I awoke to Callie batting at something on my chest. As she continued to swat, the object clattered and rolled, eventually smacking the cement floor with a jingling rattle.

At the jarring noise, my eyes flew open and I bolted upright. Callie went tumbling and so did several white bottles. I frowned, blinking slowly, not comprehending. Glancing around my room, I half-expected to find Benji. Every once in a while, he brought his makeshift toys over and played quietly while I slept. That boy rose before the birds.

But my apartment was empty save for Callie, who was now rolling one of the bottles across the floor. I plucked one off my blanket and inspected the label: calcium supplements. My frown deepened and I snatched up another one. And another. All were either vitamins or pain meds.

I scrubbed a hand down my face, trying to jog my hazy memory. Last night had been a blur of fatigue and anger and guilt. So much guilt. I had lost my temper again, big time, and once more Reagan had paid the price. I had hoped that by squashing the image she had of me, she'd back off and be safer for it. Spending time with me would only get her hurt—or killed. Mordecai would make sure of that.

And then I'd lost my mind. Instead of firmly pushing her away and erecting the necessary walls, I'd crushed her. Completely. Unforgivably. Something in me knew, just *knew* that I'd stolen a piece of her last night, one that could never be returned.

Gaia.

I kissed her.

What had I been thinking? I hadn't. I had been desperate, needing distance from her—and not just for her own safety. For *mine*. I couldn't open myself up to that kind of hurt again, and she'd been awfully close to breaching my defenses. So I'd kissed her. *Kissed* her. Yeah, that made sense. Instead of saving Reagan, I'd ruined her.

You're bad luck.

"I know," I whispered. My gut clenched hotly.

Despite the terrible way I had treated her, it was for the best. She'd heal. Live her life in relative safety—as long as she didn't keep helping the Fae. Somehow, I needed to stop her from doing that.

I had a few connections, those I considered friends—even if I'd avoided them for three years. There were too many painful memories attached. After that awful day when my life had shattered, everything they said and did reminded me of her. Their scent, their empathy . . . their hair and eye color. Surrounding myself with them had been unbearable, like sticking my head in an oven. The heat of shame burned me alive, and the only thing I could do was shove them away. *All* of them. After the way I'd shut them out, I doubted they thought of me much anymore.

But I could send word and warn them about Reagan—they would discourage the Fae from accepting her aid. They would listen when I told them the price she would pay if caught.

Because they all remembered like it was yesterday.

Every single Fae in this city knew what happened three years ago.

Such a heinous crime could never be forgotten.

I rubbed my eyes, attempting to scrub away the haunting images that came unbidden at the thought of that day. I was tired, so tired of those flashbacks. Releasing a pent-up sigh, I stood from the bed and gathered the bottles, placing them in a bag that had been dumped on me as well.

And that's when I noticed the insignia stamped on the bag—a dragon wrapped around a shard of crystal. The same one found on doors in the mansion, the same one etched onto our hazmat suits, the same one branded on Reagan's neck. Which meant that this medicine must be directly linked to Mordecai. But he would never give such valuable supplies to a Fae—especially not me. There was one shifter who had access to the mansion and who'd overheard Benji mention an ailing mother, though.

Reagan.

I stared hard at the mess on my bed. The realization of what she must have done hit me like a ton of bricks.

Gaia, no. What was she *thinking*?

With a groan, I sunk to the floor, knees barking in protest as they slapped the cement. I dug my fingers into my hair and pulled, pulled until sharp pain bit at my skull. Air stuck in my throat and I gave up on breathing. Kneeling next to the evidence of her continued help, her *caring*, even after what I had done to her . . .

I hated myself.

If, by some miracle, she had forgiven me my horrendous words and actions, I didn't deserve it. I didn't deserve *her*. I never would. Despite being brainwashed, she was pure. Too pure for this toxic city. But I didn't know how much longer she'd stay that way, not with Mordecai gunning for her and Fae like me threatening her precarious position.

Maybe I couldn't personally protect her, but maybe my connections could. After my work shift this evening, I'd seek them out and plead my case. They had every cause to loathe Shapeshifters just as much as I did, but Reagan was different. Reagan was . . .

Special.

I blew out a breath and stood on trembling legs, shoveling the last of the precious bottles into the bag. The pills wouldn't heal Haven, but they would help. Help. Reagan only wanted to help, to make a difference, and I hated that I'd be ripping away one more piece of her by asking the Fae to stop her attempts. But I couldn't stand back and watch this city pick apart every good piece of her until there was nothing decent left, until she was shaped into—

Gaia, I was such a jerk. I couldn't believe I'd called her a "little Mordecai clone." No wonder she'd attacked me. I touched the mark she'd left behind on my shoulder and winced. The spot was still sore, but I hadn't healed the wound. I couldn't. I wanted the memory. No. I *needed* the memory.

The cost of getting close to me was scars.

It was only fitting that I should bear some of them.

Rainy season was the worst.

Not only did the whole city stink of wet dog most days—or shifter, more accurately—but the water dampened my mood. This evening was different, though. After my longest workday yet, I almost felt rejuvenated as the downpour plastered hair to my cheeks.

I thought back to the day's events, wondering what had changed my energy levels. I recalled how Jocelyn had said things would get easier, but I was certain she'd only been pacifying a disgruntled employee. No, something had happened. The only thing I could think of was the odd jolt I'd felt while handling the crystal before quitting time. I had picked up the green rock several times this past week without feeling anything, but as I'd hefted a rather large and sharp piece today, a current zapped me, like an electrical shock.

Maybe the crystal had sliced a hole in the hazmat suit.

At the time, I'd been too exhausted to care. But now . . . now I felt incredible, like I'd slept twelve hours straight—which never happened, not with Benji as a neighbor. Strangest of all though was the tingling at the base of my shoulder blades. Twin lines of incessant itching, right where my wings lay hidden. I had never felt such an intense burn before and wondered what they were up to.

But I wouldn't release them no matter how powerful the urge.

I wasn't *that* stupid.

A few of my coworkers, including Holden, had agreed to help me with my Reagan problems. I hadn't mentioned her name, but they knew someone was in trouble and that was all they needed to hear.

"We've got your back, Tarik. All you need to do is ask," Holden had said without prying for details. The one thing my kind always did was look out for each other. My coworkers probably knew all about my sordid past, including my reputation at The Pit, but they didn't seem to care. Wait until they caught wind I was trying to protect a *shifter.*

The looks of utter shock would be epic.

Currently, we were laughing about our newest guess as to what Jocelyn's shifter form was. A spider. I mean, she was always in our hair and scuttling in and out of tight spaces. Fitting. But, if she morphed into a ten-foot-tall hairy arachnid, I'd never sleep again. I chuckled, envisioning eight high-heeled shoes on a spider that stumbled and tripped all over itself.

So amused by the mental image, I almost missed the cry of pain.

We were nearing the shifter warehouse district where The Pit resided. Cries of pain were common—male shifters liked beating each other up in the side alley. Stupid, testosterone-driven meatheads. I was about to tell the group to give the place a wide berth. We had much more important business, after all. Reagan's life counted on this Fae meeting.

But the cry came again, louder this time, and I paused.

Something about the cadence sounded way too familiar. The noise wasn't human but rather a shifter in animal form. A shifter in agony. The pain-filled roar that came next froze my blood.

"Reagan," I breathed. I lurched into action, bare feet slapping against wet concrete as I charged toward that accursed alley. The alley that had caused me endless guilt and suffering. And now . . . now it was happening again.

Shouts followed my pounding footsteps but I didn't look back. Didn't dare. The lion cries were growing frantic and I couldn't breathe, couldn't think of anything but getting to her.

You're too late. Too late. Too late, the voice in my head jeered over and over.

I'm not, I inwardly yelled. I couldn't be. I couldn't do this again. I wouldn't survive.

When I slid around that final corner and saw the great winged lion—pinned, shredded, bleeding, and surrounded by frenzied shifters—my heart stopped. A giant male—half man and half wolf—wrapped a clawed hand around her neck. Without hesitation, without mercy, his other fist crashed into her jaw.

She mewled like a crushed kitten, then sagged, her large form shrinking until her petite human body fell to the ground. Naked. Broken. Alone.

For a split second, long blonde tresses replaced blue and black hair. A thin willowy frame in place of curves covered in colorful tattoos. They were one and the same in that moment.

Suffering.

Dying.

Because of me.

Through my shock and rising panic, I became aware of bodies crowding in close. I didn't take my eyes off Reagan's crumpled form, so vulnerable next to the monsters intent on killing her. Had they succeeded? I shoved the thought aside. I couldn't lose hope like that. Not yet.

First, I needed to end these pieces of filth.

"We're with you," Holden said at my elbow.

I nodded, knowing they were. Every Fae knew this alley's history. What had been done here. To her. To *me*. This alley was death, the destroyer of innocence and happiness.

But I prayed my coworkers wouldn't die tonight. I couldn't have them on my conscience too.

When a burly shifter kicked Reagan's unconscious body, a roar shook the alley. Mine. Wrenched from my lungs. Twin stabs of pain lanced my shoulders as wings punched from my back, tearing my shirt in half. I stood, shaking, filled with white hot rage and . . . and something else. Something glorious. I was going to kill them.

Kill them all.

Knowing this would hurt but relishing the pain anyway, I spread my destroyed wings wide. A few Fae inhaled sharply, whether from the fact that I'd broken the city's number one rule or from the sight of my damaged wings—I didn't care. Nothing mattered right now but ridding the world of the evil before me. I caught a glimpse of my wing's dark tattered remains as I pressed forward, shouting, "You vermin are going to pay for what you've done!"

As one, the shifters turned, furious expressions quickly morphing to shock, then horror. *Yes, that's right. Fear the scarred Fae demon.* I didn't wait for them to speak. Splintering agony shot through my raw wing muscles as they gave a mighty flap, air whistling between the featherless joints. Then I hurtled toward them.

I aimed for the one I recognized: Wolf Man, the shifter who had started me down this path of no return. The path that had brought me to Reagan. I barreled into his gut and lifted him off the ground, slamming him to the cracked cement. He groaned, and I rammed my fist into his mouth, dislodging teeth.

Two more solid blows to the face and he was out. I didn't waste time wondering how I, a lowly Fae, had knocked unconscious a half-shifted wolf man one hundred pounds heavier. My thoughts switched off as I twisted and whirled, raining blows upon any shifter I could get my hands on.

My wings, still razor-sharp at the tips where a spattering of feathers clung, sliced through flesh. Men howled and screamed, and I grinned wickedly. The whole alley was a bloodbath and I reveled in the pain. Bathed in it. Shifter blood was sweet on my tongue. All too soon, the fight ended. A few of the shifters, including Wolf Man, slunk away. But even more lay dead at my feet.

I blinked, clearing away some of the red haze. *Our* feet, actually. My fellow Fae were still with me. They hadn't dared release their wings, and a few had injuries, but none of them were dead. Once again, I pushed the shocking revelation to the recesses of my mind and searched the gore-covered ground.

There.

Reagan still lay where she'd fallen.

I couldn't tell if she was breathing and my heart twisted.

I was afraid to check. If she was dead, I couldn't . . .

I couldn't . . .

With a heavy tread, my wings scraping the ground behind me, I approached. Carefully knelt beside her. After inhaling a shaky breath, I touched her neck. *Thump. Thump-thump.*

Her pulse fluttered under my fingers and a rush of sweet relief coursed through my veins. I loosed a strangled exhale. Not caring if the other Fae saw, not caring what they thought,

I gathered her into my arms and rose, cradling her to me as if she were fragile glass.

Holden said something about hiding my wings, but all I could manage in return was a quick warning for them to get out of here. Then I was walking, not once taking my eyes off Reagan's face. A face marred with cuts and bruises.

"I've got you," I whispered down at her, knowing she couldn't hear me yet needing to reassure her anyway. "I won't let anyone else hurt you."

The entire way back to my apartment, I stared at the delicate vein in her neck that continued pumping, letting me know she was still alive. I knew, at some point, I was going to crash. The emotions flooding my body were too intense, too raw and real, and I could barely contain them. But I held them in, suppressed them so I could get her to safety.

I saved her. I saved her. I saved her.

My inner demon, normally so cynical, remained silent.

As I kicked open my apartment door, I lost track of her pulse. Panic flooded me. But then she twitched, eliciting a small moan, and I could breathe again. Ever so carefully, I placed her on my bed, grimacing when her right arm and left leg wouldn't lay straight. Definitely broken.

She didn't utter a sound as I climbed onto the mattress next to her and gently laid my palm over her heart tattoo, beginning the healing process. I didn't know how much energy I still possessed after that fight, but I'd use up every single drop of magic on her. Long, agonizing minutes later, her limbs finally straightened, snapping back into place.

My magic should have been sapped at that point, but more streamed from my veins and into hers. Halfway through, as I was starting in on the cuts and bruises, she groaned. I froze, hand still splayed over her heart. Her lashes fluttered and, as her eyes cracked open, I did nothing but stare.

She blinked at me, a line forming between her brows. And, even when her gaze ran down my bare shoulder to the hand that rested over her heart, I didn't move.

"Tarik?" Her voice was weak, tired. Her gaze flicked to where my wings were spread out behind me. "Oh. They're beautiful."

A million emotions jolted through me at that word. I sawed in a breath, the action tightening my chest. "You almost died. I suppose anything would look beautiful right about now."

"I did?" Confusion pinched her expression. "Everything's a touch foggy. But truly, you should release them more. You remind me of an angel. A dark angel, maybe . . . but I mean it. They're beautiful."

I gaped, completely dumbstruck. My heart couldn't take much more of this. And did she forget Fae weren't permitted to expose their wings? Maybe she'd suffered a concussion. I allowed my magic to thread toward her brain, double-checking for damage, but she was fine. A swallow lodged in my throat. "Uh . . ." I raised two trembling fingers. "How many fingers do you see?"

She chuckled softly. "Seven. You should get that checked."

I cracked a smile, relieved beyond measure that she was joking with me. Maybe she didn't hate me then. Or maybe she was simply grateful to be alive, and as soon as she was better, she'd remember all the vile things I'd said and done to her. I slid my hand off her chest and reached for my blanket, covering her naked form. I didn't need her making jokes about *that* next.

Now that she was awake and becoming more aware, her gaze strayed to my apartment, taking in the water stains, peeling plaster, and overall lack of decor. I shouldn't feel embarrassed, but a splotch of heat crept up my neck anyway. Careful not to jostle her body, I rose from the bed, angling my wings so they were less visible to her probing eyes. "You should, uh, get some sleep. You won't be able to patrol tonight, not with the condition you're in."

"Tarik—" Reagan adjusted herself so she could meet my eyes more directly. "I—You're right, you know. About Mordecai. And I . . . You're right. But please. Please, don't go to work in the morning. There are things I need to tell you, things you *need* to know. Hear me out before you go back again."

Gaia, her admission was a knife to my chest. She was still trying to help. Still trying to make amends. After *everything*. I could see she was struggling to stay awake—her eyes held a dull sheen. She needed rest. This conversation could wait. I bent down and, when she didn't flinch, tucked a lock of hair behind her ear. "I need to tell you things, too. Many things. But they'll keep until tomorrow. I almost watched you die tonight and—"

I couldn't stand under that gaze any longer. Retreating into the room's shadows, I flexed my shoulders, willing my wings to retract. The agony of their retreat stole my breath and I inhaled several times before heading to the window. "Get some sleep, Reagan. I'll be on the roof. No one will disturb you tonight." With that, I slid the pane up and ducked through, not waiting for her reply.

The weight of her stare had been too much.

I needed space to deal with my riotous emotions.

But, knowing that she was safe from harm, alive and well,

gave me a tiny sliver of peace.

CHAPTER 12
Reagan

My head throbbed.

What the hell happened to me last night?

I racked my mind, but came up short. Cracking my eyes open, I took in my surroundings and then shot up straight. My fingers tightened around the soft blanket spread over me as my heartbeat leaped into a frenzy. I blinked away the stars that burst across my vision and scanned the room. Nothing was familiar. My chest clenched and I stilled, inhaling tentatively. I recognized the scent that flooded my senses—like the earth after a rainfall. Like . . .

Tarik.

My shoulders loosened. I was in Tarik's apartment, a simple studio-style space without much adornment. A small lip on one wall caught my eye, laden with ceramic pots. Brightly colored flowers spilled out of them and filled the space with soft fragrance. Littered on the floor beneath them . . . toys? Small, makeshift wooden cars and a stack of uneven blocks—Benji's? I whipped my head around, searching for either of them. The room spun out of focus. Laying back, I groaned; my entire body ached. I took a breath and tried to focus, tried to remember.

The fight was fairly vivid, until a point. I had been utterly overwhelmed and, thinking back, I grew increasingly agitated that Alec hadn't stepped in. Where had he been? Clearly not on his patrol, or if he was, his eyes hadn't been on The Pit where they should have been. Or maybe . . . maybe he had simply left me to my fate? The thought didn't sit well. Did Mordecai tell him to leave me, to teach me a lesson for helping Tarik?

Maybe Mordecai really did want me dead.

A few details were stronger than others. Muscles along either side of my back groaned in protest as I stretched and lifted my arm, examining the smooth, intact limb with narrowed eyes. I could remember the bone relenting with perfect clarity; the snap, the pain. A shudder raced the length of my spine. How—? Could Tarik set bones? Even so, I would have needed a sling or cast. My thoughts were too fogged, I couldn't connect the dots. I had to be missing something.

Wait. Tarik.

Where is Tarik?

I shot up again and searched the apartment, like he would materialize in front of me. Other than his curious gray and white cat, there was no movement. Nausea roiled in my stomach and I took a deep breath. What had he said last night?

Think.

The roof. He mentioned the roof.

I stumbled to my feet, jumping for the windowsill I had seen him go through the night before. Dizziness overwhelmed me and I paused to breathe, but only for a moment. Time wasn't a luxury I had to spare. I huffed in pain as I dragged myself onto the fire escape, my bruised limbs protesting the climb.

Plants grew on every rooftop as far as I could see, and the sky was a brilliant patchwork of glowing clouds and early sun. Despite the beautiful view, dread settled in my stomach. *Please tell me he didn't go to work.* I climbed back down into Tarik's apartment, hissing softly when my legs balked under my weight. Slipping out the front door and onto the street, I tried to ignore the limp that jarred my steps. My aching muscles screamed in anger with every small movement.

I tried to refocus, make a plan, but I couldn't stop thinking about Tarik. Despite the cruel things he'd done, he *had* saved me. The rage in my chest quelled at the thought, at the memory of pain in his eyes when he said he had almost watched me die. My anger faded further—not completely buried by my gratitude, but certainly lessened. Every thought of him wasn't wrapped in fury. I needed a clear mind—I had too much to do, too much at stake.

I couldn't let him suffer the fate I knew Mordecai had planned for him. Not merely for his sake, or even for the other Fae I absolutely intended to save with him. No, I wanted to save him for me. Because *I* wanted Tarik to live. I didn't recognize the selfish thought—such a foreign idea, wanting to save a Fae for my own purposes. But I couldn't help feeling like the world would be a little darker without that fiery temper causing hell for me and everyone else in it.

The thought renewed the vigor in my steps. Nevaeh was right. I couldn't walk away when I'd helped put him on this path. At least not until I knew he was safe, especially after what he had done for me only hours ago.

A large shadow blotted out the sun.

I glanced up as a taloned foot scooped me into the air.

Alec.

Oh, perfect timing . . .

His grip tightened and I groaned. All of the cuts and bruises that still littered my skin reacted with fury at each flap of his wings. The rough pads of his foot scraped against my bare skin.

Absolute agony.

Alec flew toward the mansion. When the house loomed on the horizon, my heartbeat sped up. I didn't want to deal with Mordecai right now.

I wasn't going to have a choice.

Options swam before my eyes. Confronting him about the Fae outright was the most tempting of them all. But if I did, he might kill Tarik. Or me.

Or both.

And I had few to no allies. Nevaeh was the only one—if I didn't count Tarik. After what he had done for me, I could count him as an ally, right? Did he save me from some strange sense of obligation? Or were his motivations a little selfish, like my own?

Damnit, I wish I knew.

In front of the mansion doors, Alec loosened his grip, lowering me to my feet before he shifted. No humor lit his eyes when he grasped my shoulders and said, "I'm so glad you're alive. I've been so worried. Where were you?"

I blinked slowly. "I don't know," I lied. "I woke up on the street."

His eyes widened. "What? I couldn't have missed you. I circled the city a dozen times last night."

"Yeah, but what about during the day? When you're supposed to be on patrol, and I was jumped by a horde of angry shifters?"

"What? Are you serious?" He scanned my bruises. "Your injuries are mostly superficial, right? You're okay?"

Heat simmered through my veins. Was he kidding me right now? Still, I almost believed the concern in his eyes. Almost. "I blacked out. I don't even know how I'm still alive."

A low growl slipped from his throat. "Father's Fae were in a spat near The Pit last night. Several shifters wound up dead."

"Father's Fae?" My heart skipped. *Did he mean Tarik?*

"Yeah, his employees. Several of them, if I've heard right. Led by that damn redhead you're so hot for."

I rolled my eyes, but warmth spread up my core. If I had any hesitations about saving those Fae, at facing the risks, they were put to bed by Alec's words. "I vouched for him because I cost him his last job."

Lies. I hated how the words tasted.

His eyes narrowed. "That's your only involvement with him? Father seems to think there's more going on."

"Alec, you're in my apartment almost every morning. You know I come home after patrol and sleep all day. And I'm always on patrol at night. You usually know exactly where to find me. When would I have time to have the 'hots' for anyone?"

Slowly, Alec nodded and I could see the conclusion in his expression. The belief. "In any case, Father wants to see you. Should I— I should come with you."

"No," I said quietly. I firmly believed that guilt changed a person's mind—and Alec's was clearly spread across his face. But he didn't need to involve himself further. "If I'm in trouble,

I'll accept the consequences. You should finish your patrol."

He nodded, pulling open the door for me. I muttered my thanks. Squirrel Butler had a set of clothing waiting for me and I slid them on before climbing that accursed staircase. I didn't know what Mordecai wanted. Definitely nothing good.

"In loyalty and service to the Great Dragon."

Mordecai made me wait. My heart thundered in my ears. Ten beats. Thirty. Eighty. Still, he didn't snap his fingers. Perhaps he enjoyed the sight of me kneeling. I choked back the growl that pushed against my lips. I couldn't afford to die right now. My wings pressed on my spine, a reminder that this time I could flee if needed. I would be damned if he branded me again.

Finally, the snap came and I stood, straightening my back and clasping my hands behind me. Mordecai circled slowly, eyes tracing the wounds that peeked from the edges of my clothing. My bedraggled hair. The slight rightward lean of my posture, as I tried to reduce the weight on my still-sore leg.

"What happened to you?" he asked. His icy stare captured my gaze. Relentless. Watching for a lie.

"I don't remember most of last night," I said quietly. My fingers lifted reflexively to my lip—the ring was gone, likely lost when I shifted the night before. I tucked my hands into my pockets, suppressing the urge to fidget. "I was jumped by a large group of shifters. They overpowered me, and I blacked out. And no, I don't know how I'm alive."

Mordecai remained expressionless, then slowly nodded. "My Fae were caught in a brawl outside The Pit last night. Several shifters wound up dead, and many of my men were wounded."

"I thought your men were the shifters?" Asking such a loaded question was pushing my luck, but his temper seemed mild today. For the moment, anyway.

"Shifters who attack my daughter are no men of mine." He shook his head and growled, the sound not directed at me for once. I resisted the urge to raise an eyebrow. "Can you remember any of the specific shifters involved, sweetheart?"

"My memories are foggy," I said, stalling for time. I was loath to encourage Mordecai to more violence, even if the shifters deserved it.

"Descriptions, perhaps?"

I hesitated, then spit out a few generalized shifter traits, watching as he jotted them down on a notepad.

"I'm going to question my Fae, as well. If I can find these shifters, I'm calling for their executions. I don't tolerate disloyalty, and using group force to overtake one of my Enforcers is unacceptable." My stomach flipped. I didn't particularly want to watch half a dozen men be killed. Immune to my discomfort, he glanced up. "Do you remember where you were after the fight?"

"No. I woke up in the street nearby. I don't remember walking there, or being moved there. My mind is still a bit foggy."

Those icy blue eyes locked onto my face, studying my reaction as he said, "I heard one of the Fae carried you away. Is this true?"

I schooled my expression into one of innocent confusion, rubbing at my temples, at the very real headache rising with the pressure in my chest. The panic. But I said carefully, "I'm not sure. If so, they're as bad as the shifters. I woke up on the street."

He stepped around his desk and rested a hand on my cheek. I ignored the flinch that trembled up my spine. "I'm sorry this happened to you, my darling. I'm sorry I wasn't able to help."

"Father—" I swallowed the bile that rose at that word. "Where was Alec when this happened? He didn't help me, before or after."

Mordecai withdrew his hand. "Daytime hours have been so quiet that I asked him to help Jocelyn pick up supplies for the mines. Don't blame Alec. The mistake was mine."

I stared at him. Who was this man? The Great Dragon didn't apologize or accept responsibility like this. What game was he playing? But I said, "Yes, Father."

"That said, I have to get down to the mines." He wouldn't meet my eyes, his attention on one of the thick, gem encrusted rings he wore. "There's been a contamination issue. I'm going to find out the details right now, but Jocelyn said the men have been temporarily quarantined while we sort out the mess."

The blood in my veins froze.

I'm too late.

My heart stopped.

No. I couldn't be too late.

Tarik.

Tarik was down there—maybe already trapped. I looked up at the cold steel in Mordecai's eyes.

Definitely already trapped.

No, no, no . . .

I bit back the panic dizzying my mind. Swallowed. "Yes, Father. I hope the issue isn't too serious. I would certainly like to thank those men, if they really did have a hand in pulling those shifters off me."

"I'm sure the contamination is nothing we can't handle. I'll make sure to pass on your thanks, sweet girl." He smiled. Alarms screamed in my head.

This isn't happening.

But after he held open the door and gestured me out, all I could do was follow him downstairs and watch helplessly as he headed for the back staircase. If I followed, I could ruin everything. He might hurt them more, or sooner. My heart raced painfully. I couldn't stand still another second. When the front door snicked closed behind me, I bolted onto the lawn, shifting the second my feet hit grass.

I needed help. This was too big and I didn't stand a chance alone. But maybe with Nevaeh's help . . .

Maybe we could come up with a plan. I couldn't lose hope. Not yet.

We will save those Fae.

I will save Tarik.

CHAPTER 13

Tarik

Last night had changed everything.

I couldn't leave Reagan alone, and I couldn't push her away. Not when she needed protection. Ironic that she needed saving from her own kind. After my work shift, I planned to visit the man who'd meant the world to me a few years ago but who I currently avoided at all costs—if I could get through his sons first. The eldest would probably deck me before I could explain that they needed to treat the Night Enforcer as one of their own. But, despite their feelings toward me, if I asked them to watch over Reagan, I knew they would.

At the same time, seeing her so helpless had strengthened my resolve to keep my distance. Those shifters had attacked her because of *me*. Because her defense of me had wounded their egotistical pride. So I would fix the wrongs, but I couldn't get involved beyond that. I knew that if I did, something would start that couldn't be stopped.

She and I, we were a train wreck waiting to happen. I needed to derail and journey on a different track. Preferably in the opposite direction. Because every time I saw her, my walls weakened.

I stood from the metal table in the mine's small lunchroom. Throwing away the peels of the orange I'd eaten, I tried to formulate a plan. I knew Reagan would seek me out again—she couldn't seem to help herself—but I wouldn't discourage her attention with cruelty anymore. No, there must be a better way to get through to her, one that wouldn't scar.

I had damaged her enough.

My coworkers and I were pulling on our hazmat suits when an alarm blared. *"Danger. Danger. Make for the emergency room. Danger. Danger."* Red lights flashed in the room and hallway, the warning repeating over and over again. We all froze and stared at each other, uncertain what to do. No one had informed us of protocol in case of an emergency.

Was there a cave-in?

Jocelyn clacked into the room, swiftly for having to balance on four-inch heels. "Drop your gear, drop everything and come with me. Quickly now." She clapped, the sound almost lost to the shrill alarm.

I stepped out of the suit and did as instructed, leaving the yellow puddle on the floor. Single file, we followed the mother duck into the hallway. But instead of turning left for the stairs, we turned right, toward the heart of the mines. We passed the bathrooms, and an uneasy feeling squirmed in my gut.

My mouth opened as I prepared to announce that I'd rather take my chances above ground. If my mind wasn't half-distracted with thoughts of Reagan and what she'd said last night about needing to tell me something, I would have simply bolted for the stairs. But, I hesitated, confused and maybe a touch curious.

Jocelyn unexpectedly veered into the mysterious "for emergencies only" room we never entered. I closed my mouth as she disappeared from view, the room's lights burning so low, darkness swallowed her. Around me, heads swiveled and eyebrows raised, but my fellow Fae followed her inside, albeit cautiously.

I was the last to enter, my bare feet scraping against the cold stone floor. I peered over my shoulder and took one last look at the hallway, expecting a rock avalanche or horde of angry aliens to come bearing down on us. But all was clear. All was—

As soon as I stepped through the doorway, there was a rapid shuffling, then a groan as the door was heaved shut. On instinct, I reached for the inner handle, but my fingers only found slick steel. I blinked. There was no handle. There was no—

Boom!

The door sealed closed, encasing us in pitch black. A second later, blinding lights flicked on and I pivoted, hand pressed to my brow as I shielded my eyes from the glare. The other Fae were doing the same, glancing around the room in confusion. I searched for Jocelyn, pushing past Holden and several others as I struggled to the far back of the long, rectangular space.

She was nowhere to be found.

After hours of nothing happening, we finally went silent.

The room was plain: pale stone walls lined with narrow cots. A gray curtain in the back divided the "bathroom" containing two showers, two sinks, and one toilet. One toilet for twenty-four grown males. And no plunger. At least they'd provided us with a shred of privacy. Quite generous of the shifters who would probably squat in public.

But, now that the room had grown silent, one problem glared at us—besides being locked up with no explanation. The lights. Whoever installed them had a cruel sense of humor. The wattage was so high, we had to squint or close our eyes. Looking directly at them caused an instant headache. And the noise they gave off. A high-pitched whine, like a mosquito.

The sound was slowly getting to me. Two hours ago, I'd started chewing on my nails. Now there was nothing left to chew unless I wanted bloody skin. I contemplated doing that when a faint hiss filled the room. I jumped to my feet and strode to the door, relieved that someone was finally letting us out. What had happened out there?

But the door didn't open.

As I stared holes into its steel hide, my eyelids drooped. Jolting upright, I snapped them open, but they quickly lowered again. Panic swamped my mind. Blood pounded in my ears. I raised bleary eyes, sweeping them over the room's occupants, and my insides froze. All twenty-three men were sleeping. Some lay on their cots, some propped against the walls—a few were even bent in half, foreheads pressed to their knees.

A groan slid from my numb lips. *Numb?* Crap. I was going to pass out and I couldn't reach my cot in time. I took a heavy step forward anyway, then another. And, as my eyes rolled upward, the glaring lights finally switched off.

Freezing water splashed my face.

I gasped instinctively, then coughed as the liquid speared

down my throat. When I opened my eyes, they took several seconds to focus on my surroundings. The room was stark white and small, barely big enough for the cot I lay on. I flexed my arm muscles, straining to lift my hands, but they refused to cooperate.

A moment later I knew why: my arms, legs, and torso were strapped to the cot. Someone cleared their throat. I whipped my head to the left and there stood Mordecai, an empty glass in his hand and a gloating expression smeared across his face. "You were out longer than I anticipated. Thought you could use a refreshing wake-up call."

At his sneer, my blood simmered and my mouth started flapping on autopilot. "Thanks, but maybe next time let's try lemonade, just for fun."

The scar on his cheek puckered. "I'll consider, *if*. . ."

He let the sentence hang, and since I didn't have anything better to do, I played along. "If what?"

"If you cooperate." He set the glass down on a tray situated behind him. Other things lay on the tray too, but he moved, blocking my view.

I allowed the corners of my mouth to tip up before replying, "Well, from where I'm standing—Oh wait, I'm lying down, that's right. From where I'm *lying*, strapped to a cot, I don't seem to have much choice."

His nostrils flared ever so slightly, like he was trying to stay calm but impatience was leaking through the holes in his body. "Your limbs might be tied down but your tongue is not. If the words out of your mouth prove to be useful, I might allow you to keep that foul thing when all this is said and done."

I leaned upward an inch, the only wiggle room I had.

"Maybe you should tell me what this is all about first."

He paused, gaze roving my face, then reached behind him and picked up an object. Despite my best efforts to play it cool, my heart hammered wildly.

"All in good time, Tarik Hail. I'm in no rush." At that, he held up the object, its silver length flashing brilliantly under the harsh fluorescent lighting. My heart almost gave out then. A scalpel. The devil was holding a scalpel. He gingerly touched the blade's sharp tip, saying casually, "Why, are *you?* Is there a certain someone you wish to see?"

I sealed my mouth shut. When I did, his blue eyes glittered. "That's what I thought. But there's a price for your silence." He lunged forward and grasped the hem of my shirt. With one long stroke, the wicked blade cleaved the linen in two. Peering down at my exposed chest, he tutted. "So many scars. The stories they could tell . . ."

An uncontrollable tremor shook my body as he continued to inspect my skin, like I was a slab of prime meat. I half-expected him to poke me, see how juicy tender I was. Through clenched teeth, I snarled, "I'm glad you're enjoying the view. I didn't think you swung that direction."

His eyebrows raised. "Funny you should mention that."

He grabbed the waistband of my pants and got to work cutting the material from my body. My chest heaved as I struggled to inhale air, scared witless that I was about to be castrated. I mean, he was evil, but was he *that* evil?

When he was done, leaving me naked and vulnerable before him, he carefully returned the scalpel to the tray. "Now that I've taken your pompous Fae dignity, maybe your tongue is feeling a little . . . freer? What do you say, Tarik?" He crossed meaty arms over his chest, clearly pleased with his handiwork.

Shame washed over me as the room's stale air fanned my exposed flesh, but something else washed over me, too. Something far stronger. Determination. This madman would not break me no matter what he had on that tray, no matter how much pain he inflicted on my body, because one thing was crystal clear in my mind.

If I broke, Reagan would pay the price.

Didn't mean I couldn't take Mordecai on a joy ride, though. I licked my lips. "I'm feeling free all right. Free as a bird. But since I plan on telling you everything I know, why don't you start off this little love fest with an explanation? Because this wasn't in the job description."

He considered me, humiliated me by raking his gaze down my body, then up again. "You know what's pathetic about you Fae? You have such a glaring weakness. It's why you don't deserve to be in power. Shifters carry their strength within them, but your kind? You rely on a hunk of rock."

I remained silent. Maybe he'd reveal his plans and maybe, just maybe, I'd live long enough to pass along the information. Mordecai picked up another object, this one easy for me to decipher. The syringe was pumped full of green liquid, and he flicked the needle.

"I've never been good at the injection part. I always miss my target," he mused. Heat lapped at my skin and I couldn't stop myself from jerking against the constraints. He looked at me and smiled, that hideous scar stretching his grin a mile wide. "This here will tell me all I need to know about you. What you're made of. Still, I would have liked to know what your intentions were toward my daughter. She says thank you, by the way, for rescuing her."

Rage was a live wire in my veins. I pulled against the straps that held me prisoner. He knew. Of course he knew of the rescue. But what had Reagan told him? She said I'd been right about Mordecai, but a part of me wondered if she truly believed that. I hadn't apologized for how I'd treated her the other night, when I'd called her a little clone and cruelly kissed her. What if she took her hurt out on the Fae in return? What if she said we'd been the ones to beat her and Mordecai was only messing with my head, trying to get a confession out of me?

My thoughts whirled as that needle lowered toward my bicep, as the tip rested on my skin. "Any last words?" he said, grabbing hold of my arm.

"Screw you," I whispered.

His top lip curled, revealing a row of gleaming teeth. "Then let's begin."

He plunged the needle into my flesh.

CHAPTER 14

Reagan

I was so distracted by my own thoughts that I nearly missed the tiny blond Fae waving up at me from the ground. When I focused on him I realized he wasn't greeting me, but beckoning. His eyes rounded as I landed, taking in the full size of my lion form. I dwarfed him; he didn't quite reach the top of my legs.

"Whoa," he whispered.

I shifted, crossing my arms over my chest. "Hey, Benji. I'm Reagan. But I feel like you know that already."

The little Fae nodded, hiding his eyes behind his hands. *That Fae modesty starts young, I guess.* He peeked out long enough to say, "Tarik says you're not like the others. He says you want to help."

I knelt so I was closer to his height. "He's right. Is something wrong?"

"I have friends who want to meet you. Don't worry! They're friends of Tarik's too. They said to tell you they want to help you. We haven't . . ." His throat bobbed, his small smile falling. "He was supposed to say hi yesterday, and he didn't. We're worried he's in trouble."

My eyes widened. The timing was convenient. With everything going to hell, this could very well be a trap. Yet, when I looked into the child's deep brown eyes, I could see the sincerity. And children, they could sense things. He would know if this was a setup.

Hopefully.

"All right, Benji. Take me to your friends."

Benji extended a small hand, passing me a blindfold. "You have to wear this. Sorry."

I pushed down my hesitation and secured the dark cloth over my eyes. While I was fairly certain the Fae weren't aware of Mordecai's experiments, I couldn't imagine they would have sought me out if they didn't have *any* information.

The small Fae gripped my fingers in his, leading me along a twisted path that looped past alleys filled with rancid-smelling trash and divets that caught the toe of my boots. I couldn't track where I was being led but I understood the caution.

Idle thoughts filled my mind in the easy quiet. I didn't know how much time the captured Fae had, and the thought of Mordecai torturing Tarik . . . I clenched my jaw until my teeth ached. Mordecai would have his sadistic idea of fun with Tarik.

Fun.

My stomach flipped, a shudder racing up my spine.

"Are you okay?" Benji asked.

"Yeah, fine," I lied.

He stopped abruptly, and I worried he was going to ask more questions until I heard a soft, rhythmic knocking. A code? Silence fell, quickly broken by a soft click and the squeal of a door hinge. Whispering filled my ears. Warm breath hit my neck and I recoiled.

"Gaia . . ." a voice muttered beside me. I felt fingers brush across the dragon brand and tried to hold steady—I didn't want to scare them. A lump formed in my throat. My hands shook. They were asking a lot of my trust.

I was tugged forward a few steps. A door closed, several locks clicking behind me. I stiffened.

"Night Enforcer, I'm going to remove your blindfold."

White light filled my vision and I blinked several times, trying to adjust. When the starbursts cleared, I scanned the room around me warily. We were in a Fae apartment, or so I assumed from the rampant similarities to Tarik's own. They hadn't furnished this room beyond a table and smattering of chairs; several of which held men I had never seen before. Large, intimidating Fae men who looked like they were itching for me to step out of line.

One—tall with blond hair that fell into his face—stared at me with an intensity that made me want to flee. But it was the dark-skinned Fae behind him, with muscled arms as thick as my legs, that gave me the most pause. I swallowed, inhaling a shallow breath to calm the panic fogging my mind.

They invited me here.

I'm safe.

I'm not afraid.

My legs still burned with the need to move. Run. Shift. Ignoring the latter was the hardest, especially as my mind replayed the snap of my arm breaking. Pressure grew along my spine and I took a deeper, steadying breath. Shifters had done that to me. My own people. Not Fae.

I wondered how much time needed to pass before I would

feel comfortable surrounded like this again.

Mentally, I shook off last night's horrors and cast another look around the room. A few of the seated men were rubbing at their necks, holding their gazes pointedly above my neck. Another fair-haired Fae, one with thin-rimmed glasses perched on his sunburnt nose, cleared his throat uneasily.

Clothing! I should have dressed. But even in their discomfort, their eyes never completely left me. Watchful. Distrusting. I couldn't blame them.

"Reagan!"

I knew that voice. My head whipped to the side and I stared, incredulous. "Nevaeh?"

She moved, scooping me into a hug before shoving a pile of clothing toward my arms with a pointed look.

I blinked at her slowly. "What are you doing here?"

Nevaeh's glance flitted to the Fae around her, resting on a golden-skinned Fae with spiked black hair who had finally switched his attention from me—to her.

"I . . ." She looked at the clothes I hadn't taken and nudged them toward me again. "You should get dressed first."

"Right—"

"Fae modesty," we murmured together.

The corner of my lips twitched, even as I studied her nervous expression. Nevaeh was never nervous. I slipped into the ripped black pants and cropped band t-shirt—and could actually feel the tension level lower. Over bare skin. Ridiculous. I couldn't resist smiling.

"Nevaeh, I don't understand. What is—" I gestured to the room, stumbling on my words.

Instead of answering, she looked to the middle-aged Fae

standing beside me. He was handsome, with bright blond hair and a warm smile. For a split second my attention snagged on the laugh-lines that edged his sparkling blue eyes. His mouth twitched in amusement. "Welcome to the Fae Rebellion, Night Enforcer."

"Reagan is fine," I murmured. My eyes shot around the room again, pausing on each form. Fae Rebellion?

What did I walk into?

"I'm sorry, Reagan," Nevaeh said. She fidgeted with a loose thread on her shirt. "I wanted to tell you. I really did. But I couldn't."

"That's right," the man said. "She's a good little spy and has never once ratted us out."

Nevaeh snorted. "That joke *does* get old, you know."

Several of the Fae snickered. I tried to gauge the room. Despite the tension, the joke had set them more at ease. This didn't feel like a newly established group. Nevaeh jabbed me in the side, narrowing her eyes in concern.

"Sorry, I'm—" I considered the right word to use. "Surprised. I guess I didn't really know what to expect when Benji approached me."

"Understandable," the blond Fae beside me said. He had to be in charge. "We don't exactly broadcast our organization. You can call me Rebel Leader, by the way." He winked and a few of the Fae chuckled.

When he stuck out his hand I hesitated, then accepted the offer. His grip was firm as we shook and I said, "Nice to meet you."

"Don't worry." He smoothly released his grip. "We don't bite. Well, except Nevaeh maybe."

My eyes fell to the crescent mark on my arm and my eyebrow lifted at the irony. But I said, "I guess the biting falls more in my domain, huh?"

"As a rule, yes, but some Fae have fetishes of their own." His broad smile dimmed a little. "But let's get down to why we asked you here. Our little spy brought us word of your father's new Fae employees. Is the information accurate? Are they under quarantine lockdown?"

"Actually, that's why I was so eager to accept your invitation." I swallowed and met his inquisitive stare, the words flowing before I could filter them. "Mordecai is claiming they're under quarantine, but that's not the case at all. He has terrible plans and I . . . I need help."

Rebel Leader glanced at the other Fae men in the room, silently communicating, then scratched his chin. "I'm listening. Tell us what you know."

My heart pounded against my ribs. I took a steadying breath. Treason. This was treason. Once I told them what I knew, there was no going back. If I told them Mordecai's secrets, I was firmly taking a side. Good or bad.

I blinked slowly. For a second, the only thoughts that fluttered through my mind were of one Fae in particular. Of the scars that littered his body, the damaged wings he was forced to hide, the silly blush that climbed up his neck whenever I was around . . .

I told them everything.

Every detail of what I had seen on that locked computer, a brief description of the mansion's layout, including the mines; anything and everything I thought might be relevant. The words spilled from my lips. Toward the middle of the story,

Nevaeh's hand gripped my arm. I kept talking. When I finished, my gaze fell to the floor. Even though I knew I had made the right decision, my chest was heavy. I was still so worried about backlash and betrayal. From both sides.

When did I become so afraid?

Rebel Leader regarded me with kind eyes, as though he could read my thoughts, but a calculating light shone behind them. He rubbed at his chin a second longer, then motioned to Nevaeh. They must have done this routine before because she turned to me, gently drawing me into a corner as Rebel Leader moved for the other Fae.

While they quietly conversed, Nevaeh picked at my hair and blew out a gum bubble. When she started to braid the blue and black strands together, I batted her hands away.

"What the hell are you doing?" I whispered.

"Trying to comfort you. You look stressed."

"Yeah, maybe a bit." I narrowed my eyes. "I just found out my shifter best friend is spying for the Fae. Even after all these years of warning *me* to be careful." Nevaeh winced a bit but I added, "How long have you been a spy? Are you keeping anything else from me?"

Her nose twitched. "Three years. And no, nothing else. I wouldn't have kept this from you if I had a choice." She glanced over her shoulder. "They're a good group. And smart. Some of the brightest minds I've ever met. They might stand a real chance."

I stared at her, stunned into silence. She met my eyes for a moment and whatever she saw there made her sigh. Her fingers never stopped moving, braiding my hair, strand over strand, despite my protesting swats. Then there were footsteps and Rebel Leader peered over her shoulder, shaking his head in amusement at the braids.

All he said, though, was, "Table, please."

Nevaeh's hand slid to my arm, dragging me along to a chair and pushing me toward it before dropping into the one alongside. That golden-skinned Fae fell into place on her other side. I shot him a glance and he offered a small smile, his eyes landing on the galaxy tattoo that swirled up my arm.

"Akeno," he said, extending his hand behind Nevaeh.

I shook it. "Reagan."

"Oh, we're doing introductions? Hi." That large, dark skinned Fae dropped into the seat beside me, dark locs streaked with amber tumbling over his shoulder. "I'm Caspar."

My smile was genuine this time, surprised that the massive Fae studied me with warmth in his amber eyes; a softness and kindness that was so at odds with his intimidating frame.

"We have a lot to discuss," Rebel Leader said, gesturing for the other men in the room to join us.

I sat on the edge of my chair, trying to hide my nerves, but a Fae dropped into the seat across from me with a thump and a glare. He shared Nevaeh's light brown skin, his hair rich and sandy blond, close-cropped to his head. His eyes were unwavering, lasered onto mine.

"Don't mind Flynn. He enjoys being a complete creep. We think he's overcompensating for something." Caspar chuckled, leaning across the table to slug Flynn's shoulder. The man didn't break eye contact with me, stiff as stone.

Rebel Leader waited patiently while the others settled. He opened his mouth to speak, but was abruptly cut off.

"I'm starved. Can we eat while we talk? Listening to you

all yammer always makes me hungry." The Fae near the end of the table clapped his hands together twice. "Sebastian, fetch us some food."

The long-haired Fae who had been watching me before pinned a glare on the disruptor, but tipped his chair back and left the room anyway.

"My apologies," Rebel Leader said, looking to me. "My twins have apparently decided to act like beasts today."

"And everyday," Akeno said.

Rebel Leader sighed. "Reagan, this is Elias." He gestured to the Fae with the burnt nose and glasses. "The knuckleheads at the end are Malachi and Micah." He pointed to the twins, but I knew in a glance I would never be able to tell them apart. They grinned at me in unison, like they knew.

"And the one who—" I pointed toward the door.

A different sort of smile passed Rebel Leader's lips. "My second in command, and the eldest of my four sons, Sebastian."

I didn't know how I had missed the resemblances. The blond hair and blue eyes matched in each of the five faces. But I nodded, and murmured a soft greeting. Both of the twins leaned forward to speak, but Rebel Leader shook his head.

"Focus boys, this is important." At the twins grumbled consent he continued, studying me intently as he spoke. "I wanted you here specifically because you've been seen on more than one occasion with a mutual interest of ours. Do you know whom I speak of?"

I squirmed under the circle of eyes pinned to my face. The room was suddenly very warm. "I'm assuming Tarik?"

He nodded. "Yes. If you don't mind the intrusion, we were all curious what he is to you, exactly?"

Heat flushed my cheeks. How was I supposed to answer him? I was a glorified stalker, but beyond that? My eyes flew to Nevaeh who smirked and shrugged. Traitor. I nervously scanned the faces around me, watching the various flickers of amusement and impatience. Clearing my throat, I said, "Um. I haven't known Tarik all that long. Not . . . not personally, in any case. He's a friend, I guess. And I really don't care to see him hurt."

My fingers gripped the seat of my chair. I secretly prayed the floor would crack open and swallow me whole, especially when Caspar snickered quietly.

Rebel Leader seemed impervious though as he rested his elbows on the table and steepled his fingers to contemplate. "I see. The thing is, you seem to matter a great deal to him. Last night, we were told he had made plans to pay us a visit. But our sources say that before he could, he was . . . distracted. Now, if you know Tarik even a little bit, you know he doesn't like shifters." One of the twins—maybe Malachi—burst out laughing, but one look at his father's stern face shut him up.

With a sigh, Rebel Leader continued. "As I was saying, Tarik would never rescue a shifter, even one being beaten to death. So the fact that he saved *you*, especially given who you are, says a lot. Simply put, his actions tell us we can trust you. And so, if you're making plans to rescue *him*, we are at your service."

They were mistaken. The moment he had said I mattered to Tarik, my mind filled with images of that kiss—the angry way he had pulled me from him, the harshness of his words. My rage dwindled at the reminder that he had saved me, though. And before leaving me to climb to the roof, he had paused, an unfamiliar emotion in his eyes—one I still couldn't identify.

My chest grew heavy as that memory faded. I lowered my eyes to the table. "Thank you."

"You're welcome," he said. "It would seem we have something in common. Can't say I've ever said that to a shifter before, but there's a first time for everything." Nevaeh huffed. He glanced at her. "You're a given, Nev."

He opened his mouth again, hopefully to lay out a ready-made rescue plan, when Sebastian came back and plopped a large round pan on the tabletop. The twins whooped and reached for the food. Sebastian whacked both of their heads and they paused, hands frozen midair. "We have a guest," he ground out between clenched teeth.

They deflated, then looked at me expectantly. I eyed the green stuff that was smothering the accompanying cheese and red sauce. Vegetables. Nope. "Don't stop on my account. Go right ahead."

"He didn't poison the food. Pinkie promise," one of the twins said, blond eyebrows raised.

"I believe you. Nerves though—they kill my appetite." Small lie. I glared at the vegetables. And a worthy lie at that.

Caspar shrugged his big shoulders before diving in. "No problem, tiny shifter. Nerves make me extra hungry. I'll eat your share."

I waved him on and watched with amusement as the twins glared daggers in his direction. The tension in my muscles had lessened, but I was still waiting for the next step. Unconsciously, I rubbed at the dragon brand.

"Where'd you get that piece of work?" one of the twins asked. Man, they were nosier than *me*. "The design doesn't really jive with the rest of your look." Several throats cleared uncomfortably as they were no doubt remembering my earlier entrance.

"No, this one wasn't my choice." I coughed, trying to loosen the knot in my throat. I knew the twins weren't the only curious ones though—all the Fae had taken turns eyeing my bruises, the unhealed cuts. "Mordecai has an interesting way of . . . claiming ownership. Even of people."

A fist slammed on the table, making me jump. "That sadistic piece of—"

I looked up at Sebastian's irate face, only then realizing how very tall he was. And how genuinely angry.

"Sit down, Sebastian," his father ordered, turning to me apologetically. "Forgive my sons their intrusive questions, and my own. You're an anomaly is all. Practically the right hand of Mordecai himself and yet, here you are."

"There's nothing to forgive." I shrugged quickly to put them at ease. "Ask your questions. I need your trust more than you need mine, especially if we stand any chance of saving Tarik."

Elias watched me for a long moment as he fiddled with the side of his glasses, then nodded slowly. "I can see why Tarik likes you." I stared at him, unsure what to make of his words. He lifted his shoulder, adding, "We all need someone who's willing to fight for us, even on the bad days. Especially on the bad days."

Rebel Leader studied his son with a touch of pride. "You're right, Elias. Which brings me to what I must ask of you, Reagan. If we are to successfully rescue those trapped Fae, we need your . . . special talents."

"I'll do anything," I said quietly. "I know the reputation I have with the Fae, but I need you to know that I'm not what I've been trained to be. I want to help your people, not harm them."

He leaned back in his chair and smiled slowly. *Uh oh.* What had I volunteered myself for? "I'm glad to hear that, because this is what I need you to do . . ."

CHAPTER 15

Tarik

"All right, he's under. Start the procedure."

The foggy words came from down a long tunnel, distant, echoing. Ghostly. My body floated on nothing, my mind losing touch with reality. The pain washed away, replaced with sweet, calming peace. I wanted to stay here forever, escape the guilt and suffering that living etched on my soul.

At first, the tug bordered on pleasant, careful and controlled. When the incessant tingling between my shoulder blades started, I was almost distracted from my blissful peace. But I slowly adjusted to the sensation and drifted off once again. Then a loud *rip*, followed by splintering agony, destroyed my world.

My mind screamed, raking at my brain. Demanded I join the living and save myself.

I don't want to. I inwardly curled into a ball and did my best to ignore the frantic shaking, the yelling, the pleas.

You're dying! my mind whimpered. *Fight back!*

I shook my head. *No. Living is too painful. I can't bear it any longer. The world is better off without me.*

You're a selfish coward. What about those who need you?

I thrashed, trying to dislodge the plaguing voice in my head that never rested. "No one . . . needs me."

"Hold him down!" a female barked.

"I'm trying! He's fighting the anesthesia!"

Wait. Anesthesia?

My mind stilled as that word sunk in deep. *Don't move.*

"Are we good to go now?" the female asked.

A pause, then, "Yes, he's fully under now. Proceed with the wing experiment."

A beat took up residence in my skull. A shrill whine in my ears. My wings. Gaia help me, they were *not* going to touch my wings. For once, my mind and I completely agreed. When I rejoined the living, I became aware of hands on my shoulders and spine—prying, digging, searching . . .

They were trying to pry out my *wings.*

I exploded.

With a flex of my shoulders, my wings snapped straight. The action felt like a thousand needles impaling my back. I almost went under again. But at the shrieks of surprise, my body tensed, ready for more.

You're the master of your pain.

Fight back.

As my eyes cracked open, slowly sweeping the pristine white medical room, I whispered, "Always." And unleashed myself.

Or at least, I tried to. The dismount from the examination table was wobbly at best. My legs felt strange as I balanced on them, like they weren't mine. Like I was in a different body, actually. I glanced down at my still-naked form and frowned.

I didn't used to have a six pack.

My gut roiled. Had they transplanted my head onto someone else's body?

Pounding feet came from the hallway and several shifters barged into the room, sliding to a halt at the sight of me in all my glory. I almost struck an Alec pose but didn't have time. They were already swarming—guards and doctors and nurses alike formed a loose circle around me.

"Let me guess," I slurred, my tongue dry and heavy. "This can go down the easy way or the hard way? Because I'll tell you now, hard is what I get when a pack of shifters surround me." At that, they all looked down at my—I rolled my eyes. Idiots.

I launched forward, promptly stumbling against an exam table and knocking over a tray of shiny objects. Objects that they were using to pry out my *wings*. Rage, familiar and welcome, bubbled up my throat and I roared at them all. Those dressed in white paused, the whites of their eyes rivaling their smocks.

Gaining momentum, I flapped my wings sharply. The noise distracted them as I pretended to take on the three guards. But, as they settled on their haunches and I brought up my fists, I veered toward a lone doctor blocking the exit.

A female. Her garb spattered in bright red blood. *My* blood.

I let out a war cry and charged, watching her face leach of color and her limbs lock up. I didn't hesitate. Bowled her over with a single shoulder strike. Her high-pitched shriek as she smacked against the white tile was a beautiful song, ringing in my ears as I burst through the exit and into the hallway.

Freedom. So close. I breathed in the stale air with relish. But, as I bolted for the stairs that would take me up and out of this hellhole, I slowed at the sight of that still-locked "for emergencies only" room. *Fae stick together.* The loyalty was ingrained in me, even though I'd wrestled against my nature for three solid years.

These Fae had helped me save Reagan from being beaten to death. They didn't have to. But they did. In return, could I really leave them here to suffer a cruel and twisted fate?

Hissing a curse, I skidded to a stop in front of the steel door, and with my new arms—densified with corded muscle—I yanked at the handle. The door held fast. I could hear shouts now and scrambling footsteps. I was throwing away my chance at freedom as I continued to pull and kick and curse.

But I couldn't leave. I would never forgive myself.

"Tarik Hail."

At the sound of my name on that demon's tongue, I shivered. Maybe I should have run, because now . . . now . . .

"Give up, boy," Mordecai said. From the corner of my eye, I saw him raise a black object. "That door only opens for those who know the code. Not even your full Fae strength can break through."

Full Fae—

Something stabbed my neck and I jerked back, bringing a hand up to find a dart lodged there. I pulled the point free and blinked, the hallway already darkening. "Crap, not again."

I groaned as the world turned black.

Burnt coffee. Toast. Cinnamon.

The smells swirled around me, tempting, coaxing me to leave my dark haven. I stopped breathing. Because the next time I opened my eyes, I knew who would be there.

"I know you're awake, so you can stop faking."

I exhaled through my nose and squinted up at a hovering Mordecai. Smoke puffed from his mouth as he flicked ash from his cigar onto my chest. "No, thanks. I don't . . . smoke. It's a . . . n-nasty habit."

He peered more closely at me. "You know what's a nasty habit? Irksome Fae screwing with my plans. The more you cooperate, the less painful this will be. But since you seem to learn things the hard way . . ." He wiggled a ring off his finger and inspected the face, then showed the design to me. "Beautiful, wouldn't you agree? A dragon's eye. Always watching. All-knowing."

Bringing his hands together, he pressed the cigar's orange glow against the ring's grooved surface. In the silence that followed, my trepidation grew. The ring shone brightly as the gold heated, hot enough to—My chest heaved. Reagan's raw and blistered neck, branded with a dragon mark, flashed in my mind's eye.

"I've been curious how you found out about my daughter's mark. But if you won't tell me *how* you know, then you're leaving me no choice. Shifters don't help Fae, but you know what? I don't want a dirty Fae helping my daughter, either. May this be a reminder that you are nothing more than property under my watchful gaze."

Mordecai casually stuck his cigar between his teeth and grabbed my wrist, twisting until the sensitive inner skin faced upward.

"Any last words?" he mumbled around the cigar.

I breathed in deep, preparing myself. "Yes, actually." He

paused, the hot ring inches from my flesh. I could feel the warmth and my muscles trembled. "I only have one thing to say to you. Suck my—"

He thrust the ring onto my skin, pushing, pushing, pushing, until I thought the metal would burn a hole clean through to the other side. My fingers formed claws as I fought against the urge to scream my pain and fury. The vinyl straps holding me down flexed and creaked, groaning as I pushed upward.

Mordecai leapt back, eyes wide. For a glorious moment, stark fear bleached his face. He quickly smoothed his features, dropping the ring onto the tray behind him, but it was too late. I had seen. I had scared the stupid piece of filth.

I started laughing, low and half-delirious as the pain from the mark pulsed with a second heartbeat. Whatever had been done to me, whatever they'd injected me with, made me physically stronger. And the substance was green. Not green like grass, but green like—

Emeralds.

I laughed harder.

A loud clank from the ominous tray quieted my outburst, and I blinked up at a seething Mordecai. How mad would he have to be to unleash his inner dragon? I wanted to poke him some more and find out.

"Whatever you're doing to me, you might want to stop. I'm gonna bust out of these restraints any minute now." As if to warn him, I jerked upward again. The straps across my shoulders squealed as they stretched thin.

His jaw slackened; the cigar fell from his mouth. Then he raised a trembling arm. My gaze slid up the sleek tattoo curling along his skin to what lay clutched in his hand. My mind blanked. His lips curved wickedly. "Go ahead. Break free. Let's see you walk away from this."

And he brought the silver hammer down on my knee.

The world splintered, stealing my breath and sanity. I screamed, spine arching off the cot. Hot and cold currents streaked through my body. Bile filled my mouth, choking me. Then he shattered my other knee.

I wanted to die when the hammer snapped my left leg bone in two. But, for once, I didn't pass out. I felt every single hit. Every break. Heard him snap bone after bone, until my strength was crushed. Until I was a shivering heap of blind agony.

Until I was nothing more than a piece of property under his watchful gaze.

CHAPTER 16

Reagan

The sky had fallen dark only an hour ago, but I had begun my patrol early. Made sure Alec, spying from a distance, saw me circle the area and fly back for The Pit. I landed long enough to prowl and act generally threatening, making sure the shifters saw that I was on patrol. Every step was part of the carefully laid plan.

Adrenaline buzzed in my veins. The thunder of my pulse was almost loud enough to drown out the steady rhythm of my wings. So many people would die if we failed.

I can't think like that. We won't fail.

My eyes were locked onto the mansion as I made another round. The light that glowed from Mordecai's room unnerved me. He was usually asleep by now.

Damnit.

Rebel Leader had detailed his plans before blindfolding me again and leading me away from the Fae hideout. Precautions, he had said, and I understood. Trust and blind trust were two very different things.

The whole group had tailed us, and I had felt their eyes on

me when I burst into my lion. I had worried that I would scare or at least intimidate them, but they handled the change well. Most were fairly neutral—widened eyes and a couple cautious pats. Caspar had immediately started scratching my ears and cooing about "what a good kitty" I was. The smirk on Nevaeh's lips had me glaring in her direction.

Now, several long hours later, the men of the Rebellion awaited my signal.

I killed some time scouting out The Pit. When a shifter strolled outside and cast a scowl in my direction, I tensed. My first visit seemed to have scared a few of them off—unsurprising, since Mordecai had announced the executions of a few shifters that morning. I wasn't even sure if he had the right ones. He wouldn't care, and everything was a bit too fresh for me to be entirely comfortable. Too many still ran free. Or maybe not enough, with the violent streak Mordecai was on. Maybe he would simply kill us all.

After I assumed enough time had passed, I leapt from the building and climbed into the air. This time when I glided by the mansion, the lights were off. Time to go. I flapped once, heading back toward the ruined, crumbling section of shifter territory—my sacrifice to the mission, offering Rebel Leader a closer place to hide but outing my little sanctuary. They had marked a rooftop with a single candle. When I located the small flicker of light I stopped, hovered, glanced around as though surveying the area. Seconds passed. A minute. The candle blinked out and I flew to the mansion.

The large backyard was silent. I shifted, the wet grass slick under my human feet. For the first time my exposed skin felt like a vulnerability as I glanced up at Mordecai's dark bedroom window.

With trembling fingers, I pulled a key from the hidden spot along the fence. My presence here wasn't abnormal, I reminded myself. All I had to tell Mordecai was that I'd been hungry mid-patrol and he would leave me be—that wasn't a new excuse. Right on cue my stomach growled. I hadn't eaten since yesterday, now that I thought about it. The men had been kind and generous, but the idea of ingesting tomatoes, broccoli, onions, peppers . . . I gagged.

Snatching a granola bar from the kitchen was the work of a minute. I scarfed it down while I waited and, when I returned from tossing the wrapper in the trash, the men—and an already-shifted Nevaeh—were crowded on the back doorstep. I carefully slid the locks loose, one after the other until I could slowly ease the door open.

We were doing this.

No going back now.

My chest tightened. I took a breath, plastering on a grin before I swung the door open. "About time," I teased.

Caspar shouldered his way in first. I relaxed a little. His calm demeanor set my nerves at ease. Or, at least a little. He mock-scowled at me. "Reagan, this is no time for joking. Get your head in the game."

I smirked. "Why so serious?"

Sebastian came next, eyes narrowed on us. "Are the two of you going to be a problem? Because I'll separate you if I have to."

"Shhh, Sebastian," I whispered, pressing a finger to my lips and flashing him a smirk. As I glanced behind me I added, "You're going to get us caught."

He sighed, blond hair falling across his face as he shook his head, then, "You're right. From here on in, complete radio silence. Hand signals only." The group around us groaned and he jerked up a fist. They fell silent.

I raised an eyebrow. "But wait, I don't know the—"

Sebastian raised his hand again. My jaw snapped shut. Caspar patted me on the head. "*Good kitty,*" he mouthed.

Flynn stepped past him, eyeballing me for a moment before he shoved a wad of material in my arms. Oh. Point taken. I flicked the locks closed behind us before I dressed. The corner of my lip lifted at the sight of them painstakingly averting their gazes.

I stepped in front of Sebastian, waving my hand exuberantly. He rolled his eyes, but followed. I had to admit, I was impressed by how quietly they moved. In an afternoon, all I had seen from this group was frenzy. Chaos. For the sake of what we had to accomplish, I was grateful they were disproving my doubts. And I was doubly grateful when Akeno whipped out a lock picking set as we hit the door to the mines.

The looping staircase was silent except for our soft footsteps. That familiar tug jerked at my stomach as we stepped into the dimly lit cavern. Mordecai didn't bother with more than a few lights in this chamber—he rarely used it. When I looked toward the hallway where I knew the Fae were trapped, my stomach plummeted.

Tarik's alive, he has to be alive . . .

I pulled my hair into a tie, glancing back at the men behind me. Their eyes were wide, and Caspar nudged me. Jabbing his finger at the long hallway, he mouthed, "*Creepy.*" I nodded.

Nevaeh clambered onto my shoulder, her tiny rat claws

poking at my skin. We crept to the far wall where the shadows were slightly denser, and I paused to listen. I shot a glance at Nevaeh for confirmation. Nothing, except the few soft shuffles from our own group.

We crept closer. My heart was going to leap from my throat. When we heard quiet noises ahead, it certainly tried. Nevaeh darted from her perch and dashed down the curved hallway, out of sight. I started to follow, but Sebastian gripped my arm, holding up a finger. My jaw clenched in protest. This was what she did, I reminded myself. Helped them, spied for them, as she had been doing for nearly three years. The news was still a shock to my system.

Only a few moments passed before the purple rat reappeared, rapid-shifting into human form as she approached. She motioned with two fingers to the right side where the crystal cavern's first entrance was.

Two what?

Akeno began to pass out tiny straws before I could ask. *Straws?* My trembling stilled, replaced with pure shock. He offered me a little cloth pouch filled with . . . darts? I arched an eyebrow incredulously and he grinned. Raising one, he demonstrated, slipping the dart inside and pretending to blow toward Sebastian. I bit back a chuckle, but loaded my own.

Soft chatter echoed from down the hallway. Guards, in human form. Flynn slipped past our group, clinging to the lessening shadows. A slight hiss echoed down the corridor, and then a tiny pop. The dart sank into the guard's neck. Flynn repeated the action before the first guard finished falling, but none of us were fast enough to stop them from collapsing with a loud thump. No one moved. Nevaeh shifted again, but even she waited, ears twitching rapidly.

Two more guards rounded the corner. Akeno shot at the same time as Flynn, their darts passing each other as they met their marks. Flawless. Almost too easy. Another two guards went down, then three more. I crept ahead of the rest and bit back a yelp when sharp pain lanced through my foot. Akeno slipped forward, plucking a shiny object from the ground—a dart, similar to ours but made of glass and steel. He examined the side for a moment, his brow wrinkled, before he glanced up at me. Pressing his hands together, he mimicked a sleeping pose—a tranquilizer dart. In the hallway? I glanced down the length of the corridor. Had one of the Fae escaped?

My stomach churned. Tarik?

We stopped in front of the "for emergencies only" room, and I started to wave the men over when a ripple of shadow on the steel door caught my eye. I knelt, pressing my fingers against the small dents. The others looked as confused as I felt. Why would there be dents on the *outside* of the door? What had Mordecai done?

One of the twins—I needed to get them ID bracelets—mouthed "*Whoa*" and flexed, pointing at the door. I nodded in agreement. Caspar unslung a pouch from his back, tugging out what looked like a miniature laptop along with several small silver instruments.

"*I need time*," he mouthed at us. "*Keep watch.*"

Sebastian pointed at various spots along the hallway, then swirled a finger in the air. When no one responded, he rolled his eyes and repeated the gesture, brow furrowed. He rapidly pointed in all directions and flicked his hands in a *shoo* gesture. Oh. The men dispersed, each finding a lookout spot.

Caspar flipped open the small computer, attaching wires to the keypad of the lock. Lines of numbers filled his screen as a bright red light blinked on above the door. The light shifted, squares falling away until a number remained.

3:00

And counting down.

Behind me, Sebastian swore softly, motioning for the others to stay where they were. Caspar's amber eyes flicked up. "Well, that's just splendid," he muttered, his focus on the screen renewed with vigor.

I paced the hallway, the quiet throwing my nerves into a frenzy. Three minutes. Caspar could beat that if the mines stayed undisturbed, right? This couldn't be all, though. Did Mordecai really think himself so untouchable? Did he really believe everyone was so afraid of him? Alec had told me stories growing up, tales of the great black dragon who had taken to the skies to "rid us of the Fae overlords." Stories were biased to the side that told them. The older I grew, the clearer that became.

"Any luck?" I asked Caspar quietly.

He shook his head. "That time limit is bad news. I'm entering codes manually to speed the process, but I'm not sure we want to know what will happen if we can't figure this out."

Blood pounded in my ears. I looked up at the timer. 2:00. "You need more combinations?"

"As many as you can think of."

"I may be able to do you one better." I slipped to where Elias stood, watching the crystal cavern. Earlier, he had been reading a book about quantum relativistic theories. If Caspar—who had been locked in conversation with him about the subject—couldn't figure this out, maybe Elias could.

"Can you go help Caspar? He's trying to speed up the process, and he's running out of numerical combinations."

Elias' blue eyes lit with gratitude. "Glad to help."

Leaning against the rough wall, I took his post, watching as the two men puzzled over the combination. I started to pace again. All of fifteen seconds passed before I let my feet carry me back to them, listening as they frantically threw codes out.

1:00.

"Anything?"

"No," Caspar whispered, voice strained. "Literally thousands of numbers and nothing yet. The code is eight digits. I can't imagine what he used."

Eight digits . . . Oh. Surely he wouldn't. I licked my dry lips. "Try 08252021."

"That seems fairly specific," Elias said, glancing up at me.

"It's my date of birth."

Caspar arched an eyebrow. "Well, aren't we cocky?"

"Try the combination," I growled. My fingers tightened into fists that shook at my sides. Mordecai would truly have to be a monster to use my birth date—like it meant something to him. Like *I* meant something to him.

"Oh damn, we're in."

Sebastian shot a quizzical look in my direction as he moved to help Elias push the steel door aside. Caspar hurriedly put away his tech. Nevaeh shifted beside me, pulling lavender hair out of her face. We all flinched, stepping backward as blinding light filled the hallway. Our eyes took several long, agonizing seconds to adjust, but when they did—

Damn. The room was filled, almost wall to wall, with Fae

strapped down to cots.

Too easy. This all felt too easy.

I scanned the rectangular space and shoved my apprehension to the back of my mind. The others filed past me to unstrap the helpless Fae, but my senses shut off.

"He's not in here," I muttered.

Nevaeh gripped my arm. "What?"

"Tarik. He's not in here." I searched the room again, straining to look past the Fae being helped to their feet. No shock of red met my eyes, no snarky remarks about wanting to be released. Bile rose in my throat. What had Mordecai done to him? Was I too late?

Elias wrenched a gray curtain aside at the back of the long room, paused, then strode toward Sebastian, saying, "He's not here."

"What?" Sebastian whisper-yelled and Caspar shushed him. The mission leader turned frantic eyes our way. "Nevaeh, see if he's down here."

Nevaeh nodded stoically, squeezing my arm before she shifted. She raced into the hall, nose twitching as she tried to find a scent. After a moment, she let out a short squeak and I trailed her to the lab room, Elias at my heels. We searched the room frantically but there was nothing. No trace of him. My eyes burned as Nevaeh shifted again, rapping her fist on a small section of wall. "He's in here."

I stared at her, but Elias moved forward. "How do you know?"

"I can hear him breathing."

Relief washed over me, stained by resounding terror. What hell had Mordecai inflicted on him that he was alone in a hidden room?

Maybe this was why security was so lax. Mordecai must have assumed that if I tried anything I wouldn't find the one Fae I couldn't leave without, so he would have time to apprehend me.

Elias pushed at the edges of the wall, looking for a way in. I stepped forward, pressing on a few different stones. Nothing happened. There didn't seem to be a switch. I growled in frustration, slamming my foot into the wall. Pain shot through the already angry leg and I swore softly.

But the panel opened.

Blinding light filled our eyes. I blinked rapidly, desperate to clear my vision, desperate to know for sure.

The room was small, but Tarik . . .

Tarik was here.

Tears sprang to my eyes. Mordecai had stripped him bare. Anger rippled through me, knowing what that meant to the Fae, how he must have felt. He was sprawled over a small cot, wings spread wide cramped and twisted in a way that looked painful. His arms were strapped down.

My attention fell to his legs. Ice slammed into my veins, and a sob shuddered through me.

That animal, that monster, that . . . the rainbow of words that assaulted my senses were nothing compared to the agony that ripped open my chest. My hands slid to my mouth.

Tarik's legs laid at awkward angles on the crimson stained sheets, a mess of blood and bruises. Devastation. Utter devastation. I scanned the room and, when I caught sight of the silver tray nearby, my tears fell unrestrained.

A hammer.

Mordecai had beaten him, broken his limbs, abused and tortured him far beyond what he had done to the other Fae. I had known, or suspected he would, but this . . . My heart crumbled. *How could he do this?* Elias and Nevaeh had moved past me to unstrap his arms. I crept closer, sitting tentatively on the edge of the cot.

A small red spot caught my eye and I gently lifted Tarik's wrist so I could examine the mark. A dragon's eye. I thought of the brand on my neck. That rage flared again. This one was personal, to him and me both.

Mordecai had attacked Tarik because of me.

Because he assumed I *meant* something to Tarik.

I knew, and I had done nothing. *Could* do nothing. I didn't want to look down, to examine his legs more carefully. Even from the door I could tell the damage was beyond my abilities to heal, and the helplessness that welled up was suffocating. Still, I prodded gently at the wounds, confirming my worst suspicions. Fire surged through my veins, burning away my sadness. This was *wrong*. And I wasn't going to stand by and let this happen again. To anyone.

"Are they broken?" Elias asked, breaking my thoughts. His face was pale. When I nodded, he held up a finger, stepping out of the room. Nevaeh and I exchanged a glance when the sound of aggressive vomiting reached our ears.

"Can you help him sit up? We need to see how aware he is." Nevaeh jerked her head toward the door. "I'll check on Elias. We can tell Sebastian."

I nodded gratefully. She stepped around me, her quiet chatter filling the lab. Turning my attention back to Tarik, I brushed a finger up his arm. The muscles quivered under my touch, a small reassurance.

"Tarik?" I whispered softly, leaning closer to his face. "Can you hear me?"

His head turned slowly in my direction. He swallowed, then grimaced as though even that small action pained him. I waited, barely breathing as his eyes cracked open. Vivid, beautiful green. My heart skittered when they landed on me.

"Stalker," he breathed.

The corner of my mouth quirked, but the tears renewed. I ignored them and reached out a tentative finger, brushing his forehead gently as I pushed away stray locks of hair. "Can you sit up? I'll help you."

He tried to smile and failed. "Oh, sure. No problem." His arms shook as he propped himself up on an elbow, teeth clenched tight.

"Pull, and I'll lift you." I looped his arm around my waist, waiting until his fingers gripped my side to wrap my own around him, careful not to brush his wings as I tugged. When he was upright, I asked, "Can you tuck in your wings?"

A weak laugh left him and he flinched. "You ask a lot out of a guy, but since you're trying to—" He hissed as he caught sight of his brutalized legs, then wrenched his gaze away. "Yeah. One sec."

I waited, watching him struggle for a long, agonizing minute before his wings finally retracted.

"Thank you," I whispered, shuffling myself around to face him. For a moment I simply watched him breathe, grateful, so grateful that he still did. I wanted to ease his pain—but what could I possibly do to fix this nightmare?

As my eyes darted over his face, I realized there might be one small consolation I could offer. Maybe I couldn't help his pain, or heal him, but maybe I could start making this right. Carefully, I tilted his chin up, sliding my hands up to his cheeks. His expression was curious when I gently kissed his nose. I pressed my forehead to his. "I'm sorry. I'm sorry I wouldn't leave you be. I'm sorry I bit you. I'm sorry he did this to you. I'm . . . I'm so sorry, Tarik. For everything."

His eyes slid closed and he sighed, leaning into my touch. "You don't have anything to be sorry for. But I'll take it all the same."

"You didn't deserve this," I murmured, rubbing a thumb over the soft stubble that graced his jaw. "I'll make this right. I don't know how, but I will."

He opened his eyes then, pulling away slightly to better see my face. "No, Reagan, you've done enough. This is too dangerous. You shouldn't even be here. If your father finds out what you're doing right now—" He cut himself off. Cursed softly. "I need you to do something for me, though."

"Anything," I said quietly, dropping my hands to my lap.

"I need you to get me a piece of the Genesis Crystal. I—" He grimaced, arms shaking again. "I need it."

"Why, what do the crystals do?"

"They make me—" He panted, eyes growing distant as pain consumed him. "Stronger."

I hesitated. Mordecai could have created an addiction, or he could be delusional with pain. In either case, I whispered, "Okay."

Before I left the lab, I snitched a pair of surgical gloves. Whatever affects these crystals caused, I wanted no part. Mordecai had warned me against touching them since I was young, and since the men wore hazmat suits, there had to be more that I didn't know. No one was in the hall as I crossed, but I could hear Elias complaining that Sebastian wasn't moving fast enough—and Nevaeh, her voice low and comforting.

The crystals in the large cavern were everywhere, embedded in the walls and abandoned in mining bins—scattered haphazardly, a reminder of how hastily the Fae must have been tricked into the "for emergencies only" room. I grabbed a piece, eyeing the sparkling green suspiciously. My hand tingled. My skin crawled with the need to repel the crystal, to get it away from me, even through the glove. *What is Tarik playing at?* If this could help him though—if he knew something I didn't . . .

I held the crystal at arm's length as I walked back through the lab room, flinching when the rock fell into Tarik's open palm.

His body jerked and I grimaced. He must have fallen asleep. A gusty sigh left him as he fisted the crystal. "That's the stuff. Mordecai, you fool."

My eyes rounded. I was right—the crystal was an addiction. I tried to pry the rock from his hand but his fist only tightened further. "Wait. It's not hurting me, you'll see."

I had my doubts, especially when his brows drew together, lips thinning. His eyes slid shut and he groaned. Loudly. Then I heard a snap, the eerie sound echoing in the small space. I searched for the source, but found nothing out of place. The tray hadn't moved, the cot's straps lay dangling over the edges as before.

"Tarik? What are you—" My question fell off.

A crack came next and he hissed through bared teeth. "Healing," he panted, "myself."

I looked down to his mangled limbs and gasped. His left knee was slowly straightening. I watched in morbid fascination as the kneecap reformed, popping into the socket.

Tarik grunted. "That feels better."

For several minutes I stared, glued to the sight of broken limbs reforming, bones adjusting beneath skin. When he finished, Tarik slumped forward, red hair shadowing his face. Air caught in my lungs. I brushed my fingertips over his shoulder. "Are you okay?"

"Yeah." He huffed a laugh. "But. Uh. I need you to do me one more tiny favor."

I raised an eyebrow, suspicious. After what I had watched, I wasn't so sure I trusted that 'tiny.' "Yes?"

His head lifted, but he wouldn't quite meet my gaze. "Can you find me some pants?"

For a moment, I gaped at him, dumbstruck. Then I laughed. The tension of the day, of the hour, poured out of me as I realized how simple, how *normal* his request was.

"I can do that." There was a drawer of clean clothing in the lab, I remembered. I grabbed a set that I guessed to be around his size and brought them back to him, pushing the wad into his arms. "Wouldn't want me to see *you* naked—all that skin, what a *scandal*."

"Thanks," he mumbled, placing the clothes on his lap. I stared, waiting, but he fidgeted with the hem of the gray shirt. "Uh . . . could I have some . . . privacy?"

"Oh good grief," I huffed, rolling my eyes. Still, I complied. From the lab, I could almost make out the soft instructions Sebastian was feeding the Fae. Almost ready to leave, I assumed. Behind me came a thump. Tarik cursed.

"You okay in there?" I peered over my shoulder.

"Don't look!"

I turned back around, snickering.

Several grunts and mutterings later, a presence warmed my back. I tried to face him, to see for myself that his legs were healed and whole, but he whispered, "Not yet." His fingers trailed down the nape of my neck before he bent, brushing a featherlight kiss on my cheek. He lingered, and my heart felt two sizes too large. His voice was a low caress in my ear, warm and soft, as he said, "Thank you for saving my stupid Fae butt. I wouldn't blame you for saying 'I told you so.'"

My heart skipped a beat. The voice in my mind—the one wanting to scream about his betrayal, to remind me of that stolen kiss—was oddly silent. Relieved, perhaps, that he was safe. Alive.

I almost spun to face him, to throw my arms around him. I could have. He had opened that door. Right? No. He was still Fae. And I was still a shifter, the thing Tarik himself despised most in the world. Heavy weight settled in my chest.

No. I better not.

Instead, I turned, gathering his hands in mine. "I'm glad you're alive."

When I met his eyes, free of pain and filled with gratitude, I almost caved. But I held still, even when he disentangled one of our hands and ran his fingers along my cheek, tucking a loose strand of blue hair behind my ear. His breath hitched, voice gruff as he whispered, "I didn't think I'd ever see you again."

"Are you sure he's not your boyfriend? Because from where I'm standing . . ."

I jerked my gaze to the lab's entrance and there stood one

of the twins, casually leaning against the doorway. Heat raced up my neck and cheeks. I took a step back.

"Micah?" Tarik pulled away and, with a slight limp, strode to the blond Fae. Before he could reach him, Micah moved, wrapping Tarik in a hug. I heard muffled chuckling, then, "Easy, man. I'm kind of fragile right now."

Wait, Tarik can tell the twins apart?

Micah held him at arm's length, scrutinizing him from head to toe. "Yeah, I heard you were busted up. Gnarly. Good to see you, bro."

"Hold the touchy-feely family reunion moment," Sebastian interrupted, poking his head around the corner. "We're not out of this yet."

Shouts sounded and our faces folded in confusion. I shoved past the men, moving down the hallway as quickly as my sore leg would allow. Weaving in and out of the rescued Fae, I caught sight of glasses and stopped next to Elias. "What's happening?"

"Akeno spotted someone coming," Elias whispered. "We need to get out of here, and fast."

As the Fae spilled into the cavern that contained the stairs, a shadow slowly strode toward us, cutting off our exit. I squinted, then raised an eyebrow. Squirrel Butler? As he hit the center of the large room, he glared in my direction.

"Oh, mistress Reagan. I always knew you would be a disappointment." I froze. My instincts screamed that we couldn't kill him, but he had seen me. I couldn't think of another way if we didn't want Mordecai to find out. He removed our options, though, when he added, "Tis of no consequence. I will see you dispatched, even if it will displease the master. He will understand."

I almost laughed, imagining tiny squirrel fisticuffs. But as he shifted, I realized that his animal form had been another of Mordecai's secrets. He grew and grew, until a massive brown wolf, at least three times the size of my lion, dominated the cavern. His eyes glowed bright orange, a perfect match to the flames that licked out from between his teeth.

"Get anyone who's injured out of here," I said to Sebastian, eyes sliding to Tarik. "That means you."

As he opened his mouth to protest, I shifted, hurtling forward to slam myself into the wolf's jaw before he could snap them closed around one of the twins. I growled at him, taking his attention away from the Fae. This was between us. I would die if doing so gave the Fae a chance to escape, and live.

He barked in my direction, fire licking at my legs. The stench of burnt fur bit at my nostrils. Stinging pain spread up my legs but I gritted my teeth, sweeping my wings at his next burst of flame. Effective, but he launched forward and slammed me into a wall. I slumped to the floor, pinned under his snout, his hot breath choking my lungs.

I shifted. My smaller form slid free, then I rapid-shifted back into my lion as soon as I was underneath his belly. I latched onto his front leg, ripping flesh and muscle from the back of his knee. Hot blood spurted over my snout. Jaws snapped at me and I pulled myself free with a flap of my wings.

A dart whizzed past my face. I spared a half second to see Flynn lurking not far from me. The wolf spotted him in the same moment. Before he could attack the Fae man, I barreled for him and flung my wings wide. Fire tickled down the curving feathers and I winced, dropping into human form when the flames fizzled out. I needed to get him away from Flynn.

"Come on, you brute," I yelled, racing across the floor. I jumped for him at the last second, rapid-shifting. As I launched into the air, I could feel the tug on my muscles, the lag in my responses—I wouldn't be able to rapid shift again.

I swatted his jaw away only to have him slam me to the ground beneath a paw. He growled, a low, victorious sound that vibrated through my body. I couldn't get free, my wings splayed across the ground beneath me. Flames burst to life in his maw again. I clawed frantically at his nose, but the wolf didn't flinch.

A million images flashed through my mind. One lingered—a glimpse of emerald eyes free of pain and filled with gratitude—and I held onto that image as I squeezed my eyes shut.

This is it.

This is how I die.

CHAPTER 17

Tarik

When Reagan bolted from the medical room, I went the opposite direction. After fixing my broken legs, I had discovered that the Genesis Crystal's energy wasn't bottomless. This would be my last chance to acquire some more. It made me stronger, it made my *healing* ability stronger, and I couldn't waste the opportunity—not when I knew of someone who desperately needed the crystal's power.

Micah followed me into the Green Room, babbling questions, asking if I required assistance walking in the *right* direction. I ignored him even as I marveled that he was here. That they *all* were—despite the hurtful things I'd said and done to push them away. Maybe I was simply a byproduct. Maybe their mission had been to free the other trapped Fae, and I just happened—

"So, is she really your girlfriend? And a shifter, too. How did *that* happen?"

His newest question gave me pause. I picked up a crystal—uncut and foolishly left out in the open—and strode across the massive cavern, hoping to never lay eyes on it again. "Now is not the time, man. Ask me questions when we get out of here."

If we got out.

Because as we drew closer to the stairs, as we squeezed past dozens of my nervous coworkers, something in the chamber ahead chilled my blood. What used to be an unassuming, squirrely little butler had transformed into a hideous, fiery-eyed beast.

"Crap, Bushy, I thought you'd be cute and cuddly."

"What?" Micah asked. I must have said that out loud.

I scanned the shuffling and bobbing heads for blue hair. The search took way too long, her short frame swallowed by the crowd. When I got to her side, she was already barking orders, her Night Enforcer tone brooking no argument. I opened my mouth, but before I could stop her, before I could tell her about the crystal, she shifted.

Several of the Fae leapt away from her, pressing themselves against the walls as a great white lion filled the hallway.

"Malachi!" Micah shouted in panic, and I saw his twin next to Bushy, about to be snapped in two.

I lurched forward, but Reagan was already there, smashing into the beast three times her size. I became aware of Sebastian ordering the Fae up the stairs, telling them to hug the walls and avoid being burnt alive. If I wasn't so focused on the two animals tearing into each other, I would have rolled my eyes.

A shot of flame burst from Bushy's maw, singing Reagan's fur. She thrust those brilliant wings wide, snuffing the fire out, but I knew she was in trouble when he slammed her into a wall. At the sound, my wings strained against my skin, and I let them rip free.

"Flynn!" I yelled to the silent Fae I'd recognized amid the

growing chaos. "Distraction."

He nodded, pulling out darts as he slipped to the far side of the cavern. By now, the crystal's mysterious power had leached into my bloodstream, infusing my muscles, my very bones with strength. I lunged for the frothing wolf as Reagan shouted. The beast chased after her and I caught nothing but air. He tackled her, pinning her lion form to the ground. Maw open, he readied to spew bright orange fire into her growling face.

The world stilled as a deadly calm stole over me. No, calm wasn't what wrapped around my bones, giving me courage and strength. Giving me purpose.

Rage was.

I unleashed my fury on the foul beast who dared threaten Reagan's life. With a snarl, I slashed a wing toward his one front leg still uncut, severing the muscles at the back of the knee. Blood sprayed on my face. He howled and his front legs collapsed.

I knew what I needed to do next.

Send a message.

I wrapped my arms around the beast's thick neck, grappling for a better position. He shook his head and almost launched me from him. Not caring if he blasted me with fire, I latched onto his snout instead. Securing his maw shut with one arm, I dug something out of my pants pocket.

And, without hesitation, thrust the scalpel through his eye.

"I'm glad you're not a cute little squirrel," I grunted. "Or I might actually feel bad for doing this." He continued to thrash, so I continued to thrust, deeper and deeper. Until at last, the blade penetrated his brain.

We crashed to the ground and I rolled off, flinging the

already-shifting butler to the side. A pink, gooey substance dripped from my hand and I grimaced, wiping the slime on my stolen pants.

Reagan lay on the floor, naked and bleeding, but alive. A relieved sigh shuddered through me and I bent to help her up.

"Come on. We have to go," she said breathlessly, already pulling me toward the stairs before I could straighten. I looked one last time at the room and hallway beyond, making sure none were left behind, then followed, wishing I could breathe fire.

I would raze this mine to ash.

We burst through the mansion's back door and Reagan quickly secured the lock, then asked me to bust through. Gladly. More things to destroy. Rage still simmered in my blood, making me jittery, making me want to do something rash, like storm up to Mordecai's room and take the devil on myself. But she was staring up at me with those big blue and gold eyes, expectant, and I rammed a fist into the metal, snapping the lock clean off the door.

Her brows arched and I paused, realizing in that moment I couldn't go home. Mordecai would know I'd been a part of this, what with a scalpel protruding from his butler's eye. Besides, I was a fugitive employee now.

No. I wasn't.

I quit.

I scratched my neck, watching Flynn and Micah lead the rest of the straggling Fae to safety. Knowing they would find a place for them to hide. But . . . I blew out a breath.

"What's wrong?"

I looked at her again and blinked. Gaia, when had she become so beautiful? I debated what to tell her. How much did she know? She was running around with the very Fae who were supposed to keep her away from our kind. My plans had backfired terribly. Again.

Bad luck.

I chewed on my lip. Why was this so *hard?* "I guess this is goodbye. For real this time." At her widening eyes, I plowed on. "I'm a fugitive now. Associating with me would be a death sentence. And I'm not gonna allow you to take more risks for me."

Reagan snorted. "The first time I saved your 'sorry Fae butt' I signed that death sentence. Pretty sure we're well past that line." She paused, scanning the dark mansion nervously. "Stay with me. I have a guest room, and everything you could want. I can get your cat. You'd be safe, at least long enough to figure out something more permanent."

A million thoughts scrambled for attention. What about Benji? And Haven? I couldn't sit on my hands, watching TV on her flat screen while Mordecai did who-knew-what to the Fae community. A light flicked on in a window above us and Reagan gasped, her eyes pleading with me. Hurry. Hurry. We were out of time.

I was going to regret this. "Lead the way, stalker."

Heaven.

I had finally died and gone to heaven.

In all my twenty-three years of deprived life, I'd never smelled anything so divine.

I inhaled again, filling my lungs to capacity. Mouth-wateringly rich, the strong scent had dragged me out of a deep sleep. And not simply a deep sleep, but a void filled with nothing. Absolutely nothing. No tossing and turning, no mumbling, no fitful jerks or cries of pain. Best of all, though, no thoughts of the night that had stolen everything from me.

Everything *good*, anyway.

I heard distant humming, the sound slightly off-key, and a grin spread across my face. Maybe there was still a bit of good after all.

Last night, Reagan had somehow smuggled me up to her apartment without anyone seeing. Then had left as she headed off for patrol again. Not that anyone would notice me, not when they could ogle her naked body instead. My smile slipped. Wasn't there a way to shift and keep your clothes on? I would have to look into that. Maybe she had a Shapeshifter dictionary or something.

It was morning now. Or afternoon. I didn't know. For the first time in as long as I could remember, I hadn't woken with the dawn. Which reminded me of Benji. Was he worried? My chest tightened and I sat up. I had to get word to him. I didn't want Reagan heading over there, not even to collect Callie. The place was no doubt being watched.

I would probably have to sneak out of here at some point while she was off on patrol. I looked down at the stolen clothing that I'd been too exhausted to remove, still blood-spattered from my encounter with Bushy. Who would have thought that such an unassuming man was hiding such a big secret?

From somewhere in the apartment, Reagan yelped, letting fly a string of curses.

I jumped out of bed and bolted down the hallway as if demons were on my tail. I found her in the kitchen, her back to me. Completely and utterly stark—

The carpet tripped me up and pulled me down. I was up in a flash, scanning the immediate surroundings for the threat.

Reagan glanced over her shoulder, eyebrows pulled together. "Everything okay?"

"No. Yeah," I panted. *Why am I panting?* I pointed at her hand. "Why do you have a weapon?"

"These?" She waved the silver object around, clacking the ends. "Tongs. I'm making bacon. You want some?"

I raked a hand through my hair, looking everywhere but at her. Bacon. Bacon. Why did that sound familiar?

"I don't know. I just—" I cut off when she turned back around and I caught a glimpse of that long, naked spine. That blazing red and orange Phoenix wrapped around her—

Crap.

I cleared my suddenly dry throat. "Are you sure you're not in danger? I heard you yell."

"Oh, that?" She waved a hand dismissively. "Yeah, I should know better than to cook bacon after patrol. I'm far too hungry to fuss with clothing." She snickered. "I'm covered in tiny grease burns, you'd think I'd learn. But yes, I'm perfectly fine."

I sputtered as my gaze drew downward again. What was wrong with me? Then my mind latched onto a word she said. Burns. I sucked in sharply, stepping nearer. "Let me see."

"Why? They're teeny. You can't even see them. Seriously, they're my own fault. After patrol I'm lazy, hungry, and man, can you *smell* this bacon? Worth it."

My eyes rolled to the ceiling and I inwardly groaned. Stubborn woman. Always thinking she deserved the pain others inflicted on her. "I've heard of bacon, but what is it exactly? A fire-breathing pet? Do I need to stab this thing with a scalpel too?"

Reagan turned around, a strip of—was that leather?—in her mouth. She ripped a chunk off with her teeth, chewing as she said, "Seriously? You don't know what bacon is? Try this." She held out the strip.

I raised my hands, palms out, and took a slow step back. "Whoa, there. Hold on a sec. Is that meat? 'Cause that's a shifter thing, not a Fae—" My stomach lurched as I thought about what she had done. "Are you eating your pet?"

She fidgeted with the stove's burner, lowering the flames. Then she sashayed around the counter, arm still out. "I will force-feed you. I don't have a pet." She grinned slyly. "Anymore."

Ah crap. Now she was coming at me with her full body on display, a playful look on that adorable face. I was screwed. I had no choice but to retreat. Without looking—because there was no way I could pry my eyes from what was heading toward me—I backpedaled. She kept coming, her eyes twinkling mischievously.

But I made a grave mistake in not watching where I was going.

The living room was sunken in.

My left foot found nothing but air and I was falling, falling. *Oof!* I looked up at a grinning Reagan still holding that red strip of disgusting mystery meat.

"We're ten stories up, and I have a key to every room in the apartment. One bite and I'll leave you alone."

Bite.

My mind went places it shouldn't, remembering that night when she'd bitten my shoulder and I bit her arm. I glanced at that arm now. Sure enough, the mark from my teeth was still there. Warmth pooled in my gut at the sight of those crescent scars and I wrenched my eyes away. What did she think of that scar? Of being marked by a Fae? By me?

At the thought of the pain I'd caused her *after* that bite—when I'd been so tired and furious and stupid—I gave in. Gaia, I gave in and opened my mouth.

Her face lit in delight as she inched closer, ripping off a third of the strip. Gently, cautiously, she pressed the piece to my bottom lip. Before I could even slide the thing called bacon all the way into my mouth, I knew I was forever changed. Smokey, salty, sweet perfection exploded on my tongue and a surprised moan left me. Flames of embarrassment heated my neck at the look Reagan was giving me—self-satisfied, like a spoiled cat. But when I bit down and heard a crunch, my eyes slid closed and I moaned again without reservation.

So this was what meat tasted like. I was a fan. Definitely a fan.

"Told you so," she said, and I watched greedily as she finished off the last bite. "Now, do you want some bacon?"

Still munching away, my mouth tipped into a frown. "Am I not eating bacon?" I paused in my chewing. "Then what am I eating?"

"You're hilarious. And now you're not getting more." I stuck my bottom lip out and rounded my eyes at her. "Pouty lips don't work here. You'll have to try harder."

She turned on her heel, waltzing back to the kitchen. The

stovetop clicked back on and a sizzle filled the room.

I lay there, studying the back of her head, not entirely sure what to make of her words. *Harder.* What did she want me to do, exactly? Beg? A grin tugged at my mouth and I jumped to my feet, striding toward the kitchen. I sidled up behind her, my chest lightly brushing against her—

I stopped my mind from thinking of what stood right in front of me. What I was doing. Gaia, what *was* I doing? Crap. Too late to back out now. I was doing this, even if the heat from the stove was boiling me alive. Bending down so my lips grazed the shell of her ear, I whispered, "Please?"

Reagan jumped, giggling as she batted at my face gently. "That tickles. Stop, you can have more."

At the carefree sound she'd made, my breath stalled. Giggling. Eyes lit with mirth. A blade stabbed my chest and I stumbled back. Breathing became impossible. I couldn't look at her. I couldn't—

"Do you—" My voice cracked and I roughly cleared my throat. "Do you have something I could change into? I'm kind of . . ." Unable to finish, I pointed at my blood-stained shirt.

Her eyes narrowed as they skirted the length of me. "Yeah, I should have offered sooner, sorry. You can shower. The bathroom is in my room and there's spare clothing in the guest room." Her gaze flicked back to my face. "Are you all right? You seem . . . antsy."

As I inched toward the hallway, still unable to meet her eyes, I said, "Yeah, yeah. Fine. I've had a rough couple of days." I continued backing up until a wall hid her from view, then whipped around, practically jogging down the hallway in my attempt to create distance. Lots and lots of distance.

I found her room and refused to explore, striding straight to the bathroom. Inside, I quietly closed the door and leaned against it, finally releasing my breath. She was messing with my head. This arrangement was no good. I couldn't stay here. Something in me would eventually explode being trapped like this, forced to confront growing feelings I shouldn't have. Didn't *want* to have.

Pushing away from the door, I stripped off the filthy clothing, wadding them into a ball and tucking them in a corner. In that corner was a . . . I blinked in surprise. A plant? As far as I knew, shifters repelled nature. They surrounded themselves with concrete walls and little else. Seeing a touch of green in this pristine white room skewed my perspective of Reagan even more.

My eyelids began to burn and I pressed my palms against them, cursing. How could this short, slip-of-a-girl have so thoroughly burrowed beneath my skin? I blinked rapidly, clearing my vision, and focused on the small fern again. *I bet she has a catnip plant stashed in her bedroom.* The thought made me chuckle.

After several minutes of poking and twisting at the shower's many knobs, I stood under a cold waterfall. And as faint pink swirls slid down the drain, I prayed that these dangerous feelings I had for a five-foot-nothing female shifter would slip down the drain just as easily.

"So . . . I have to tell you something. Don't get mad."

Great.

Did she know me at all? If she thought I would get mad, I probably would. No. I would. Hands down.

I shoved another piece of bacon into my mouth, washing it down with orange juice before I grabbed a square of something she called waffle. Reagan watched me, thankfully with clothes on this time, a faint smirk on her lips.

"What?" I asked, my mouth still full.

"Well, Alec was here this morning while you were asleep. He has a bad habit of dropping in before his patrol." Her eyes dropped to the table. "And I have to meet with Mordecai before I go out tonight."

Abruptly, I swallowed. Bits of bacon lodged in my throat. Choking, I pounded a fist on my chest. "Wait—" I coughed, taking another large swallow of orange juice. "That was . . . that was a lot to digest all at once. *Alec* comes here? Came here while I was sleeping, and you're only telling me this *now?*"

"Alec does what he wants. But you're safe enough. He won't go beyond the living room unless I'm home. Never does. And I chase him out every time. I'm sure you'll see—hear—what I mean." Reagan poked at the edge of her plate. "And yes, he was only here long enough to deliver that message. It was a nice change."

I couldn't quite organize my thoughts, so I simply sat there, gaping as she stared at her plate. Yeah, his presence here was a huge complication and I almost bolted for the door, but what glued me to the chair was her last words. *Nice change.* This was none of my business, I warned myself, yet my one encounter with him still sat like bile on my tongue. What he'd said about her . . .

"When you say he does what he wants . . . what does he

want, exactly?" I asked carefully, watching her expression.

Her eyebrows pinched together, lips pressed into a firm line. "Something he can't have," she growled.

In the next instant, I was up out of my chair, hands slamming against the tabletop. "Has he touched you?" I thundered, incapable of lowering my voice. "Because I swear I'll kill him. I don't care who he is, I'll—"

I jerked upright before I could say more, pushing past the table and into the living room. Facing the sliding door, I stared at the sprawling city below. Everything was blurred shapes. I had overreacted just now. I knew that. But the words had dredged up memories. Ignited a fire I couldn't control. Behind me, all was silent as I worked on slowing my raging pulse.

Fingertips grazed my arm. "Hey. I'm okay. He gets handsy, but he leaves with broken parts every time he does."

Broken.

Broken.

Screams. Pain. Helplessness.

A flame, so pure and good.

Snuffed out.

Broken, broken, broken.

The word was a pounding beat in my skull. Over and over it played. I couldn't think. Could only re-imagine a beautiful, broken girl, dying in more ways than one at the hands of—

In the next moment, she was wrapped in my arms. I pressed my mouth to her hair. Breathed her in. Sweet and spicy, apples and cinnamon. I held her like that, clutched tightly to my hammering chest, never wanting to let go. Afraid she would pull away. But she didn't. Her slender arms wrapped around me in return, and my heart almost burst.

What are you doing? my mind hissed.

I buried my nose in her hair.

She's not your girl. Snap out of it. You're only going to ruin her.

I squeezed my eyes shut, trying to ignore the voice, but the thoughts were relentless.

And right.

My demon was right.

Reaching up, I took Reagan's shoulders and gently pushed her back. Not meeting her eyes, afraid of what I'd see there, I whispered, "Sorry. I shouldn't have done that."

She slid her hands over mine, squeezing softly. "Don't stress over a hug. Someday I'll break you of that Fae modesty."

But she wouldn't look at me either.

CHAPTER 18

Reagan

My eyes burned with exhaustion. I hadn't slept. At first I had been too wired from the night's events. Then worried about Tarik after—

No. I didn't want to dissect the layers behind that hug. Tarik was never so vulnerable, and while I had always imagined he had the capacity for it, to see the raw emotions firsthand . . .

I wanted to push him. To force that side of him out into the light. But I worried he wouldn't be able to fight off that dark, angry persona and I would end up the victim of that nasty temper. Again.

A shifter must have hurt him badly to leave such deep, invisible scars. He reacted too impulsively, driven too much by those concealed emotions for me to believe otherwise. When he was scared, or concerned, he pulled me in. Then he spent the rest of his time shoving me away. I was stuck in a game of tug-o-war that usually left me in the mud.

Honestly, after that kiss, I might be better off running far away.

If nothing else, Tarik was filling a lonely void I hadn't realized existed in my life. I had Nevaeh; the only person in the universe I could say with absolute certainty loved me as much as I loved her. Our friendship meant more to me than anything, and she was always there when I needed her . . . but she didn't visit often.

And Nevaeh didn't make me feel flustered. Nervous. I didn't think about her all the time, didn't feel warmth bloom in my stomach when she looked at me with concern in her eyes. I didn't know what that meant.

I had to admit, having someone to talk to was kind of nice. To share new things with, even silly things like bacon. I had always been perfectly fine on my own . . . but maybe I was simply used to solitude. When the options were Mordecai or Alec, there really hadn't been much choice.

Shaking my head, I lowered my eyes to the large dark-wooden desk in front of me. These were thoughts for another time. Mordecai was late. I had been standing in his office for well over fifteen minutes. Alec hadn't mentioned why the Great Dragon wanted to see me, but I imagined he wanted me on the hunt for his Fae fugitives while I patrolled tonight. I huffed a laugh at that. Fugitives. That was how he treated them.

Tarik had to be frantic by now. The panic that had blazed in those emerald eyes when I had strode for the balcony . . . Was he really worried about me? Or himself?

Either way, I promised him I would be back before sunset. The sky was a brilliant shade of pinkish orange, though, and here I was. Waiting.

Worry began to darken my thoughts when the door finally banged open. Every muscle in my body tensed, my stomach twisting into knots. Mordecai's expression was lit with fury, eyes flashing in my direction as he crossed his arms and waited expectantly.

I knelt. "In loyalty and service to the Great Dragon."

"Is that so?" he snarled. Before I could look up a fist slammed into my jaw, sending me backward. "Where were you last night?"

I stumbled to my feet, not daring to glance at his face, resisting the urge to reach for the jaw that now throbbed in agony. "Father, I was on patrol all night."

Mordecai circled me. I kept my eyes on the floor, eager to stop him from lashing out again. He shoved a long, white feather under my nose. My heart stopped and I fought to keep my face smooth. "Then why did I find this in my mines?"

"I don't know, Father."

A slap this time, one that vibrated through my body. I stiffened, hands clenched into fists at my sides. This time, though, I wasn't restraining fear. No, I was holding back anger. Rage. Fury over all the things he had done to me, to Tarik, to an entire race of innocents. To a little girl with sparkling amber eyes that haunted my every nightmare. I backed away a step, then another, stopping when I bumped into his desk.

When I glanced up, he grinned wickedly and leaned forward. "Did you release those Fae? Were you involved in the death of my butler?"

"No, Father." Lying was easier with poisonous anger flowing through my veins.

"You're a liar," he spat. "How else would this feather have shown up next to his body?"

"Maybe one of the shifters who attacked me the other day planted one of my feathers. They were all over the alley the next day. If they could make you think I was guilty, you would finish the job for them and no one will stop *you.*"

"What have I told you about telling lies, Reagan?"

Mordecai moved too quickly. I couldn't stop him as he latched onto my hair. His hand jerked forward, slamming my face into the corner of his desk. Pain splintered from my cheekbone, lancing through my eye, and surged up the side of my head. Instead of crying, I ignored the pounding in my head. Let the fury win.

I growled.

Low, inhuman.

In the flash of time it took for his shock to register I had shifted, lion's teeth bared as I snarled. He backed away quickly, straight into the bookcases.

Come out and play, dragon. I've had enough.

"Reagan, stop."

I roared angrily, taking a step closer.

"Reagan. Leave now and I'll consider this indiscretion forgiven."

Forgiven? I should be the one forgiving *him.* Heat and rage warmed my blood.

I lunged for him, pinned him against the shelves. My nose was an inch from his face, my teeth ready to sink into the flesh trembling before me. I scanned his face, registering the unbridled terror at my animalistic fury.

"Reagan, my daughter, my dear sweet daughter. I'm sorry. My temper gets the best of me, you know this. Of course you weren't lying. I'm sorry."

His eyes glistened. I wondered why he didn't shift; the Great Dragon could easily destroy my lion. Instead, I stared at him until my breaths became shallow. I could kill him. I could kill him right now. Destroy his legacy and set the Fae on a path to fight for their freedom. I could rip his throat out for all he had done. All he would continue to do, if I didn't.

But I hesitated. The only one here was me. Directly, I was the only one in any kind of danger. And even knowing what kind of person he was, I simply couldn't bring myself to kill him. Maybe he had trained me too well. Maybe I still considered him too much of a father figure. I couldn't bring myself to do it, to enact that kind of violence on a cowering man.

Maybe I was too weak.

I growled again, a warning, and shoved open his balcony doors. Even though I wasn't entirely sure what had happened in there, I did know one thing with absolute certainty.

That was fear in Mordecai's eyes.

Fear.

Of me.

"That son of a—" Tarik pulled at his hair and growled at the ceiling. He took a few breaths that did nothing to calm him, then stormed toward me. Rage still simmered through my own veins. My arms trembled, but I tried not to move.

He reached for my face and, despite my best efforts, I flinched. The reaction gave him pause, his hand hovering mid-air. "I would never—" A tremor shook his fingers. He slowly curled them into a fist and let his arm fall. His voice was low—lower than I had ever heard it—as he said, "What. Happened?"

"That wolf—I mean, Squirrel Butler, in the mines. He must

have torn one of my feathers out. Mordecai found one down there and went off." I gritted my teeth. "I handled him. I'm fine."

"No," he barked. "You're not *fine*, Reagan." He started pacing then, cursing under his breath. "You can't stay here. *We* can't stay here. It's too dangerous, and if Mordecai finds more clues of your involvement last night, he'll kill you." He stopped and stared a hole through the carpet. "I think we need to go into hiding. The rebels have a safe place."

I brushed my fingers over the swollen spot on my cheek. The whole area was tender, from my cheekbone to my eyebrow, and I wondered how bad the bruising looked. I sighed. "Tarik, I can do more in my Enforcer position and you know that. Right now I have enough power to make things happen. Take that away and what do I have? This is my life." I looked away from him, anywhere but at him. The rage was sputtering into tension. Bursts of energy zipped through me. I rocked on my feet. "You can leave if you want to. But I don't think Mordecai is much of a threat to me."

I told him everything—the entire meeting, from Mordecai being late, to his tantrum, to the fact that I had shifted—not excluding the fact that I had never shifted on him before. Never. I hadn't dared. I stammered when I reached the end, the part that revealed my own cowardice. He was braver than me. Tarik wouldn't have hesitated. But I pushed on.

When I finished I glanced up at Tarik, trying to gauge his reaction.

He chewed on his lip, so aggressively that I wondered if he drew blood. After a full minute, he deflated, shoulders drooping. "This is your decision. I can't force you to leave, but . . ."

He sighed, searching my face. "Promise me something?"

"What?"

His eyes narrowed. "Promise me you'll be careful. Promise you'll never turn your back on that devil. There's something . . . off about him. When I was strapped to that cot and he was—" He looked away, throat convulsing. "He's desperate for something. Desperate people are unpredictable. And extremely dangerous. Promise you'll keep your head down."

My hand twitched. In my mind, I strode across the room and touched his arm, his face. Comforted him. In reality, I resisted. He had drawn lines, ones that he kept erasing and redrawing. I wasn't ready to meet another dead end. A lump grew in my throat. Even if comforting him felt appropriate to me, he would retreat. I knew he would. So I did nothing.

I sighed. "Sure. I promise."

"Good," he murmured, gaze resting on my swollen right cheek, then my jaw where another bruise was probably showing. He deliberated, opening and closing his mouth. Abruptly, he turned on his heel and strode for the hallway, throwing over his shoulder, "Come here. I need to show you something."

Confused, I trailed behind him. Tarik had slipped into the guest room and sat on the bed, his hands held nervously behind his back.

"Sit." He gestured to a spot on the mattress next to him and I perched timidly on the edge. What was he up to? His gaze slid over me, then jerked to the ceiling as he muttered to himself. All I heard was "skin." I glanced down at myself. What? He yanked his shirt off and thrust it at me. "Put this on or I can't have this conversation."

I rolled my eyes, but did as instructed.

Then waited.

And waited.

Tarik shook his head, pulling his hand out from behind him. "I've been able to do this for as long as I can remember and . . . I want to show you. May I?" He gestured to my injured cheek.

I swallowed. "Um. Sure?"

He scooted closer and brought a knee up onto the bed, boxing me in. Without taking his eyes off mine, he whispered, "Here goes nothing," then raised both his hands, gently cupping my cheeks.

My heart tried to force its way up my throat. Lines. We were crossing lines. Weren't we? No, this was innocent. But something tugged at me, a reminder that Fae weren't keen on touching, especially not shifters. No. I couldn't think like that. Instead, I held his stare. Waited.

At first, nothing happened, and I had the urge to fidget. Then a warm tingle spread over my swollen cheek and eye, making me jump.

"It's okay," Tarik said. "I'm only taking away the pain and a bit of the swelling. I'll leave the bruises so Mordecai won't suspect anything."

Before I was ready, he pulled away. I brushed a finger across my cheekbone. Smooth. The swelling was effectively taken care of. My eyebrows pinched together. "How?"

He shrugged, looking a bit uncomfortable. "I was told stories about the first Fae to cross into this realm, how they were able to perform miracles. I know many of your kind still think we're witches, that we have dark magic. But I've never met another Fae who could heal with a single touch. Then last night, when my legs were nothing but pulp orange juice, I was able to heal them completely. I've never been able to heal an injury *that* severe before. And so . . ."

He held up a green rock with a flourish, it's multi-faceted surface winking. "I came to the conclusion that this Genesis Crystal stuff has hidden magical powers or something. Boosts my healing abilities, if you will."

I leapt to my feet, backing away a step. "Isn't that stuff dangerous?"

He looked at the rock, then me. "Well, I'm not growing two heads or anything. At least . . . not yet." A smirk tipped his lips. "Why, is the big bad Night Enforcer scared of a rock?"

"Maybe." I swallowed, eyes locked on the green crystal. I retreated another step.

A wolfish grin stretched his mouth wide as he slowly stood. He stuck the crystal out in front of him and pursued me as I backed out into the hallway. "One little touch and I'll leave you alone. I know where you keep the waffle batter. I'd hate for *that* to go missing."

I looked up at him, catching his eyes for a split second. I resisted the urge to smile. "You don't play fair. I knew for sure that bacon wouldn't kill you."

"But *I* didn't know that." He sighed, exasperated. "Reagan. This rock isn't going to kill you. It *gives*, not takes. Are you saying you'll face off with the Great Dragon but not touch this itty bitty harmless rock?"

"Yes, well. I know he can kill me. Maybe. That rock is a total unknown." I chanced another glance at his face. "You have no clue what the Genesis Crystal does, exactly. And Mordecai always told me not to touch the stuff."

"You're right, I don't. But I'm ninety-nine percent certain

you're safe since you're not Fae. I think." He chuckled, tossing the rock in the air. The green stone shimmered under the bright penthouse lights. Then Tarik looked at me almost . . . victoriously. "Think fast."

And the rock came soaring toward me. My eyes widened. I didn't think. Instinct reacted. My fingers curled around the crystal, clutching the sharp edges against my palm. The strange tingling I had felt last night through the gloves intensified, vibrating through my hand, my arm, spreading through my veins.

Then I was on fire.

I gasped, doubling over in pain. My whole body was engulfed. Flames burned in my veins, my lungs. I couldn't breathe. My knees slammed to the floor and I desperately tried to pull in air. Failed.

The room spun.

As my vision began to cloud I inhaled sharply, cool air flooding my lungs. The tingling was back. My body felt energized, invincible. I could take on the world.

Another breath and the flames returned. I curled in on myself, forehead pressed to the floor. Burning. I was burning from the inside. Razor sharp pain sliced up my back, on either side of my spine. Through gritted teeth I screamed into the carpet.

The flames diminished into cooling tingles again. I felt strong, even as my body trembled. Pressure spread across my back, gently at first, then insistent. Oh no. My wings. *My wings.*

Fire raced through my spine and splintered outward, cascading across my back. My wings screamed in protest as they tried to burst through.

Stuck.

They were stuck on my shirt. Tarik's shirt.

I focused, pushing every bit of energy I had into shoving them past the fabric. With a loud rip, my wings tore free, exploding to their full span. They roared with the same fire that furiously coursed through my body. The shredded shirt fluttered to the carpet.

Relief.

A last wave of tingling energy washed through me. Then ceased. I lay panting on the carpet, wings splayed across the floor, bracing for the lion that never took over. Shock pulled at my slipping mind. I couldn't summon only my wings in human form—they weren't a feature I could partial-shift. Once they were free, there was no stopping my full shifter transformation.

What was happen—

I inhaled a long, shuddering breath before the world fell dark.

CHAPTER 19

Tarik

"Reagan!"

I was officially the biggest jerk on the face of this planet.

As she fell to her knees, writhing in agony, my whole body froze. Completely unresponsive despite my brain screaming at me to move, to undo what I did. She curled forward, shaking like a leaf, and all I could do was think that I had killed her. Would my decisions forever cause death and destruction?

This was all my fault.

She screamed, and my limbs finally burst into action. I lunged for her hand, the one still gripping that stupid green rock. What had at first been playful was morphing into a nightmare. One I couldn't wake from.

"Let go, Reagan!" I tried prying the crystal from her fingers but they were locked in place. Vices. Everything was a blur after that. With a rip, the shirt I'd given her fell from her trembling body. And then I was ducking and rolling as wings shot straight out. White. Brilliant.

I waited for the rest of the shift. Instead, she collapsed unconscious, her wings splayed wide on top of her.

The first thing I did was remove that blasted piece of rock from her slackened grip. I was tempted to throw the crystal off the balcony, but forced myself to pocket the object that had caused so much misery. Reagan had experienced adverse effects, but I had to test it on Haven. I knew she would be willing to accept the risks.

What surprised me was the half shift. She had never revealed her wings without her lion form before. Had the crystal caused a shift malfunction?

Kneeling next to her, I reached toward the left wing, curious if the feathers were as soft as they looked, then snatched my hand back. I doubted she wanted me to touch her, not after the cruel trick I had played.

But I couldn't leave her on the floor either. Naked, once again. I groaned. She really needed specially-designed shifter clothing. For several moments, I simply watched her, the way her wings silently rose and fell with each breath. All by itself, my hand inched for those feathers again, gliding a finger down the length of one.

Softer than silk.

So different from my own.

A low huff of air caught my ear. "Oh no, please don't. That tickles. And they're so heavy . . ."

"Reagan?" My heart sped up. She was going to be okay. She had to. "Where do you hurt? Hold on, I'll heal you—" But I stopped myself from touching her. Swallowed. Forced myself to say, "If you want me to, that is."

"Honestly," she began, swiveling her head in my direction, "I feel okay. You're a prick, by the way, but thankfully I don't have to hold this against you. I feel . . . rested. Energized. Is that normal?"

"Uh, yeah, I think that's normal. I get the same energy boost after touching the crystal. Are you sure you're not in any pain? I thought . . ." I cleared the lump in my throat. "For a minute there, I thought you were dying."

Her expression softened. "I'm fine, Tarik. Really. These wings, though. I might need help. This hasn't happened before."

I blinked. She needed help? "Do you need me to . . . uh. What do you need help with, exactly?" I knew what *I* needed: a punch to the face.

"Well, let's start with standing. If I can get my balance, I should be okay."

Right. Standing. Standing would be good. And she was naked. And awake. And staring at me expectantly. I suddenly had a terrible urge to flee. *Stand your ground, man.* Stand my ground. Yes. She was a . . . a *cat.* A cat with graceful arcing limbs and long, flowing—

Crap.

After a deep inhale, I jerked my body into motion, latching onto her biceps. In a flash, I had us both on our feet and quickly dropped my arms. A second later they were up again as she tipped forward and didn't stop. Closer, closer—*Wham!*

"Well *that's* new," she mumbled.

I could barely catch the words, what with her mouth mashed against my chest. Heat flared up my neck when I realized my shirt was gone and her lips were pressed to my skin.

Warm. Moving. Breathing.

Gaia, shoot me now.

"Uh, that—that's okay," I stuttered, righting her once again.

This time, I kept my hands planted on her shoulders as she teetered back and forth. "Can you retract your wings?"

"Can I—" Her eyes widened. "No. I don't know how. I've never had to. Not like this."

Great. Just great.

I blew out a long sigh. This was going to be interesting. "I'll walk you through the process. Hopefully. These things kind of come . . . naturally to Fae." What was I saying? I wasn't an aerial flight instructor. And I certainly didn't know how to explain the complex art of wing usage, not when we weren't allowed to reveal them, let alone use them. "Okay. First, you need to learn balance. Widen your stance and slightly bend your knees."

As she moved beneath my touch, I rolled my eyes to the ceiling. This wasn't happening. *Note to self: don't look down.*

"Done," she said.

"Okay. I'm gonna let go now. You ready?"

"Ready."

My hands left her shoulders, and I took a giant step back, hoping the distance would force her to focus solely on standing. From my peripheral, I saw her wobble, but she didn't fall. When she straightened, I maneuvered around her, finally allowing my gaze to rest on her wings.

Now what?

"I'm guessing the reason you don't know how to retract your wings in human form is lack of muscle memory. So first, I need you to be aware of what muscles to focus on."

My attention drifted to her skin, and I frowned at the faint white lines there. They didn't cover her body like mine did, but I knew a scar when I saw one. A mix of curiosity and anger thrummed through me. This wasn't the time to prod into her past, though. I gave myself a few moments, clenching and unclenching my fists, then gently grasped the base of her wing joints.

She shivered, mumbling, "Tickles."

I couldn't stop from cracking a grin. "Sorry," I muttered, laughter in my voice. Clearing my throat, I got back to business. "This right here is what you need to focus on. Not the fact that several feet of bone, cartilage, and feathers need to retract inside your body." My thumbs lightly stroked where her joints met skin, and she shivered again.

Soft. She was so soft.

If I had to endure much more of this, I was going to lose control.

"Want to try again?" My voice came out all wrong. Deep, rough, shaky.

"Sure."

Her back tensed where I still touched, and I helped rein in that focus, rubbing slow circles at the base of her wings. She hunched next, feathers rustling as her whole body trembled. At her soft grunt, I let go and swiveled to face her, worried she was in pain.

I froze.

That face. All shriveled and puckered in concentration.

I burst out laughing. Once I started, I couldn't stop. I hit the carpet, rolling back and forth, forever imprinting that image of her on my brain.

"Wait, what's so funny?" she huffed. I couldn't catch my breath to answer. She crossed her arms over her chest, and I tried hard not to look. "That's rude, you know."

"Sorry," I gasped out. All was silent as I managed to swallow some air. Then I broke into more laughter. I hadn't laughed like this in . . . forever.

"Well, since you're so busy rolling around on the floor, I'm going to have some fun." And she strode for the living room.

I snickered, letting my gaze rest on the lion tattoo spanning her right back thigh, the mane a mess of pink, blue, and yellow flowers and feathers. But when she passed the couch and made for the sliding glass door, my laughter died.

"Reagan, what are you doing?" Her only answer was to slide the door wide. A stone dropped into my gut when I finally realized her intentions. I jumped to my feet and hurtled through the living room. "Reagan, no!"

As she stepped onto the balcony, twin lines scratched down my back and I let my wings punch free. But they couldn't carry me more than a few feet. Not in their current condition. If she fell . . .

With an extra burst of speed, I lunged. Wrapping my arms around her waist, I dragged her away from the ledge and certain death.

"Oh, *now* you stop laughing. Great."

I held her to me, maybe a little too tight, her feathers lightly tickling my stomach. "Reagan?" At the humming noise she made, I growled, "That was not cool."

She wiggled, tugging for freedom. "I want to try them out!"

Her body intimately rubbed against mine and I froze as a blast of heat shot through my core. Gritting my teeth, I quickly released her and stepped back. Then clamped a hand over her shoulder so she wouldn't attempt a suicide flight again.

"You're going to die doing it that way. Your wing muscles

haven't been conditioned to fly in your human form. They're used to carrying a heavy lion." She looked up at me with big, pleading puppy eyes—or kitty eyes?—and I groaned.

She was going to kill *me*.

"I have an idea. Come with me." When she didn't immediately follow, I added, "I won't make you touch any more rocks."

"I'll force feed you the rock next time," she grumbled.

A slow grin spread across my face. "You could try."

Her deep growl shook the room, like a pissed off kitty cat. My smile broadened.

Before my thoughts could sharpen on what I was about to do, there was a more pressing matter that needed attention.

"Do you have a pair of scissors?" I glanced over my shoulder and noted her quizzical expression.

"No, why? Stay away from my wings."

I slammed to a halt, realizing how the words must have sounded. "Reagan." I scrubbed a hand down my face. "I'm not going to cut your wings. You think I'd do something sick like that?"

"No." She paused. "Reflex, sorry. I have knives?"

Reflex. I huffed out a sigh. This girl . . .

"Yeah, I'll take a knife." When she passed me one, I strode down the hall and into her bedroom. Then whirled to face her. "If I'm going to give you flying lessons, I have one rule: no nudity. So grab a shirt you don't mind me tearing into."

A crease formed between her brows, but she shrugged and tossed me a black t-shirt. I wasted no time digging the knife into the material, cutting the back straight down the middle. "I need a pair of shoe strings, too." After a moment of rummaging in her closet, she threw them my way, then proceeded to pull on a pair of black cut-off shorts.

Making a couple holes in the shirt, I threaded the string through and tied the ends off. I crooked a finger at her and, when she came over, motioned for her to turn around. "Slip your arms through the sleeves."

She clucked her tongue and grabbed the knife, cutting off the sleeves. "Better."

Better for who?

When the shirt was draped across her front, I grasped the shoelaces, preparing to tie them together below her wings. She gathered her hair over a shoulder and that's when I noticed a cutesy sea otter tattoo almost obscured by her right wing. The little creature was gripping a fish, looking ready to chow down.

I smirked and lifted a hand toward the spot, but stopped myself just in time. What I couldn't stop was my mouth. "Is this your spirit animal or something?" And then my stupid finger touched the otter's tail.

Reagan lifted her shoulder, the animal's body stretching with the motion. "Not quite."

My curiosity was piqued now. I pursued. "A pet then?"

"No," she said softly. "She's a memory. A reminder."

I glanced at her thin scars again, and a rock tumbled into my gut. I hadn't expected her to say that. If her memories were anything like mine, the tattoo similar to why I'd kept my scars . . . "I get that. You don't need to tell me."

"She was Fae," she began anyway. "I was . . . I screwed up. And Mordecai . . ." Her words trailed off. Then she added, her voice barely a whisper, "She wasn't even six . . ."

Unease churned in my stomach as I slowly threaded the

shoelaces together. She didn't continue and I struggled to keep my mouth shut. Questions pushed at my throat, but with difficulty, I swallowed them. After several beats of weighted silence, I simply said, "I'm sorry." Another few seconds passed and I blurted, "The tattoo is cute, though."

She huffed a laugh, shivering as I finished tying the strings. I inwardly sighed, relieved. Talking about my past demons wasn't something I did. Maybe Reagan was the same way. "There," I said smugly, stepping back to inspect my handiwork. "Problem solved."

Her eyes narrowed as she looked down at my brilliant creation, then reached for the knife again. As she ripped away the material covering her stomach, I groaned. "You're killing me here, Reagan."

"You left too much. This is better. More mobile, too."

Too much. Mobile. She might as well strip naked again. *No.* This would do.

"Okay, I have to do one last thing before this disastrous flight attempt can proceed. Just . . . don't go anywhere. I'll be out in a minute." My heart was already an out-of-control drum in my chest. It had been so long. Was I really going to do this? What if . . . what if it didn't work?

I didn't wait for her reply, already making for the spare bedroom. The door snicked shut and I blew out a shaky breath. For a full minute, I stared at nothing, my mind completely blank. Behind me, my wings lightly scraped against the walls, as if to signal their purpose, their strength. Even now, when only their frame and a few lethal feathers remained.

You're a master of your pain.

Determination pumped hot through my blood.

I was ready.

Sitting cross-legged in the middle of the bed, I let healing energy stir in my veins, let the magic recently enhanced by the Genesis Crystal thread itself toward my tattered wings. For the last three years, I convinced myself that I didn't have the healing power to fix them. I wasn't strong enough. But in truth, I'd never tried.

That night, when everything had gone wrong, I'd survived. I had *lived*. But that didn't mean I could go on living and forget. I had to remember the cost of my mistakes. A price I hadn't been willing to pay, but one I now atoned for every miserable day. So I'd kept my scars. Hadn't tried to heal them. Including the wings that had failed me. That had failed *her*.

Now, one room away from me, so close I could almost hear her breathing, Reagan needed those wings. Actually *needed* them. Old, familiar shame threatened to undo my newfound determination. But maybe, once my wings were healed, their future use wouldn't hinder my need to remember past failures. I had to try. Because a part of me, a part that was growing louder each and every day, begged to live this moment.

With Reagan.

When the healing was complete, I didn't peek at what I knew rested behind me. Wings with feathers that resembled sleek, obsidian blades. Fixed. Whole. I simply rose and walked out of the room, seeking the girl who needed a flying lesson.

I found her sitting on the back of the living room couch, wings tucked behind her. Reagan's eyes widened when she caught sight of me. She slipped down and strode closer. Her lips parted as she tentatively reached out, like she would stroke one of the streamlined feathers. She jerked her hand back at the last second.

"Tarik, your wings are incredible. I thought they were beautiful before, but . . . they're glorious."

My stomach clenched hotly. Not only from her words, but from her hesitation. I had wanted to feel her touch. Actually *wanted* it. I mentally shook myself, dispelling the ache. "Right. Let the flying commence. Although, there's a good chance I'll fall, too. I'm a bit rusty."

"We'll be fine." She grinned, eyes bright with excitement. "I can do this at least." She stretched her wings out and flapped. If only that were all she needed to know.

I strolled to the open sliding door, turning around when my feet hit the balcony. Caution tugged at my common sense then. Was I really going to fly? In *shifter* territory? I shoved the feeling aside. When had I ever exercised caution? Besides, night had fallen—my wings should be near invisible against the dark sky.

So, instead of using my brain, I tipped my lips up and said, "Even baby birds can flap their wings. Right before they fall out of the nest," then fell backward off the balcony's edge.

Wind whistled past my ears as I plummeted for the cement below. For a split second, fear crashed through me. What if my wings had weakened? Flexing my back muscles, black wings snapped out, catching my fall. With a great flap, I shot into the air, popping up in front of a stunned Reagan.

I hovered, waiting for her to call me out on my theatrics—maybe call me an arrogant Fae prick—but she was a frozen block of ice. Seeing her so vulnerable sent a jolt of protectiveness spearing through my gut, and I carefully landed beside her. Large eyes stared up at me, her earlier excitement snuffed.

I gentled my voice, saying, "See? No problem. Just like riding a bike."

"You dropped like a stone. You're right, there's a difference. My lion . . . I'm too bulky. I don't drop that fast." She gulped. "Help me."

"I can do that. But maybe for the first time, you should, uh—" Warmth smacked my face when I realized what needed to happen. I didn't know if I could go through with it. But her expression, so afraid yet so determined, gave me the courage to try. "Here . . ." I picked up her arm and looped it around my neck, then did the same with the other. With our height difference, I had to curl forward, bringing my head close to hers.

Wrapping an arm behind her, securing her to me, I said, "Ready?"

Reagan choked out a laugh. "No."

I raised a brow. "You know what they say about trust?" Her eyes widened as I finished with, "You have to take a leap of faith."

Jumping into nothing, I took her with me, flapping my wings hard so we wouldn't plummet. She clung tighter, arms like vines around my neck, and I laughed.

"I won't drop you," I said, still chuckling. I shouldn't—I really shouldn't—but when she continued to strangle me, I couldn't help adding, "Did you know mama birds push their babies out of the nest?"

"Do you know that I can rapid-shift in a split second?" she growled.

The corners of my mouth twitched. "Can you now? Let's see."

She shook her head, hair thickening into bright white.

I almost dropped her. I chuckled again, nervously. "If you become a huge cat right now, there's no way I can carry you. I mean, how much would you say your lion weighs?"

"That's incredibly rude. You can't just ask someone how much they weigh." But she winked and shook her head, hair returning to the familiar blue and black.

"Point taken." I stared at her for a moment. The night sky was clear around us, studded with twinkling stars, the city below surprisingly quiet. Only us, with the world at our feet. Her fear of falling had all but melted away, my dumb jokes drawing out her sass. I almost wished things were different. That three years ago, I hadn't lost my ability to care on a deeper level.

Because *this*. There was something special about this.

I didn't want this moment to end.

You can't have her.

"I know," I whispered.

"Tarik? You okay? Your eyes got all sad on me."

I snapped back to reality, to what we'd come here to do. I mentally slapped myself. *Get yourself together, man.* "Must be the wind in my face. Anyway, your turn to fly. We can start by hovering. You know how to hover, right?"

"Never heard of 'hovering.' Could you explain?" She batted her lashes at me, lips stretched into a smirk.

I huffed. "Very funny. But I don't think this teaching thing is going to work. The best way to learn is by *doing*, so . . ." I let my grip on her loosen, and she slid down my body an inch.

She groaned. "All right, fine. Do what you must."

My mind blanked.

Then went places it shouldn't.

She seemed to have no clue how her words came across

sometimes. Or how her nudity affected me. She was seriously messing with my ability to think.

I slowly exhaled. Focus. *Focus.* "I'm not going to let go—not until you're ready. Start by stretching out your wings as far as possible."

She did, her white wings catching the city light's below. I raised my free hand and stroked one of the feathers under the guise of bringing her attention to them. But I couldn't resist touching her wings—so supple compared to mine. "Now, feel the wind flowing along the length of them. Wind is your friend. It'll keep you from dropping like a stone when I let go." I paused. "Do you feel it?"

At her nod, I flapped higher.

"Still feeling it? Good. Because I'm letting go now." I lowered my arms and hers wrapped tighter, strangling me once again. "Flap your wings," I raised my voice over the rushing wind. After a few test flaps, she loosened her grip. "You've got this. You can let go."

And she did.

For a heart-stopping second, she dropped. I tucked my wings, prepared to catch her, but her wings caught a draft, lifting her higher.

She whooped in delight, circling me, and my stomach flipped.

Because for a moment, she looked Fae.

Fae or not, she was the most beautiful thing I had ever seen.

I couldn't get that night under the stars out of my head.

Even two mornings later as I lounged on her plush sofa, watching a ridiculous TV show about a couple who couldn't communicate to save their lives. Those accents. Cringe-worthy. Who spoke like that? It was better than watching the local news channel laden with typical shifter propaganda, though.

After the flying lesson, everything naturally clicked into place for Reagan. She could retract her wings and shift into lion form at will, interchanging the two when needed. Every time she allowed the wings free while still in human form, my heart stopped, then sped up too fast, stealing my breath.

Any minute now she'd return from patrol. I pushed on the remote control again, trying in vain to change the channel. Or turn it off. If she caught me watching this garbage—

"Hold still, Tarik. I want to remember this image *forever.*" Laughter filled the room behind me.

My legs jerked, but I managed to stay seated, even as heat crawled up my neck. I played it cool, not daring to turn around. "Are these characters supposed to mimic real life?"

She continued to snicker as she said, "No, they amp up the drama. After a few seasons, you'll be able to call every plot twist."

"What a waste of time," I muttered, dropping the remote beside me. "So." I swiveled to face her naked form, knowing I would never get used to her casual morning entrances. "Can you make some bacon?"

"In a few. Alec's on his way over. I saw his dragon as I dropped in." She made a shooing gesture. "Go to my room, lock the door, and promise me you'll stay in there. Please?"

I stood, crossing my arms. "Only if he behaves. Because if

he crosses any lines, all bets are off."

"I'll be fine. Shoo, go."

Turning on my heel, I made for the hallway, then quickly backtracked with one of her discarded sweaters. I liked this one because it covered her to mid thigh. When she didn't take it, I said, "I don't want him seeing you like that." As her eyes rolled upward, I fitted the sweater's neck over her head myself. She grumbled but stuck her arms through and pulled the material down.

I nodded, satisfied, then jogged to her room, locking the door behind me. But I wouldn't sit back while the fool dragon shifter strutted around Reagan's apartment. I pressed my ear to the door, not caring in the least that I was eavesdropping.

A boom sounded directly outside, then a squeal as the sliding door opened.

"Hey, babe, you're looking particularly delicious this morning."

I hissed softly. That cocky piece of—

A snort. "Get out of my apartment, Alec."

"Is that any way to greet your favorite dragon?" he crooned, and I clenched my teeth.

"I'm not particularly fond of either of you."

A pause. "So what father said was true, then. You shifted on him."

"And if I did?"

"I mean, I've never really seen you as the take-control type. It's honestly kind of hot." I heard heavy footfalls as he made his way toward the kitchen.

Their voices lowered then, as if the tension had grown. I strained to pick up Reagan's next words.

"Alec, I am not in the mood."

"You're never in the mood." Something about that statement—as if he'd said the words dozens of times before and his patience was wearing thin—raised the hair on my arms.

"Get out." Muffled sounds—like furniture being knocked into—broke the silence, and then, "Alec, I'm warning you. I will cut your manhood off."

"Your apartment smells like dirty Fae." A pause. "And since when do you wear clothing in the morning? Got company?" At that, I quietly wrapped a hand around the doorknob.

"What's with the third degree, Alec? I'm wearing a damned sweater. Get out."

"Is it just a sweater, though? Because shifters talk, Reagan, and I've been hearing some really interesting gossip at The Pit about a certain Fae and *my* girl."

"You really trust rumors from the drunken idiots at The Pit? And I was never your anything. You're disgusting. Now I'll warn you one more time. Leave."

"You're *mine*." Alec's voice was low, threatening. "And I better not hear another word about you even looking at another man."

A snorted laugh, then, "I'm getting a knife. I warned you." For a moment, I lost track of the sounds and conversation. Then came a loud thud. Reagan gasped. "Let me down, *now*." At the panic in her voice, ice shot through my veins. She didn't sound in control. She sounded—

"I've had enough of this game, Reagan. I'm an alpha, and alphas get what they want. Who they want. If I can't have you, I'll *take* you."

Splintering rage exploded through me. I wrenched the door

open to find Reagan pressed against the wall, feet dangling, Alec's hand locked around her throat. At the sight, I threw away every ounce of restraint. Allowed the demon inside to swamp my mind, control my actions, do whatever it pleased. Because Reagan.

He had Reagan.

With a roar, I was on Alec, ripping him away from her. My wings snapped out and the tips raked across his exposed back. He screamed and rushed me, but my feet danced. He couldn't touch me. Time lost meaning then. Had undoubtedly stopped to watch me pound my fist into his face over and over. Even when he pleaded with me to let him go, I was insatiable. I wouldn't relent, not until every last drop of blood was squeezed from his body.

From far away, I heard my name being called. The voice of an angel. She spoke to my demon, her tone soothing. But it shoved her aside. We didn't want to be soothed. We wanted rage. We wanted vengeance. We wanted this sick animal's blood.

Fingers gripped my arm, gently at first. Then tightened, pulling hard. "Tarik, please. Please! Stop! I can't watch you like this. Not because of me. Please."

The pounding in my ears dimmed enough for me to catch her words. But I didn't like them. I growled, not caring how inhuman I sounded. I wanted to kill. *Kill the shifter.* My fist raised, trembling with a violent ache to end this pathetic human—if he could even be called that—but there it stayed. Chest heaving, I allowed Reagan to pull me away. I didn't tear my gaze from Alec's bloody face, though.

He couldn't see me, his eyes long since swollen shut, but I

knew he could hear me. I didn't recognize the voice that came out of me next, but the words felt right as they expelled from my mouth. "If you ever touch her again, you'll wish I had killed you. Because what I'll do to you is too horrendous for words."

On autopilot, I turned and stumbled down the hallway. Our cover was blown. *Hurry, hurry, hurry.* Everything here could be replaced except the Genesis Crystal. I shoved the rock into my pants pocket and lurched for the hallway again, already forming an escape plan.

And came up short.

Reagan blocked the way, looking lost and confused and—

Gaia, she was walking toward me and wasn't stopping. She crashed into me, burying her nose in my chest. I froze, shock coursing through my body. But when she twined her arms around my back and squeezed, I jerked into motion, gathering her to me. Inhaled her greedily. Kissed her hair. She trembled and I murmured random things, only aware of saying, "You're okay. We're okay," over and over.

All I knew was that she needed me and I poured all of my being into our embrace.

We stayed that way for a full minute. Too long. Her warmth was intoxicating and pulling away hurt. But we were out of time. "We have to go." I locked my eyes on hers, willing fire into her veins. This wasn't over yet. "Can you release your wings? Because we need to fly."

CHAPTER 20

Reagan

The end of my cigarette was withering, and I had only taken a single drag. I sat outside in a little area Rebel Leader had offered up when he noticed me flicking my lighter open and shut. He hadn't forbidden me from smoking inside, not directly—maybe he thought I could use the air to clear my head. My thoughts *were* full, my mind trying to sift through the overwhelming pile of events and emotions that had slammed themselves into my life.

Akeno had found Tarik and me as soon as we had dropped into the Fae district a couple days ago. He was one hell of a spy. Benji had been ecstatic to see Tarik again, eagerly chattering about how well he had been taking care of Callie. I knew Tarik wanted to check on Benji's mother soon. Every time she was mentioned, his hand would slide into the pocket where that crystal lay.

For now, we were safely hidden with the Fae. Rebel Leader had extended a generous invitation, but I didn't know how long they could actually let me stay. Both dragons were pissed at me now. Anyone I associated with was as good as dead—

Mordecai had made that clear when he instituted a stricter curfew on the Fae, barely clearing working hours. A wanted poster had begun to circulate the city. Mordecai was saying I had been abducted by Tarik.

Lies.

I couldn't escape his lies. He had Alec out on extra patrols, no doubt looking for me. Waiting for me to slip up. Alec—

My heart hammered angrily every time I thought about Alec.

For once, I was grateful for Tarik's stubbornness. If he had listened to me . . .

I swallowed hard. Yet again he had saved my life, damning his own all the more.

We were making a terrible habit of this.

Still. No one would be allowed to take anything I didn't want to give. Not now, not in the future. No more mistakes.

"You all right? You're about to burn yourself."

Nevaeh interrupted my thoughts and I glanced down. Sure enough, the cigarette had burnt itself low, almost out. I dropped the butt into the grass and snuffed the ember, tugging another loose from my case before I answered, "I have a lot on my mind."

"Yeah, I can imagine." She plopped beside me, assessing my face with those alert brown and silver eyes. "Want to talk about anything?"

I shrugged. Nevaeh knew what had happened. We had spoken as soon as I had arrived at the Safehouse, and she finally had the chance to answer a few of my questions—like explaining that Akeno had brought her into the rebellion because he had caught her spying on unruly shifters one afternoon. She had warned him away, explained the danger, only to realize the information she had given him was exactly what he had come for.

Rebel Leader had filled in several blanks too, and in return I had offered my story to him and the rest of the crew. At least, as well as I could. Tarik had filled in the parts I struggled with. Repeating the worst of it was no easy task.

"I might leave Nathra City," I said. "I saw an underground tunnel system on Mordecai's computer, the one that he uses to import goods from other cities. The entrance is right below The Pit. I could make a real fuss, rile any guards, make sure they were mad enough to run back to Mordecai about it. Then maybe he'd lift his obnoxious curfew. I was always faster than Alec. I'm not worried about him."

"You know that won't work. And maybe you should be a little worried. You've always played off Alec's visits like they were nothing, but he's been bordering that edge for years. I'm glad Tarik was around when he finally tipped over."

"I know. That entitled dragon and his obsessive need to take anything he can't have . . . I should have realized how far south things were going. There were signs, and I didn't see. I panicked and forgot how to react. Forgot to even try to shift. All I kept thinking was *I can't breathe*, over and over . . ."

A lump formed in my throat, pressure I couldn't quite force down. "I don't think he's used to being denied. Either way, I won't make that mistake again." I sucked in a long breath, blowing out slowly. "As for Tarik . . . well. That subject is a fresh kind of hell all its own."

"Tarik? Why?" She stole a cigarette from my case, lighting the end before offering to light the one I still clutched between my fingers. I shook my head.

"I want him around as much as I want him to leave," I admitted quietly. "I want him to go, to be safe, to not have a warrant on him because of me. In the same breath, I want him to stay. A fiery prick he may be, but he's grown on me and I . . . I don't want to lose him. Especially not to the dragons."

Nevaeh's eyes softened. "So tell him that. All of that."

"He pulls away, Nevaeh. He tugs me closer to him, lets me in, and then literally shoves me away. I don't know what he's been through, but I don't know how to help when he won't let me in. And then, I still haven't forgotten that kiss." I flicked my lighter open, lit the cigarette, and took a long pull. When I had exhaled the smoke, I said, "The way things are heading, he's going to shatter my heart."

"Aw, Reagan." Nevaeh leaned her head on my shoulder. "You really like this guy, huh?"

I paused, considered. Tarik . . . He filled most of my waking thoughts, even when I tried to focus them elsewhere. I should have fled in terror when he attacked Alec, when I saw how primal his anger could be. When I saw his limbs shaking with rage, the fury a blazing flame in his green eyes. Instead, I felt the opposite. That anger had all been channeled into protecting me and, minutes later, when I had asked more of him, he hadn't hesitated. He had flipped to that vulnerable side I wanted to coax out. Because I needed him. Needed the comfort of knowing he was okay. That *I* was okay.

I needed him.

And I knew what Nevaeh was really asking, that she wasn't merely talking about friendship. The question was as laden as the ones that sprang into my own mind, turning over every facet of every interaction I'd had with Tarik. But good or bad, my answer was still the same.

"Yeah," I admitted finally. "Yeah, I do."

"So tell him."

"And get pushed away?" She nudged my arm, a do-it-anyway jab I was all too familiar with. "Nevaeh, you're better at this stuff. I can't. I'm not like you."

She nodded, purple locks spilling onto my shoulder. "No, you're not. You care more, about everyone and everything. And if you tell him how you feel and he walks away? He's a fool, and you're better off."

I stared at the wisp of smoke dancing off the end of my cigarette. "Yeah, maybe."

Even I didn't believe the words. I was too deep into this now to really feel like I would be better off; I rarely felt true, unbridled fear, and after Alec attacked I had run straight to Tarik. I didn't know what to do with that. What was happening to me? I was the big bad Night Enforcer. I didn't need people. Maybe Nevaeh, but I hadn't initiated that friendship. She had latched onto me, and after a time, I refused to let her go. But I had grown used to disappointment. Emotions were more easily managed when you didn't pour all of them into people who simply crushed them in return.

Now Tarik was in my life. This foreign entity. This challenger who drew out my sarcasm but constantly needed rescuing—as much from himself as from the problems that came with knowing me. And, truthfully, he had done his fair share of crushing too. Yet, he was also a solid force at my side when I really needed him. He was the person who, with a touch, could send all my bravery plummeting into my stomach. Who would literally dive in front of a dragon to keep me safe.

Nevaeh squeezed my hand, as though she could read my thoughts, before she left me alone to sort out the tangled strands of my mind. Of one thing I was fairly certain—I wasn't going to tell Tarik anything.

"Is there anything I can do to help?"

Tarik paused in his task to glance at me. "Um, no. Just lay low, we've got this." Beside him, Caspar opened his mouth, but Tarik gripped the large Fae's shoulder, silencing him with a look. "We gotta go to a meeting, actually. See you later."

"But Tarik—"

He kept walking. I clenched my jaw, frowning.

A week. I had been stuck here in the Fae Safehouse for a week. Tarik was off helping the rebels with who knew what, while I sat here smoking and twiddling my thumbs. Even when I had poked at them to give me tasks to do, they had brushed me off. Encouraged me to stay hidden. *Safe.* I couldn't take the boredom anymore. There had to be *something* I could do. Tarik's face was plastered all over the city, not mine, and I was shoved into a box?

I inhaled a sharp breath and reined in my anger. His work with the rebellion wasn't what frustrated me, not really, and I knew that. He had avoided me all week too. Wouldn't so much as glance in my direction most of the time, and when he did? Not a word. He hadn't spoken to me in days. I was stuck on a wheel, running and running, going nowhere.

My fist slammed into the wall and I hissed at the sting of

pain. If no one would give me any direction, I would make my own. Sitting around certainly wasn't helping me take my mind off the situation. Off *him.*

In a recent meeting, Rebel Leader mentioned that Mordecai had loosened Alec's reins. He was terrorizing Fae for no reason, many now too scared to do anything beyond working and hurrying home. Their supplies, food and otherwise, always ran low. I couldn't imagine the limited schedules had helped that situation.

Sure, Alec hated the Fae, probably more so now, but I couldn't help wondering if he was trying to distract us from worse plans. Mordecai wasn't the type to simply stop when he failed. Maybe I could find out what he was up to, waylay the dragons from finding the Fae. At the very least, I had to get out of here, even for an hour or two. I couldn't stand feeling so damned useless.

Not like anyone would notice if I was gone.

I was being bitter and petty and obnoxious.

With a huff, I glanced down. The Fae had given me clothing—of course—as soon as we had stepped through the door. But they were bulky and long, clothing tailored for much taller bodies. The fabric hung off my limbs. *I'm wearing a tent.* I picked through the kitchen drawers, but there didn't seem to be anything I could use to modify the clothing. *Hands it is.*

I tore off the majority of the thin linen shirt. Sleeves, stomach, collar—the parts that would make rapid-shifting nearly impossible if I was caught and needed to escape. I left a bit, enough that Tarik could restrain his clothing frenzy.

Ugh. Tarik.

I need to get out of here.

No familiar faces were around as I slipped out the door. I shouldn't be surprised; they were busy, even if I didn't know exactly with what. But today . . . today, I would help.

While they were off gallivanting around, I was going to check on the Fae that bordered the shifter districts. I couldn't get too close to The Pit—Alec apparently kept near-constant watch on the building these days, circling at random intervals. I wasn't sure why. Neither Tarik nor I had any friends who frequented that cesspit.

Stop thinking about him.

The path I took into the city might be familiar but I couldn't remember a time when I felt more out of place—the moon in the daytime sky, exactly where I belonged but still not quite right. Strange, the change of tide, considering I had once strode about without regard to where I fit. I treated the city like I owned the place—and part of me wondered if I still could have, if I had killed Mordecai. I should have. Everything would be easier, and I could deal with the guilt of murdering an unarmed, pleading man later. On my own.

I thought I was so strong. Virtually untouchable, in the ways that mattered.

But look at me now.

My fate, and the Fae's, clenched in the fist of a man I could have simply ended. In either case, decisions had been made. Too late to turn back now. I shook my head, lengthening my hair into my lion's mane. Thick and white. The bright Fae clothing should keep people from recognizing me immediately, even with my visible tattoos, but if I could lower the odds I certainly would.

Loading up on supplies took all of five minutes, and I paid

with a wad of cash I had grabbed before leaving my penthouse. Virtually untraceable. The routine was like clockwork—the same aisles, the same supplies I had bought so many times before. Doing supply drops for the Fae had always made me feel like I was taking a step in the right direction. They were worth the risk.

But even with that certainty in my mind, when the cashier did a double take my heart burst into motion, pounding against my ribs. She finished bagging the groceries, though, and didn't look up again. My fists slowly unclenched.

After I was finally concealed in the shadows of the alley, I shook my hair back out. If only my clothing didn't scream "fugitive." A glance at the bags on my arms, though, and my stomach flooded with warmth that pushed aside my fear and relaxed the tension that lingered in my shoulders.

The matter of navigating back through the city and dividing up the supplies took maybe an hour. My confidence was up, my heart full, when I heard the loud whoosh of dragon wings behind me.

Damnit.

I ducked into an alley, tucking myself into the shadows. Blood pulsed in my ears. Alec never patrolled this far into Fae territory. While I knew I could face him hand-to-hand, a wave of shame still rolled over me from our last encounter. I had failed, miserably, and cowering in the shadows was my penitence.

When the wings passed over, I waited several long seconds before I crept to the next building. Alec circled around again. Damnit, how many times a day did he do this? The game of cat-and-mouse continued for several more minutes as I inched closer to the Fae Safehouse, trying to still my trembling limbs. His circles grew so persistent at one point that I hunkered down in the shaded area next to a weathered shanty, prepared to wait him out.

A low voice broke the silence beside me, making me jump. "Mind explaining what you're doing out here?"

I whirled, shoulders sagging in relief when I met familiar green eyes staring down at me. Then I noted his rigid stature, arms tight over his chest, and the feeling was gone. I frowned. "Not at all. I was bored. Now shoo."

Tarik's left brow ticked upward as he slowly uncrossed his arms. "Bored? *Shoo?* Did you forget that the shifter circling above us is looking for *you?* And don't forget what he'll do if he finds you." A deep crease formed between his brows at that.

My teeth ground together. "Thanks for the reminder, I'd completely forgotten. But I've been out here for a couple hours, and I'm still alive. You did your duty, I'm clearly safe. You can leave again." I held my ground even as my chest tightened, sliding past him to take advantage of a break in Alec's circles. I crept closer to the Safehouse. Tarik's footsteps trailed me though, and I sighed.

"You can't waltz around this city thinking no one will recognize you," he said. "There's a *reward.* Even people you thought you could trust might turn you in for a few coins. *Think*, Reagan. You're not safe on these streets, not even in the Fae district."

My emotions spiraled through a quick one-eighty. *Arrogant, irritating prick.* He only ever showed up when he felt like it. Or when I was in peril, like he could sense I was in danger, like he gravitated to trouble. Well I sure as hell wasn't going to play his damsel in distress. I could see the last building before the Safehouse now—so close.

Pausing, I debated the cost before I snapped, "All I've done for days is *think*, Tarik. I can't sit around by myself all the time. I'm bored and miserable. But then again, I guess the only way you'd notice something so trivial is if I managed to be in danger at the same time."

Conflict roiled in my stomach. Part of me wanted to ask why he only showed up when I needed him. Why not before, why not after? I inhaled, then blew out a breath to expel my growing nausea.

When I moved forward again, he doggedly followed me, a splash of annoyance coloring his words now. "You have Nevaeh. And I've seen how several of the Fae children in the Safehouse respond to you. I *do* notice. But I'm . . . busy."

I sighed. Relentless, and missing the point. Why couldn't he leave me alone? Hell, I should have stayed in the Safehouse. He definitely wouldn't have bothered me there. I could have shut down my riotous emotions, turned off the feelings that bloomed in my stomach whenever he was near. Tarik was pain—and trouble—waiting to happen. And if I had stayed behind, I could have started to repair the damage he had already caused.

Instead of saying any of that, though, I said, "I love the children, but I can't sit and wait for you all to take care of my family problems." I snorted at the thought of Mordecai and Alec actually being my family, but pressed on. "Even Nevaeh has things to do. I'm dead weight. So I found a way to help. But I mean, you're right. At least she's spoken to me. Busy or not."

Behind me, he sighed—or huffed. I couldn't tell. "Let Rebel

Leader deal with your *family*. That's what we've been working so tirelessly on. If you need something to do, ask and we'll put you to work. Somewhere *safe*." He paused, and I thought he was done, then, "I wanted to talk to you, but . . . I can't."

I froze, hung up on his emphasis of the word safe. That was the problem, though. Safe didn't fix problems. I didn't want to be safe if that meant hiding away, locked in a cage. I shivered, carefully considering my words. Replaying his vague excuse. Finally, I shook my head in frustration. "Nah. Not today, Tarik. I'm not playing this game with you anymore."

I slipped over the last little gap to safety and slid inside, slamming the door behind me. My heart thundered in my ears, my breathing uneven. I couldn't keep riding his emotional teeter totter. If I caved today, the back and forth would never end.

The door whooshed open and in stormed a scowling Tarik. He marched up, glaring down his nose at me. "Did you seriously slam the door in my face? What game are *you* playing at? Because I'm supposed to be the one with the nasty temper, not you."

"I don't play games, Tarik. That's why this stupid little back and forth we do? I'm done playing."

Shock morphed his expression and he took a step back. "What?"

"This thing we have going on"—I gestured between us, ignoring the burn behind my eyes—"is harmful and unhealthy. I'm done. With it. With *you*. Done."

He straightened, shoulders stiffening. For several seconds he simply blinked as if dazed, then slowly said, "I don't—There's nothing going on, Reagan."

"I—" My voice caught and, unbidden, tears slipped free. I

furiously wiped them away and clenched my jaw.

After a moment, words spilled from me, angry and raw. "You heard me. I can't do this. I can't have you ignore me for days at a time because you don't know what you want from me. I can't have you showing up in my life when the timing is convenient, or when you think you can save me. And to what end? Because it suits your fancy? Or because you're *worried*, whatever that means to you. You pull me close and push me away in the same breath, and here we are again. You've shoved me away for a week, but the second, *the second* I do something you don't like, here you are, trying to keep a leash on me when the rest of the time you don't even seem to want me around."

I balled my hands into fists—angry at him, angry that I couldn't stop crying, angry that more words escaped my lips before I could stop them. "I care about you, Tarik. Like really care, in a way that makes my knees weak and my stomach flutter and my chest tighten."

Choking in a breath, I said, "But I don't let people into my life, because they do *this*. This back and forth. People take and take, and I'm *so* tired. I don't have enough pieces left to give if I want to keep standing. My life is too complicated right now as it is. I can't do this with you anymore."

Planning to squeeze past him, I took a step forward, only for my traitorous mouth to open one last time. For the words I had been holding in to spill out, for everything—every emotion, every heartache—to be laid at his feet. "You kissed me—kissed me like I was *nothing*. And all the while, I can't stop thinking about you. All day, every day, all the time. All I've really wanted this week was for you to be there, even once, to talk so I'd know what you're thinking. How *you* feel . . . if you're safe.

I'm driving myself crazy. But you don't seem to care. So you heard me. I'm done."

My jaw clenched as I shoved past him, opening the door and slipping into the city again. I didn't care if I was caught. I was pretty sure that baring my soul to Tarik hurt me more than Mordecai or death ever could.

Maybe Mordecai was right.

Maybe love is pain.

CHAPTER 21

Tarik

I didn't go after her.

I couldn't. My intestines were on the floor. At least, I was fairly sure they were. Her words had ripped me open, leaving a gaping hole behind. And an ache unlike any I'd ever felt before. I had screwed up. I had screwed up bad. I hadn't realized she'd started to reciprocate my growing feelings toward her. The feelings I trampled again and again in hopes that they'd eventually disintegrate.

And now I'd trampled *her.*

A hand squeezed my heart and I embraced the pain. Let myself feel every bit of that piercing agony, because I deserved to. I deserved to rot in hell for what I had done to her.

For a split second, relief swamped me, relief that she felt as I felt. But the feeling was savagely replaced with shame. And guilt. I didn't deserve her.

She's not your girl.

"I know," I muttered. I knew what I wanted—I knew with a fiery passion—but I couldn't have it. I couldn't have *her.*

Destruction followed me wherever I went. She didn't deserve that. I would never be good enough for someone like her. So kind and giving. So innocent.

She had wanted something from me. *Me*, the screw-up with a short fuse. In a world surrounded by men whose only goals were to use her, she needed someone who would give instead of take. Who would give her their heart. Gaia, she wanted *my* heart.

But I couldn't give her something I didn't have.

She's not your girl.

"I know!" I roared and punched the door frame, pain jolting up my arm.

"After what that girl said, are you really going to let her walk away?"

I whirled, blinking as Rebel Leader strolled toward me, hands in his pockets. I still couldn't believe I was under the same roof as him again. And in one piece. I had expected at least one of his sons to take a shot at me for all the terrible things I said after I'd left. His name wasn't actually Rebel Leader—we only called him that to protect his identity on the rare occasions he left the Safehouse. I avoided speaking his real name either way. It made the distance I'd created between us over the years more bearable.

I inhaled through the pain consuming my chest, saying, "You heard all that?"

He nodded and pulled his hands free as he sunk onto the stairs, placing elbows on bent knees. "You two were pretty loud." He chuckled, patting the stair next to him. An invitation to talk. Something I had planned to avoid until my dead corpse turned to dust. "Come on, Tarik. I can't stand seeing you like this anymore."

My lips pinched together. There was no way I'd share my problems with him. No way—

"Like what?" I clenched my teeth. Stupid, idiot mouth.

"Like a mountain crushed you, yet you still found a way to shoulder the weight. Like you think you deserve to carry that burden for the rest of eternity. Your penance."

I couldn't endure his all-knowing gaze a moment longer. I stared at his bare feet. "I *do* deserve it."

"Why?"

I blew out a frustrated sigh, glaring up at him. "You know why."

His expression clouded, eyes growing distant. "So that's what this is about," he whispered. For a moment, he looked lost. Then his face cleared. "After all these years, you haven't forgiven yourself."

The statement was so abrupt, so certain, that I sputtered, "Wh-what?"

"You haven't forgiven yourself for that night—the night they took Leilani from us."

At the mention of her name, I flinched, hunching under the weight it pressed down on me. Anger bubbled beneath my skin. Anger that he would so casually dredge up her memory. My eyes narrowed to slits. "Would *you?*" I snapped. "Would you forgive yourself for not being there when she needed you most? For letting her suffer under the hands of those foul, disgusting beasts while you stood there and watched it happen?"

My voice had risen to a shout, arms shaking with rage. But his expression was the exact opposite of mine. Sad.

"Tarik," he said softly. "You didn't stand there. You fought to save her with everything you had and were barely alive when we found you—we didn't even recognize you. But for days and weeks afterward, you didn't let anyone tend your wounds because of the guilt. And when you look at your scars, evidence of the injustice you yourself faced, you see them as failure. Your burden and shame to endure forever."

He stood then, and my heart pumped so hard a wave of nausea swept over me. Slowly approaching, as if knowing I was about to disappear like I'd done three years ago and every day since, he continued. "But none of that is true. You don't have to carry the burden of her death anymore. Let go, Tarik, or you will never leave this hell on earth you've created for yourself."

Carefully, he reached out and clasped my shoulder, that soulful gaze seeing into the very heart of me. My eyes burned when his filled with unchecked tears. My voice shook, but the words needed to be said. "She'd be alive if not for me. If I'd come home on time, she wouldn't have worried and gone out looking. I—I killed your daughter."

"No," he said firmly, even as tears tracked down his cheeks. "No one could have stopped that. Sometimes evil wins the day. Sometimes—" He stopped, dragging in air. "She wouldn't want you to suffer this way. She'd want you to *live*. She'd want you to chase after that girl you let slip through the door because, Tarik, she'd want you to be *happy*."

My tears finally spilled. They fell in droves and I couldn't stop them.

Leilani's father drew me into his embrace and I stopped fighting. I allowed the tears to soothe the rage heating my blood, a balm to the guilt and shame I had inflicted on myself. The pain was still there, the ache of losing someone too soon, but the torture I'd put myself through . . . washed away.

"I did fail you in one huge way, Tarik," he said, voice muffled where his mouth rested on my shoulder. "I never told you that I'd forgiven you. That I never blamed you. When you left, I thought you needed space to cope with the pain. I'm sorry, my son. I'm sorry you carried this burden on your own."

We stayed that way for several minutes, soaking in the silence. Healing. My mouth opened, then closed. Opened again. "Thank you, Liam."

He chuckled and I frowned, pulling back. His eyes were ringed in red, but . . . *lighter* as he said, "I haven't heard you say that in three long years."

I huffed a weak laugh, dragging a sleeve across my face. "What, 'thank you' or your name?"

"Both." He laughed. I joined him, at first ashamed that I was laughing so soon after remembering Leilani. But I set the feeling aside and allowed myself to feel something new: peace. I took a breath, filling my lungs to capacity. The air tasted different. Sweet. Clean.

He clapped my shoulder again and gave me a shake. "Now, enough of the past. I'm not going to stand by and watch you ruin your future. And that's exactly what you'll be doing if you don't exit through that door in the next few seconds."

My heart rate picked up. Reagan. "But—"

His hands gripped both my shoulders now, squeezing. "Don't make me look like a fool, boy. I placed a sizable bet on you two getting together, and I will *not* lose."

I choked on a laugh. "Bet? With *what?* It's not like you have any money."

"Chores," he growled. "I have to clean the dishes and scrub

the toilets for three months if I lose."

Gross.

"You're cracked, old man."

"I'm going to crack your idiot skull wide open if you don't get out of here in five seconds. Now go!" He shoved, sending me staggering back.

I shook my head, walking backward. "Have you been working out, pops?"

"Three seconds!"

Smirking, I yanked the door open and bolted into the dusky evening, my heart filled to bursting. Just as quickly, I jerked to a stop, heart sinking. Reagan. I had no idea where to find her. She could be anywhere. Searching the immediate surroundings, I spied her friend, Nevaeh, lounging on a stairwell as she smoked.

She pointed north. "She went to the old ruins. Look for a collapsed building that has a three-headed mermaid painted on the side." As I stepped in that direction, she added, "Oh, and Tarik? If you break her heart, I know where you sleep."

I thanked her, then took off at a jog, betting she would follow through with that threat. How did she know who I'd been looking for? Was I that obvious? Maybe to everyone but Reagan, that is. I stuck to the growing shadows, keeping both ears open for the boom of dragon wings. The *last* thing I wanted right now was an Alec confrontation. Without Reagan holding me back, I didn't know if I could restrain myself from killing him. Or maybe I'd settle for tearing off his—

All thoughts switched off as I caught sight of her. She was tucked into a dark corner shielded by the partially collapsed floor above, perched on a heap of filthy rubble, her body curled into a ball. My chest tightened to the point of pain. I couldn't breathe. I couldn't do this. Straightening, I forced my legs to carry me toward her, up and over debris, around potholes. I halted a few yards away, unable to close the gap.

She must have heard my approach. I didn't want to spook her, so I'd been extra loud. But she didn't lift her head from her raised knees.

My pulse hammered in my throat as I struggled with what to say. How could I undo all the damage I had caused? She probably hated me now. *I* would hate me now. I would have kicked myself in the balls, if that were possible.

I took a tentative step forward and her shoulders stiffened. I froze. Would she run? Would she flee this city and never come back? At the thought, pain lanced my stomach and I gasped for air. No, she couldn't leave. She had grown on me. Had burrowed beneath my skin. When she smiled, warmth bloomed inside me. When she laughed, I burst alive.

She needed to stay.

I needed her to stay.

Because I—

"I need her," I whispered. A sigh shuddered through me. Admitting that out loud gave me the courage I normally lacked. The strength to take a step, then another, until I was carefully lowering myself beside her. And now the hard part. The part I had failed at again and again.

The bravery to be vulnerable.

To bare my scarred and bleeding soul.

"She died three years ago," I started softly, haltingly. A decided tremble shook my voice, but I wouldn't stop. Couldn't. "Right before she died, I found her. She was . . . she was naked.

And alone. No one to save her from the pack of shifters intent on—"

The image flashed before me and I jerked, unable to breathe. Somehow, past a closed throat, I forced the words out anyway. "The shifters overwhelmed me, too. Made me watch as—as they brutalized her. Raped her. And then, when it was over, they beat me to within an inch of my life. Shredded my wings with their talons, leaving me naked and broken in that accursed alley outside The Pit. I'm sure they thought I'd die, too."

Reagan stirred next to me, but didn't speak. I was relieved that she didn't—I might not be able to finish otherwise. Plowing shaky hands through my hair, I continued. "But I didn't die, even though for three years I wished that I had. When you found me in the alley that night, bloodied and beaten, I thought that would be the end. I wanted it to be, but . . ."

My breath hitched. "But you saved me. And then, despite everything I did to discourage you, you saved me again. From there, I was lost. I was torn up with guilt over destroying my girlfriend's life and not being there when she needed me most. I was also struggling with feelings I didn't know I could still possess."

I inched closer, letting my knee brush against her thigh. "Reagan, I didn't—I didn't want to destroy *your* life, too. I'm bad luck. *Was* bad luck. I'm—I'm seeing now that maybe . . . maybe I wasn't seeing things clearly. That maybe I feared getting close because I didn't want to lose you, too." I stopped, chest heaving. The air was thin, thinning still. So many words, so many feelings dropped into the unknown void. I was naked before her, more vulnerable than I'd ever remembered feeling.

And I didn't know.

I didn't know if my words were too late.

"I'm sorry," Reagan said, her voice muffled against her bent knees. "Losing someone you care about in passing hurts badly enough. I couldn't imagine losing someone I loved, and carrying that guilt for so long. I'm so sorry."

Her words gutted me yet again. I had dropped my sorrows into her lap and didn't once apologize for all the wrongs I'd done her.

I didn't deserve her or her forgiveness.

But . . .

If I walked away right now, I'd regret it for the rest of my life.

I moved, knelt in front of her. I still couldn't see her face—didn't know if she wanted me to leave—but I opened my mouth and held nothing back.

"I hurt you. I hurt you so much. I thought that by pushing you away, I was saving you from me. That you'd be better off. But I couldn't stay away. I came back again and again, hurting you more and more. Reagan," I choked out her name, not caring that tears were falling again. I didn't want to lose her. I would cry a million tears if only she'd look up at me one more time.

Just once.

"Please, Reagan. I'm sorry. I'm sorry for kissing you like you meant nothing. I'm sorry for shoving you away over and over. You aren't nothing. You're *everything*. But I didn't think—I didn't think I deserved you." I paused, heaving in air through a raw throat.

And in that pause, she looked up and met my eyes. Only for

a moment, but one was enough.

Then she moved.

Throwing her arms around my shoulders, she buried her face in my neck.

A shuddering sigh shook my entire body and I clutched at her, fumbling, grasping, until she firmly rested in my arms, going nowhere. *Ever again.*

We stayed that way a minute.

Two.

I would stay for however long she wanted.

CHAPTER 22

Reagan

The soft sizzle of bacon filled my ears. I leaned my hip against the stove and casually poked at the long strips of meat with a pair of tongs. A soft pop made me jump, shaking me from my thoughts. The burn never came, though, and I narrowed my eyes. There were small benefits to clothing, even if I would never admit it to a certain Fae.

Bacon for breakfast was Tarik's idea; when Akeno and Nevaeh ran for supplies this morning, Tarik had asked them to grab a package. The moment I woke up he asked me to cook it, saying the others needed to try the glory that I had introduced him to.

Now he sat, shooting glances at me in between slowly prodding Sebastian's glass of orange juice closer and closer to the edge of the table they occupied.

While I waited for the slices to darken, I pulled my cigarette case from my pocket, gripping the end of one between my teeth before I tucked the case away. I hadn't shifted since we left the penthouse, and the feeling was starting to gnaw at me; we needed to shift regularly or the animal might pop out, regardless of what we wanted.

Maybe this afternoon I could slip outside and shift for a few minutes—I didn't need to accidentally become a lion in the Safehouse and terrify the innocent Fae. I flicked my lighter to life. The end glowed bright as I inhaled, slowly releasing the smoke. Better. The shifting tension eased.

A second later, the cigarette was plucked from my mouth.

"House rules," Tarik said in my ear, tapping the cig end on a paper towel. The towel started smoking and he jabbed the cigarette against the kitchen counter several times, swearing softly. "Besides, all that smoke isn't good for your body."

My wings pressed hard against my spine, white hair spilling into my eyes. I shook my head and inhaled, focused on stopping the transition. When blue and black strands fell over my shoulder again, I smirked. "You know what's not good for your body? Taking a cigarette from an edgy shifter."

He looped a strand of my hair around his finger and tugged. "I'll risk it." Then he was gone.

"What are we risking?" Caspar asked. He leaned against the door frame, the electronic chirp of an arcade game blaring out of the handheld his eyes were locked on.

"Entire limbs, if Tarik's not careful."

"Do you have to play that noisy thing so early in the morning?" Tarik grumbled from the table, adding, "It's not natural."

"Yes," Caspar shot back. "Just to annoy you." He grinned, but dropped into a chair and rested the device on the table. "So when do we eat? And what are we eating?" He sniffed the air. "Smells good, whatever it is."

"Something that'll change your life," Tarik said. "And put hair on your chest. Or, in your case, more hair."

I nudged a strip of bacon, deeming the piece finished, and dropped it onto a paper towel beside me. Tarik was there in a flash, snatching the piece even as I warned him he would burn himself. He rounded on his first target, Sebastian, who had been stoically ignoring us as he flipped the pages of his book.

"Hey, man, you *have* to try this," Tarik said, waving the strip in front of Sebastian's face.

Startled, the blond Fae snapped the book shut. Sniffed. "That does smell—wait, is that leather?"

Tarik guffawed before he broke a piece off and slowly bit down with a crackling crunch. "That's what I said too. Meat tastes a lot better than it looks, I swear. Try a piece."

This time, he stuck the remaining portion under Sebastian's nose and the blond leaned away, hands raised. But Tarik was relentless, tracking his movements with the bacon. Finally, his victim shot out of his chair and inched backward. "Look, no offense to the shifters in this room, but the thought of eating meat makes me want to hurl. I'll stick with fruits and vegetables."

"I'll try your meat, Tarik," one of the twins said, a sly grin curving his lips as he elbowed his look-alike.

"This is an adults-only experience, Micah," Tarik said, pointing the bacon at him. "Wait another year." The twins protested loudly as Tarik took another bite, chewing noisily.

Nevaeh brushed past the small crowd gathering in the doorway, rolling her eyes and tossing her gum in the trash bin. Hopping up on the counter, she watched me impatiently as I dropped one strip after another onto the paper towel, snitching two before Tarik could beat her to them. His eyes narrowed. She shrugged. "Too slow." Her eyes scanned the room. "Anyone else gonna eat, or are Tarik and I going to battle for the bacon?"

A long beat of silence passed. Akeno eyed her warily, his jaw opening, then clamping shut like he couldn't decide, when Elias said, "I will." Sebastian lowered his hands, eyes wide. The twins fell silent, and even Caspar tore his attention away from his game for a moment. Elias looked around, then shrugged. "What? I trust Tarik. Maybe it's time for change. Maybe we've been missing out on something amazing all these years."

An emotion flickered across Tarik's face. His throat bobbed. I wagged a strip of bacon toward him, gripped between the tongs. He slipped the piece free and strode over to Elias, pulling him into a tight hug. "I missed you, man. Now eat this while it's hot. It's the only way."

He did, and the surprised delight that lit his face encouraged the others on. At one point Flynn passed through the room, his expression blank, utterly oblivious to the chaos of several Fae men now trying to gang up on poor Sebastian. Even Nevaeh joined in, prodding Akeno and Caspar to pin him down. I turned my back to finish cooking the last of the package when a shout rang out, and Sebastian bolted from the room.

"Tarik, Elias, I'm warning you," Sebastian yelled, sliding around a corner with both men hot on his tail. From the next room, he roared, "Get that thing away from me."

"You'll never be the same, Seb," Tarik practically crowed. "Just one bite!"

I shifted, laying myself out on my side with my wings

tucked carefully behind me. After our eventful morning, I insisted Tarik let me go out for air; the sweet morning breeze was positively glorious after the heat of the kitchen. The sun warmed my fur enough to stave off a real chill and I stretched my claws, a low rumble of contentment rolling from my throat. My mind dimmed, falling to the cusp of a nap when I heard the door snap shut.

Someone gasped dramatically and I raised my head enough to see Tarik approaching, hand clasped to his chest. "You gave me a fright. For a second there I thought you were a real lion. Then I reasoned, no, lions aren't usually so pigment challenged. You're getting the hang of it, though. But be careful not to stay out too long or you'll get sunburnt."

I lowered my head to the grass, loosing a growl.

"Really?" A huff. "Fine." He plopped down next to me. My side twitched where he rested his head, then adjusted himself into a more comfortable position.

Tickles.

I crossed one of my paws over the other, relaxing into a sun-stupor. My eyes drifted closed, breaths slowing, nap in sight.

"I need to tell you something." At the interruption, my eyes slid open, narrowing. "Can you shift?"

Another low growl vibrated out of me. I swatted him lightly with a paw, my tail flicking in annoyance. *Shhh, Tarik, nap time,* I wanted to say.

"Reagan." I ignored him. "Reagan, this is important." Another tail flick.

All went silent and my mind switched off. A light caress ran the length of my rear paw—my leg jerked. The tickling continued and I batted at the intrusion. Warm air blew in my ear, making it flick back and forth. I groaned.

"Come out, Reagan. I know you're in there."

With a huff of frustration, I shifted. The moment my vocal chords were human, I scoffed, "What do you think happens when I shift? A lion flies in and eats me?" With a frown, I added, "I'm not a common house cat you know. I am fierce. *Fierce.*"

He smirked down at me. "Sure you are. And my tiny Fae brain has a hard time understanding how a large cat is curled up inside your little—" His words cut off as his gaze trailed over my naked body.

I reached out a finger, tilting his chin up. "It's skin. Focus. You interrupted my attempt at a nap. This better be important." I considered, then added, "And I mean, shifting doesn't tickle. Having your bones extended and snapped into new locations is actually kind of painful. If you wondered."

Grimacing, he said, "I wondered, but now I have a clear visual. Thanks for that." He shuddered. "So does your brain become a lion's too when you"—his finger twirled in the air—"do that thing you do?"

Rolling my eyes, I sighed. "No. Not usually, anyway. Mordecai used to tell me stories about shifters whose animals took control when there was no other way for them to survive." A shiver rolled down my spine. "I don't care to find out if there's any truth to them."

Tarik gave his head a small shake, then huffed a laugh. "Wow. Well, let's hope a day never comes when you see me as prime rib." Jumping to his feet, he reached a hand down. "And it is important. Come with me."

I sighed. Goodbye, delicious sunshine. Goodbye, nap. I accepted the hand that was offered, following him inside.

A few steps in, he stopped abruptly. "Uh, wait here," he said, dashing outside and quickly returning with the clothes I had forgotten about. "You might want to put these on."

Inhaling, I released a long breath. Today was exhausting already. Whatever he was up to, I seriously considered shifting and returning to my attempted nap. *Let him try to drag a lion away.* At least my shifter nature wasn't trying to burst out of my skin now. But I relented, tugging the clothing on. "This better be worth the effort."

He chuckled. "I hope so, too. I don't want to become catnip."

I turned in his direction, slowly running my gaze down the length of him and back up. "You still might."

His brows rose in surprise. A beat later, his lips tipped up, and he leaned in close, whispering, "Is that a promise?"

Warmth hit my cheeks and I leaned closer. "And if it is?"

He erased the space between us, breath tickling my ear. "If it is . . . you'll have to catch me first."

I growled loudly as he disappeared around the corner. *Prick.* But I grinned, glancing at the empty kitchen before I stepped into the dining room. Rebel Leader had set out picnic tables instead of more traditional seating—kid-friendly and seated more people, he had said. The concrete walls were plastered with children's art, one of the few things he encouraged them to "destroy." Nevaeh spent hours with them when she could, teaching them to paint and draw.

The rest of the room beyond had been made into a communal lounge—couches, recliners, and a single television dotted the space. A few Fae waved as I passed, a couple tilting their heads pointedly in the direction of the covered garden out back. I grinned and nodded my thanks before I stepped outside, pausing to admire the handiwork.

Rebel Leader had done really well by this garden. The top was concealed so that nosy dragons couldn't see in, but the space was still open enough that sunlight poured through. The plants grew in plethora. Despite my aversions, I couldn't help but appreciate the beauty—even in the vegetables. I spied a bobbing head of red hair behind the tomato vines and slid around the corner. Tarik sat cross-legged and met my eyes as he took a bite out of a giant tomato.

I gagged, turning away. "No, ugh. You're tainted catnip now. Your loss, sorry." I swallowed hard before I glanced back over my shoulder.

He stopped chewing, eyes round with shock. Then burst out laughing. A thin trail of tomato juice dribbled down his chin and my stomach lurched. Finally, after a full minute of rolling on the ground, he said, "For that, I'm putting you on tomato-picking duty. Say hello to your new job."

"I can pick them but please don't make me eat them." I gagged again, sticking my tongue out for effect.

His face turned serious. "I'm sorry, Reagan, but I can't promise that. You see, Fae have this ritual. One involving tomatoes and shot glasses."

My hand fell to my fluttering stomach. "If I puke, I'm aiming for you."

He scrambled off the ground. "Noted. Good thing I was joking about the shot glasses. There may actually be a bathtub involved."

I dry-heaved, pleased when he had the decency to look slightly concerned. "What are we actually doing out here?"

"Well, I was serious about putting you on tomato-picking duty, but more like garden duty. You said you didn't have anything to do, so I asked if they'd let you help here. Outside seems to be your preference, so . . ." He spread his arms wide. "Here we are."

I met his eyes and held them for a long moment. This time when my stomach fluttered, the cause was very different. The corner of my lips rose. "This is perfect. Thank you."

He smiled softly. "You might not be thanking me when you pick a rotten tomato and guts splatter all over your face."

"Are you speaking from experience?" I considered, nose wrinkling. "How do you even pick a tomato so poorly that . . . You know, never mind."

He sidled over to me, grin firmly in place, and bent his head down. "Good luck. Exploding tomatoes are no laughing matter." Then he strolled on by, whistling a merry tune.

I stepped from the shower, grateful for the removal of dirt and grime from helping in the garden all afternoon. Filling my day with work made the time go so much faster, and lightening the load of the Fae already working outside filled my soul with joy.

"The clothing though," I grumbled, tugging on another set of modified Fae clothes. Nevaeh had offered to retrieve a handful of mine, or to lend me hers, but on the off chance someone spotted me outside, I was much less noticeable in the Fae garb.

Still, this was one part of Fae life I would never adjust to. Why didn't they all want to run free, let the wind caress their skin . . .

A knock broke my train of thought. The showers were loosely communal, split by curtains. Any of the women could have come in. I dried my hair a touch more and slid the towel onto a rack before I pulled the door open—and met a wide-eyed boy and an ever-silent man. I had tried to crack Flynn—told him jokes, pried into his personal life. Nothing. Stoic as ever. Benji was the one who drew my attention though, tugging at my makeshift shorts.

"Tarik asked us to get my mom and bring her back here. Can you come help? I need to get Callie too, and"—he lifted his shoulders—"maybe you can keep her from escaping. Since you're a cat and all . . ."

I grinned, reaching out to ruffle his hair. "Sure, Benji, lead the way. Where's Tarik? Are you sure he's okay with this?"

"Rebel Leader pulled him away. They wouldn't tell me for what. But yeah, he's fine with you coming!"

"Oh, okay." I glanced up at Flynn, who lifted a shoulder and jerked his head in confirmation. "Well he probably had an important meeting, then. We'll help you, right Flynn?" The man's hazel eyes were locked onto my face, but he didn't reply. My brow furrowed. "That's creepy. Seriously."

He shrugged. I frowned. One day I would crack this one. Tarik told me not to get my hopes up, but . . .

Benji had already disappeared around the corner. I cast another glance at the sullen Fae trailing me, but continued downstairs and out the front door. Lately, we had to check for Alec constantly. As the days went on with no word of my whereabouts, his patrols had become more frantic. Benji's home wasn't far though, and the sky was quiet. For now, at least.

Flynn ushered us inside the small apartment, sliding over to where Haven lay on the bed. He signaled to me, holding out a clean dress for her, and I nodded. While I helped her dress, he disappeared out the door, motioning for Benji to stay put. Haven glanced up at one point, her deep brown eyes the match to her son's.

"Where are you taking me?" Her voice was soft, weak. She seemed so frail beneath my hands, so light. I understood why Tarik felt like she was his responsibility. I didn't know her and I already wanted to protect her.

"The Fae Safehouse."

She struggled against my grip, pushing me back. "But this is my home."

I paused and sat down on the edge of her bed. She relaxed, relieved that I seemed to be relenting. Instead, I said quietly, "Why don't you want to go there?"

"I—I don't want to become someone else's burden. I'm fine here. Tarik checks on me at times."

"You're no one's burden, Haven," I said gently. "And if it helps, Tarik sent us."

"Where is he?" She tried to look past me. "Why didn't he come himself?"

"He's been really busy helping the other Fae. He didn't want you to be alone." The sound of dragon wings caught my ear. My heart bolted to life. We needed to get back. This wasn't safe. My thoughts flicked to Tarik, to the crystal. "Tarik might have found a way to help you, really help you. But he hasn't been able to slip away long enough to come down here. He'll bring you back home if you want, after he tries."

Haven stilled. As the booming sound passed overhead, my breaths quickened. I bit my lip, hoping against hope that Haven would come with us. She nodded. When the wing beats faded, Flynn barged through the door with Callie in his arms.

He motioned to the sky and I nodded. "Flynn's going to help you, Haven. I'm Reagan, by the way."

I traded places with Flynn, gripping Callie to my chest and grabbing Benji's hand.

"Have you got her?" Benji asked.

I nodded. "Stay with me outside, okay? Flynn will take good care of your mom."

"Okay!"

The second we stepped out the door, the whoosh of wings returned. Close, too close. I darted into a shadow, pulling Benji with me. Callie shrunk against my chest, as though she too knew we had to hide from that dragon.

We waited, silent until Alec passed again, then slid to the next set of shadows. Again and again. I didn't like how close the blue dragon had flown on the last round, but I held open the door to the Safehouse, breathing a sigh of relief when Flynn slipped past me.

Close. Too close.

CHAPTER 23

Tarik

She came in trembling, close to tears. I stopped what I was doing and went to her.

"Thanks, Flynn, I'll take her from here." The silent Fae nodded, carefully depositing Haven into my arms. She peered up at me, so many questions in those tired eyes, but words failed me. I knew she would hate being brought here, but at the moment, my worry was greater than her need for independence.

She could scold me all she liked when she was better. *If* she got better. The crystal practically burned in my pocket, fully charged. I could almost feel it tugging at me, asking to be used. And I would. I would drain all of the crystal's power before laying hands on the frail female before me.

Too long she had suffered. For three years, I'd watched her health decline, watched her skin stretch thin and bones break again and again. I hoped that today would be her last one filled with pain. That tomorrow, she would walk again without crying. Without breaking.

"You'll understand soon, Haven. Trust me," I whispered, but a tear of frustration slipped down her cheek anyway. I wordlessly communicated with Reagan to distract Benji, to keep him away from his mother while I attempted the impossible. If all went wrong, I didn't want him to see. In the back of my mind, I tucked away the knowledge that Reagan had left the Safehouse again. A cocktail of fear and anger swirled in my gut, but I shoved it down—for now. I would deal with that later.

There weren't many Fae in the living quarters this time of day, most at dinner, so when I lowered Haven onto an unused cot in the women's dorms, we were alone. As I fussed with the pillow beneath her head, she wouldn't look at me. Inwardly, I sighed. She was mad. Mad at *me*. I clenched my jaw, reminding myself to apologize later. But this had to be done, and now.

Come tomorrow, I didn't know where I'd be. If I'd be alive or dead. Or worse—a prisoner. When she was as comfortable as I could make her, I slipped the stone from my pocket, the familiar jolt of power zipping through my veins. I made sure Haven got a good look at the crystal. "See this? Only a week ago, this crystal healed my shattered bones."

Her eyes widened and she sank further into the pillow, as if to flee the green object. "Is it dangerous?"

I thought of Reagan, curled on the floor in agony as her wings tore from her back. Inhaling deeply, I blinked away the image. "No, because you won't be touching it. But I need to touch *you*. Will you . . . will you let me?" I'd never asked before. Shame twisted my gut. What if she didn't want to be healed?

"Of course, Tarik." When I looked at her, she smiled faintly. "You never have to ask. I know that you've been making me feel better all these years. Healed me, even. I don't know how, though. I've never seen a Fae do what you can, but . . ." Her eyes flicked to the crystal again.

But my healing attempts hadn't been enough. Maybe today, with the help of the Genesis Crystal, she would at last find relief.

When I laid a hand on her arm, the familiar weight of her ailments pressed down on me. So much damage. So much wrong. She was still young, barely in her thirties, yet she felt so old. With the crystal's strength coursing through me, I spread my magic throughout her body, seeking, mending.

What I hadn't been able to fix before, I was able to repair. Brittle bones became hard and smooth. Her skin regained elasticity, hiding a network of blue veins. A healthy flush stained her cheeks as the red blood cells in her body multiplied. Sweat beaded her forehead, but she kept silent.

Just when I dared hope she was healed, I felt the wrongness creep back in. It was like a disease attacking the good, healthy parts of her. Every time I repaired the damage, a new bad cell would pop up, slowly undoing my work. I bit back a growl of frustration.

Too soon, my magic depleted. Sweat slid down my neck as I slowly rose to my feet, exhaustion sweeping through me.

"Rest, Haven. I'll be back to check on you in the morning." Her eyes drifted shut before I'd finished the sentence, her expression almost peaceful. But as I quietly left the room, a fresh weight settled on my shoulders.

You failed.

"I know," I whispered.

Our new relationship dynamic was fragile, but I didn't seek Reagan out. I knew I should, but instead, I avoided her. And not only because she had left the Safehouse on a mission that could have exposed her to the dragons. My inability to fully heal Haven had left a bitter taste in my mouth, and I wanted to be alone. She had relied on me all these years and I'd failed her. I didn't think I'd ever have the strength to heal her completely, even with the crystal's help.

And so maybe I was wallowing. Pouting. Whatever.

But I needed space.

Reagan wouldn't find my hiding spot in the men's communal bathroom. I turned the shower on scalding hot, needing to cleanse away the sickness and hopelessness of another failed healing. As I stepped under the spray, I wished the water could melt away the helpless feeling in my gut. The feeling that Benji would soon be an orphan and there was nothing I could do to save him from that fate.

"So why exactly did you think I wouldn't want to know about this little adventure you've been planning?"

Startled, I knocked an elbow against the stall's tile. Then cursed under my breath. She found me. "Can we talk about this later, Reagan? I'm kind of busy right now." Thankfully the white shower curtain hid me from view.

"I mean, now seems as good a time as any." Her tone was clipped, agitated.

"Now isn't a good time for *me*," I ground out. Then reined in my riotous emotions. A little. "It's been a stressful day. Give me a minute?"

"Sure. One minute. I'll be outside." A short pause. "You've got to talk to me, Tarik. Trust me. Or this won't work."

"Yeah. Talking. Sure," I muttered. *Like the way you told me you were leaving the Safehouse again?* I chomped down on my tongue to keep the words from leaking out.

She left as soundlessly as she came, and I thunked my head on the tile. I had been dreading this conversation, so I'd put it off. I knew she'd be mad, but now I was too. Not a good combination. With a creak, I shut the water off and slowly towel-dried, donning my clothes. I would tell her, but I'd take my sweet time.

She was right outside the bathroom door, waiting. I breezed past her, heading for the stairs. "Let's walk and talk," I said over my shoulder. "I have to prepare. What have you heard and what do you want to know?"

"Wait—how is Haven?"

I grimaced. "Better. Now what have you heard?"

Reagan huffed. Oh, she was mad all right. "I've *heard* that you're planning to make a run for the mansion. And I want to know why you left me out of this plan."

Who had told? I swore under my breath. No one could keep their mouth shut in this place. I descended the stairs two at a time, leaving Reagan to scramble as she tried keeping pace with my longer strides.

"The last place you should be is under the same roof as Mordecai. This is simply a quick mission we've been planning. Grab as much crystal as we can and retreat before anyone's the wiser. We don't need you on this mission."

"Okay, but Mordecai is still my problem. I can help. I know that mansion better than any of you could ever hope to." She went silent for a moment. "I mean, do you even know where Mordecai's armory is? He added guards to the mansion's rotations. Are you going to be ready with dart guns as your only defense?"

I stopped dead in my tracks. Then picked up the pace again. No. She wouldn't weasel her way into this mission. "What armory?" Crap. I needed superglue.

"The one filled to bursting with weapons that you *need.* The one he locks. Luckily, I know where the key is. But I can't tell you everything, I suppose."

My teeth clenched. Evil girl. We didn't need weapons. Actually, we desperately did. Akeno's peashooters were almost useless in a fight—they'd done nothing against Bushy. We had our wings, but that was like bringing knives to a gunfight. Shifters rarely used weapons, but if there were armed guards . . .

Crap.

Landing on the ground floor, I wove through groups of Fae lounging and dining in the common areas. Some threw curious glances my way, probably wondering why the lion shifter tailed me like a cat sizing up its next scratching post, but I ignored them.

I wished Reagan understood I needed space right now. If she insisted on talking, then I needed to blow off steam before I verbally blew up at her. She might give up on me for good if I did that, so I banged open the doors to the rec room and strode to the far corner. Pulling on gloves, I said, "Reagan, you're not going."

She threw her hands on her hips. "Like hell I'm not."

I struck the punching bag, pretending the thick leather was my throat. If I couldn't breathe, I couldn't speak and say things I'd later regret. No such luck. "You're staying here where you're safe, and that's that."

Reagan laughed. "Oh, I'm sorry. For a minute there you seemed to think you have some kind of control over me. You can't stop me from going, Tarik."

"Oh yeah?" My eyes narrowed on her. "Call this settling the score for leaving the Safehouse in broad daylight without telling me first. No way are you going on another dangerous mission today. I'll tell Rebel Leader not to let you go." I threw another punch, harder this time.

"I specifically asked Benji if you were okay with me leaving and he said yes. He asked for help, do you really think I was going to say no?"

"What?" I caught the bag mid-swing so I could level her with an incredulous look. "I didn't tell him it was okay for you to leave."

"Regardless, I don't need your *permission* to do anything. Maybe you could use a reminder that I'm my own person." She scowled, crossing her arms over her chest. "In either case, that's between you and me. You shouldn't punish the others for it. A lion is awfully handy in a tight spot, especially when she knows more about what you're trying to do than you do."

"That may be, but I still can't let you go. There's . . . there's too much at stake." I gritted my teeth, hating how my words came out. Hating how she viewed me. But I couldn't seem to say what really needed to be said. "You can help the Fae best from here."

"I'm not some helpless little girl," Reagan spat, arms trembling. "I'm not going to sit here and wait for the men to solve all my problems. I'm going. I'll plead my case to someone who will listen if I have to."

With that, she spun and stormed out.

I growled and punched the bag one last time, needing the shot of pain the contact brought. Yanking off the gloves, I pursued her. Faces blurred past but I saw nothing. Only a spitfire shifter with blue and black hair charging into the night. As I burst into the gardens after her, she disappeared from view. My heart plummeted.

This couldn't be the end.

Not like this. It would wreck me. I wouldn't be able to complete this mission with her hating my guts. I scanned the rows of fruits and vegetables, becoming more and more desperate with each empty row. Finally, I saw a glint of blue, and ran.

"Reagan!" I shouted, but she kept going. If she didn't stop soon, she'd expose herself to the night sky. To Alec. Crap. I reached out and grabbed her arm, swinging her around.

"Let me go," she growled. "You clearly don't want to talk and I'm *not* staying behind."

My breaths came too fast. I didn't know what words to say, let alone *how* to say them. "I can't. I can't let you go."

A muscle in Reagan's jaw twitched. Her eyes narrowed. "I didn't walk out of Mordecai's cage to walk into yours."

Just like that, panic crushed me. Her words jarred my bones, collapsing my rib cage. Exposed my raw and bleeding heart. A cage. She thought I'd put her in a cage. Had I? What was I *doing? Screwing everything up, as usual.* I would lose her if I didn't get this right. The urge to hide my deepest emotions raged within me, but she needed to hear them. See them. Because if I left her in the dark—if I didn't open up—why was I even pursuing her?

"You're right," I said, voice strained. I glanced away. Looking into her eyes, so full of anger and confusion and hurt—I couldn't get the words out if I held her stare. "I've been trying to put you in a little box. I can't bear the thought of you getting hurt, so in order to protect you, I tucked you away for safekeeping. But that's . . . that's not how I want to treat you, like you're this fragile thing that can't take care of herself. I *know* you can."

I relaxed my grip on her arm, sliding my fingers down to hers. Laced them together. When she didn't pull away, my eyes began to burn. I heaved a sigh, locking my gaze on hers. "You can come on the mission. You're needed and wanted. But . . . but if something happens to you, I don't know what I'll do, and—"

I searched her blue and gold eyes, hoping for answers. Finding none. My final words were barely a whisper. "It hurts to think of losing you."

She scanned my face for a moment, then exhaled a long breath. "Oh, Tarik. I'll be fine. No, don't look at me like that. I'll be fine because I have you at my side. We make a good team. Isn't that the point?"

"A team." I nodded, swallowing roughly as a new emotion punched my gut. Determination. "I won't fail you tonight, Reagan. Even if we're walking into a trap, I'll get you out of there alive. And I know you'd do the same for me."

The truth in those words still staggered my mind. But as she looked at me, the hurt and anger melting away, all too willing to forgive, I knew there was still one thing left undone. Watching her reaction carefully, I slid my free hand behind her neck. My heart pounded out of control. I didn't know if the timing was right. I didn't know if she wanted this, but . . . "I owe you something," I said softly.

Her throat bobbed. "What could you possibly owe me?"

Through the tremor in my voice, I managed to say, "A kiss. That I stole. I want to give it back."

Reagan's breath hitched. After a moment, she whispered, "You have to catch me first." Her grip on my fingers loosened as mischief sparked in her eyes.

Before she could escape, I captured her lips with my own. She stilled and I focused on her mouth. Soft. And utterly perfect.

This.

I belonged here.

And here I would stay.

I wrapped an arm around her, drawing her to me, and she came willingly. When she dug her fingers into my hair, bringing me close, closer, my heart exploded. She couldn't get enough either.

My blood warmed, raging hot, hotter as her mouth moved against mine, tentative, teasing. I mirrored the movements, then grasped her hair, tipping her head back. She moaned and I almost lost control, almost went too fast. I wanted her, every last tattooed inch of her, but I knew she wasn't ready. So I slowed, rolling my tongue along her bottom lip—soft, then hard as I found her metal lip ring.

Bad idea.

I immediately became addicted to her taste and wanted more. I growled against her mouth, asking, pleading. She opened and I swept my tongue inside, seeking hers. When they touched, the world ceased to exist. *She* became my world. I explored her and she let me, gasping softly when my teeth grazed her lip.

"Tarik, are you out here, man?"

I broke the kiss, barely, brushing my lips against hers. She pushed upward, asking for more. I groaned softly and gave in, lowering my head.

"We have to go, Tarik. So if you're out here doing *things*, finish up now. We're leaving in five." I heard Malachi snicker, followed by a hoot from Micah. I was going to kill them.

I inched back. When I met Reagan's gaze, she looked as lost as I felt. "We're not done here. Once this mission is over, we're picking up where we left off."

She nodded mutely, slipping her bottom lip between her teeth. Nibbling. Crap. We needed to go. The timing was terrible, though. What I wouldn't give to spend the rest of the night out here with her.

Soon, I promised myself.

After this mission, things would change. And maybe, just maybe, we would earn ourselves more moments like this.

A few seconds after we were safely inside Mordecai's downstairs study, Reagan appeared with a golden key.

Rebel Leader motioned for her to open the hidden armory, and we—Caspar, Akeno, the twins, and I—watched as Reagan approached the floor-to-ceiling bookshelves lining the room's inner left wall. Flipping a book open, she inserted the key. *Click.* The whole shelf-back cracked open. Caspar and Akeno swung it wide, careful not to let the hinges squeal.

Inside was a whole new dimension. A dangerous one. The

rectangular room was top to bottom white, but peppering that white was row upon row of silver and black glittering weapons. Rebel Leader gestured at us to grab what we could comfortably carry, nothing more. We still had to collect the Genesis Crystal, and that was far more important than basic technology.

Nevaeh hadn't come on this mission, neither had Flynn, Sebastian, or Elias who were left to guard the Safehouse. The responsibility would be good practice for them, Rebel Leader had said. They'd grumbled but agreed, except for Flynn who simply shrugged.

I slipped a knife through my belt and slung a gun over my shoulder. Not a gun with bullets, though. They couldn't always penetrate the hide of a shifter, so I'd opted for a long-distance taser gun. High volts of electricity knocked anything down. When the team was bristling with weapons—especially Caspar, who had three gun straps criss-crossing his chest, his pockets bulging with . . . grenades?—Rebel Leader waved us forward, Reagan taking point.

The overprotective part of my nature balked at seeing her petite frame in the lead, exposed to whatever lurked in this tomb of a place, but I didn't pull her back. I knew the action would undo the progress we'd made but an hour earlier. Surprisingly, the mansion had been deathly silent as we'd crept inside. Had Mordecai hired a new butler? I wondered what their shifter form would be. Maybe an elephant with venomous tusks.

Once we were down the stairs leading into the mines, I readied my gun. Security had probably tripled since the great Fae escape. But as we inched toward the Green Room, we found nothing. Absolutely nothing. Chills prickled my flesh.

Something wasn't right.

I was about to break our code of silence—convince Rebel Leader we were walking into a trap—but Reagan was already entering the large cavern, slipping from my sight. Panic tightened my chest and I pushed past a stunned Akeno, mouth opening to call her back. My fumbling caused a domino effect, the twins pitching forward onto Rebel Leader. In a tangled rush, we spilled into the soaring green cavern, clutching at our clanking weapons.

Several yards ahead, Reagan whirled, hands on hips. She eyed us, arching an eyebrow. I shrugged sheepishly, moving to join her. As a unit, we made for the far wall, pulling out thick burlap sacks to hold the crystals. If there weren't any loose pieces left out like last time, we'd have to search the place for a hidden cache. That or it was pickaxe-wielding time. Adrenaline hummed in my veins and I had the strongest urge to bolt across the large space. Too open. Too exposed.

Too quiet.

Trap. Trap. Trap, my mind screamed.

From behind came a resounding *thud!*

Weapons clicked as the team swiveled toward the noise. At the sight that greeted me, my face blanched. In that moment, as the gangly creature rose to its full height, I would have rather faced a rock slide. Or a horde of angry guards. Or a dozen Bushies. But this?

I raised a trembling finger, pointing at the . . . at the . . . "S-spider," I stuttered.

"No kidding, genius," Caspar blurted, unslinging two guns, one in each hand. "Stand back. I'll pump the sucker full of lead." Sporadic gunfire popped from his waving weapons, ricocheting off the floor, the walls, the . . .

"Caspar!" My limbs unfroze and I lunged for the crazed lunatic, jerking the guns from his hands. "The crystals. The bullets are rebounding. You're going to hit us, you blundering idiot. You don't even know how to shoot!"

"I do too!"

"Video games don't count," I snarled, and he looked at me like I'd mortally wounded him.

The spider skittered closer, hissing out a laugh. I cringed as the long, black legs made a clicking noise similar to that of high-heeled shoes . . .

No way.

"Jocelyn?" I swallowed the bile climbing my throat. The spider, taller than any of us, raised two legs and brought them together as though clapping. A shiver that felt way too much like crawling baby spiders shook my entire body. "Crap. I was hoping you'd be a seal."

Hissing again as though I'd insulted her, she leapt into the air and landed a few yards in front of us. The group scattered, Micah yelling as he pulled free a sword he must have snatched off Mordecai's study wall, "A jumping spider? Really? Come on!"

Jocelyn ignored them all, her multiple black eyes focused on me. I dropped Caspar's weapons and unslung my taser gun. I had no idea if the electricity would work on this hideous creature, but I'd give it my best shot. One glance at Reagan beside me and I knew she wasn't going to take that risk.

"Let me try something before you go all lion on me," I said to her. "Jocelyn and I have a score to settle."

She nodded, as if she personally understood how I felt, but didn't back away. My jaw clenched. I would have to be right about this. And quick. The giant spider that resembled a house-sized black widow scampered toward me. As I dove out of the way, a tiny whimper left my mouth.

"Heard that!" Malachi shouted.

"Tarik's afraid of spiders!" Micah chortled.

"Shove off, guys, or I'm sending her your way!" I grunted, leaning back as a sharp leg swung over my head. She hissed, snapping her pincers together. Pincers? Venomous ones? My eyes flicked upward, and I almost dry-heaved at the sight of her bulbous red and black underbelly.

I aimed at the disgusting creature, volts of blue electricity sizzling against her shiny body. Jocelyn shrieked and reeled back, ramming a leg into my stomach. I wheezed, forcing myself to a stand, and sent another bolt arcing through the air. One of her eight limbs buckled.

"Aim for the legs!" I yelled, ducking as another one darted toward me. The men surged forward, most with blades in their hands, slashing at a furious, hissing Jocelyn. Two more of her legs gave out and relief crashed through me. She could be defeated. I wouldn't become her next meal. Wait, what did she eat? I threw up a little in my mouth.

I was about ready to send a bolt into her face—which would hopefully blind her temporarily—when she jumped straight up, latching onto the cavern's ceiling. Several of the men groaned. I heard Caspar mutter, "Anyone have a very long broomstick?"

Out of the corner of my eye, Reagan crouched, her expression focused. "Don't," I warned, which earned me a scowl. "She'll knock you out of the air."

And then Jocelyn moved. Everyone shuffled aside when she hovered over their heads. Prey. She was looking for easy prey. A quick pounce, bite, and retreat.

"Micah," I whispered, never taking my eyes off the creeping spider. "Throw me your weapon. On my count."

"Are you sure, man? I might accidentally slice off your—"

"Just do it," I hissed, as the black, leggy creature positioned herself right above my head. This was going to bite. Hopefully not literally.

In the next second, she dropped, rotating her body midair so all I could see was red and black and thin, grasping legs. So many legs. Gaia, help me.

"Sword!" I bellowed and wrenched my gaze from the spider as the weapon sailed toward me. Catching it, I slammed my back to the ground, raising the sword high.

I squeezed the hilt tightly, arms jerking as she impaled her underbelly on the blade's sharp tip. A loud, wailing shriek echoed throughout the cavern as she shifted. I blinked up at a naked Jocelyn, quickly rolling out from beneath her. Blood leaked past her red lips as she laughed, the sound cut off as she choked on her own blood.

"You may have—" a wheeze and more leaking blood "—defeated me, but Mordecai is at this very moment destroying what you sought to hide from him." She laughed again, red-painted fingers resting on the blade still protruding from her stomach.

"Where is he? *Where?*" I growled, a thread of panic lacing my words. Something wasn't right. The mine was still too empty. Too quiet.

As her eyes glassed over, one last word slipped from her lips.

Shock, then fear lanced through me, through all of us.

We bolted for the exit.

CHAPTER 24

Reagan

Safehouse.

The word echoed in my mind, over and over. My heart pounded against my ribs. Pressure spread across my back, my wings anxiously trying to rip free. *Go, go, go.* I could beat them all there. *Maybe.* I could save the Fae. *Probably not.*

Would Tarik forgive me if I left him behind? The Fae could fly—and judging from the desperation on their faces, the wing ban wasn't even a thought in their minds. They would catch up. And fast, more than likely.

He would have to forgive me.

I would beg him if I had to. If we survived.

The moment chill air hit my face I shifted, slamming my wings open and taking to the sky. I didn't wait for an updraft, pumping my wings in a panicked frenzy. How did Mordecai find the Safehouse? Had I inadvertently led Alec there? Yesterday flashed through my mind, Alec's circling as Tarik and I argued. And then again, when Flynn, Benji, and I had rescued Haven.

Did I lead the dragons there?

I was guilty in either case. They wouldn't be bothering the Fae if not for me. Not like this, in any case. *No, they'd be torturing them. Experimenting.* I growled in frustration, at my frantic, warring mind. I should have gone to Mordecai, should have turned myself in for treason. Shouldn't have endangered them.

I should have stayed.

All of this was my fault.

For a shining moment I had thought I could escape. A selfish thought, I realized, when Tarik and the Fae were the ones playing shield. An already broken, scattered shield that I asked too much of.

The world, my mind, my heart—all three stopped when I spotted the building. Bathed in blood. Shifters were tearing Fae from the doors and windows, brutally ripping them apart before their wings could unfurl. Crimson sprayed up the walls, pooled in the street. Agonized screams crowded my senses. I shoved away the accusatory words that bubbled up. Not now. I had to stop this.

Alec was terrorizing a pair of Fae up the street and I dove for him first, slamming myself against his thick scales. He roared in anger, eyes flashing when he realized who had attacked him. I tried to lure him away; flew around him, batted at him.

He knew. In the smallest of glances he knew exactly what I wanted, what I was trying to do.

Those Fae didn't stand a chance. Alec swiped them from the sky, tore their wings to ribbons.

No hope for escape.

Fury vibrated through my bones. I didn't have time to stop Alec, couldn't spare the minutes to lure him into human form.

My claws and teeth were useless against his natural armor, and he had been trained well to guard his weak spots. As if sensing my turmoil he spun on another innocent, a wicked twinkle in his eyes. My breaths came in shallow, rapid bursts. I was utterly helpless to stop him.

I can't save them. Not from this. I can't help.

My stomach heaved when he snapped the Fae between his jaws, spraying my nose with the same blood that dribbled from between his teeth. Bile raced up my throat and I shoved the acid back down. I looked away, eyes falling to the Fae fighting for their lives behind me.

They're alive. I can still save them. Go.

I spun and flew to the Safehouse, ignoring the shock of pain that splintered through my bones at my hard landing. The first shifter I saw had the legs of a bird—caught mid-transformation. I pinned him to the ground, tearing his still-human throat out in one swift motion. Shaking my mane, I grimaced at the metallic taste that lingered on my tongue.

I tucked my wings and burst into the building, lunging at shifters as they passed. A familiar-looking coyote nipped at my ankles. I snapped open a wing, pinning him to the wall before I pounced, slicing my claws down his middle. He didn't even twitch.

Nevaeh.

Sebastian. Flynn. Elias.

Where are they?

I searched the room quickly. Nothing. No sign of them. Every inch of me trembled with rage and fear . . . and guilt. So much guilt. Dead Fae littered the common rooms. Innocents. Children.

I shook my head, blinking away hot tears. *Focus.* I needed to find the others and get rid of Alec.

A flash of movement caught my eye. What I thought was red hair vanished up the stairs, and my lion's determination reignited at the sight. Every shifter that moved met the fury of my claws and teeth—tearing, shredding, ripping, destroying. Not enough. They still came, crawled out of the woodwork. Still killed. *Murdered.*

There was no sign of the four that had stayed behind. Not in the kitchen, or the main common area. I growled in frustration. My ear caught the softest whimper. Behind one of the recliners, a Fae child crouched, trembling. Damnit. I couldn't get her out as a lion. *Damnit.* She was only a child.

My mind latched onto that word. Child. *Children.* Fae children had grown scarce in more recent years. My heart slammed to a halt when I realized Mordecai had targeted them, knowing exactly what they meant to the Fae. What they meant to me.

Wait. I scanned the room.

Where's Benji?

Damnit.

My anger renewed. I held myself together and gently nudged the child toward another fleeing Fae. I watched them from a window, made sure they were outside and safely past Alec, before I continued my search. I shoved my way into the gardens, scanning the area.

Nothing, more nothing, and then—

A familiar form lay crumpled on the ground.

Elias.

Covered in blood, gripping his chest in pain. His glasses lay shattered on the ground beside him. The air vanished from my lungs, and my eyes burned.

My fault, my fault.

I started to shift, to help him, when something plowed into my side. A snarl slid from between my teeth as another lion shifter—smaller and brown—prowled toward me. Sought another blow. I pushed him away from Elias, back into the main house, then slammed him to the ground, slashing at his face. He turned, slid free. His long claws dug into my side. Crimson sprayed across my white fur, blood pouring from the wound.

Before I could swallow the sound, a small yowl escaped. A second later, Caspar slammed the butt of his gun into the lion's snout. The animal slumped to the ground, unmoving, before he slid back into human form.

"You're welcome, tiny shifter!" the large Fae called, before disappearing into the kitchen.

I huffed a thanks. Then remembered Elias. I turned for the gardens, but Nevaeh shifted in front of me.

"Reagan . . . upstairs. You have to go upstairs," she panted. "Mordecai . . . You need to stop him. He might listen to you."

Before she could finish, I was charging up the stairs. Right into a harried-looking Sebastian who flinched instinctively as I approached. I shifted, dropping into step beside him.

"What happened?"

"I-I don't know," he stammered. "All was quiet and then . . . and then Alec. Now Mordecai's . . ."

"Where's Benji? Flynn?"

"I don't know . . ."

I put a hand on his arm and squeezed gently. "Get to safety. Help Elias—he's in the gardens. I'll take care of Mordecai."

Sebastian nodded as I bolted past him. Mordecai wasn't

hard to find—he was terrorizing one of the larger family rooms, a small child locked in his grip. The second I strode through the door, his eyes widened and he grinned.

"I thought this might motivate you out of hiding, sweet daughter," he crooned.

I stared. Didn't dare move. "Release them or I'll leave again."

Mordecai paused, considered. "You'd leave them to die?"

"If I have to." I wouldn't. He knew I wouldn't. Apparently he didn't want to take the chance, though, roughly shoving the child to the floor. The boy scrambled to his family. I made sure they reached the stairs before I prowled a bit closer to Mordecai. Our eyes locked.

"Reagan. Enough of this game. Come home."

"Anywhere you are isn't home. You think I'd want to come with you? That this display of wanton violence would what, pacify me?"

He laughed, but his attention slid to the door. I spared the half-second glance. Tarik. Damnit. I growled at Mordecai.

"So the Fae managed to brainwash my beautiful daughter, hm?" His cold gaze lingered on Tarik and I stepped more firmly between them. "You really did a number on her, if she thinks whatever this is could possibly be superior to the comfort she's used to."

Tarik scoffed. "The Fae might not have fancy apartments, but we don't lie. Unlike you, who's been lying to the entire city, all while sitting on the truth. Yes, I know what the Genesis Crystal does. What you've been hoarding, *dragon*."

Oh no. No, no, no. I shouldn't have let Tarik talk, should have known better. The glint in Mordecai's eyes made my stomach curl, reinforced my fear. He lifted his foot to step forward and I rapid-shifted, throwing my wings out between them.

"Reagan. *We do not help the Fae.* How many times do I have to drill this into your thick skull?" Mordecai seethed, then inched closer. I bared my teeth, another angry snarl slipping free. I balked at the honeyed tone in his voice when he added, "Sweetheart. I'll stand right here. Let's talk."

I hesitated. I didn't trust him, but I had the energy for another rapid-shift, if needed. Possibly the last I could manage for the day. I could hear him out, right? When I shifted, Tarik swore softly.

Mordecai's face lit with glee.

"There, see? Now we can discuss this like civilized people. But first . . ." He crossed his arms and stared at me, pointedly.

"Not a chance in hell," I spat, teeth grinding together. "I'm never going to kneel to you again. Why are you hoarding the Genesis Crystal? What do you want with caverns of green rock?"

"I don't want the Fae to have it," Mordecai said simply.

The admission caught me off guard but I didn't miss a beat. "Why? And if that were true, you wouldn't have been using Genesis Crystal to experiment on them."

Mordecai took a step closer, his expression flipping like a switch. Manipulation mode. "I have no idea what you're talking about, Reagan sweetie. You're confused, but you've had a long week. We were trying to help them, my daughter."

Confusion blurred my thoughts, my mind responding to that softened tone, wanting to believe him. Because believing him, believing that I was crazy, was an easier net to fall into than the one I was currently scaling. His voice was in my head, had been for so long, and reflexively I wanted to fall into the routine he had conditioned me for.

That's abuse, my mind screamed loudly, in a voice that sounded oddly like Tarik's. But it was enough to force my doubts to stumble and falter. *If you can't trust yourself, trust Tarik. You don't have to accept abuse as remittance for living.*

My body shook, fists clenched at my sides. Pain shot through me and I winced, blood dribbling from the claw marks spanning my ribs. A steady warmth pressed against my arm. I glanced up at the angry, impulsive Fae beside me. *He really does have a death wish.*

No. It was more than that now.

He was *my* angry, impulsive Fae, and with the smallest of glances he confirmed what I already knew. He wasn't going to let me do this alone. Wouldn't let me face *him* alone.

Because we're a team.

My chest warmed, even as renewed waves of fury flooded my veins. "Liar," I growled, snapping my full attention back to Mordecai. "You can't even be honest with *me?*"

Mordecai turned his lethal stare onto Tarik again. Deflecting. Baiting, as he said, "What have you done to her?"

Tarik shrugged. "Not much. Yelled at her a bit. Kissed her a couple times." Unconsciously, I slid my lip ring between my teeth as his own lips curled back. I bit down when he snapped, "But I didn't stick a hot brand on her neck. I didn't beat her face in. I didn't take a hammer to someone's legs. No, that was all you."

"Reagan doesn't belong to *you*," Mordecai bellowed. He exploded with a roar, teeth gnashing as he launched himself at Tarik. In the span of a heartbeat I shifted, slamming my paws into his chest. I shoved him to the ground, snarling in his face as he tried to squirm free.

"You're a wasted investment," he seethed. "I tried to change you, tried to make you reach your full potential. But no, even I couldn't save you. Your mother's blood runs too deep. Filthy, disgusting *Fae* blood."

Time seemed to jolt to an abrupt halt, then jumped back to full speed.

My mother was Fae?

The wheels in my mind wouldn't turn, wouldn't do the math. Mordecai knew my real mother. Knew her, and apparently hated her. Or maybe he was lying yet again. Was she alive? She couldn't be if she had left me to be raised—to be trained and broken—by *this* man. But who—?

Booming wings broke through my whirling thoughts. The walls crashed in around me. Alec's blue dragon form smashed through, pinning my wing to the floor. I shifted as he swept a clawed foot inside. He shoved me backward before securing Mordecai in his grip, launching them into the sky.

The smooth floor offered no purchase and I skittered across, smacking into the wall, my body barking in agony. After a moment of painful panting, I eased onto my back. My side burned in protest and I groaned as the rubble on the floor bit into my skin. I turned my head, searching for Tarik, only to find him stumbling around the debris. The world tilted and I closed my eyes, taking in slow, deep breaths until my head calmed.

"Imagine that," I murmured. The words wavered, despite my best efforts. I glanced toward Tarik. "Guess I'm a little bit of a Fae prick too . . ."

Tarik knelt beside me, red hair shadowing his face. Carefully, he touched my arm, and I felt his healing magic begin knitting my wounds closed. He stayed like that, silent, for several long moments. He was simply . . . there.

Finally, he raised his head and I caught sight of red-rimmed eyes. A fresh wave of guilt struck me. Before I could cry, or pull away, or do anything, he smiled softly, saying, "I'm not surprised. I didn't connect the dots, though. Probably because you're so short."

Despite myself, an airy laugh escaped. The sound of frantic voices broke the moment and I sat up. My stomach plummeted as images flashed through my mind. Bodies. Blood. Elias. Children.

Children.

Tears welled in my eyes and the urge to flee shuddered through me.

My fault. All of this. My fault.

If not for me, none of this would have happened.

Still, I would help the Fae clean up. Carry the injured away from here, heal them as much as my rudimentary skills would allow. After, I would leave. I would run, try to flee the city, maybe through that underground passage. I could draw Mordecai and Alec away. If I couldn't . . . Maybe I should return to the manor, try to distract them and minimize their attacks on the Fae. My eyes met Tarik's and I pressed my lips into a hard line, concealing the sob that pushed at my throat. He would never forgive me, but he would be alive. Pain wrenched at my heart and shivered through my body. I looked away before the tears sprang free.

"Did anyone find Benji?" I whispered, voice quavering. I probably didn't want to know the answer.

The hand on my arm began to tremble. Tarik's voice was strained as he said, "No. Flynn is missing, too. And . . . and—" He made a choking noise. "Elias is dead."

My heart shattered, splintered into a thousand tiny pieces that pierced my veins. Tears slid loose, trailing through the grime on my cheeks. I wanted to comfort him as much as I wanted to steal his comfort for myself. I withdrew. Kept the feelings brimming in my mind to myself. I didn't need to be his burden, not right now, when I had cost him so much. Cost all of the Fae so much.

Not when it was all my fault.

At the southern end of Nathra City, a field stretched as far as the eye could see. Beyond was a network of mines, distant enough to not feel threatening, but unquestionably there, hidden beneath the grass. The expanse of green glowed beautifully under the moonlight that broke through the darkness. Here, under a towering willow, we held the last ceremony for the lost. Several of the Fae came down earlier in the day to hang tiny lights from the tree, in recognition of the final rites.

Fae funerals were beautiful. They believed that in death, they should be returned to the earth. Early in the morning they had begun the ceremonies, small funerary pyres lit at varying times and places in the field. Normally, they would have done them all at once—the Fae had permission to use this section of field for their funeral traditions—but since most of us were fugitives, it was risky to be out in the open like this.

I hated that I saw beauty in any part of this disaster. Hated that I was the reason for so much death. That I hadn't left well enough alone—left Tarik alone.

And now . . .

I tried to convince myself that I had done what I could. I had saved a few of them, and that was enough.

But no. Nothing I had done was enough.

They hadn't deserved the havoc wrought on them by yet another shifter. I was exactly what Tarik had always feared of me.

And we still couldn't find Benji.

My stomach churned. The feeling grew, and I almost retched when the Fae passed prayers and offerings over the final funeral pyres. They buried the scent of death with incense, but even that couldn't mask the ache I felt over the losses—every single one of them—burning my soul. In all the world, there wasn't anything that would make up for the lost children. Or Elias. My chest squeezed painfully at the thought of Elias on one of those pyres.

I stood alone, far to the back of the group. Tarik was beside Rebel Leader, comforting him in a way I didn't know how. I couldn't help any of them. Hell, I could barely even look at Sebastian, whose tears fell freely at the loss of another sibling. Or at the twins, offering him silent support.

Why did I always have to be so stubborn? I could have listened to Tarik and stayed behind. Fought more, saved more, *done* more.

Several of the Fae had thanked me for protecting them.

Thanked me.

My eyes burned at the memory.

Bright orange flames licked at the night sky and I almost

crumbled. If I could take everything back and suffer the pain myself, I would. All of these broken hearts, these falling tears, these sorrowful eyes. I did this. Not Tarik, not even solely Mordecai. I was the reason they had lost so many friends and family members.

I brushed a tear from my cheek.

Nevaeh already knew what I was planning to do after the funeral. I couldn't cause more grief, more pain, so I was leaving. Fleeing, like the coward I was. I didn't know where I would go—maybe to learn more about my mother. Knowing that she was Fae should have given me some kind of comfort but, staring at the fires in front of me, the knowledge only made me feel worse.

My gaze lingered on Tarik as the plan ran through my mind again. I knew how much this would hurt him, even if that wasn't my intention. My heart ached every time I looked at him.

He was better off. They all were.

I closed my eyes. Snuffed out the sight in front of me. Nothing helped. Elias. Benji and Flynn. Hundreds of Fae, missing or dead or hiding in the tunnels under the city.

Their memories would haunt me for a long time to come.

I couldn't wait much longer. If I did, I wouldn't leave. If I did, the thought of hurting Tarik would cripple me. Would hold me here. My thoughts skipped over his voice, his touch, the brush of his lips. We were building something. Slowly, with our fair share of bumps and confusion and uncertainty—but something.

My breath stuttered. I couldn't linger. He glanced in my direction, like he knew my thoughts. I let my gaze roam over his handsome face, memorizing the lines, the freckles, his nose, his mouth. The green eyes that flickered with fire light. I absorbed every tiny physical detail that made Tarik who he was, down to the beautiful jagged scars that marred his cheek and jawline.

When he turned away I slipped off, into the dusk, letting my feet lead me back to the city.

Away. I was going away.

Where I couldn't hurt anyone ever again.

CHAPTER 25

Tarik

I knew what she was doing.

Every single molecule in my body knew. I didn't go after her, though, and that decision killed me.

She needed space to process, to make sense of the foreign emotions flooding her system. If I pressed, she'd blow up. If I hovered, she'd shut down. I knew all of this, because when I'd glanced across the field, I saw myself in her eyes. I had looked away for a moment, and when I'd turned back, she was gone.

When I couldn't find her after the funeral, I'd panicked and grilled every single Fae I ran across. No one had seen her. Coming to my senses, I'd asked her friend Nevaeh. By the way she dodged my questions, I knew she was aware of Reagan's whereabouts.

One day I tailed the purple-haired rat shifter as she left the tunnels, a bulky pack slung over her shoulders. She knew I followed—she wasn't the rebel's little spy for nothing. And she led me straight to Reagan anyway. I hadn't gone inside the crumbling building, but I'd paced outside for hours. Debated going in. Forced myself not to. I had lingered like a stalker.

Rebel Leader slapped a piece of paper on the scuffed table before me, disturbing my memories of the past week. Sound returned. The steady *plink* of a leaky sewage pipe, the nearby rustling and low murmurs of too many people forced into the cramped underbelly of Nathra City. Most of them hadn't seen the sun in days—it was already taking a toll, adding more fuel to the growing fear and tension.

"I know it hurts, son, but she needs time," Liam said, clapping me on the shoulder. I didn't bother asking how he knew my train of thought. He *always* knew.

"Yeah." I sighed tiredly and stared at the paper without actually seeing. "But time won't heal if you hold onto the pain. She's doing exactly what I did, Liam. That look on her face . . ."

"Which is why," he said, taking a seat across from me and tapping the paper, "you'll be asking her to come along on this mission."

My eyes narrowed on the paper until shapes and symbols appeared. "Mission? Don't you think it's a little soon? I mean, our numbers were cut in half, our resources all but depleted. Many Fae are missing, including Flynn and Benji." Saying the boy's name out loud tightened my throat, and I swallowed roughly. Haven was inconsolable. If we didn't get him back soon, I worried for her rapidly declining health. She seemed to have stopped trying. "We've been forced underground to live in tunnels. You lost your *son*, for Gaia's sake."

As my temper rose, so did his. He slammed a fist onto the table and I blinked. He was never angry. "And that is *exactly* why this mission is so important and has to happen now. When tragedy strikes, you pick yourself back up again. You *do* something about it. When Leilani died, I made plans to build the rebellion and Safehouse days later. Threw myself into being useful, into making a difference. If I had done nothing, I would have wasted away in my sorrow."

His words were a blow to my heart. He had suffered as much as I had, but he'd risen above. I, on the other hand, had let the misery bury me. And watching him now with that angry spark lighting his eyes, I knew I couldn't let him down again.

I studied the old, water-stained paper, not comprehending its contents. "What is this?"

"A map." He leaned back in his chair, crossing his arms. "You have that green, rechargeable rock of yours still?" I nodded, gut twisting every time I thought of that failed mission when we had come home empty-handed. We hadn't collected a single crystal that night, too panicked to think straight. "Good. Because that crystal is the key to opening the veil."

My brows furrowed as I looked up at him. "Huh?"

He chuckled, his old humor returning. "I took the liberty of exploring Mordecai's study when you all were loading up on weapons, and hit the jackpot. Information on the Genesis Crystal and what it can do, a map leading to the land our ancestors came from, proof that we've been lied to all these years. We weren't cast out or abandoned by the gods. We've simply been trapped, the knowledge of our freedom hidden from us. Our elders were massacred during The Shift, no doubt Mordecai's doing so they couldn't tell us how to tip the scales.

"But now . . ." He grinned wide. "We have the key."

"The key to what?" I held my breath. Something told me his answer would change everything.

"The key to a land teaming with our own kind who can

help us stop Mordecai. The key into Daranil, the Fae realm."

She hadn't left the city yet.

But today, that's exactly what she was doing. Nevaeh told us about the map Reagan had found of an underground passage—coordinates that we still needed if we were to leave the city ourselves. She'd also helped Reagan scrounge together supplies so she wouldn't be completely helpless traveling to strange new lands. And now, she was ready. Nothing holding her back. I could feel the familiar well of anger roil in my gut, but I tamped the emotion down.

She may be leaving without even a goodbye, but she was hurting. I knew all too well the conflicted emotions she was drowning in. So when she exited the rathole she'd been slumming in for the past several days, I didn't storm over to her. Didn't grab her and shake sense into her. Didn't curse and yell.

No, I snuck up behind her while she was lighting a cigarette and casually leaned against the building's graffitied wall, despite feeling anything but calm. "You're needed on a mission."

Reagan jumped, nearly dropping the cigarette from between her teeth. She pulled it out long enough to say, "Tarik . . . I can't."

And started walking.

I kept pace easily, marveling at her short stature. I had missed this. Walking beside her. Matching my stride to hers. I missed watching the wind tease strands of her blue and black hair. Missed the way she nibbled on her lip ring. "The mission will be dangerous. In uncharted territory. We need the strength and expertise of the lion shifter."

She shook her head. "You don't need me. You'll be safer if I'm gone."

I stifled a sigh. She sounded exactly as I did a month ago. The table had flipped and I wasn't used to being on the top. "Maybe we're safer, maybe we're not, but that isn't the point. We *want* you to come along."

Reagan slowed. Then stopped, stamping out her cigarette before she peered up at me. "I can't do this, Tarik. I'm sorry."

That look in her eyes . . .

Pain. I wanted to wipe it all away. Unable to hold back a moment longer, I reached out and stroked a thumb down her cheek. "Please don't leave." My chest tightened. "I want to help you through this."

"I miss you," she admitted quietly. Her throat bobbed, eyes glistening as grief welled to the surface. "But this, all of this . . . Everything hurts."

I dared to move closer, sliding my fingers into her hair. "I know. I know it hurts so bad that breathing is sometimes impossible. I know the images revisit you in your nightmares. I know the guilt is a living thing inside your chest, eating away at your sanity. But"—I carefully pressed my forehead to hers—"running away won't fix any of that. Actually, running makes everything fester and spread until the hurt completely consumes you. And so I'm begging you. Begging you not to go. Let me help you heal."

Tears spilled down her face. "I should have listened to you," she whispered, a hiccup breaking her voice. "I should have stayed behind and let you handle your mission. I could have stopped the dragons. If I leave now, they'll follow me. If I leave, you'll all be safe."

My thumb brushed away her tears. "You're just another conquest to them, Reagan, a piece of property. You think that by leaving, the injustices done to the Fae will disappear? That Mordecai will leave us alone? Because he won't ease up when you're gone. His terrorizing stems around us and the Genesis Crystal—he's trying to figure something out. I don't know what, but he isn't finished. He won't stop. Not until we *make* him. That's what this mission is for: to put an end to his tyranny."

I pulled back, needing to see her expression. "So if you want him to pay for what he's done, join us."

The invitation hung between us, and although I watched her closely, I couldn't tell if my words had an effect or not. My heart rate climbed when I realized this might be the end. She might very well turn me down and leave this city behind—and everyone in it. A sinking sensation grew in my stomach.

"All I've ever wanted to do was help," she said at last, a shuddering sob trembling through her small frame. "And I ruined things so completely. All those lives—their blood is on my hands. Their deaths are my fault."

And there it was. Hearing the guilt was a spike through my heart. I knew the burden she carried. The burden that shouldn't be borne.

"Reagan," I breathed, sliding an arm around her shoulders. I pulled her in, tucking her head against my chest. "It's not your fault. The world is a dangerous place full of dangerous people. Bad things happen and we can't always stop them. A wise old man once told me: sometimes evil wins the day. But instead of giving up hope, we can fight for a better tomorrow. Fight back with me, Reagan. Come on the mission."

She turned her face into my chest and inhaled deeply. I waited, refusing to breathe, worried that my words hadn't been enough. That this was goodbye. But when she spoke, it was a whispered, "I'll go with you."

Relief almost bowled me over. I wrapped my other arm around her, locking her in tight. Breathed her in—apples and cinnamon. Perfect. Gaia, I'd missed this. She fisted my shirt, effectively scattering my thoughts and narrowing my focus to her. And me.

Us.

But the moment couldn't last—we were behind schedule as it was. I took a quick steadying breath and let out a piercing whistle, pulling Reagan in closer when she startled.

Right on cue, several heads popped out from various locations down the street.

As they ambled toward us, I lightly tugged her hair, saying, "Look."

She turned her head, cheek still pressed to my chest. A small sound left her lips, either surprise or horror. Hopefully the former.

"Kitty cat!" Caspar called, amber locs loose and swinging. Sebastian shushed him, aiming a fist at his shoulder, which the big Fae dodged.

Micah and Malachi came next, cooing and smooching at us.

"*You're dead*," I mouthed at them.

Nevaeh and Akeno were last, the latter staring a little too hard at the purple-haired rat shifter. Interesting.

When they gathered around, each in turn greeted Reagan, welcoming her to the "cool club." I explained that they were joining us on the mission.

She raised her eyebrows. "What's the mission?"

I chuckled. Explaining *that* to her was going to be fun. "Let's walk and talk. You have a lot to catch up on."

As we moved out, she reached down, lacing her fingers through mine. I raised our linked hands, staring at the sight. At the rightness.

She's your girl.

Startled at my mind's certainty, I almost tripped over a loose brick in the street. But then I grinned, so wide my cheeks throbbed.

"I know," I whispered back.

Acknowledgments

First of all, I want to thank my co-author Tyffany Hackett for approaching me two years ago with the idea of co-writing a series together. The timing couldn't have been more perfect. I was in a dark place, and from that darkness, Tarik was born. We spent endless nights creating these characters who hold many of our inner demons. We let down our guards and let these characters tell pieces of our own stories, our scars and burdens laid bare. This experience has been challenging and eye-opening, filled with give and take. But most of all, it brought two people together who were more alike than they realized. It created a bond not so easily broken. And I will forever be grateful for that.

I also want to thank our beta readers for their contagious enthusiasm as they read this book. Grace's special-sauce notes, Shiza's love of the cute, Hannah's consistency radar, Chelscey's world building expertise, Marissa's keen eye for error—you ladies helped shape this book into something incredible. To our early readers, Melissa, Becky, and Jessica, thank you for shipping our characters!! To my local critique group, Russell, Lyn, and Stephanie, thank you for finding the weak spots and making this book shine.

Many many thanks also goes to the bookstagrammers who jumped at the chance to share this book with the world. We are blown away by your excitement and willingness to help! To our street teams and ARC readers—you rock our socks off. We appreciate you to the moon and back! A huge thank you also goes to the artists Gabriella Bujdosó, Carrow Brown, and Hanna Sandvig for bringing our characters to life with their gorgeous illustrations. And Jane for making them smell amazing with your Wick and Jane candles. We love them so much!

And thank you to our readers for supporting us and loving on our characters. We hope you enjoy Tarik and Reagan's world and the adventures that are to come!

And here we are. There will never be enough words for my gratitude to everyone helping make this author dream a reality. But . . .

To my coauthor, Becky; without whom this series would absolutely not exist. I'm so proud of this book, and us! I never could have imagined where this insane journey would take us but I'm so glad it's you along for the ride! Little pieces of our souls went into these pages, and I wouldn't have it any other way. <3 Love you!

To my husband, Corey; for being a rock without whom I absolutely could not be chasing my dreams. Thank you for supporting my crazy adventure, in every way. I love you!

To my son, Ethan; Nothing will ever motivate me like wanting to do better for you. I love you kiddo, forever and ever and always and more. Times infinity.

To Matt, Chris, Wayne, Jessica and Ally; I couldn't ask for better friends or cheerleaders. You guys are seriously everything and my life is so much more wonderful with you all in it. Love you!

To our beta readers; Grace, Jessica, Becky, Chelscey, Shiza, Hannah, Marissa, & Melissa. You guys provided so much great feedback, and listened to us talk about these characters for so long . . . thank you. We couldn't do this without you!

To my street team; you guys stepped up like champs when I dropped a surprise book launch on your laps and I am SO eternally grateful for every single one of you. Thank you for being amazing supporters and friends.

To everyone who helped share on social media, especially the crew on bookstagram; I don't have words. Thank you. You know who you are. You're amazing.

Special thanks to the artists—Gabriella, Carrow, Hanna, and Jane—who helped bring our characters and worlds to life just a little bit more. <3

And last, but never least, to our readers; for taking a chance on these books and being so damned fantastic. Thank you, thank you, thank you. You're everything. *Everything.* ;)

ABOUT THE AUTHOR

- Tarik -

Becky Moynihan writes sass, romance, and action. She's also the award-winning author of *The Elite Trials* trilogy (a YA dystopian romance), and co-author of the *Genesis Crystal Saga*, with author Tyffany Hackett.

She spends her days staring at her picturesque backyard—wishing there weren't so many bugs outside when her goldendoodle insists on playing catch—scarfing down chocolate, and sipping on Mountain Dew. In her spare time, she draws fanfic of her characters, designs book covers, and reads all the books. She lives in central North Carolina with her family.

SIGN UP FOR BECKY'S NEWSLETTER

Be among the first to find out about other upcoming projects!

https://www.beckymoynihan.com/newsletter

CONNECT WITH BECKY:

www.BeckyMoynihan.com

Instagram.com/Becky_Moynihan

ABOUT THE AUTHOR

- Reagan -

Residing in New York's Southern Tier, Tyffany Hackett is the award-winning author of *The Thanatos Trilogy* as well as co-author of the *Genesis Crystal Saga* with Becky Moynihan.

She spends her days chasing after her rambunctious toddler and her nights trying to make the words go. In her down time you can find her killing reapers, darkspawn, or battling for the horde.

SIGN UP FOR TYFFANY'S NEWSLETTER

Be among the first to find out about other upcoming projects!
https://www.tyffanyhackett.com/newsletter

CONNECT WITH TYFFANY:

www.TyffanyHackett.com
Instagram.com/Tyffany.H
Twitter.com/Tyffany_H

Also by Becky Moynihan

THE ELITE TRIALS:

- REACTIVE
- ADAPTIVE
- IMMERSIVE

Also by Tyffany Hackett

THE THANATOS TRILOGY:

- IMBER
- TELLUS
- VENTUS

Dawn Till Dusk Playlist

TOP TEN SONGS

- Angel With A Shotgun — *The Cab*
- Hate Myself — *NF*
- Jar of Hearts — *Christina Perri*
- Feel Invincible — *Skillet*
- Girl That You Love — *Panic! at the Disco*
- Demons — *Kurt Hugo Schneider*
- World Away — *Tonight Alive*
- Radioactive — *Imagine Dragons*
- Before I'm Dead — *Kidneythieves*
- Heart Attack — *Demi Lovato*

Bonus:

- Lover. Fighter. — *Svrcina*

Full Playlist on Spotify

https://spoti.fi/2AXYKGD

Made in the USA
Columbia, SC
07 May 2020

93554495R00209